The Chronicles of Borea

Book II

The Making of a Bard

Gigue

D1523356

By Joseph E. Koob II

Illustrations and Cover by Robert Haselier

Seven-Book Fantasy Series

Book I – The Making of a Bard – Preludio

Book II – The Making of a Bard – Gigue

Book III – The Making of a Bard – Siciliana

Book IV – The Making of a Bard – Ciaccona

Book V – IXUS – Corrente

Book VI – Civil War Threatens –Tempo Di Borea

Book VII – The Great War – Grande Finale**

**The book sub-titles reflect the musical emphasis in the series. Taken from the Baroque period, all except the Finale are found in J.S. Bach's *Three Sonatas and Three Partitas for Solo Violin.* *(See Next Page for descriptions)*

ISBN: 978-1-072-37620-0

Sub-Titles

Preludio (Prelude) – short introductory piece of music, improvisatory in style, usually begins a work of several movements

Gigue (Giga, Jig) – a lively dance often serving as the final movement of a suite of dances in the Baroque period

Siciliana (Siciliano) – Baroque Dance/movement in an instrumental work in a slow $^6_8$ or $^{12}_8$ time with lilting rhythms, that resembles a slow jig or tarantella, characterized by dotted rhythms and usually in a minor key. It can elicit a pastoral mood.

Ciaccona (Chaconne) – series of variations over a ground bass (short, repetitive bass line) that sets the harmony

Corrente (Courante) – triple meter dance, often found in the Baroque suite

Tempo Di Borea (Bourree') – lively dance in duple meter with an upbeat quarter note

Grande Finale (Finale) – ending section or movement of a larger work – sonata, suite, etc.; often with thematic material from other movements and related in Key to the whole

Acknowledgements

Much thanks to everyone who has influenced me over the years.

Thanks to: my wife, Lisa; my children, Nathan and Elise, and **Pat**, son-in-law, who have been readers throughout the development of this series and helped me in innumerable supportive ways with this project; Anne Duston, one of my regular readers; Carolyn K.; as well as other readers and friends. Special thanks to my good friend and expert editor, Steve Bridge, who set me on the path to righteousness early on in this process, and who has been instrumental in making the final editions so much better. Thanks also to Stephanie H. of SLL Editorial Services for her early editing; Phil Lang for his work on the cover; and my cousin, Robert Haselier, for his wonderful illustrations and cover art.

Website: **chroniclesofborea.com**

Blog: chroniclesofboreabooks.wordpress.com

Contents

Map of Borea

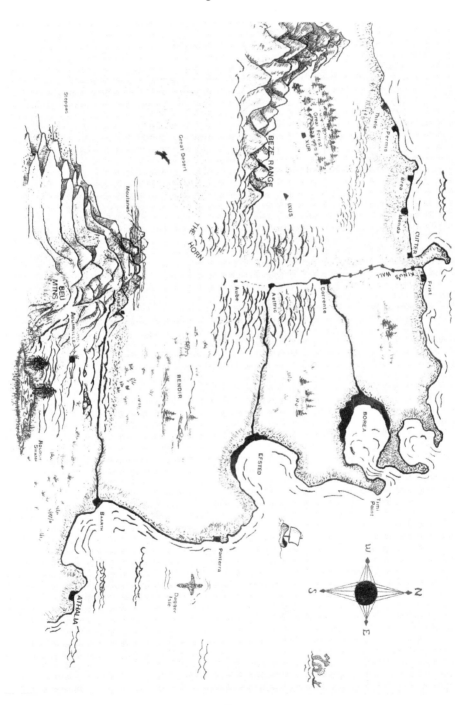

First Year

The Hall of Bards

Jared followed the old man through the courtyard toward the ornately-carved, paneled doors that led into the Hall of the Bards. Shifting his knapsack higher on his shoulder, he stared about as he walked. He had accumulated little enough since hastily leaving his village during the Qa-ryk assault: one extra pair of clothes, his lyre, his polished yew bow with quiver of arrows, and a few odds and ends. He felt lacking in so many ways as he realized how little he knew about the place he was about to enter. He was a boy from a wilderness town, and the complex he was facing could easily have fit his whole village in its center.

He had heard of the magnificence of this cathedral of learning from passing minstrels, yet he never would have imagined the overwhelming impact the buildings would have on him. The stonework was carved from the finest white marble. Each beam and brace, each piece of siding, window trim, and molding was crafted from the richest woods and polished with a protective sheen using the best oils. The main building extended to his left and right further than he could see, and it stretched far above his head. The marvel of the place was further enhanced for him by the wondrous cacophony of sounds that tumbled from every window and open shutter.

Jared swallowed, determined to make a go of it. As he climbed the steps to the main door, he shifted his entire focus to the one thing that he would always understand intuitively. For a moment, he paused to breathe in the music. Melodies from instruments of every description swirled into the courtyard. And such sounds: richly clad tunes performed on resonant lutes; caressing harmonies floating down from delicate harps and lyres; and voices, voices as he had dreamed of yet rarely heard – tenors and sopranos, the deepest of basses, and luxurious altos. All this somehow supported, or perhaps better phrased, were uplifted, by the interspersing tones of horns, fiddles, and drums.

He was almost mesmerized by the mix of emotions that swirled through him as he stood there. Thistle, the girl he loved, was gone to the Borean Palace to be tested by, and perhaps become apprentice to, the great White Wizardess, Meligance. His father and many friends were dead, killed by terrible beasts in the west, and the gods only knew where his brother was. And he had survived an unlikely series of events that somehow had led him here to the one place in all the kingdom where only the best of musicians could study, to become, as he had never dared even dream it – a Bard.

Jared could have spent hours listening, picking out this tune or that, and wondering, learning, being with this experience. The old gatekeeper, however, seemed to ignore both the glorious building and the effluence of music coming from it. He pressed ahead toward the mahogany doors and stood patiently waiting for Jared to follow.

Once there, Jared would have wished to pause again to study the intricate designs of the many instruments that had been carved into the dark wood; yet, the gateman, his bushy white eyebrows raised and his face heavy and tired-looking, sang a phrase as Jared approached. "Speak the password and you shall enter the Hall of Bards."

The man's penetrating bass resonated so that almost half of the music coming from windows immediately around the doors stopped. Heads began popping out to look down on the new arrival. His voice had once been of excellent quality; time had added a roughness to the upper edge of the final three tones as the musical phrase ended in a question. That he was to answer the question musically was immediately obvious to Jared; and in spite of having no formal training in music, the three-note response came to him naturally. He wondered what words he should sing. During this pause, if he had bothered to look up, he would have noticed that all of the boys and young men above had stopped their practice and were looking down with smiles on their faces. Jared quickly decided. Smiling to himself, because he remembered a joke his brother had once played on him, he sang, "The Password," in his light tenor voice.

The old man's eyebrows raised even further. He bowed deeply. "You may pass; new Bardlings, third door on the left, past the fountain."

Jared returned the bow. Then, ignoring the excited whispers from above, he pushed on the large door panel. Surprisingly, it opened with the lightest of touches. As he started forward, the white-haired man touched him on the shoulder and whispered, "The words did not matter, but I like that," and he chuckled deeply. "I really do like that." He turned away, still chuckling, back to what seemed to be his post at the golden inner gates to the Hall of the Bards.

Jared entered a large hallway with a church-like arched ceiling. He could see dark oaken beams crisscrossing some thirty feet or more above his head. Again, he stood and simply breathed in the aura of the place. The wide passageway stretched ahead to a small fount about forty paces from where he stood. Spaced about every ten paces or so were doors on each side of the hallway. Though muffled, Jared could still hear a myriad of instruments and voices blending into a pleasurable mixture of sounds that somehow fit with what he had imagined this place to be.

As he walked slowly down the center of the large hall, Jared was only partially aware of the light polished woods that were used here to contrast with the richer, darker wood he had seen outside. A part of him ached at having to say goodbye to Thistle, and at the same instance to have said goodbye, in a very real way, to his entire past. There would be no attempt now to rebuild what had been. His home, his wilderness life in a furring and farming community, were gone forever. Yet here, a dream he had never envisioned as possible was unfolding for him. In this revered hall, the building spoke of wonderfulness, challenge, and growth. It was a language that he slowly began to realize he desperately wanted to learn. At the same time, it awed and humbled him. Truthfully, he felt unworthy of this place.

Jared came to the third door on the left and found that he had not yet reached the fountain. Hanging on the light oaken panel from a tiny brass nail, at eye level, was a small carved sign that said, "Not this door." An arrow pointed further down the hall.

Jared shifted his pack and lyre once again and turned back toward the fountain. He stopped when he reached the fount, admiring the finely detailed base, which depicted a Bard sitting with his lyre. He also marveled at the clear, pure water that bubbled up from the center of the marble bowl. Even with closer study, he couldn't figure out where the water was coming from, or where it went. Shaking his head, he turned back down the hall.

At that moment a bell began to clang from somewhere above. Within seconds, almost every door in the hallway opened; and a flood of students poured into the open space. Soon Jared was surrounded by streams of boys and young men pushing this way and that. Several clapped him on his shoulder or tousled his hair as they passed. "Record time." "Good show." "Welcome to Bard Hall."

At each welcome, Jared turned to speak to the boy who had greeted him; but the fellow would be off, waving as he passed. One did manage to get out a second phrase, "Class; can't be late." And as quickly as the hall had filled, it emptied. All the doors closed, leaving Jared standing where he had stopped.

He went on, down two more doors, where he finally stopped at a panel that had another sign on the front. It said, "This door."

Knocking tentatively, Jared stood back waiting for a response.

Nothing happened, so he knocked a bit louder.

With still no response, Jared pulled on the brass handle. The door opened out, so he drew it wide and peered into the room. Across from the open door was a large mahogany desk, behind which sat the same old man who had met Jared at the inner gate and sung him the entry tune. Puzzled, Jared stepped in. He could see no other entrance to the chamber. The whole room was lined with bookcases that were filled to the brim with volumes and volumes that appeared to be identical to one another. The large tomes were all bound in a medium blue soft leather; the words *Introduction to Music* were embossed in silver on the binder and cover.

"Took you long enough, young man. You're not going to become a Bard if you stand around lollygagging at everything. Here…"

The old fellow took a book from a shelf and handed it to Jared. "You will need this. Everything you should know for the first year. Or maybe I should say, everything you better know by the end of the first year." He smiled from under those big bushy eyebrows and his equally bushy mustache. "I'm assigning Simon-Nathan as your mentor and roommate. He is a second year and will help show you the ropes. You'll meet him at lunch. Your seat assignment is 456 in the lunch hall; your room assignment is the same number. Lunch is in thirty-five minutes. So, find your room, get settled, and follow the swarm to the dining hall. Simon-Nathan will take it from there. Any questions?"

The old man didn't allow Jared enough time to open his mouth before he rattled on. "Now you're a bit behind, coming this late in the term; but you seem to be a bright lad. Study hard, ask questions, you'll catch up, I'll warrant. And!" The old man paused, "Stay out of trouble." He raised one of his big white eyebrows as he looked down his nose at Jared. "Any questions?"

Jared did have millions of questions, and this time he did manage to get his mouth open; that was as far as he got.

"Take the stairs across the way," a gnarled finger pointed out the door. "Go up three flights and turn left. Numbers are on the doors. No keys. I have to get back. Welcome." The old man stood, stuck out his hand. Instead of allowing Jared to shake it, he shooed him out the door. "Go, go. Time's a-wasting."

Jared managed a slight bow, which would have looked pretty silly to anyone who might have seen it, because the old man had already turned away.

It's All New

Jared suddenly felt very small in the great hall. He was overwhelmed by the enormity of what he was attempting to undertake. He stood for a couple of seconds outside the doorway. The rush of good feelings he had while everyone had been swirling about him, when he had simply been drinking in the ambiance of it all, had been overcome by self-doubt and a sense of powerlessness. Finally, willing himself to take a first step toward whatever lay ahead, he managed to move away from the door toward the open portal on the other side of the hall.

The old man in the room he had left raised both his eyebrows and muttered, "Hmm."

Resigning himself to at least get through lunch before deciding whether to flee back to an equally uncertain future in the wilderness, Jared climbed the long flights of steps to the fourth floor. After a few minutes, he figured out the numbering system – evens on the south corridor, odds on the north. He headed west down the long line of rooms, until he was about two-thirds of the way down the hall.

Doing some quick math in his head, and assuming that the top three floors were all dormitory rooms, he calculated that there were some four to five hundred boys studying to be Bards. That number was overwhelming; for some reason he had thought he would be unique, at most one of a few. Five hundred seemed like a huge number. There hadn't been more than several hundred souls in his village during his entire life.

Coming to the correct numbered door, Jared tried the ornate brass doorknob. It turned easily. When he pushed on it, the door swung inward revealing a long narrow room. Moving into the open doorway, he paused at the edge of the tiny foyer that set off what he assumed were two closets, with wooden doors to his left and right. Jared scanned the room.

There were two beds, one on either side. Both beds were neatly made with light blue sheets and a dark blue coverlet, each with two pillows with light blue cases. One bed had a neat pile of clothes on the end that Jared recognized as the uniform he had seen many of the boys wearing. Though the colors appeared to have varied considerably in the mass of movement as the boys had rushed from one class to another, the doublet, shirt, pants, and socks on the bed were varying shades of yellow. The doublet was such a bright yellow that it almost made Jared wince.

Past the beds were two desks, with a chair nestled under each. Their design included a small desk in the center that was surrounded by a wooden lattice shelf composed of a variety of compartments, drawers, and shelves that allowed one to store all sorts of items. The desk and shelves on the left were filled to overflowing with a variety of books, scrolls, quills, and papers. The one on the right was almost empty, except for a few papers strewn about the flat surface. At the far end of the room was a window that looked out across an open space to another building.

Walking slowly into the room, Jared went between the desks to the window. He looked out to see an elaborate courtyard with statues, fountains, and stone benches. The scene was bleak. In the late fall the fountains had been emptied, and the plants had all been trimmed back; however, some older students and faculty looked to be enjoying the opportunity to be outside on a sunny day.

Turning back around, Jared scanned the plaster walls. They were plain and drab, except that someone had begun to paint a scene onto the wall above the bed with the clothes. It was a summer landscape with a unicorn nibbling on the grass amongst a picnicking family. The mural was only partially complete; the artwork was still impressive.

Not sure what to do with himself until lunch, Jared sat on the edge of the empty bed and opened the book, placing his small bag of belongings and his bow and quiver next to him. He left his lyre strapped to his back; it was the one thing that gave him any sense of stability at this point.

The book was written in the common tongue. The preface stated that it was an introduction to the study of music meant only for the serious-minded student, and that so-and-so had done such-and-such and so on. Jared flipped the page and continued with the Introduction, which delineated in brief form all that "the serious-minded student" should learn during his first year. These included Theory, History, Basic Lore, Understanding Instrumental and Vocal Music, Basic Accompaniments, Poetry, and more.

Jared was about to turn to the first theory section on note reading, when another boy came sweeping into the room through the open door. Out of breath, the smallish, round-faced fellow tossed a pile of books next to Jared, and said, "My bed." Then he stuck out his hand grinning, "Simon-Nathan, at your service. You must be Jared."

Jared stood up, taking the other boy's hand, allowing his to be pumped enthusiastically. His face must have bespoken his question, as Simon-Nathan added, "Your bed is that one. That is your uniform. Sorry, freshmen are yellow. Yellow 'til you mellow, or more precisely until you pass your first-year equivalencies. It's lunchtime. Lunchtime! Let's go eat. Oh, yeah, take your book, instrument, and bow and quiver with you. Don't worry about the uniform, you can wear it tomorrow. I'll drop you off at your first class after lunch. That'll be singing with Swenson – real bear; he's a good teacher though. Come on."

All this time, Simon-Nathan continued to pump Jared's hand up and down, and now he pulled him toward the door. "It's bread, meats, and cheese day, my favorite." Jared stumbled after him, joining the stream of boys now heading in one direction toward the eastern stairway.

Jared almost had to sprint to keep up with the smaller boy. After descending three flights of steps and making several turns, they came to a massive foyer that led to three sets of open double doors into which boys, young men, and girls were pushing.

Girls? He had never heard of women being Bards. Certainly, women sang, and he guessed, yet he didn't know, that women played instruments, because his mother had given him his first lessons on the portative harp. On occasion, he had heard her play a few beautiful haunting tunes, when she believed she was alone in the house. But a woman becoming a Bard?

His thoughts were interrupted by Simon-Nathan's tug on his tunic. "Come on. First come, first served." They pressed forward into the masses.

The dining room was huge. As they pressed inside, Jared quickly raised his estimate of the number of students several fold. Long, solid hardwood tables and benches stretched for several hundred feet in both directions. Everybody except Jared seemed to know the ropes. Hundreds and hundreds of young people were crowding down the long aisles. Amazingly, everyone got settled quickly. Simon-Nathan directed Jared to a bench about sixty paces along the table closest to the southern wall. Clearly marked on the back of the bench were the numbers 450, 450, 452, 452, 454, 454, 456, 456. His roommate plopped himself into the furthest 456 and gestured for Jared to sit next to him.

The tables were already set with food and drink. Jared had only seen a repast like this during the fall harvest celebration at his village. The wood planks were piled high with platters of a wide variety of smoked and dried sausages, salamis, and pates, cheeses of every description, and aromatic breads hot from the oven. Simon-Nathan immediately began filling his plate with slices from the different platters, managing to stuff his mouth full in the process. Between mouthfuls he mushed out to Jared, "Helpss yoursselfs."

Still taking in the whole atmosphere, Jared took a few more moments to become immersed in the experience. The roar of a thousand and more voices had diminished considerably as almost all the students had settled and were already eating. Jared tentatively sipped at the drink in front of him, discovering it was a strawberry flavored tea – slightly sweet, and cool and refreshing. Glancing about, he noticed that this great room was also finished with the finest of hardwoods. The walls were richly paneled and hung with elaborate tapestries depicting a wide variety of scenes; all somehow, from what he could see, were dealing with music and musicians. Above the paneling was a two-foot carved escarpment of polished walnut that ran around the entire room above the doors and windows. It appeared to be a collage of hundreds of different instruments, both old and new.

Jared could see a long table far to the front of the room that was at a right angle to the student tables. Here several men and one woman, who he presumed were faculty, were settling for lunch as well. Jared noted that they were each ordering food, and that they were being served individually.

Finally, taking a few deep breaths, he settled back onto the bench. Though he did not feel hungry – he was too tense – he selected a few different meats and cheeses to go with a slice of whole grain oat bread. He had not eaten since the night before and he knew he should get something in his stomach.

The whole luncheon experience was over far too quickly. It was not long before he found himself being tugged along once again by Simon-Nathan down another corridor. His roommate chattered as they hurried, "You'll have singing next. That's Swenson, as I mentioned earlier. He's strict, almost mean some of the boys think; but actually, he's pretty fair. He knows his stuff. He'll ease up a bit with time. He was just anointed Bard. Pay attention, do what he says, and you'll do fine.

"We change classes by the bells – two bells for changing classes, three you better be there. Which can be a trick, because we often have a-ways to go from one place to another. You'll get used to the other rings for convocation, and so on. Luckily, your next class is two doors down. It's the instrumental hall, where you will have basic instrumentation and performing. It's two periods long; so stay there until the bell rings, and I will be along shortly."

Simon-Nathan paused long enough to take a deep breath as they rounded a corner. "Basic instrumentation is all about getting familiar with as many types of instruments as possible your first year. At end of the session, that's in June, you'll get to pick two or three instruments that you want to study more seriously. Ah, do you play any instruments well? Because you will be a bit behind in trying things out."

Jared nodded, then managed to say, "Yes, the portative harp or lyre, some lute, and I've fooled around with the fiddle, rebec, fife, and recorders a bit."

"Good, very good. Well, be sure to mention all of that. They'll probably get you branching out from there. Have fun. This is where you want to go." Simon-Nathan pointed to a large door. "Instrumentation is two doors that way," he pointed to the left. "After that, I'll meet you out here in the corridor. All novices and second years have weaponry in the late afternoon every day. We probably won't be in the same class, as it's based on ability and skill level, but I can get you there. They'll put you through the paces to see where you belong. See yah."

"Thanks, Simon. I really appreciate..."

His roommate was already scurrying away, waving as he went. "It's Simon-Nathan. I prefer the...," and he was around the corner.

On the Spot

Jared followed some other students through the door and into the classroom. The room was large and rectangular, with an arched amphitheater comprised of raised platforms set curling around the walls. These were focused toward a rostrum with a music podium facing in the center. A man stood there waving his arms and bellowing, "Places, places. Move it everyone, we have lots of work to do today. Places."

Not sure what to do, Jared stood watching as several hundred students, seemingly of all ages from young boys to almost middle-aged men, moved to assigned spots on the risers. The movement was chaotic with everyone jostling for position, but eventually they all managed to find their places.

"You," the teacher bellowed; he pointed a long baton at Jared. "Where do you belong?"

Jared, embarrassed that the master had singled him out, squeaked out, "I'm new, sir."

"What's that? Speak up, boy. This is singing. We vocalize in singing. You want to be a singer or a crow? Speak up! Who are you and what are you about?"

Color rising in his face, Jared cleared his throat, then said forcefully, "I'm Jared, lately of Thiele. I'm new, sir."

Many of the students snickered, and Jared blushed even deeper.

"Well, Jared of Thiele, at least you are polite. Half of these whippersnappers have no manners at all. Come, come, we'll need to hear you sing, so we know where to place you. Johns, give him the music to 'Adele, My Pretty Lass is Running.'"

Jared walked hesitatingly forward toward the podium. He had certainly been at the forefront of many a village dance and celebration, yet those had been his close friends and relatives. He had never been put on the spot like this – to sing before hundreds of strangers, all of whom probably knew far more about music and song than he did. A young man handed him a page of music. Jared stared at it blankly, desperately wanting to run. The scratches on the page meant nothing to him.

The music master signaled to another boy sitting patiently at the Virginal keyboard. The boy began to play. Jared stood gripping the sheet of music tightly, fighting back tears he definitely did not want to shed.

"Sing, boy. Let's hear what you've got."

Jared didn't move; all of this felt completely wrong.

Finally, the music master gestured, cutting off the keyboardist. "Cat caught your tongue? Or are you only an instrumentalist, my boy? You know what we call those who can't sing? 'The Toads,' because they croak so well. We have a special section for them." He gestured toward the left side of the bleachers. More snickering.

Jared was now blinking back tears. Finally, choosing between what he considered to be two equally embarrassing solutions to his dilemma – to run or to admit the truth – he said haltingly, "I cannot read music, sir."

There were no snickers this time, only a grand silence that Jared took to heart as the ultimate judgment. In truth, however, most of the students in the room were now feeling embarrassed for him.

The master recovered quickly and smoothly, "Ah, well, what songs do you know, my boy? How about, 'The Lads and Lasses Sprightly Go,' or perhaps, 'Gentle Goes the Night.'"

"Either would be fine, sir." Jared's embarrassment was now beginning to be replaced by a rising ire. He knew Thistle would want him to fight through this. What was this compared to battling Qa-ryks or evil priests? He drew himself up, and as the keyboardist began the introduction to "The lads and lasses…," Jared cleared his throat.

His first few words were tentative, but once he found his voice he sang clearly and strongly in mid-tenor. It became obvious very quickly to all in the room that the new-comer could carry a tune, and his tone quality was exemplary. To the more experienced and discerning, one could tell that there had been little, if any, formal training. The instructor knew that the lad's voice would become even fuller and rounder in quality as he matured.

Finishing the first chorus with, "a falling, a falling, a falling," on a descending cascade of notes, Jared began the next verse. The choirmaster cut them off. "Good, good, well done," he said, which was accompanied by enthusiastic clapping from the students. "You have a fine instrument there, my son. It needs work, nevertheless definitely some potential."

"Stevens, take him under your wing. Get this young lad started on scales, arpeggios, and the usual exercises. And while he'll get tutored in theory on his notes, run him through the program I've developed. He'll get there faster… Jared."

"Sir?"

"Join the mid-tenors, row two, right side." He gestured toward the risers. "Follow-along as you can for now. Keep in mind, though, that I will test your sight-reading thoroughly at the end of term. Welcome to Bard Hall."

"Thank you, sir," Jared said with relief. He joined the boys on the risers and appreciated the pats on the back as he was ushered toward an empty spot. Already he felt completely drained, and he had just started. He did not want to think what the next class period might bring.

Luckily, the rest of the hour the choir master focused his attention elsewhere. Jared did note that he was never averse to putting a student on the spot who wasn't measuring up to his strict standards. Jared made a mental note to apply himself to his singing studies.

17

More than Enough Instruments

Dreading a repeat of the past class's introduction, Jared slunk into the next classroom following a group of other boys and girls all wearing the bright yellow garb that had been sitting on his bed. He almost laughed as they looked like a flock of molting canaries milling about. He slid far to the back of the room, hoping to stay out of sight for at least one course, so he could learn the ropes. The room was large, with the walls and edges filled with stored instruments of every type Jared had ever heard or seen and a good many he had no experience with. Yet, the class was a fifth the size of the singing class.

As he watched, most of the students began removing instruments from various bins or closets. They were forming into loose knots around the room. Unslinging his lyre from his back, Jared decided to join a group of young men and one woman with other non-bowed string instruments. He brought over a small wooden folding chair and settled himself in their midst.

Some of the boys, who he guessed might have been in choir as well, nodded to him as he joined them. For the most part, they were all either tuning his or her instrument or playing little ditties to warm up. Jared followed suit.

After a few minutes of playing, Jared warmed to his portative harp. This, at least, felt familiar and comfortable. He enjoyed the feeling of his fingers flowing over the strings. As he played, he noted a freckle-faced, red-headed girl join their group. She settled on the floor with a small lyre cradled between her legs. She smiled brightly at Jared and began to check her instrument's tuning.

Just then, a young-looking man entered the room clapping his hands. Jared figured he must be an assistant to the music master, because he didn't look any older than some of the lads in the class. The percussive pop echoed through the room; everyone immediately stopped what they were doing.

"Attention, today I'll see what you have managed to accomplish on your current instrument. Today," he smiled wickedly, "the bowed strings are first!"

There were some good-natured groans from that corner of the room, and many of the students in the other groups clapped. Jared immediately liked the young man. He hoped that he was indeed the actual instructor, though he still had his doubts. He also felt a bit better about continuing his subterfuge. He figured the fellow would find out soon enough that he was new, simply because he and the instructor were the only ones not wearing yellow.

The red head, whom Jared had to admit was quite cute, leaned toward him and whispered, "That's Julingo. He's really young for a Bard, but also amazing. He plays all of these instruments really well! They say he is one of the youngest ever to become a full Bard. He's the son of the son of the son of Baringo – you know, of the southern Baring clan – *The* famous Bard! The... well, never mind," she said, seeing Jared's puzzled look. "You'll learn all about that in Lore – my best subject. Well, that is if you don't count music theory." She smiled brightly. Jared couldn't help smiling back.

"Practice everyone," Julingo announced. "You might be next."

Jared wasn't sure what to do, so he practiced several popular instrumental pieces that he had learned by rote. He chose ones that would show off some of his technical skills, in hope that it would be enough to at least demonstrate that he knew something about music. Finally, he settled on "The Chase," a tune that, if one believed the story he had been told, was a ribald tale about young men chasing young women in the meadows.

The plucked strings were the focus of the master's attention next. Julingo immediately recognized Jared as having just joined the class. "Welcome, welcome. I see you have some familiarity with the portative harp. Good. Relax for a few minutes while I hear the rest of this disreputable lot; after that, you can play me something. I'm Master Julingo," he said with smile. Jared liked him even more. He bowed slightly from his seated position. "I'm Jared of Thiele."

The next ten minutes went quickly, with the young Bard listening carefully to scales, exercises, and brief tunes that each student had been asked to prepare. Jared was relieved to discover that most of the students obviously had little familiarity with the instruments they were trying to play. When the last student had finished his little performance, Julingo turned to Jared. "Play me something you know, and we'll take it from there. Don't worry; the whole purpose of this class is to get you familiar with different instruments, so you can choose those that you might have some talent for."

Jared nodded; then he broke right into "The Chase." He started softly and slowly, building up to the faster tempi of the middle and end of the song, his fingers flying across the strings. By the time he hit the abrupt clashes of the alternating dissonant and consonant chords at the end – supposedly depicting the young men's success by throwing their captured lasses onto the grass – most of the rest of the class had stopped to listen. He glanced up questioningly.

"That was quite good, young man! You have a talent there, though your choice of song is amusing." Julingo's eyes twinkled. "Who have you studied with?"

Jared didn't really understand what Julingo meant, so he answered truthfully. "My mother taught me to play, elsewise I have not had any formal training. I have played with several wandering minstrels that came through our village – Josquin and Vertalin. They gave me a few pointers, some years ago."

"Vertalin? Yes, I remember him, quite a versatile player. Well… even more impressive. I will commend you to Therin. He teaches the grand harp, lyre, and kithara. He will want to hear you play sooner than later, I imagine. You're quite rough around the edges, but you have a fine start. For now, I want you to stick with the plucked strings. I'll have some of our better players work with you on getting familiar with the other instruments in this group. I doubt you will have any trouble transitioning from one to another. Have you played any other instruments?"

"I have done a fair amount on the recorders – they are the staple of the western villages – and a smattering on the fife, rebec, and fiddle. Oh, yes, also, a variety of percussion, but they are not my strong suit." Jared flushed, feeling a bit conspicuous. Now that he had stopped playing, he realized everyone in the class was listening.

"Good," Julingo said, standing. "We are over two months into the term, but you should have no trouble fitting into class." He turned slightly. "Karenna, work with Jared on the kithara for the rest of this week. Next week, Markus, you can introduce him to the grand harp. After that, if all goes well, Jared, you can jump into the upper wind group and get acclimated with whatever you haven't tried before."

Karenna, it turned out, was the pretty redhead. Jared groaned to himself. He didn't want to consider what Thistle might think of his working closely with a good-looking young lady his first day at school. It was a sacrifice he would have to make.

19

Might isn't Always Right

Jared stood in the hallway waiting for his roommate. His head was buzzing with new tunings, fingerings, and another introduction to reading notes, which Karenna had insisted on showing him. Simon-Nathan, as hurried as ever, dashed around the corner. He beckoned Jared to follow.

After a maze of turns and long corridors, jogging all the way, Jared found himself staring through an archway onto a wide-open compound that was alive with running students. Simon-Nathan pointed toward a tall figure in the middle of the expansive yard. "Talk with Elwind. He'll get you started. Good luck."

"Wait!" Jared said, grabbing Simon-Nathan's shoulder. "Are those elves?" He nodded toward a small group of tall, white-haired young men standing to the side conversing.

Simon-Nathan shook his head sideways, pulling away from Jared's hand. He was obviously anxious to get to his group. "Mostly, but not. I'll explain later. True elves don't study here anymore. See yah."

Jared wondered at his roommate's response; nevertheless, he decided it was not an important point. He stood there taking it all in. He could feel a cool breeze coming from the west, which he decided was a good thing, because this looked like it would be an energetic end to his first day of classes. Already students were pairing off to spar with a variety of weapons or joining groups that were going through what he knew were standard forms for developing strength and agility with a given weapon.

He smiled as he stepped toward the center of the paddock. This he was familiar with and confident about. He had studied weaponry with one of the greatest swordsmen in the kingdom. While his father had been hampered by the loss of his arm and his advancing age, he had put both his sons through rigorous exercises with a wide variety of arms. Jared and Ge-or** had practiced for hours on end the strengthening and flexibility of the standard forms for swords of all types, blunt weapons, thrown weapons, spears and halberds, and the like, and also with both longbows and shortbows.

Stopping in mid-stride, Jared's thoughts turned to his brother. Where was he? What was he doing, right now? Would he understand what Jared was doing and why? He stopped, and for a few minutes allowed himself to reminisce about their training as youths; unfortunately, the shock of all that had happened returned. Though Sart had promised to check on his brother, Jared knew Ge-or was headstrong. He would be mono-focused until he either recovered their father's great elven sword or died in the bargain.

"You! Don't stand there in the midst of this ruckus. Where do you belong?"

Jared jolted out of his reverie, blinked twice, and looked around to see who had spoken to him; almost everyone appeared to be focused on their weaponry work. Jared's gaze fell on a broad figure leaning on a two-handed sword in front of a group of older students. "Sorry, Master." Jared bowed. "I'm new."

**Considering the unique linguistic characteristics of Old Borean, and Ge-or's heritage, historians have agreed that his name would have been pronounced "Gay-or" in contrast to the current popular vernacular "Gee-or" or the more vulgar "George."

The man nodded. "See Elwind," he boomed, pointing toward the same figure Simon-Nathan had indicated.

As Jared turned, he saw the tall master gesture for him to approach.

"Name?"

"Jared, half-elven, of Thiele."

"Thiele? North-west coast?"

Yes, Master."

"Yes, I know it – small town, compact. I was through there in 1481 as a Journeyman. Pleasant place."

Jared did some quick math in his head. That's seventy-one years ago, he calculated. Though he was surprised at first, he noted the elven characteristics in the man's face and ears. He bowed low. "Tu honara me."

"I hope your family and town prospers."

Jared flushed. "I'm sorry, master; Thiele is no more. It was destroyed by a Qa-ryk band and red-dragon assault two months ago."

"I am most sorry. I offer my condolences." Elwind bowed low to Jared.

Jared acknowledged the master's deference with a nod. He also noted that those within hearing range had stopped their conversations and were now staring at him. "I appreciate your kind words, Master." He wondered if those listening were interested more in how he had survived the attack, or whether it was simply the mention of a red dragon being part of the battle that had raised their curiosity.

"Well, my young half-elf, what are your abilities with arms? Are you familiar with swords? Spears? Bows?"

"I have been trained in all forms of weaponry, Master. I believe I am competent in most."

"Well, I guess we have to determine what competency means to a young half-elf from the west." Elwind raised his arm and gestured toward the group of elves that Jared had noted earlier. The four "almost elves" approached and bowed, a bit cursorily, Jared felt, toward Elwind.

"Elanar, take Jared and Rosc here. See what they can do with the staff to start. After that, let's move them to the long sword corral. Allin, take these others to the beginning knife class. Rolin, assist with the advanced long-bow section. Joelin, you will assist me today. Young Jared, I will be around soon to see how you are doing."

Jared followed Rosc and the elf -- he decided to give Elanar the benefit of the doubt -- toward a small paddock at the back of the large enclosure. Elanar gave each of them a padded long-cudgel. Standing in the center of the sparring area, he waved at Rosc to approach him first.

Jared watched the match with keen interest and practiced eye. This had been the first weapon their father had allowed the two boys to spar with, except they had never used padded staffs. Rosc obviously had some training in the long stick's use but was no match for the elf. Elanar was fast and he was adept at all the standard moves. Yet, Jared could see many holes in his approach. He did not seem to have the knack to be creative outside of what he had been taught and had mastered.

Rosc was soon gasping for breath and could not defend himself well against Elanar's moves. Though he was game and determined, he got lightly buffeted numerous times. Stepping back after a few minutes and lowering his staff, Elanar gestured to

Jared.

Jared moved forward, holding his cudgel lightly in his grip. In these times, unlike the shorter version used decades before, the cudgel was a heavy long staff, roughly made, typically of ash or oak. It was approximately five to seven feet in length, depending on one's size and preference. Jared had been given a six-foot staff that suited his frame. The stick gave him a certain amount of added weight and strength without overbearing him or being too cumbersome for lightning moves.

He and Elanar circled each other for a minute. When the elf struck, Jared easily parried. While his heritage was both elven and human, Jared had inherited more of the elvish characteristics -- he was quick and flexible. His brother, on the other hand, who was also quick for a human, had broad shoulders and a power that Jared would never develop. Their sparring had always been interesting: Jared capable of quick and decisive moves; Ge-or dominating in strength and endurance.

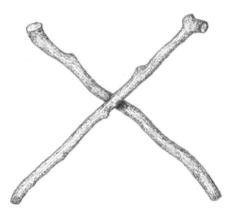

Jared was easily able to contain all of Elanar's attacks. He knew the standard repertoire by heart. It had been two years of work with the heavy staff before his father let them touch another weapon. Two years that had helped him develop speed, strength, and flexibility. Plus, he had learned to be creative in what he did. He had always excelled at the unexpected. He had also helped his brother, through the application of numerous bruises, learn to expand his own horizons in weaponry.

After three minutes of a steady spar, Elanar increased the speed of his attacks. The elf was now making a concerted effort to break through his defenses. Jared did not go on the attack, except to parry an aggressive strike. He felt it was not the purpose of the exercise. Spinning under a Hargrave swing, Jared noticed that Elwind had come to the edge of the paddock and was watching them. Elanar saw the master, too. He immediately raised the stake again, pressing his attacks even more.

A few moments later, Elwind raised his hand to stop them. Jared, accustomed to the seacoast air and the constant training he and Ge-or had put themselves through, was barely breathing hard. Elanar was now gasping for breath. "Well done, Jared. You have good form and know the repertoire. I want to see you on the attack. Be creative. Show me what you can do."

Jared bowed low, first to Master Elwind, then toward Elanar, a sign of respect for both.

Two minutes later and Elwind raised his hand again. In that time span, Jared had "touched" his elven opponent six times. Elanar did not look happy with the outcome.

"Good, excellent. You have been well-trained, Jared. Who were your instructors?"

"My father, Manfred of Borea, lately of Thiele, Master."

Elwind raised his eyebrows. "I knew your father. We fought together in the early Qa-ryk Wars. We will speak sometime together." He waved for them to follow him. "Come, to swords."

The long sword was a weapon that needed a fair amount of room to wield. Here in the paddock that was not a concern, but Jared had always preferred the lighter short sword. It was heavy enough to do serious damage, yet easier and much faster to swing in close quarters. Unless he needed the weight or extra length of the longer weapon, the short sword was by far his choice for combat. While he had also been trained in the lighter bladed weapons like the rapier, they were not the best weapons for fighting the beasts of the west.

His father had told them that in the capital the lighter swords and the more powerful longer and heavier weapons, such as the long sword and the two-handed sword, were more romantic; therefore, they were what everyone wore. Few of these so-called warriors had ever heard of Qa-ryks, nor faced gzks or goblins in close quarters. He and Ge-or had learned to wield all of these weapons and to wield them well.

It took a couple of minutes before Jared found a sword in the bin that was somewhat satisfying in his hand. These were training weapons, and Jared knew the type. He and Ge-or had used them in their early training, but they had long ago graduated to better quality blades. His father had insisted they learn the basics of sword-making; and in the many hours they had spent at the forge over several winters' time, they both had become capable of producing a decent weapon. The two of them had also gotten considerably more muscular as a result of the hard labor.

Jared spun the weapon in his hand a few times. Then he went through a series of moves to get used to the heft, weight, and balance of the sword. The weapon was dull and blunted with cork at the tip; though one could inflict bruises in a mock battle, it would not do any serious damage, unless used as a club. When he felt he understood the blade's features, he bowed low toward Elanar and waited for a signal to begin.

Over the first few minutes of their spar, Jared noted the elf's strengths and weaknesses. Again, Elanar was adept at all the formal choreography, yet had little true inventiveness in his attacks or defenses. Jared was able to easily stay with him. He found himself enjoying the exercise immensely. Competent as he was with a staff, the blunt weapons were of little use in combat with large beasts – Jared had always preferred the feel of a bladed weapon in his hand.

After a few minutes, Elwind again signaled for them to stop. He encouraged both of them to press their attacks. Jared did not want to further infuriate his opponent, as he knew he could best him easily; neither did he want to give a wrong impression. Initially, he let Elanar mount several offensive series. Jared used the opportunity to show his creativity in defense. Finally, quite reluctantly, he spun into a lightning series of strikes that used his maneuverability and control to overwhelm his opponent. Within a few seconds, he touched Elanar three times. He backed off, lowering his sword to indicate a truce.

As Jared's blade dipped near the ground, Elanar, who certainly knew the signal for a break in combat, suddenly lunged forward and touched him hard in the lower right chest, with the now un-blunted tip of his blade. The hit drove the breath from Jared; and though the blade was dull, it cut through his tunic and slid along his left rib, opening a long, shallow gash. Had the blade been sharp, the attack would have easily crushed the rib and gutted him. Jared reacted as he would to any attack; he spun immediately away, then attacked. In two strokes, he disarmed Elanar and had his blade, still corked, at his opponent's throat.

Elwind, in a soft, firm voice, said, "Hold." Jared froze in place. He withdrew his blade, bowed toward Elwind, ignoring Elanar. He strode angrily to the sword bin, tossing in his sword. He had expected far more from the students here. So far, it did not seem that anything he did here was turning out well. Again, he doubted whether he should be in this place.

What he didn't see when his back was turned to the sword arena, was Elwind dismissing Elanar with a flick of his hand. The master was angered with his advanced student, but it was a matter that would be dealt with later. When Jared turned around, Elwind said, "Are you injured badly?"

Jared shook his head, 'No." He knew he would have a heavy bruise, but there was little bleeding. Because of the pendant he wore, the blood now oozing out would stop momentarily; yet he would be quite sore for a couple of days.

Still very controlled, Elwind said, "Jared move to the archery range. I will put you in the hands of Selim, a master of the shortbow. Show him what you can do. Move to thrown weapons when you are done there. Return to me when you are finished."

Selim turned out to be a gnome with a long white beard that constantly brushed the ground. So astonished was Jared that the small fellow was a master archer, that he held his deep bow, staring at the dirty brown tip of the gnome's beard.

"Up, up, my young sir. While I am old and due a modicum of deference, I assure you, I am neither so old nor so revered that you need to abase yourself in my presence." He raised his bushy eyebrows high and turned around to stare at some of the other students nearby, adding, "…though some here could learn something from your obviously well-trained manners."

Jared immediately liked the twinkly-eyed fellow. He liked what he saw of the training area as well. It was designed for the type of practice taking place. Students were firing short and longbows at targets set deep against the far wall of the compound. The two areas were divided by a high, solid wooden wall that allowed the longbow archers the freedom to set up further back so they could practice shots out to a hundred paces. In the shortbow area, shooting lines were set five paces apart. The current rank of archers was firing from fifteen paces. The results, Jared noticed, were less than stellar, even at that close a range.

"I see you have your own bow, elf-kin. Would you care to join the current file and show me what you can do? Fifth target from the left, start after the next retrieval. Six shots and wait."

Jared began to turn away; but, on inspiration, he bowed low to the gnome and held it. He was grinning when he straightened up. Selim "Tut-tutted," breaking into a

24

broad smile himself.

Jared knew archery protocol. He waited patiently while the archers finished their line. Once they were done. he strode forward at a signal from the line monitor that it was safe for them to retrieve their arrows. He moved into position in front of the fifth target, removed six of his arrows from his quiver, and set them in the wooden box-quiver at the right of each shooting position. He strung his bow quickly while the others in the line got in position for their first shots. Testing the gut and satisfied that it was still in excellent condition, he set his first arrow to string and eyed the target.

These targets were massive to his trained eye, fully three feet across with a center spot of four inches in diameter. Jared felt like he was aiming at a bull's eye the size of a dinner plate. He and Ge-or had used a five-inch target for years, with a center spot the size of a gold imperial – less than an inch across. Their long-bow targets had been only a foot-and-a-half in diameter. Their father had insisted on them practicing out to ranges exceeding a hundred and fifty paces with the longer-ranged weapon.

Shooting easily, and with a focus and calm that he took on with his first breath, Jared nocked his arrow and drew in one smooth motion, bringing the bow to eye level in process. He released as his aim centered on the mark he set in his mind's eye. He had long ago learned not to hold on a target for any length of time. An archer's best accuracy came from being able to launch an arrow as soon as he had the mark in line with his aim. This was not only important technically; it served in combat to disavow any distractions that might thwart your aim. Plus, unless you were well-trained, archery students tended to find it difficult to focus and to maintain an aim for any length of time, drifting left and right or up and down the longer it was held. Jared suspected many of these students were facing that very concern right now.

He launched all of his arrows before most of the line had gotten to their third. His target displayed his accuracy. He had painted a neat pentagon with his first five arrows in the yellow center circle. He had placed the last in the dead center. If he had wanted to really show off, at this range he could have placed all six arrows in a row with the shafts touching each other. But there was a risk that one of his painstakingly crafted arrows would have suffered minor damage. After the retrieval, the other boys were wondering who this new arrival might be.

Selim, sensing that this student was something special, moved the line back to twenty-five paces. He told Jared to attempt the same feat. Jared easily complied. He knew he could place five practice arrows in an imperial at this range. So far this had simply been a warm-up for him.

The gnome moved Jared out to the forty paces line. At this range, Jared had to pay more attention to his surroundings -- the slight breeze that fluttered through the yard, the tilt of the target, and to the humidity in the air. All could affect the flight. He almost instinctively noted the subtle variations that would make a difference to his aim. Stepping to the line, he shot with the same fluidity and confidence he had shown at the shorter distances. He was the only one shooting. The other students were all standing behind and to the side, marveling at his skill.

After Jared once again formed the neat pentagram with the arrow in the center, Selim bowed low to him. "You have great skill, my young master."

Jared bowed in return, satisfied overall with himself, though he had been disappointed by his first shot of this flight. His arrow angle had caused the nock of that shaft to be slightly out of alignment with the others.

"Are you experienced with moving targets?" Selim asked.

Jared nodded. "Rabbits, squirrels, field mice for practice."

The gnome raised an eyebrow. He turned and directed one of the boys. "Botham, man the rail-deer."

The rail-deer turned out to be a mock-up of a deer. It was made of leather and straw that was set on a rail, so if it was pushed from the side, it would "run" across the target area. Selim told Jared to pick a distance and shout when he wanted the target sent on its way.

Jared stepped back to the fifty-pace marker. This target was so big he could have hit it from sixty paces with his shortbow, but that was pushing the accurate range of the compact weapon. After placing six arrows in the deer's vitals, Jared stepped back. "Master."

Selim's eyes twinkled. "You have me convinced. Botham, bring out the mobile."

Whatever that was, it set everyone watching into a buzz. Jared stood relaxed and confident. So far, none of this was as stressful as waiting to shoot a Qa-ryk in the eye. He watched to see what would come next.

The archery mobile turned out to be a contraption that, when it was set in motion by a crank, sent six different small round disks spinning about each other in a seemingly random motion. The disks varied slightly in size from two inches in diameter to about five. Each was painted a different color. Selim instructed Jared to go to the twenty-five paces marker to shoot. He explained that the disks would fall backward on a hinge when hit, and the arrows would drop to the ground.

Jared watched the spinning wheels for a couple of minutes before raising his bow. He noted that there was a pattern to their movements, but it was complicated. He wanted to be positive he had it down before he shot. When he was ready, he shot as smoothly as he had before – he nocked, aimed, and fired -- one arrow after another. Not only did he hit each of the spinning disks; he hit them in order of largest to smallest, finding the exact center point on all except the next to last, where a sudden gust of wind slightly deflected the arrow after he released it. Jared chastised himself for not anticipating the change in the breeze. He could hear his father shouting in his ear, "Sense -- always sense what was, what is, what will be."

When Jared returned with his arrows, the other boys were chattering excitedly. Later he would find out that he was the first student to have ever scored a perfect mark on the mobile. Master Selim made it a point to demonstrate each term that it could be done.

This time it was Selim who bowed low and held it. "You have been well trained, young sir. I salute you. How is your ability with the longbow?"

"I am trained in it as well," Jared offered. "I prefer the short for combat."

"Combat?" Selim looked deep into his eyes, "Yes, I see you have experience in these matters. Well, enough for today. You can shoot longbow for me tomorrow. Elwind wants you to move on to the thrown weapons. I will be honored to shoot with you, Jared of Thiele."

Jared bowed low once more. He felt he had met a friend in the place that would be kind to him. Someone who understood what he had been through the past few months.

Jared was a little less skilled at some of the throwing weapons, having only

26

trained with knives, spears, and axes. And a bit with buoas. He proved again, however, that his father had versed him and his brother well. He even managed to impress with his spear work. It had been the one weapon he had never quite taken to -- the weight and bulkiness he felt uncomfortable throwing with his slight frame. Ge-or, on the other hand, with his powerful build, had been really accurate with the various-sized and weighted shafts his father had made them form and throw.

Simon-Nathan caught up with Jared as he headed toward the gates of the compound. "You've created a bit of a stir," his bouncing roommate said. "You may not have the music down yet, but no one is going to question your ability with weapons. Impressive, quite impressive by all accounts. News spreads around here like wildfire. I caught a bit of your shooting. Maybe you can help me out. I'm a dolt when it comes to bows. Well, actually pretty much any weapon. They're not my forte. Any help you can give me will be appreciated. I like the history side of things. Quite fascinating..." He continued to ramble on as they left the arena.

Jared felt exhausted. He soon slid into a reverie of part-listening, part-following, and partially giving in to the enormity of what was happening to him as they walked back to their room.

Thistle

Sart and Thistle had walked for what seemed like hours through a maze of opulent corridors in the massive Borean Palace. Thistle was awed by the gilt facades, long mirrored hallways, rich tapestries that hung from twenty-foot ceilings and stretched to the floor, the marble floors, and stone statuary of a wide variety of colors and shapes.

Sart pressed ever forward toward their goal -- the apartments of Meligance, White Wizardess of Borea. He did not appear to notice the lavish, overly ornate style of the late Borean Empire nor any of the magnificent things they passed. He kept pulling Thistle along when she stopped to admire a particularly interesting sculpture or piece of furniture. He knew Meligance was waiting; and she did not brook delays, even from her friends.

They finally came to a halt before two fifteen-foot tall, richly stained oaken doors. Sart reached out with his staff and struck the brass door plate three times. A booming sound echoed down the corridor. Waiting and counting under his breath slowly, the cleric then struck the plate again: four quick raps, another wait, and three additional hard strikes. The doors began to swing outward on their own. Thistle and Sart drew back as the two panels separated, slowly revealing a wide chamber that stretched as far as they could see. Thistle noted the sun had crept around to the south and was peeking through the windows set between the arches of the cathedral ceiling of the hall before them.

The grand Magicians Hall was divided into many smaller areas by what appeared to be movable wooden screens set on wheeled dollies between marble pillars. As Sart drew her down the center corridor, Thistle noticed a flurry of different activities taking place in each of the separated areas. The men and women in their respective stations were busy with a wide variety of tasks. Some wore long green robes and were huddled over smoking braziers; others in dark blue regalia studied large tomes or long scrolls set on reading easels; and others in yellow and brown appeared to be practicing a wide variety of conjurations, standing freely about a section devoid of any apparatus or furniture at all.

Thistle paused at one opening to watch. Several magicians were practicing with glass balls, making them float up and down, or disappear and reappear with the wave of a hand. Further into the room, she could see older students working with what appeared to be energy bursts that flew from their hands or fingers and struck metal plates set into the far wall.

Sart drew her away, moving her forward again. "You will have time enough to understand all of this and more, my child. Come, the White Wizardess awaits. She is very powerful; she is also kind. She has called you, and would that I knew what that meant. It is, above all else, an honor. So be respectful and answer her honestly and directly.

"All this you see here are the trappings of magic, illusion, and the alchemical. What you will learn, should she take you on as an apprentice, will be up to Meligance. I will warrant that she will leave little to chance in your education. There are two key points to remember in your studies here – these above all she will teach you: 'Respect the power,' and, 'To the best of your judgment and ability, use it for good.' All else is secondary.

"Know also this, Thistle – she has never taken an apprentice. If she chooses you, you will be unique. All these you see about you here," Sart gestured at the many working diligently in the sections they passed, "are apprentices to the kingdom. They are instructed by the mages, witches, alchemists, and illusionists employed by the king. Your lot will be to learn much of this... and far more."

Thistle pulled to a stop, glancing about, tears began to fill her eyes. "But I know none of this. I am not powerful, nor do I have a shred of magic. I... I am nothing compared to these. I don't belong."

Sart reached out to her, drawing her under his arm. "Child, child, you have far more power than you think. I sensed something when I first saw you lying in that thicket. I saw the evidence of it in the protection you were able to produce from the sending. Then, you were able to remember and use energy, albeit subconsciously, to protect me in a battle that I myself could not win. While it may have been dangerous to do so, you wielded a type of energy that only the most powerful wizards and wizardesses dare try. You may not recognize your power or ability, Thistle; nevertheless, it is there. Else we would not be here.

"Trust in your path, my child. For good fortune or ill, it has been laid before you. You may be asked to make a choice. Choose wisely; most importantly, choose from your heart."

"Will you be near?" Thistle pleaded. "I feel the need of a friend. I miss my family so much. I am so alone, so overwhelmed here..." Her voice trailed off. She fought the tears that wanted to flow freely as her emotions swirled.

"My duties are here for now," Sart replied. "I plan to search the archives in the palace vaults. I want to try to understand this stone that young Jared has acquired. It has power, perhaps great power. Aberon and the Black Druids had a reason to want it destroyed. We won an important victory by destroying the Altar of Kan, yet there is still great evil in that dark dungeon below his former fortress. There is some other power behind the rise and strength of the Black Druids that we must discover. Perhaps this artifact is one we can use in other ways to help the kingdom. I am well versed in lore, but I have heard naught of this stone.

"I will come, weekly, to see how you are doing, or more often, if feasible -- at least until I am called elsewhere. Meligance, however, may have other uses for me where it concerns you. I defer to her wisdom when I can. I will check in on Jared as well. You and he, along with many others, are the future of this kingdom. Come, my child, the unknown can bring us both danger and treasure. It often depends on how we approach it."

Thistle wiped the tears from her eyes with the rough cotton sleeve of her stained travel tunic. Though she and Jared had acquired some new clothes at Xur, it had taken them weeks to reach the eastern palace. Now, at the moment of meeting the great Wizardess, she realized that she was wearing garments that had last been cleaned with rough soap in a stream some days ago. They would have to suffice; she had nothing else to put on. Looking down, she noted that her worn, sweat-soaked sandals and roughly used feet would probably not add to her presentation. She laughed.

"What is it, my child?"

"I was thinking that I am nothing more than a mess. Perhaps Meligance has poor eyesight?"

"Not likely. She sees everything – what is obvious and what is hidden. Her powers are immense. Fear not, I am as travel-worn as you; and she is not concerned with our appearance, at least not outwardly. Come, she awaits, and I have much else to do this day."

Meligance, White Wizardess of Borea

After traversing the length of the great hall, they came to an unremarkable wooden door set in the far wall. Sart paused before finally, with a deep sigh, tapping lightly on the dull brass plate that said simply, "Do not Disturb without Good Cause." He mumbled under his breath, "I trust our cause is good," a frown on his face, which changed in an instant to a broad grin, and finally to a slight frown. "I can never quite forget my first run-in with her... Ah, but that was when I was young. Now, I warrant, she will be glad to see us."

"Come." The voice that echoed from above their heads was strong and commanding, yet obviously feminine.

Sart cracked the door open, using the unadorned wooden knob to gain entrance. The disembodied voice boomed again. "Come, my good cleric. I shan't roast your rump a second time without good cause."

Sart grumbled under his breath as he pushed the heavy door inward. "It still smarts on occasion," he said. He pushed Thistle ahead of him. They entered what was a small, empty, circular chamber. There was a slight shift to the light, and suddenly the two of them were facing a long, ornately carved, rectangular desk in a similarly shaped, much larger room. If one could believe the view out of the large stained-glass windows, they were seeing the palace proper from high above.

Sart whispered to Thistle, as she oriented to the new room they were standing in, "I'm sure you will get used to that trick of getting up here. Even after all these years, it occasionally makes my head spin."

It took Thistle a few minutes to get used to the strange lighting -- partially from a cascade of multicolored rays coming through the stained-glass windows, and the rest caused by a variegated radiance effusing from fuzzy balls of light that floated here and there about the room. She finally settled her gaze on the woman behind the desk. A lithe figure, dressed in a flowing gown of the lightest purple, accented with satin white, was bent over the manuscript-strewn desk. She was peering intently at a darkly-stained scroll, using a small flat piece of glass or quartz, which was illuminated magically from within, to facilitate her perusal. Meligance's long, straight blond hair flowed about the parchment as she moved the viewer from side to side. "Be with you both in a second... Ah, here it is. This will be of interest to you, my good cleric. It is a reference to a stone of some power. I read it in my youth and remembered the reference. See here..." Meligance turned the scroll toward Sart. He stepped forward and bent to study the illuminated section with her.

"Yes, I see... 'gold, with an oval greenish-blue stone, almost turquoise; power to ease suffering of the mind.' No, no, similar, but what Jared has is light blue at its core. It is oddly shaped -- cut, yet in no design I have ever seen – irregular. A diamond, I would hazard, pure at first glance, strangely murky when you look into its depths. It appears to promote healing. It is a powerful artifact, from a bygone era, I would think."

"Well, you seem to have work to do." Meligance waved her hand over the crystal, and the light faded. She stood up, straightening to her full five-feet, eight-inches in height. She looked intently into Thistle's eyes.

Thistle had a strong urge to flinch; she fought the impulse to draw back. The Wizardess' gaze, however, held her in a grip stronger than any shackles. She felt Meligance's grey-blue eyes penetrate to her soul. For a moment, Thistle felt like she was going to faint. Eventually the sensation left, and she felt at peace – simply a young woman standing in front of a senior who could have been a nun, or mother, or even a mentor. The words came flashing quickly through her mind.

The White Wizardess of Borea said rather oddly, "Come to Mama, Baby. Come." At first Thistle thought the words were meant for her; but then she felt Yolk slide down from his perch on her stomach and out from under her tunic. He slid onto the desk and flowed over to where Meligance stood with outstretched hands. "Good boy." She scooped up the brownish, pancake-like creature and stroked the lump of its head. Much to Thistle's surprise, the ovietti began to squeak and chirp excitedly at Meligance. "Yes, my pet, she is wonderful and, yes, you are hers now. I only wanted to welcome you back. Go…"

Meligance's voice had changed to a high pitch, and she continued in the common tongue. Thistle saw Yolk rise up in the center and open his eyelids to stare intently at the Wizardess. After she stopped speaking, he flowed out of Meligance's hands, across the table, and back to Thistle.

Eyes wide, Thistle accepted Yolk's return. When Meligance addressed her again, the creature folded itself back under her tunic to rest against her chest and stomach.

"You have great power, my child. And you have the potential for even more.

32

Your friend…what do you call him?"

"Yolk," Thistle mumbled, suddenly embarrassed at having given the wondrous creature so banal a name.

"Yolk? Yes, that fits," Meligance chuckled. "Yolk has chosen you to be my apprentice and his friend. It is a great honor to be chosen by an ovietti. They are one of the most naturally powerful magical creatures of our world." She paused, as if to let Thistle say something; when she didn't, she went on.

"So, to business. I would like you to become my apprentice; you must think carefully on your answer. You will work hard, harder than you have ever imagined, and there will be many trials. While you may not realize it, you have powerful natural abilities in magic, and some deep insights, as well as instincts, in the art. There is, however, much to learn that goes beyond our nature. It is control – control of the gift you carry – that will make or break you as a mage." Meligance paused again to let her words sink in. Thistle, this time, took the opportunity to speak.

"Truly your… your highness…" Thistle felt completely flummoxed by what Meligance was saying to her. "I know not of what you speak. I can do none of the things I saw being practiced by the students below. What magic I may have shown in the wilds came from you. I did nothing more than speak the words of your sending. I feel lost here. I do not belong." Thistle bowed her head, not wishing to gainsay the Wizardess; but she also did not want to lie about what she knew about herself.

Meligance's wisp of a smile widened. She glanced toward Sart, asking what the cleric took to be a rhetorical question. "Does she not know of the power she tapped in receiving and wielding the sending?"

He did not respond at first, only shrugged his shoulders. Yet, when Meligance kept looking at him, he answered. "I think, milady, that the power is so natural it lies calmly within her, ready to use, already well-controlled."

"Ah, if you are right, my good priest, she is special indeed…Thistle!"

"Yes, your highness?"

Meligance smiled again. The gentle upward curve of her lips made her look more beautiful in the variegated light. She was a stunning woman by any measure, even if you discounted the obvious power about her presence. She chuckled softly. "My dear girl, whatever you may have heard, I am not 'your highness,' and never will be. You may address me as, 'milady,' 'ma'am,' 'mum,' or even 'Meligance'. Formalities are unimportant, only truth.

"Here, catch this." Meligance drew one of the colored balls of light from the air, somehow caused it to flare to a brilliant golden sphere, and tossed it toward Thistle.

Surprised, Thistle held out her hands and caught the sparkling ball, as she would have caught a brambleball in the child's game -- lightly and cautiously. The globe of light danced in her palms. She held it easily, marveling at the slight tickling sensation it made in her hands.

"Now, throw it to Sart."

"Oh, milady, canst thou…" Sart groaned.

Thistle did as she was instructed. She cradled the ball in her right hand, then tossed it underhanded to the cleric. Instinctively, he reached out to catch it. When it touched his hand, it exploded into a million tiny sparks. Sart yelped. "Ouch. For goodness sake, Meligance, must I always be at the receiving end of your educational devices!" He shook his hand, looking at her ruefully.

33

She smiled at him. "You are right, my good cleric. I am sorry for the painful demonstration; but it made my point, and yours, effectively. She has power, true power in the art; and she does control it effortlessly, without ken. That, my dear," and she turned back toward Thistle, "can be both good and bad. You will need to learn to recognize your power and understand the means you use to control it.

"To give you a perspective of what happened: Sart is a powerful cleric, yet he could neither catch nor control the power of that magic ball. You did so without even knowing how. I could take almost any one of the magic-users and illusionists you passed on your way to my door; not only would they not be able to control the ball, they would likely sustain far more injury in trying than our dear cleric here, who got a nice prickling jolt. The few who could catch and control it would have done so only with great effort. For you, it was natural, as easy as catching a wicker ball.

"So, what say you, my child?" Meligance looked into Thistle's eyes, almost as if challenging her. "Do you wish to study under my guidance or no? It will be a long, hard road if you accept, and there will be little time for frivolities."

Thistle's first thoughts were of Jared. She wondered how he was, what he was doing, and mostly, how he was feeling. She wondered if he felt as lost as she did right now. A pang of loneliness shuddered through her body. How was he faring at Bard Hall? She knew his studies would be long and arduous, as well, though they hoped they would be able to see each other soon. Now she was the one with the choice to make; their relationship would be theirs to deal with.

The other consideration she felt she had to face right away was her family and whether she could be of any help to them. She and Jared had taken a quick side trip to Permis on their way to the capital city. There they found that her parents had taken in several additional children from the devastation at Thiele, which made their lot even more precarious. Such was the honor of the wilderness bred – you helped your own. It was a new burden for her relatives.

Yet, Thistle had chosen to continue on their trek to seek her own fortune. According to Sart, she really didn't have a choice. She had to know whether she had this supposed power or talent, lest it hurt herself or others. Her parents certainly did not need one more mouth to feed. But all of this? How could she help them if she were studying to become a mage? Somehow, she needed to feel she could aid her sisters and parents in some way.

Thistle answered hesitatingly. "To study with you, milady, is a dream beyond any dreams I ever had. Though I do not ken any of this, I am willing to try. Until only a short while ago, I sought only to be well-married for my family and to live a simple life in our village. I...I am deeply honored that you would consider me of value in any sense. I cannot justly take on this responsibility without finding some means to help my..."

"Your family?"

Thistle answered meekly, "Yes."

"Sart and I spoke on this in a sending while you were journeying here. Your sisters will be well cared for. I will have the seneschal of the western province send your mother and father a stipend for their upkeep and education. I will also have a company of young soldiers assigned to your village for a period to help reinforce their defenses." Meligance paused, clearing her throat, as if to emphasize a point. "There is also, is there not, the matter of the young half-elf? Jared, now at Bard Hall?"

Thistle lowered her eyes, her cheeks reddening slightly. "Yes, milady."

"You will be able to see him, though rarely. Your studies will be all-encompassing and draining. These things are best learned while free of emotional attachments. I will not, however, stand in the way of your true feelings. Only know this, your chastity is crucial in focusing and understanding your power in the early years, else you could hurt yourself or another. Can you promise me this?"

"Yes, ma'am," Thistle answered, blushing even more deeply.

"Good, it is decided." She turned toward the cleric. "Sart?"

"Yes, milady?"

"You will be in the library for some days?"

"As long as I can, until I am called elsewhere."

"Good. It will be helpful to have you around to help educate our young lady in the type of power you wield."

"I am at your disposal…ah, that is as long as I'm not disposed of, if you get my drift."

"That will be determined by your behavior, my good cleric. Stay with me a while. Thistle, you may return to the magic academy. Sart will be down in a bit to show you about. We will start your tutelage early on the morrow, here… Oh, yes, I nearly forgot. Do you read and write?"

"The common tongue, milady, none else."

"Well," she looked at Sart, "get her started on the old language. I know of no one better suited to teach it -- two hours in the evening until you must go. If she is as bright as I ken, I can take over from there. Go, child."

It was a request and a command. Thistle did not have to be told twice, but she had no idea where to go. There were no doors in the room. She was still rooted in the spot she had "landed in" after they had been magicked here.

Meligance offered instructions. "Turn around; walk toward the wall; envision the entryway; and if you feel you must, wave your hands about impressively."

"Meligance," Sart chided. Yet, he knew, too, that there was always method to Meligance's way of doing things. Thistle would learn from this simple lesson that magic was not about gestures and extravagances. Those were things only for show, for an audience. Magic was about power; tapping power from within oneself, as well as from without.

Thistle turned on her heel, took a step toward the wall of stone, and envisioned the plain circular room they had left. An instant later, she found herself standing before the door they had left ajar twenty minutes before.

"See, she didn't even have to wave her hands." Meligance smiled at Sart.

"Yes, but where is she? She could be in the seventh plane of hell with those instructions. Sometimes, you worry me, milady," the cleric fretted.

"Tut, just another test. You do worry too much, my good man. Now come here and give an old lady a bear hug."

35

The Uses of Magic

Thistle paced the hallway for almost an hour, waiting for the cleric to return. Her thoughts and feelings were completely jumbled, one thing tumbling upon another as she tried to sort things through. She was relieved that her sisters and family would be cared for. Staying had seemed ludicrous. She would have been another burden, and they would have wanted to marry her off as soon as was practical. Now, after all she had been through, that was something she definitely did not want. Yet, as the eldest, she did feel a responsibility toward her family. Times in the west were getting tougher. She was happy that the extended family would be provided for while she studied here in the capital.

In some ways, Meligance had been daunting; but the Wizardess had also been kind. Thankfully, she did have a sense of humor. Thistle did feel she could devote herself to her mentorship and to this new life. Yet, she was still unsure of her supposed talent. The demonstration with the orb had proved interesting; but innate or not, she did not sense this power she obviously had.

The truth was she felt really lost. Her closest friend, Jared, was now out of reach; and she had no idea when they would be able to see each other again. The closeness they had shared over the weeks since the battle at Xur had been youthful and innocent. They had held hands and kissed lightly and shyly in the few moments they had alone. On rare occasions, they had been able to lie together and lightly touch each other, fully clothed. It had been deeply sensual, yet they had maintained control.

Meligance and Sart had both spoken seriously of control – of the importance of controlling magic -- really controlling its power. If she had control of her inner energy, her "magic," she did not recognize it. If anything, she felt powerless and far from in control. She felt like she needed a long cry in her father's arms. Sometimes, she desperately wanted to go back to what was a far simpler life in the seacoast village. Here, she wondered if she…

Sart suddenly appeared in the doorway, interrupting her musings as she spun for what felt like the thousandth time to continue her pacing. She stopped abruptly and tried to smile up at him, but the emotions suddenly reached a saturation point. Tears began to flood down her cheeks. "Oh, Sart…"

"Come, come, my child. Come to Father Sart." The cleric reached out with his long arms and enfolded her in the warmth of his voluminous robes. "Come, let us rest a bit. I have summoned us a cold lunch. It should be here soon." He led her to a bench by the wall; then he drew her down, letting her sob onto his broad shoulder. "Sh-h-h. All will be well. You have impressed our lady, and soon you will be on your feet here in your new life. Rest awhile."

Thistle was feeling much better after their light repast. The two glasses of fine southern wine she had drunk had her giggling at Sart's silly antics. When the cleric indicated it was time to proceed with Meligance's admonition to "show her new apprentice around," Thistle stood up. Taking the cleric's big, rough, callused hand in hers, she helped pull him off of the low bench.

"Ah, to be so young and agile again. Middle age is creeping upon me much faster than I would wish," he groaned as he stood.

"Well, young lady, let us take a brief tour of parts of the palace; after which, I shall show you to your quarters. Soon you will know this place better than I; but for now, try to get a sense of what it is all about."

Their first stop was a section on the right of the magic hall. It was teeming with students of various ages, practicing what Thistle took to be fundamental magic tricks. When she asked about the magic involved, Sart answered with a smile. "No, my child, what you are witnessing is not true magic, simply legerdemain – deftness with the fingers. Come, I'll have one of the more advanced students show you some tricks.

"Maskel?" He gestured toward a tall lad, who was amongst a group near the entrance. "Come here, if you will, please."

A tall handsome young man of perhaps nineteen or twenty separated himself from a group of students who had been doing a variety of coin and ball disappearances and reappearances. "Maskel, this is Thistle, Meligance's new apprentice. Please show her how a couple of your tricks work."

Maskel's eyes widened at Sart's introduction. He bowed low to them both, though he held his bow more toward Thistle than Sart. "I am honored, Sart. I heard you were out west. You brought back a prize indeed. I am honored to meet you, milady."

Thistle blushed and murmured, "The pleasure is mine."

"What would you like to see?" Maskel asked.

"A few sleight-of-hand tricks with a coin; then explain the techniques," Sart said.

Maskel took a silver imperial in his hand, holding it out for Thistle to see. "The basics of our art are to be quick and stealthy enough to appear as if we are making objects appear from nowhere and disappear into thin air. Like this…"

Maskel tossed the coin in the air with his right hand; he immediately snatched it out of the air with his left. When he opened his hands for them to see, the coin was back in his right. He did several other tricks for Thistle, including pulling coins from her hair, behind her ear, and much to Sart's chagrin, from the cleric's nose. Thistle laughed delightedly at his antics during the demonstration.

Next, he showed her the deft hand movements required for the tricks. He performed the sequences in slow motion, even showing Thistle the distractive movements he made when he wanted her eyes focused elsewhere. His skill was impressive. When he redid the tricks at speed, Thistle could still not follow his motions.

"Would you like to try, Thistle?" Maskel asked, bowing again.

"Oh, I couldn't. I would fumble terribly," Thistle answered, blushing again.

"Just for fun." Maskel tossed her one of the imperials he was using. "Try tossing it in the air and switching hands."

After explaining the moves two more times, he finally persuaded Thistle to try. Thistle laughed as she tossed the coin in the air. Focusing intently, she reached up to catch it in her left hand. The coin suddenly disappeared in midair. Maskel stared at her, blinking in surprise. "That was amazingly good. Are you sure this is your first time? Show me the coin and do it again."

Thistle opened both her hands; there was no coin in either. She shook her head. "I don't know what happened. I was ready to grab it, and it disappeared."

Sart groaned. "We definitely need to get you started, my dear. Oops…" The silver imperial suddenly dropped from the air in front of him and landed in his lap. A firm feminine voice spoke through the ether. "Control, control!" It was Sart's turn to blush. "Ah, yes, well, sorry to disturb, Maskel. Thank you for the demonstration. You are much improved. Good day."

Embarrassed, Thistle bowed toward Maskel. The young man, reddening himself, managed an awkward bow in return.

"Come, my child, let us simply look into the different areas. I'll explain what is happening. Perhaps we better avoid demonstrations until you have had a few sessions with Meligance."

Thistle agreed, more than happy to defer any more such situations.

When they left the magic hall, Sart gestured expansively. "You have witnessed an array of skills – some the result of physical and mental acumen, others truly magical in that the wielder taps power outside herself." He stopped and gave Thistle a long look from under his brown brows. "So that you appreciate that power and ability come to us in many ways, know that I have studied long and hard to understand what I can use directly from this world to help in healing: herbs, potions, salves, and ointments, as well as techniques in wound care, surgery, and so on. I also use my personal inner force to help heal. Perhaps, if I continue to grow in wisdom and ability, I will reach ever-higher levels of skill through practice. I also hope to learn to draw even more power from the earth. It is my life-long endeavor to develop myself to my fullest as a healer.

"I cannot speak, my child, to the power you have within yourself. Meligance will guide you in understanding that better. All true mages have a gift, or talent, that helps them to tap into other sources of power. In a sense, it is akin to how I tap into the power of the earth, of living things. However, as I understand it, it is also fundamentally different. It goes beyond life to the root of it all – or that is how Meligance has described it to me. Hence, your ability to catch and throw the magical ball, in contrast to my inability to do so. As Meligance indicated, I was at least able to fend off most of the power with my inner force, though I could not control it directly as you did.

"Come, let us walk. I want to get you to your rooms so you can rest. This evening we shall begin your studies in the old language."

They walked down the long hall and took several turns into other corridors. Thistle tried to focus on where they were going, but the maze of rooms and passageways looked to be endless. She gave up trying to remember.

Sart finally stopped after they rounded a corner. "Ah, here we are – your rooms, milady." He gestured at an ornate door that had strange symbols carved in its surface. "Before we go in, one other caution about the use of magic. You will learn quickly that there are many limits to power: what you have the strength to wield, what you can draw upon and how, how the use of power is personally draining, and so on. Those who see power as a means to personal gain and glory often find themselves destroyed by that which they would gain. Be wise, my child. You are already cautious, and that is a good thing. Understand first, then learn control. Listen to your mentor; she is far wiser than I about these things."

Sart turned the handle on the door and pushed it open. "Now, go into your chambers, freshen up, get settled, and try to rest a bit. I will find your chambermaid. Since we broke our fast late, I will have her bring us dinner after dark. While we eat leisurely together, we will begin your study of the ancient tongue. I will return anon."

When Sart had gone, Thistle paused in the doorway, not believing what she was seeing. She gaped at the lavish room before her. Brilliant tapestries hung on both sides of the foyer. These drew one into an expansive chamber that was filled with ornate furniture and plush pillows. Silken draperies hung alongside a wide window, which overlooked a large courtyard. Thistle had never seen anything so luxurious. Her life in Permis had been basic, almost hand to mouth. She stood staring at this opulently-layered scene, which was such a contrast to her worn and stained clothing.

She finally took a deep breath and moved into the chamber. A minute later, she stopped again, realizing that this was merely the first of several rooms. She set the tattered traveling bag containing her few possessions in the middle of the floor on a dark area of the plush rug, so that it might not show dirt from the road. Then she poked her nose into the rest of her rooms, which looked more and more like an exquisite suite the further she explored. The living space was larger than her family's entire extended cabin.

Her needs appeared to be provided for. She discovered she had a private bath with a large copper tub centered on a plush oval rug, a larger bedroom equally lavish in its décor and furnishings, and a den complete with a desk with dozens of spaces and drawers built in for placing books, scrolls, pens, and anything else she would need for her studies. In the closet, there were a dozen sets of robes and dresses of the finest fabrics. She reached out tentatively to touch a green, velvety full-length gown to feel the texture. Suddenly, she drew her hand back, embarrassed when she felt another presence come in from the doorway to her right.

"Excuse, milady, I am Alicia, your chambermaid. Would you enjoy a hot bath before you rest?"

Thistle turned on her heel, flushing at having been caught looking at the rich clothes. "My... my chambermaid? You are here to serve me?"

"Why, yes, milady. I am at your call. My room is across the hall. If I am not here, you can ring me with the bell cords." She pointed to one hanging by the right side of the bed. "Did you not know I was coming?"

"I'm sorry, no... Well, yes, I guess Sart did mention it. I'm sorry; you said your name is Alicia?"

"Yes, ma'am."

"Alicia, I have never had a chambermaid. I have never had a servant or been waited on. This is really strange to me. I... well, please call me Thistle. And please, please dispense with the formalities, shall we? Let us be friends as we may. I so desperately need a friend here. Can we do that?"

"Yes, milady... Ah, I mean yes, Miss Thistle... ah, Thistle. That seems awkward, milady."

"There, good, Thistle it is. What do your friends call you?"

"Alley, milady, ah, Thistle. Like the cat, the alley cat. I was always sneaking about as a child, you know?"

"Alley, it is, or better, Alli. A-l-l-i. Do you read?"

"No ma'am... ah, Thistle. They don't teach servants to... well, it isn't important for chambermaids to learn to read."

"You can learn with me. I have to learn a new language, and you can learn your letters, too. Anyway, yes, a bath would be absolutely wonderful." She turned, looking about the room again, still stunned that this was to be hers.

She turned back toward the closet and asked, "Alli, are these mine to wear?" Thistle gestured at the clothes.

"Yes'm, and you have laces and underthings in that chest." Alli pointed to an ornate, dark walnut drawer chest in the corner of the room. "And slippers and shoes in there," she gestured toward a floor chest in the closet. "You can ask one of the palace tailors should you need anything further. I brought them all up this morning. They were expecting you, you know."

"Well, actually, no, I didn't know. Oh, Alli, I am so lost here. I..." Thistle swallowed, then blushed, realizing that her chambermaid was dressed far better than she was in her stained, worn clothing.

"Yes, please, bring me water for the bath. And while I am getting all this travel dirt off, why don't you pick out a matching outfit for me. I imagine I will have to learn what is appropriate to wear at the court."

Alli's eyes danced with merriment. "I would love to help in any way. Please sit, relax. I will be right back with the water for your bath. It will only take me a few minutes to prepare it. I was told you had travelled a great distance and to have everything ready. Welcome, milady. I am so happy you are so nice." She curtsied and left.

Thistle sighed deeply. How her fortunes had changed. For a minute, she almost didn't miss Jared.

Study

Jared sat on the end of his bed working through the exercises that Stevens had given him after dinner. The older boy from choir had sat with him for a few minutes and explained the basics. Once he understood the staff, clefs, accidentals (or sharps and flats), and the basic scales, the concept was fairly simple. However, he knew that it would take him a while to be able to read notes easily.

Right now, Jared was working through a page of treble clef music, writing down the names of the notes lightly under the staff with his graphite stick. It was a bit tedious, but he could see the value in the work. Already, he was past the stage of having to count lines and spaces; except, when the notes went above or below the staff, he still had to think them through.

He stopped at the end of the page and looked over at his roommate. Simon-Nathan was deeply engrossed in a voluminous tome entitled, *The History of Music, Part V.* Jared had *Part I*, which he had been given by the first-year history master. An hour ago, he had tried to wade through the first chapter which was auxiliary reading to his basic text, *An Introduction to Music*, the book he had received from the old man the previous day. "How can you read that stuff?" Jared asked. "I almost fell asleep after two paragraphs of the first book."

Simon-Nathan, placing his finger carefully on the spot where he had stopped reading, looked up and smiled. "I know, I'm a bit weird. I love this history stuff. That's what I want to do – research and write about the old Bards, the development of music. I find it all fascinating. Someday I hope to be Master of History."

"You don't want to be a Bard?"

"Never really considered it. As you already know, I don't have the weapon skills to…"

"What…?"

"Actually, most students here don't plan to be Bards, Jared; and my father… Ah, by-the-way, how's the note-reading going?"

Jared puzzled a second over why Simon-Nathan suddenly seemed a bit uncomfortable; he decided to leave it for another time, "All right… Well, fine actually. The concepts are pretty basic. I think I'll pick this up fairly quickly. I'm a little confused about the application though. I can use this in choir right away, at least after I learn the tenor clef a bit better; but what about my lyre or lute? I don't know where to start. You don't play one note with one finger, do you? Do I have to memorize every possible finger with each note?"

"It's not that bad, Jared. Here, I'll show you." Simon-Nathan grabbed his lute from the bottom of the bed and set it in playing position. Now take this note…" He put his first finger on a string and plucked.

"A 'D,'" Jared said.

"Yeah, that's right. How did you know that?"

"A couple of months ago, a Journeyman Bard I was with asked me to play in the Key of D. I didn't know what he meant by 'Key;' nevertheless, he started on that note or nearly that note. Yours sounds a wee bit low."

Simon-Nathan raised his eyebrows. "You must have darned good pitch, maybe even perfect pitch, to remember that. Well, that makes this easier.

"As you know, I can play this note with any of my four fingers, and for complicated pieces, I might even use my thumb, right?"

Jared nodded.

"I learned, as many musicians do, to read notes as I learned to play," Simon said. "I started on the lute, and moved to keyboard instruments. So, I learned on the lute to play 'D' with my second finger initially. Only later, when I learned other positions, did I learn to play that 'D' with another finger. You have an advantage in that you learned to play first, before reading notes, though you will struggle for a while coordinating the two.

"Don't worry about that. The truth is that when you really know an instrument, you get beyond hand positions and what finger you play something with. The instrument becomes a part of you; you choose the easiest and best-sounding way to play a passage, regardless of 'fingerings' or 'positions.'"

"Oh," Jared said, although he didn't quite get it.

"Well, don't worry about it. I tend to overdo explanations. Trust me; it will come to you in a rush once you learn your notes and chords."

"That's another problem, too. I read about intervals, chords, triads, sevenths, and so forth in the theory section. My head is swimming."

"Jared, my friend, I am not a theorist; yet I do understand the historical end of how theory developed during different eras.

"Let me try to make this simple. Learn your notes and clefs. It will take you a while to become truly facile at the movable clefs, but you'll get it quickly enough. Apply the clefs and notes to your voice and instruments as soon as you can; then it will all start to fall into place.

"Beyond that, keep in mind that what you are studying in first year is all about intervals: most importantly, the octave and third. After that you will start with the triad, which is a three-note chord, each note a third apart, and from there basic harmony. In other words, how those triads relate to each other. Those are the basics."

"Harmony seems…"

"Yeah, I know, Jared, it's really confusing. Better ask Karenna about all that. She's a real theorist; loves the stuff. I tend to like the old music. You know, the contrapuntal compositions. But the new music is the thing now, so we have to learn both.

"Here, I'll tell you a couple of things.

"First, and this is important, the theory/harmony you will learn this year and next is all about the new, modern system. What is becoming known now as the major-minor tonal system.

"The old system, which is based around polyphonic music – multiple melodies

– has as a foundation the 'perfect' intervals of the ancients: the fourth, fifth, and octave, and the old scales known as modes.

"Get this..." Simon-Nathan suddenly looked energized by what he was talking about. Jared, unfortunately, had been lost from the start. "The modern harmonic system grew out of the old polyphonic system when... Darn, there I go again.

"How do I explain this fundamentally? Ah...?" Simon-Nathan frowned, trying to think of a logical, simple explanation.

"Well, today's system..." Simon-Nathan continued on for another half-hour trying, relatively unsuccessfully, to explain the new theory in relationship to the old polyphony. He succeeded in giving Jared a bigger headache.

That night, as they were getting ready for bed, Simon-Nathan noticed the large welt on Jared's chest when he removed his tunic. "What happened there?"

"A cheap shot from Elanar. It is nothing. It'll heal quickly."

"Shouldn't you have it looked at in the infirmary, Jared? It looks nasty."

"I'll be fine. It will be mostly healed by morning. I have this." Jared took the pendant from around his neck. He held out the irregularly-shaped stone so his roommate could see it.

"What is it? It is oddly-shaped and pretty murky inside. What does it do?"

"Don't really know. I took it off a Qa-ryk officer I killed. I was... well, I was desperate. My village had been destroyed. I guess at the time I thought I might be able to sell it for supplies. At any rate, it seems to have some power to heal. I was badly wounded by another Qa-ryk; see this scar." Jared pointed at the long wide scars on his shoulder that ran from almost the top of his neck around to his armpit. "I put this around my neck when I took it off the beast. By the second morning after I was wounded, this had healed over. Later, I met a cleric and he said it had healing qualities. He urged me to keep it safe.

"Please, Simon-Nathan, don't tell anyone about it. It is now my charge. Sart, the cleric, is searching the lore to find out more about it."

"Absolutely, I'll keep it to myself. No worries there. You killed a Qa-ryk? What..."

Jared ended up telling his roommate about his village's destruction and the adventure that eventually led him to Bard Hall. Though tired, they talked long into the night.

Jared's theory and history classes the next morning did make his mind spin, yet he was determined to do his best. It turned out that Karenna was in his theory class. She volunteered immediately to help him with his studies. After class, she enthusiastically grabbed him by his arm and suggested an hour study session that evening. Jared wanted to groan; but she was so bubbly and intense, he felt obliged to set the date.

All he wanted to do, really, was crawl back to his room and immerse himself in his studies. Then stay there, at least until he could emerge some months later caught up with everything, when he was no longer embarrassed by his inadequacies. He knew that was unrealistic. He needed all the help he could get. Karenna's offer was great; the only problem was that she was so cute.

43

The Power Within

Thistle paced in the hallway below Meligance's "entrance," waiting for the White Wizardess' summons. She had spent a relaxing and quiet evening in her rooms. The bath had been fantastic; and in spite of all her protestations, Alli had insisted on waiting on her, combing her hair, helping her dress, and generally attending to whatever she wanted.

Shortly after Sart arrived, a meal was delivered to Thistle's door by a kitchen servant. Thistle thoroughly enjoyed the delicious dinner of fish, fruits, cheeses, and breads, while the cleric introduced her to High Elvish. Though the scripts varied, and the words were somehow more flowery and severe at the same time, she discovered that there were many similarities between the old language and the vernacular of the Borean Empire. She had always loved to read, and she was fascinated by all that Sart imparted to her that first evening.

As promised, Thistle had Alli sit with them. Sart, always enthusiastic as a teacher, helped her begin learning her letters. She appeared to be a bright girl and was eager to learn. Thistle was happy to have Alli. At least now she did not feel so alone. The two of them spent the last half hour before Thistle went to bed reviewing with each other all they had learned.

Before dawn, Thistle was woken by a gentle prodding from Alli. "Your mistress wishes to see you anon. I have set out a basin with warm water, your hairbrush, and mirror. There is also a cup of blackberry tea by the side. However, she wishes to see you before you break your fast."

Thistle didn't know what Meligance meant by "anon." She assumed, by Sart's statements yesterday, that the Wizardess was not one to keep waiting. She hurried through her morning ablutions and quickly sipped the fragrant and honey-sweetened tea.

She let Alli lead her through the maze of turns and corridors to the Magician's Hall. There her handmaid left her, obviously not comfortable in the presence of so much overt magic. At the last minute, Alli pressed into her palm a detailed map of that part of the palace complex, as well as the brief note from Meligance requesting her presence: "Come to my work chamber before daybreak. Your training will begin." Her signature, with the royal Borean crest swirled within, was at the bottom. Thistle waited at Meligance's stoop, wondering how soon she would be called.

It wasn't long before a voice came from the ether above. Though it wasn't booming, it did penetrate to one's core. "Don't stand there, girl. Come in. Come up. The day waits."

Thistle opened the door, hugged Yolk, who was as usual on her lower chest under her cloak, and stepped forward. An instant later, she was standing before Meligance.

The scene was much the same as the day before, when she had been there with Sart. The magical balls shed a kaleidoscope of lights across all the surfaces in the room. Meligance sat, as if unmoved from the previous day, at the long table/desk working diligently at a piece of parchment. This time she had an odd-shaped pair of spectacles balanced on the end of her elegant nose. The triangular lenses on the device appeared to be interchangeable, for the Wizardess occasionally shifted the various frames up and down on both sides. Seemingly annoyed, she took them off altogether. "Some of my former colleagues took their subterfuge much too seriously. If you're going to leave something for posterity, leave it so it can be deciphered easily. Tut...tut," she sniffed in frustration.

Suddenly she appeared to have an idea. "Come here, child, look at this. What do you see?" She pushed the paper around, shoving it across the table toward Thistle.

Thistle looked down at the page of vellum. At first, she saw nothing; it was simply a blank sheet of parchment, darkly yellowed with age. As she stared, a fine row of lettering began to appear from the bottom to the top. The script was elven and quite fine. She already knew most of the characters from last night's tutelage, so she was able to pick out a few words.

"Milady, it appears to be a note from a person named Barkus. I think, perhaps it is to the king or another royal person. I do not know enough of the language to be confident what..."

"You can see script?"

"Yes, ma'am. It appears to be elvish, a fine hand."

"That bastard, Barkus! It is age defined. He probably expected some mage would try to read his memoirs some day, and decided to confound them by an age limited script. These so-called readers..." Meligance picked up the odd spectacles and tossed them across the table toward a large bin stuffed with crumpled papers, parchment, and an assortment of other objects, "are a ruse to throw one off. Ah me," she chuckled. "I would have dearly loved to have met that old codger. He had a sense of humor."

An idea suddenly came to her, and her eyes sparkled. "Well, well, here is a good chore for you to take on. You can practice what you are learning. Take these with you when you go today." Meligance pressed a stack of parchment across to Thistle. "Use them to practice your new skills with the old language. Barkus is one of the great mages of the past age; his writings are an amusement for me. Occasionally, they yield something worthwhile. I have never been able to decipher this lot and now I know why. He has ever been a challenge." She paused, eyeing Thistle as if trying to figure something out.

"Before we begin, know this. Thistle, you need to understand first and foremost your own gift. Once you understand your power – the power within – and are able to control it fully, you can begin magical training – or, as I assume Sart has instructed you, the use of power derived from outside oneself. In order for you to understand your own gift, in other words the innate talent you possess, you will spend a great many hours over the next months observing yourself. You may find this tedious, but the time and effort you expend will be dependent on how well you learn to focus inwardly. That means, how quickly you can define for yourself who you truly are. Today is lesson one. It is the lesson of the utmost importance to your success; all else depends on what you learn from this.

"This is not unlike," Meligance mused, "what I assume your friend, Jared, is going through right now at Bard Hall. He is learning to understand and control the innate talent he has for music, as well as the many other gifts that need to be developed to become a Bard. The two of you are along similar, yet widely divergent, paths.

"What I want you to do right now is to close your eyes and relax. I want you

45

to note everything you can about how you feel. Focus on what you sense about your body, from the top of your head to your toes. Note all the physical sensations you have, and try to bring all of that to a focus in your center, your core." Meligance pointed to the center of her chest and upper abdomen. "It is why your little friend likes to rest there. Your purpose is to understand exactly how you feel right now, and Yolk can help you with that. I will be quiet for several minutes while you do this. Try not to be distracted by anything without...

"Now!" It was a command.

Thistle did as she was told. Within a minute's time, she was able to remove herself from the womb of the room and its dazzling effects, to bring herself within a close personal sphere. She had learned to meditate as a means to regain her focus and energy when the demands of taking care of her sisters and the stead had been overwhelming. It had somehow been an instinct that she had pursued to find some personal peace.

Rather than going completely within to a point of deep rest, this time she did as Meligance had suggested. She began to slide her mind's eye down from the top of her head, slowly toward her toes. Thistle noted each area of her body and how it felt as she focused her attention. She could almost count the strands of her hair that lay across her forehead; the slight trickle of sweat down her temples stood out and beg to be wiped; her throat felt as if the honeyed tea had coated it thickly, and she felt the urge to swallow. Each part of her body seemed to speak to her of what it was and how it felt at the moment in time she focused on it. Even so, when she tried to bring all of that together into her core, it all slipped from her tenuous grasp. So, she stayed with the peace and focus that had brought her back to her core.

"Thistle, open your eyes and catch this." Meligance once again plucked one of the glowing balls from the ether; she tossed it toward her apprentice. As she had on the previous day, Thistle caught it and balanced it between her two hands, still not understanding how she was able to do it.

"Good. Now go within again and go through the same process while holding the ball. Take your time. I want you to be able to tell me precisely what is different when you are done."

Thistle slowly closed her eyes and went within again. Immediately, she noted that there was a tingling in her hands and arms that extended into her core. Rather than focus on that strange feeling, she did as she was told. She went again from head to toe and finally back to her center.

"Well?" Meligance asked, after several minutes had passed. She gestured for Thistle to toss the ball back to her, which the Wizardess quickly set to spinning back in the room's ether.

"I, well..." Thistle began to giggle and finally to laugh. Tears began to stream down her face until she couldn't suppress the feeling any longer. She began to laugh uncontrollably.

"Well, that is most odd," Meligance said. She waited calmly for Thistle to regain control.

"I'm sorry, milady," Thistle giggled. "It's that, well, I always felt that meant I had indigestion," and she giggled some more.

Meligance suddenly understood and began to smile herself. "You mean the core feeling, the buzzing, uncomfortable sensation at your center?"

46

Thistle nodded, laughing even more.

"Oh, dear," and Meligance began to giggle, too. Soon she was clutching her sides, and tears were streaming down her cheeks as well.

When they both finally managed to regain control, Meligance wiped off her cheeks, then passed the kerchief to Thistle. "Well, my young pupil, so you have felt your power before, only you didn't have any idea what it was. I suppose your mother gave you some bark tea or other concoction for your distress?" She began to laugh again.

"Yes, ma'am. I always thought I had a septic stomach."

"Well now, this is good then. At least, we know that you have been aware of the sensation of power before. Now, in all seriousness, you need to learn to focus that, my child. All of that power, that sensation, is your core energy. Once you can focus it to your center and be able to release or not release it at will, you will have made tremendous progress.

"Here is your assignment. Take one of these balls back to your room. Your task will be two-fold. Use the ball as we did today to focus your energy. Trace its power back within yourself. Because when you hold it or manipulate it in any way, you are using your power. Thus, it connects in a way with your core, and it awakens your personal power. See?"

Thistle nodded.

"Good. Spend a lot of time with this – learn how you control it.

"The second task is to begin to manipulate the power that *is* the ball. To do this you have to use your own power. The purpose, *always*," Meligance strongly emphasized the word, "is to see what you have to use to do that, and how it feels to change the ball. You can do anything you wish with it; however, remember this – though it is a small amount of energy in and of itself, what you do with it can change that. Caution – always. Do you understand how important this is?"

"Yes, ma'am."

"Good, now let me show you a simple example." Meligance pointed at a bright red ball floating a foot above the tabletop. Without any change in expression, nor any words to accompany, she flicked her right index finger. The ball shot across the room, bounced off the far wall in a shower of sparks, and careened back toward the Wizardess with increasing speed. With a slight movement of her pinkie, the ball stopped suddenly in mid-air, in much the position it had been before. It bobbed lightly in the ether. "A simple trick using my own energy," she stated matter-of-factly. "You can try almost anything, except…" she paused for effect, "adding your energy to the energy of the ball. You could do some serious damage to yourself or another. Learn to keep the two fields of energy separate: one is for control, the other to use. Remember this! It is another key to this lesson. Otherwise," Meligance's eyes twinkled as she said, "have some fun. The more fun you have, the more you will learn what I want you to learn.

"Select any of these and take it with you."

Thistle, now cognizant of the energy in her body, pointed at a lively purple sphere. She began to draw the ball toward her by focusing the trickle of power she felt waft through her hand. Once she had it cradled, Meligance smiled. "One other thing – you probably cannot harm the ball as it is pure energy, not at this stage of your development; but you can potentially dissipate its energy. If you do that, you will have to recreate it. If you can't, you will have to amuse yourself with other things until I return."

Thistle, now cradling the purple ball in her hands, looked up at that.

"I have to go away for several weeks on business for the kingdom. It may be a couple of weeks after that before we can have another lesson. This task I have set you is unending. You cannot reach a conclusion; you can only develop what you have, understand it, expand on it, and learn to use it. Be wise, be cautious. If you have need, call Sart for help. He assures me he has many more weeks to spend in the archives before he goes off on another trek.

"Go, I am pleased with today."

"Yes, ma'am." Thistle bowed to her mentor, turned, and disappeared.

"More than pleased," the White Wizardess whispered to herself after her pupil had left.

Winter is Here

For the past four weeks, since Aldred's return from the trading post, the three had worked hard to make sure they were fully prepared for what bode to be a long and cold winter. The higher passes in the hills to the south and west were already thick with snow and ice; and though they had only had a few dustings in the vale, it had turned bitter sooner than expected.

Ge-or spent much of his time gathering more wood and chopping it into serviceable pieces for the stove, so that they would have sufficient supplies well into the late spring. He also hunted several times a week, adding to their larder for times when they would not be able to get out of the valley. Deer were plentiful, and he brought in a feral pig, braces of coneys and squirrels, and two geese from a late-flying flock. They smoked some of the meat; but it was now cold enough to lay most of the cleaned, frozen carcasses and haunches in the underground storage, wrapped in skins. There they would remain frozen until brought inside.

Leona made crocks full of rabbit, goose, squirrel, chicken, and goat confit thick with fat and juices, fall and winter vegetables, and herbs. These she sealed with fat and buried in the ground in a special section of the barn. They would keep for a long time and would serve them throughout the winter and early spring. Bones and scraps of meat from the animals were added to a rich stock in a large pot that simmered almost constantly on the back of the stove. Leona used this for soups and stews that helped warm their insides when the temperature dipped below freezing outside.

Aldred spent much of his time preparing the barn, hay, and livestock for the winter. The goats had grown thick heavy coats. They would stay outside except in the worst weather. Several of these they butchered for their hides to make coats and mittens. Their meat was added to the confit jars, used for stews, and for fresh or smoked sausage.

By early December, they felt that they were ready. It proved none too soon. A southeasterly storm blew up. Combined with the moisture coming off the sea to the north, it dumped several feet of snow in the valley over a week's time. After that, their outdoor maneuverability shrank to paths laboriously cleared in and around the cabin, barn, and other outbuildings.

By then, Leona was beginning to show. Now that she was predominantly cabin-bound, she spent much of her free time working on clothing for herself and the baby. She worked with wool from the angoras to knit warm caps, sweaters, and pantaloons for the baby. She also used fabric from the robbers' loot to make other garments, quilts, throws, and shawls.

While she worked, Ge-or would often sit across from her. He had chosen some aged ash and birch for her bow and arrows. He spent the long evening hours cutting, whittling, shaving, and forming the pieces into the right shapes for the layered construction of the weapon. He also worked on a dozen arrow shafts to fit the small bow.

After dark, Aldred would doze near the stove in his rocking chair; though when he was awake, he would find an excuse to spend hours at a time in the barn, or he would whittle away at odd pieces of wood when in the house.

It was a comfortable time. They enjoyed relaxing after the hard work of the fall. Leona and Ge-or had settled into a comfortable relationship, almost able to ignore what would happen in the spring. They were kind and supportive of each other. After love-making, they snuggled warmly together on the large feather bed, drowsing through the night.

Hard Work

"I don't get it!" I don't get it!" Jared moaned. "Circle of fifths, modulations, secondary dominants, two-sharp-four-sharp-sixes? What's that? I…" He was sitting at his stool slumped over, head in his hands. Simon-Nathan sat on his bed opposite Karenna, who was sitting on the end of Jared's. Karenna, looking quite worried, jumped in. "The two-sharp-four-sharp…"

"No! No more right now," Jared almost shouted at her, his head popping up angrily. When his eyes met hers and he saw her shocked reaction to his outburst, he felt embarrassed.

"I'm sorry, Karenna. You've tried. You've both tried, but I'm too thick-headed to get it. It's not that I don't understand some of the theoretical perspective. I can't seem to equate that with the music, with what we play. I don't know what I can do. My head hurts, and we have exams in two weeks. I'm going to fail theory, miserably."

"You've come so far," Karenna offered. "You've learned your notes, all the clefs, intervals, triads, and basic chord structures. That's a lot for a few weeks here. Remember, all of us other first years have had over three months."

"Yeah, you're being kind of hard on yourself," Simon-Nathan added. "You've caught up in every other subject. You're way ahead of even second years in performance, and better than most graduate students in weaponry. Heck, you're better than some of the masters at short sword, and equal to anyone, even Selim, with the shortbow."

"Thanks," he said dejectedly. "No, really, I mean it, thanks to both of you. I sincerely appreciate all of your hard work in helping me the past weeks. It's just that I feel so overwhelmed right now. I'm so tired, and I want to get this theory stuff so badly, but I can't get it into my head."

"You know they won't kick you out if you don't pass the first semester theory exams."

Jared looked sharply over at Simon-Nathan.

"I'm serious, Jared. Give yourself some time. The new harmony is confusing to most of us. Karenna is exceptional in her understanding of it as a first year."

"I…" Jared sighed. "I guess I… Well, I guess I hate to fail at anything. I hate not being able to do well."

"*That* is your Dad talking, I'll warrant."

Simon-Nathan and Jared had spent many a late evening talking about their childhoods. Jared's roommate had gently prodded him into talking about his past. Eventually, he had talked at length about his strict, demanding father, and the many tests he had put Jared and Ge-or through, always driving them harder and harder. Jared knew Simon-Nathan was right. They had talked about this one night. He took even the smallest failure personally. He had been quite surprised when he had finally put that feeling into words. Unfortunately, understanding this compulsion hadn't made his drive to excel any less.

"Look, give me a half hour to rest; after that, maybe we can tackle this again, Karenna. I'm afraid you'll have to go back to the chord basics and lead me through it one more time."

Karenna stood up and touched Jared lightly on the shoulder. "Rest until dinner, Jared. Come on, Simon-Nathan. He's beat, and I need you to help me with that history assignment."

Jared knew that Karenna didn't need any help with history. She was tops in her classes in all the academic subjects. She had been an invaluable friend to Jared. He watched them slip out the door; then he rolled his way from the chair onto the bed. Putting his arm over his face, he tried to relax. His thoughts drifted to everything that had happened to him since coming to the Hall.

He had accomplished an amazing amount during his first month in residence at Bard Hall. History had been dull, but doable. His roommate was a fount of information on any topic dealing with the past. Simon-Nathan had helped Jared fill in any gaps in what he had not been able to glean from his books and lectures.

He found Bard Lore fascinating; though the fact that it was tied closely to music history, as well as the kingdom's history, left Jared feeling a bit cool toward the overall subject.

Theory had been a disaster once he had gotten his notes, clefs, intervals, scales, and the like learned. He could not make the leap from the maze of interweaving notes, polyphonic lines, and chords, to worst of all, keys and modulations. Perhaps he was trying too hard. There was no doubt that classes moved rapidly ahead. You were expected to excel here. There were no sluggards. Almost all the new students read notes and knew a lot about music theory before they were even accepted to study here. Jared had accomplished a great deal, yet he was still far behind.

Choir, instrumental class, and weaponry, his afternoons, were wonderful. He loved to sing, and though Swenson was demanding, Jared was always prepared. Instrumentation was a joy with Julingo. The young master was chatty, happy, and helpful. He appeared to love everything he did, and he was amazingly patient with all of them. He was also by far the best instrumentalist that Jared had ever seen. He could play all the instruments in the classroom, and he played them all well.

For Jared, weaponry was freedom and structure exemplified. His skill with weapons had allotted him a privileged position. During the first hour, he was allowed to do essentially whatever he wanted. In the second hour, he had a private lesson, usually with a different master each day. Typically, he would practice the previous day's lesson the first hour of the next day. Occasionally he would take time to work with some of the younger and less expert students at the archery range.

Jared was a natural teacher. He knew what to say, how to say it, and had the patience to help the younger lads understand what they needed to do to improve their technique and focus. His skill in archery was so impressive that Selim allowed him to practice with the longbow during their private lessons together. Often, they would stand next to each other matching challenging shots. Afterwards, they would discuss the results and what factors had influenced their shots.

His schedule was rigorous. He, Simon-Nathan, and Karenna spent long periods of time together practicing, studying, quizzing each other, and generally trying to stay on top of things. Jared was helping both of them with weaponry, though Karenna, as a girl, was only allowed to use knives. Often, he worked with his roommate on short sword techniques or on improving his archery skills.

Outside of his concerns about theory, Jared was having the time of his life. There was one small glitch – the elves – as Jared still thought of them, appeared to have a vendetta against him. Sometimes, when he was moving in the hallways between classes, he would be bumped from behind or from the side. When he spun around to look for the perpetrator, there was always someone with long white hair moving away. Jared also suspected the elves had been spreading rumors about him to some of the first years. He couldn't prove anything, but occasionally students would hush up and stare at him when he walked past. He asked Simon-Nathan and Karenna about this. Neither said they had heard anything specific; however, Jared would have sworn that Karenna blushed a bit when she had answered him.

Simon-Nathan did eventually explain the "elvish situation" to him. About a century ago, the elves, the pure race, had closed the doors of Moulanes to all except "true elves." They had actually kicked out any elves that had any other blood crossed in their background. The six "almost" elves still at Bard Hall as students were one-eighth, one-sixteenth, or even less, human or other mixture. Still, that had been enough to have them forced from their home.

Elanar was even more special in this respect. He was the rarest of blood mixtures: having, at least from what Simon-Nathan had heard, a birthright of elf, as well as human, and dwarf, with only the slightest tinge of the two "other" races actually part of his heritage. Jared's roommate had launched into a long history of his research of the family tree of the elf. It traced back to first age when dwarves, elves, and men intermixed freely, an age when dwarves spent more time above ground, and dwarf-maidens were considered comely by anyone's standards. Supposedly, there had been a binding between a stout human fighter and a beauteous dwarf maiden. Centuries later, one of their offspring, with considerably more human blood intermixed by that time, had married an elf maiden. Eventually, through many more centuries, the elven side had dominated with marriages to "pure bloods."

Simon-Nathan's research fascinated Jared. He asked his roommate what he felt was a logical question, "Wouldn't there be thousands of such offspring now?" Which he followed with an equally logical extension, "Are there really any true elves left?"

His roommate chuckled. "You don't know a great deal about elves for being half-elvish, do you?" The question had been rhetorical, so Jared waited for him to continue. "Elves find it difficult to reproduce. I'm sorry to tell you this, but as a half-elf you will probably have difficulties as well. As long-lived as they are – and contrary to popular opinion they are not immortal – elves are lucky to have one or two offspring during their long lives.

"The true elves in Moulanes know their heritage. It is a source of great pride that the pure bloods trace their family trees back to the 'sea-borne' – the elves that came to Borea across the eastern ocean. However, their glory wanes: births are further and further apart, and the elders are nearing their time. If they are not killed in battle or by disease or misfortune, elves live for centuries and centuries, some for thousands of years and more. Eventually, they do get old and die. Rumors have it that there are few of the sea-borne still alive, and those that are would be four thousand years old or more."

Jared was astounded by all that Simon-Nathan related to him about his heritage. He was surprised to discover that the elves of the plains, the Slivs, were not "true" or "pure" elves either. They had intermixed with human horsemen thousands of years before. Only recently, in a historical sense within the last few hundred years, had they drawn within their borders and set strict rules of behavior, effectively purifying their race from that point on. Even the diminutive sea-elves to the east and south had theoretically intermingled with another race far in the past, though no one had been able to trace their true lineage. Some suggested they had mixed with a race of small humans that was no longer a part of the Borean world. These had either died off or had gone back across the sea whence they had originally come. Others believed the sea-elves came from the east, already a diminutive race.

He also learned that elves were not necessarily better than humans or other races at weaponry, magic, healing, crafts, and so on. Indeed, their race was naturally agile, graceful, and keenly intelligent. The exemplary skills they possessed, in most arenas, were mainly a result of their long lives. They had many more years in their prime to develop their talents. It was one reason Jared was superior to most of the human students at Bard Hall in the use of weapons. He was older and had additional practice, under the tutelage of a great warrior, to develop his weaponry skills. The natural agility from one side of his heritage didn't hurt either.

Jared rolled over onto his back. He wasn't getting the rest he needed. Too many ideas were running through his head. Finally, he thought of Thistle. He smiled to himself, trying to bring her softness to mind, especially the feeling of her when they had lain side by side together, clothed, yet so close. A few seconds later, he did drift into sleep.

Though he slept through dinner, he needed rest; and the surprise he had when he woke was worth it.

Practice

Thistle was having a ball, literally. She loved working with the purple globe. She even gave it a name – Blinkie. When she brought it back to the room after her lesson with Meligance, Alli had chirped excitedly, "It's blinking; it's blinking."

The two girls, for both were young and still mischievous, had gotten on famously. Thistle was always amused by the deference her chambermaid paid her. Only a few months before, Thistle had been the main caretaker of her four sisters, while their mother and father worked with many of the villagers in the fields, scraping furs, and preparing other items for trade. The things that Alli did for her were things she had done innumerable times – cleaning, preparing baths, laying out clothes, combing the young ones' hair, and on and on. Now, she could hardly do anything for herself. Still, she insisted that Alli play games with her, learn her letters when Sart came for her language lessons, and go for long walks about the palace.

It wasn't long before Thistle had started to know her way about. As she found her way into various areas of the castle, she was surprised by how much deference everyone paid her. One day she asked Alli why.

"Oh, milady," she giggled. "I guess you would have to say that they are all afraid of Meligance. She is *very* powerful. So-o-o, I guess they figure you are really powerful, too."

"Hah," Thistle had laughed. "You mean they are scared of me?"

"Yes, milady, and I have to admit, I'm a bit... a bit in awe of you, too. You are so nice that sometimes I forget that you also control vast powers."

"Me? Vast powers? No, no, at least not yet, Alli."

"But look what you have been able to do with Blinkie."

"Tricks, Alli, simple tricks."

Her handmaiden was right. Thistle had been able to accomplish amazing things with the little ball of energy. Right now, she was sitting on her window ledge looking out over the courtyard, envisioning the task she had set for herself tonight. It would take a great deal of focus; so she had sent Alli away for the evening, allowing her to visit an aunt who lived on the outskirts of the city.

Yolk was also with her, though often the little fellow would perch on her window sill enjoying the winter sun. Tonight, she might need his extra boost to her own energy for what she had planned.

Thistle had followed Meligance's instructions explicitly. She spent hours each day simply standing and focusing on her energy. Often that would be with Blinkie in hand, as she was better able to feel her core energy when she was expending some of it to control the ball. Then, when she felt she had brought herself to the deepest level possible, she would begin her experiments with the sphere.

At first, she did simple things like moving the ball from place to place; changing its color, although she still preferred purple; stretching it in one direction or another; enlarging it and reducing it; and generally manipulating its form. On one occasion, she compressed its energy so much it became a pinprick of intense light that lit her entire room, as if she had lit a thousand candles. It was amazing to her, because she not only felt her own active energy when she held the ball; she somehow seemed to know instinctively how to manipulate the separate and distinct energy of the ball itself.

In some ways, it felt like she could pick up fire in her hand and twist it as she liked. Yet, she had not been brave enough to try manipulating anything other than the sphere itself. She was not positive Meligance would approve of such a diversion from the task she had set for her apprentice.

Once, when Thistle was practicing with Blinkie, Alli came in to announce that dinner was ready. Thistle had been so involved with trying to understand the source of the ball's energy, that she had lost track of the time. Alli shyly asked if she could touch the sphere.

"I... No, Alli, from what I know, it would hurt you. I..." Thistle had paused, an idea having occurred to her. "Well, maybe, let's try something."

Thistle took the glowing orb and expanded it many times its original size, until it was a large purple globe, half filling the space between the walls, ceiling, and floor. She said to Alli, "There, now I think you can touch it without it hurting you, but just use one finger and go slowly. If you feel any pain, withdraw your finger immediately. All right?"

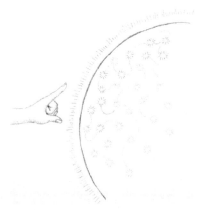

It took Alli a few seconds to get up the courage to approach the ball. When her finger made contact, she jumped back, exclaiming, "Oh!"

Thistle panicked for a moment. "Are you alright?"

Her handmaiden giggled. "It tickles." She put her hand out and caressed the side of the ball; then Alli stuck her hand and arm into it. "It really tickles, Thistle. It's funny... and scary, too."

Thistle was relieved that the experiment turned out so well. She didn't like using Alli as a test case, though she had felt strongly that there was a finite amount of energy in Blinkie. When spread out, it reduced its impact. This small experiment helped her improve her overall understanding of the sphere.

Recently, she had tried much more daring escapades with the little bundle of energy. Her first real venture into the unknown had been to try to make the globe move between one point and another, by making the ball disappear and reappear in another location. This had taken much greater concentration than anything she had done before, so she spent more time working on her focus and on understanding and being in touch with her own inner power. Once she developed that focus and control, the task was easy enough. She could fold up the energy that was Blinkie, imagine it at another point, and release it. The ball would erupt in the new location. It was as if she could send it through holes or spaces in the ether. Eventually, she realized that this could also be accomplished by sending Blinkie through solid objects, as there appeared to be "spaces" in the make-up of everything, spaces that energy could pass through.

Soon she was sending Blinkie from room to room. One day, as she sat slightly bored, toying with the globe, she thought to send it into her handmaiden's room. Folding it in, she focused on what she remembered of Alli's chamber; she released the energy. She heard a surprised yelp from across the hall. "By-the-Gods," Thistle had exclaimed out loud. "I hope I didn't hurt her."

Surprisingly, she heard Alli say, as if she was in the room with her. "No, I'm fine, Thistle. Blinkie surprised me."

From that point on, Thistle would send Blinkie to Alli if she wanted anything. The bell pulls were no longer of any use.

Thistle spent considerable time trying to understand the dynamics of sending the globe to ever more remote areas. She knew she was using her own energy, because as near as she could tell the sensation of energy she received from Blinkie never changed. It remained constant. She could also sense the energy she called upon to do the trick; she wasn't sure what happened during the transition of the sphere from one point to another. Nor did she have any idea as to why she was able to speak to someone using the sphere. It was something she wanted to ask Meligance about. Sart did not have an answer. He told her emphatically, "It is beyond my ken, child. To understand the ether, you must ask the Wizardess."

He had paused for a moment, and added, "I only know this: what we think of as air, earth, water, fire, rock, and so forth, are all made of energy. Everything has energy. The form that energy takes is what alchemical studies are all about. I can manipulate certain elements physically to change their form, or to create a healing salve or potion; yet I do not understand the foundation of what is happening to do that. Water, ice, and steam are simple examples. Their form changes with temperature. Other things may change shape, color, consistency, and so forth by adding or subtracting other elements, heating or cooling, pounding, and so on. I am afraid that our alchemical studies are in their infancy.

"See what the Wizardess has to say; she likes pondering the imponderable. She will often tell you to keep searching for answers. She likes to see people opening their minds by being willing to ask about things."

Thistle kept at her work with the sphere of energy; however, she had not been able to decipher any more about what was happening when she sent the ball to other locations. What she did accomplish had led to what she was going to try this evening. Less than a week ago, she had sent the ball as far away as her family's house in Permis. Surprisingly, though this took all her focusing powers, the energy she used to accomplish the feat seemed little more than the wee bit she used to send the ball to Alli.

To minimize her family's fear from the sphere's sudden appearance, she had chosen a late hour to try this special experiment. She did not want to scare her parents or her sisters with a bright purple ball showing up in the middle of mealtime or when they were focused on other things. She decided it was best to send Blinkie to hover over her mother's bed at night. When she was positive she had gotten it all right, and her focus was intense, she had folded the energy of the sphere and sent it. A minute later, having not heard anything, she loudly whispered, "Mother? Mother?"

Then, as if she was right there with her, Thistle heard, "Oh! Thistle?"

"Mother, I..." She had choked up, tears running down her face. It was some time before she could explain to her mother that she was "sending" this vibrant messenger. For several minutes they chatted, her father snoring loudly in the background. Thistle discovered that the family was safe, and that the stipend from the Borean treasury that arrived that month was much more than they needed. They had begun a two-room addition to the house and helped several more refugees from the disaster at Thiele. It was the wilderness way – take care of your own, always. After a few minutes, Thistle and her mother said goodbye to each other. Thistle promised to try to send again in a month, when they would all be at Yule-tide dinner.

Tonight, Thistle was preparing something special and a bit tricky. She planned to try to send Blinkie to Jared. Again, she chose a late hour, hoping that he would be in his room alone, perhaps practicing or studying. The difficult part was that she had never been to Bard Hall. She knew nothing about Jared's environs: whether he was in a room with roommates, a communal sleeping area, or alone. The sending would be her trying to locate him by her memory of his beautifully carved lyre.

She had learned that careful planning was paramount to success. She had experimented with trying to send the sphere into solid objects, like her chair or the stone walls of the palace; but the sphere had always "popped" out when she released it. So, she was fairly sure that she could not send the energy ball into another object, or tragically, perhaps, into a person. She didn't, however, want to take any chances. Her focus tonight was to imagine a space in mid-air near where Jared's portative harp would be, and high enough to be above his head if he were standing. Unfortunately, she had no idea whether he had it stored in a locker or closet. She would find out. She took a deep breath and drew into herself.

Contact

Jared awoke when Simon-Nathan returned following dinner. His roommate entered quietly, carrying a large sack in his arms; but Jared had already been coming around. The shuffling sound caused him to raise his head from the pillow.

"Sorry, Jared, I brought you some dinner. It's only bread, cheese, and a mug of wine. We didn't want to wake you, since you needed the... Whoa-a-a, what's that?"

Simon-Nathan backed up abruptly. A bright purple sphere, about the size of a large fist, had suddenly appeared hovering high up near the head of Jared's bed. Jared looked up at his roommate's reaction. Just as surprised, he sat up quickly, swinging around away from the glowing orb and placing his back to the wall. They both eyed the bright sphere as it danced above them. A voice suddenly emanated from the orb. "Jared? Jared, are you there?"

"Thistle?" Jared answered tentatively.

"It worked! It worked! I've missed you so much. Jared, can you hear me?"

"Ah, yeah... what is it?" Jared gestured toward the ball, though he had no idea whether Thistle could see him or not.

"Sorry, Jared, I didn't know any other way to get to you quickly. The purple ball is Blinkie. He, I mean "it," is a ball of energy. Meligance has me working with it. I discovered I could send it places and talk to people. It does take a lot of focus, so it is hard to keep it for long. I'll try to hurry.

"Sart, ah... Meligance isn't here right now, has given me a day off tomorrow, and permission to go about town as long as I take my chambermaid with me. Can I see you?"

"I don't know. Let me ask Simon-Nathan. He's my roommate and knows all the rules." Jared looked at Simon-Nathan, who was standing with his mouth partially open, looking at the ball, and at Jared, and back at the purple globe.

"Simon? Are you hearing this?"

His roommate, eyes wide with wonder, ignored what he considered the improper use of his given name. He nodded "yes," then "no," shook his head and blurted out, "Well, maybe you could meet her. First years aren't allowed off campus until they pass their end of year exams, but you can see visitors in the main courtyard from one to four. That shouldn't be a problem."

"Hi, Simon, I'm Thistle, Jared's friend. I look forward to meeting you... Can we meet tomorrow, Jared? I can come to Bard Hall."

"Definitely, yes!" Jared leaned forward toward the orb, as if that would make Thistle's task easier. "We have chapel until noon, and after that luncheon. We could meet right at one."

"You can stay until four," Simon-Nathan piped in. "We have required study or practice time after that."

"Jared, it will be so good to see you. I..." The purple ball suddenly flared up, then dimmed considerably. "Sorry, have to go. I'll see you tomorr..." With another bright flick of light, the orb disappeared, and despite several lit candles in the room, the boys suddenly felt like they were in complete darkness.

"Wow!" was all the talkative Simon-Nathan said before plopping on his bed. Jared sat on his own bed musing.

After a few seconds, Simon added, "That was extraordinary. You said Thistle is studying to be a magic-user, right? That seems like a pretty advanced trick for an apprentice. Unbelievable."

Jared nodded. "I really miss her, especially on days like today. I..." His voice trailed off.

"Listen, Jared. I promised Karenna I would take a walk about the grounds with her; you know, an evening constitutional. Help yourself to the food and wine. It'll give you some time to think. I'll be back in an hour or so."

Jared spent the next hour nibbling on the food his roommate had brought. More than anything, he mused about the last soft kiss he and Thistle had shared at the gates to Bard Hall.

Together Again

Jared wolfed down a light lunch, then ran as fast as he could to the main courtyard, which was set in a quadrangle north of the main entrance. He was twenty-five minutes early, so he paced back and forth before the gate. Five minutes before the outer gate would be opened for visitors, he was forced to stand still, because so many others had joined him in anticipation of the warder opening the gilded entryway.

Once the gatekeeper let them pass, Jared rushed over to the visitor gate and peered anxiously into the crowd. He couldn't see Thistle in the milling bodies, but he trusted she would be there.

Six minutes later, most of the visitors were inside and had found their counterparts. Jared stood at the edge of the entryway and watched as the last few people walked in. It was only when he saw the ornate carriage down the avenue begin to come toward Bard Hall, that he moved up to the gates. It stopped right in front. A young lady leapt lightly out and pulled down the steps, offering her hand to a person inside. Dressed in a velvety dress of azure blue, matching slippers, and a warm dark blue cape, Thistle stepped out of the carriage, looking quite elegant and stately. When both her feet were on the cobblestones, she stopped and looked around. Instantly, she spotted Jared; and with all formality aside, she ran toward him and launched herself into his arms.

They kissed lightly several times, then held each other tightly for a few seconds. Thistle finally pulled away. Her cheeks flushed when she realized how her eagerness must have appeared to others around them. Turning to the girl, who was standing slightly behind, she said, "Jared, this is Alli, my chambermaid and friend." Alli curtsied, smiling broadly. She offered her hand to Jared.

Several minutes later, after having briefly introduced Thistle to his roommate and Karenna, who had come down to meet her, they were sitting at a table enjoying the light mulled wine offered to all the guests at Bard Hall. It was a chilly December day, but Jared hardly noticed. His attention was completely focused on Thistle. She had grown in so many ways that it was hard to imagine she was the same girl he had left at the gates of the Hall only weeks before.

She was at least a half-inch taller, a bit fuller in all the right places, he would have sworn; and there was something powerful, more open, and more dynamic about her whole presence. Still, she laughed the same, and she felt the same to him. While holding her hand, he kept feeling waves of emotion flood through him. He didn't think he could be any happier; she was perfect.

They talked at length about their efforts and trials, and about the wonderment of what they were doing, seeing, and accomplishing. Thistle wanted to know the smallest details about Jared's classes and his friends. She was fascinated by all aspects of his studies. Jared, for his part, was amazed at the simplest things she had managed to do with her magic.

After some time, Thistle reached out and took Alli's hand. "Alli, would you mind going back to the carriage for a bit. I would like to spend some time alone with Jared."

Her eyes bright and her cold-reddened visage forming into a broad smile, Alli stood up, curtsied to both of them, and left.

Thistle drew closer to Jared. "I've missed you so much, so very much. I love what I am doing – the challenges, the language lessons – all of it. Yet... well, it seems so unfair that we can't be together."

Jared leaned forward and nuzzled Thistle's cheek, breathing in her lavender perfume. He kissed her lightly again. "You are the love of my life, Thistle. I know this. We have chosen these paths, or perhaps, in part, they have been chosen for us. I want you to know that I carry you here." He touched his chest. "Every day you help me get through the hard parts; just thinking of you helps me."

Thistle rose from the bench, pulling him with her. "Come, let us walk." Yet, she stayed, drawing him close into a tight embrace and a lingering kiss.

Jared let Thistle to take the lead. She pulled back, finally, and took his arm as she stepped away from the table. "There is something I must speak to, something that is going to be hard for both of us, Jared. Please listen carefully, and don't gainsay what I am about to tell you. Know this first – I love you, too. I know I am still young and probably foolish and inexperienced, yet I do so love you. I will wait for you, Jared, always... but... but I don't want you to wait for me."

Jared gasped, shocked by what Thistle had said. He started to turn toward her. Thistle held tight to his arm, pulling him back and starting to walk. He could see tears starting to fall down her cheeks.

"Jared, I must, out of needs unique to my profession, my powers, remain chaste, perhaps for years to come. Meligance and Sart have both explained to me that until I can completely control my inner energy, I could hurt someone, even kill them, if... if I lose myself in...well, in passion. We can meet and be together, even kiss and hold each other. I must, though, be very careful. I am beginning to realize how much power I do have. I... I never want to hurt you or anyone through my inability to control that which is inside me. Can you understand this?"

"I..." Jared so wanted to draw her to him, yet something held him back. He wasn't sure what it was that Thistle was saying to him. He felt afraid – for her, for them. "I..."

"Sh-h-h, listen yet awhile, my love." Thistle stopped walking. Turning slightly, she looked him directly in the eyes. "You are maturing. I can see it in the short while we have been apart. You are becoming a man, and you will have strong needs. I want you to enjoy life, live life, be life. I want you to love and be loved, as you may." She paused, reaching up to grasp the top of his tunic in her delicate hands.

"This is really hard for me, Jared. I know, somehow, that deep down our love will last through all others. Sometime, maybe in a few years, or... perhaps longer, we will be able to be together as we will; that is when our love can blossom. Please understand, I say this for both our sakes."

Tears continued down her cheeks. She reached up to brush them away, just as Jared did the same. Their hands touched; they clasped each other tightly.

"Thistle, I can promise..."

"No!" Thistle's eyes flashed. She lowered her voice. "No, Jared, don't promise me what you can't, shouldn't keep. Promise only to be honest with me; I ask for nothing else. I wish more than anything that we could be lovers now, or soon; but I can't, because I do have this power. It is not something I can give away or ignore. I realize that now. Please, please promise me only this."

"Thistle... I promise; I could never lie to you. I... I don't know what else to say." He drew her close and clung to her tightly, almost desperately, as if they might never be together again. As luck would have it, at that instant the five-minute bell rang.

They walked quietly back toward the gate, Thistle's left hand clasped tightly in Jared's right. They didn't speak. Once there, they nuzzled and kissed lightly. By the time Thistle turned to go, Jared's cheeks were wet, too, and there was a great lump in his throat. He whispered softly after her, "I love you." Then she was gone.

The rest of the day Jared spent furiously practicing and studying, trying to keep occupied so he would not think of what Thistle had told him, and of what she had asked of him. Finally, he settled down in his chair and played his lyre, going through the fastest pieces he knew to dissipate some of the energy and frustration he felt.

Thistle went back to the Palace, took a long hot bath, and wept herself quietly to sleep. Alli knew enough to stay away.

Measuring Up

Two days later, sweaty after a long workout in the yard, Jared flung open the door to his room to find Simon-Nathan sitting on the end of his bed with his head down.

"Simon-Nathan? Are you all right?"

"I'm sorry, Jared, really. I don't understand it."

"Sorry about what? What are you talking about?"

His roommate pointed with his chin toward the other bed. Jared looked over. Lying on the coverlet, he saw a bright red, gold-embossed envelope sitting neatly at the foot. "What is it?"

"It's... it's a summons from the grandmaster. It's not good, Jared."

"What? What do you mean? I... Did I do something wrong?"

"I don't know, Jared, but... well, I do know that all the students that have gotten one of those are no longer here; they were gone within a fortnight. I... I'm sorry."

Bewildered, Jared sat in the middle of his bed. He took the envelope in his hand. Opening it carefully, he drew out a matching heavy card. It said in gold florid script, "You are requested at an audience with Grandmaster Leonis at one in the afternoon on the morrow."

Jared silently handed it over to Simon-Nathan, who grimaced after he read it.

***

"Are you positive you don't want us to come, Jared? We'll vouch for you. Really, we don't mind, even if we get in trouble for missing classes." Karenna begged him with her eyes, while Simon-Nathan stood behind agreeing. They had all come from lunch, though none of them, even the voracious Simon-Nathan, had eaten much.

Jared didn't understand. Except for theory and the elves, he thought things had been going well. His father had raised him to tackle troubles head-on. He would face whatever this was as best he could. He wanted to stay here. Somehow, in spite of his difficulties with chords and chordal progressions, this all seemed so right for him. Maybe he hadn't measured up. "Thanks, both of you. You've been great friends. I'll let you know. Meet me outside of instrument class. I don't imagine that he will keep me for long."

Jared stood before the plain heavy oaken door. He had only been in this part of Bard Hall once before, when Selim had wanted to lend him a book on advanced archery skills. The masters' wing consisted of offices and studios running the length of a long hall at the southernmost point of the enclave. Jared had not, to his knowledge, ever met the grandmaster, nor was he sure he had even seen him. Other boys said that he rarely ate in the commons room except for end of year parties, and his place at Chapel on Solisdays was so far up in a private alcove from where the first years sat that Jared could barely see the top of his white head. Simon had said this was an office the grandmaster rarely used; his main studio was near the entrance to the main hall.

At precisely one, as the bells began to chime the start of the next hour, a booming voice that Jared was confident he had heard somewhere before, said, "Enter." He took a deep swallow, trying to rid himself of the dryness in his throat.

Jared turned the golden handle and pushed the heavy door in. Much to his astonishment, sitting at a plain, but well-crafted, mahogany desk in the large studio room was the old gatekeeper he had met on his first day. "Ah, Jared, my boy, so good of you to come," the grandmaster boomed, his voice friendly and open, not at all stern as Jared had expected. "How could I not?" Jared answered, hoping his assessment of the grandmaster's mood was correct.

"Ah, yes, the new boy with a sense of humor," chuckled Leonis. "I like that about you, yes, indeed. Don't lose that aspect of your personality, Son."

He isn't cross with me; what is this about? Jared wondered.

"Now, why are you here? Ah yes, theory. I am told you're having a spot of trouble with theory, in spite of our best efforts."

"Yes, sir, I mean, yes, Grandmaster."

"Well, let us see if we can get to the bottom of this. Did you bring your portative harp?"

"Yes, sir. It's here." Jared shifted it from underneath his cloak, and unstrapped it from his back.

"Good, good. Now listen to this tune." The grandmaster picked up an ornate instrument lying on its side on a velvet cloth at the center of a small stand. He played the melody to a popular drinking song, "One is Far too Few for Me."

"There, now what key was I in?"

"C, sir."

"Just so. Major or Minor?"

"The song starts in major, shifts to minor for the interval, and then goes back to major."

"Good...excellent. Now, I want you to play it for me and harmonize it as you go. Don't worry or think too much about it, just play."

Jared did as he was told. While he played, he warmed to the music. He felt a release of tension, as he realized he probably wasn't going to be sacked.

"Good, now tell me why you used this chord." The grandmaster played through the song until the fourth measure. He stopped on the first beat, "and not this." He played it again, changing only the last chord as he stopped in the same place.

"I... I don't know. I guess... well, it was more interesting."

"More sensual?"

"I guess you could describe it that way, sir. It adds more interest; it adds tension, I guess. Makes you squirm a bit."

"Good. Exactly! So, tell me what chord did you play there, and what did I change it to?"

"I played C E G B-flat and you changed it to a C E G chord."

"Good. Nothing wrong with your ears, young man. Now, what is a C E G chord in C major?"

"The root; the tonic chord."

"Yes, and what is C E G B-flat, in C major?"

"Ah... well, it's not really a chord found in C major. I guess you could call it a Tonic chord with a flat seventh, a one-flat-seven chord."

"How about if we call it simply an 'X' chord."

"X?"

"'X' as in it doesn't belong in the key. Seem reasonable?"

"Sure."

"So, can you tell me what key, the simplest key you can think of, that you can find the chord C E G B-flat in?"

"It's a seventh chord built on the fifth scale degree in F major, Grandmaster."

"Quite right, quite right, so – now pay attention, young man – what you played, what you did to make this song a bit more interesting or 'sensual' at this point was to shift keys, but only for an instant, to F major. Does that make sense to you?"

"Ah... Yes sir, I guess it does."

"And what did you resolve this chord to? How did you ease the tension you created?"

"F A C in root position."

"And what is that chord in C major"

"The four chord, sir."

"And if we were still in the key of F major what chord would it be."

"The... ah, well it's the tonic in F... Oh!" Suddenly a light dawned in Jared's head.

"Yes. Oh!

"You see Jared, modulations, secondary dominants, or one-flat-seven chords, or two-sharp-four-sharp-six-chords are all ways we make music more... well, interesting... more squirmy, I believe you said. Call them anything you like. Generically, we could call them all X chords, because they don't fit within a given key. In the realm of harmony, however, we can almost always explain them in one way or another as related to another key and its chord progressions. Understand?"

"Yes, sir." Jared was starting to smile, "Yes, I think I do."

"Good. The important thing about theory – that is if we want to be true to our musical natures – is that it grows out of what we do, how we play and sing, not vice-versa. It is all about creating tension, and releasing that tension. That is how all chords relate to each other in this new modern system.

"You have a good ear; hear it in your head. It will be easier. Figure the formal structure from there."

"Thank you, Grandmaster. This has helped; this is great!"

"There is one other thing," Leonis said, more seriously.

66

Jared thought, here it comes. Though he didn't believe he was in any type of big trouble, he dreaded what might come next. "Yes, Grandmaster."

"About your other little problem – sometimes the best thing to do is to face things head on. When you do, you may find that you will gain wisdom as you make the effort."

"Yes, sir." Jared wondered what he was referring to, Thistle, or the elves, or...?

Leonis interrupted his musings. "What are the ideals of Bard Hall, young man?" The grandmaster straightened. He now stood tall and imposing at the edge of the desk.

"Honor, Duty, Truth, Wisdom, Healing, and Joy, sir." They started each convocation with them; it was hard not to know them.

"Yes, precisely. Is there anything in there about music?"

"No, sir?"

"No, there isn't. Live these, Son, and you will make a fine Bard. Now go, you must not miss any more of your class time."

"Thank you, sir. Thank you so much, Grandmaster." Jared bowed low. Leonis dismissed him with a wave of his hand, smiling under his thick mustache.

When Jared met Karenna and Simon-Nathan, he was beaming. When she saw him, Karenna sensed immediately that all was right with the world. She grabbed Jared in a bear hug, and planted a resounding kiss, first on his cheek; and then, when he didn't pull away, full on his lips. It lasted a bit too long for Simon-Nathan to feel comfortable. When he politely coughed, they pulled apart, both of them blushing hotly.

Lesson Two

Thistle was excited with anticipation of seeing Meligance. She tried to talk Alli into coming with her, so she could introduce her to the Wizardess; but she wouldn't have anything to do with it. "No, milady, she doesn't want to see me. No, no, no! I would be so scared, I'd pee my pantaloons. You go, have fun. I'll be here when you get back." Alli backed so far toward the window in Thistle's room that she had to sit on the ledge. Thistle let it go.

Skipping probably wasn't considered appropriate behavior for a young lady at court, much less for the apprentice to *her*. Thistle didn't care. She was happy, and so alive with energy. She was also, after all, now a young lady of almost seventeen, with still a good bit of the silliness of her youth about her. That is one reason that she and Alli had so much in common.

Her chambermaid had turned sixteen a week ago. Thistle had used some of the spending money Sart had allotted her to buy the girl a beautiful smock and a comfortable pair of slippers. Alli had cried for five minutes when the two of them had surprised her with the gifts, a birthday party, and a grandly decorated cake. Sart had given her a set of the picture books, *Bunny Tales*, he had picked up at one of the many bookstores in the center of town. They had hugged all around. It had been the most joyous time, with Blinkie producing a festive light show, courtesy of Thistle's emerging talents.

As she approached the entrance to Meligance's domain, Thistle paused, wondering briefly if she had spent her time foolishly. Bother, she thought. I did what she said. If she wants more, she'll have to give me better instructions.
***

Seven levels up, Meligance also waited with anticipation for her pupil. She had purposely left Thistle to her own devices. She could have spied on her in numerous ways, either through magic, or simply by asking Sart and her chambermaid to tell her what she was doing with her time. She had resisted. Best to see what bent the girl had, and whether she could indeed learn on her own. Well, she would know soon enough; Thistle had entered the anteroom below.

The first thing Meligance noted was that she still had the globe. Not only was it still glowing, as it had when she had sent her away over a month before; it definitively had a sharper tone to it. She had managed to draw energy into it. Meligance wondered if Thistle knew how she had done that.

"Show me," were all the words she spoke when Thistle arrived before her.

Obediently, Thistle ran through the gamut of her tricks with Blinkie. She did what she now called her "standard repertoire." First, she focused her own energy, then used the orb and the routine she had developed to help her focus even more intently. She made it expand and contract, caused it to float, spin, dance, and whirl about the room, and sent it chasing around the other orbs that were omnipresent whenever she was there. Finally, she began to form it into shapes: geometric forms, animals, objects, whatever came to mind. She easily shifted the energy from one form to another, all the while garnering her own inner strength and control.

When she had completed the fifteen-minute exercise, she cradled Blinkie back into her hands in its original form and smiled at Meligance.

"Is that all?"

"No, ma'am, those are my warm-up exercises." At that, she drew the sphere in toward her, wrapped her hands over the top as if to push it down. It disappeared. Meligance raised her eyebrows as Thistle went on. With a simple flick of her finger, she brought Blinkie back into the room where it hovered over the Wizardess's head. Almost immediately, she made the same folding motion with her hands and the orb disappeared once again. An instant later, a disembodied voice said clearly, "Thistle, are you there?"

"Hi, Mom, wanted to check in and see how everything was. I don't have time to chat right now, but I am fine. How is everyone?"

"We're fine, honey. Talk with you again Solisday?"

"Yes, Mom. Love you."

She brought the sphere back into her hands with a small motion.

Meligance sat back, staring at her young apprentice. She hadn't learned that until she was ten years into her studies. Most magic-users in the kingdom couldn't do it, even when instructed how, and only after they had been given a lengthy string of syllables to help them focus. Thistle had done it without instruction; and she obviously was not taxed in any way from the effort, except for the concentration and focus it took to reach the point where she could make it happen.

"Are you tired, child?"

"No, ma'am. I do get tired if I talk for long. It is hard to hold my focus for more than a few minutes while conversing. It doesn't appear to take much general energy to send it."

"Remarkable," Meligance mused. Not only had she easily accomplished what Meligance would have labeled a Level I focus, she was well into Level II and starting a Level III. "Is Yolk with you?" she asked.

"No, ma'am. I wanted to show you what I had accomplished without help. I do sometimes have him with me when I practice, yet he doesn't seem to aid my concentration. He only adds to my power, the amount of energy I feel within."

"Good, Thistle! That is a keen observation. You are right; ovietti only add to the power we already have within ourselves. How they accomplish this is unknown. However, there is something I should tell you about your little friend. As you may have surmised, he, or perhaps I should say he/she, as they are androgynous, was sent to you by me. Well, sent to you is not quite right either. I let Yolk go out to find me a worthy apprentice – knowing he would choose a person with a strong innate energy core. You were his choice. Yolk is the offspring of an ovietti I had named Pan."

Meligance paused, and Thistle could have sworn she had just blushed. She thought, Egg and pan – ovietti – ova from the old language for egg. She blushed, too, suppressing the urge to giggle.

Meligance continued. "Pan passed away some months after birthing your Yolk. I knew she was near her time, but it was hard for me to accept. Years before, I had stopped using her as a source of power as I knew it had begun to take a toll; yet she was still a friend. Yolk, whom I had named Pan II, grew slowly. The larger he got, the more power I sensed in him. He had grown restless in his fifth year, so I knew it was time for him to choose someone. You do appreciate that you can't capture one; they choose who they want?"

Thistle nodded.

"In actuality, Thistle, I did not know of you before Yolk made his choice. I released him and he found you. Then, using much of a similar technique to what you demonstrated with the orb, I was able to know who you were and where."

"Oh!" Thistle had wondered how Meligance had been able to find her in so remote a village, and how she could have known of her innate gift of power when she had not even known herself.

"You are right, child. It is wise to understand your own power without Yolk's assistance. Yet, as you found out a few months ago, there are circumstances where his help will prove invaluable. You could not have cast the spell to help Sart without him; it would have destroyed you."

Thistle flushed, still a bit embarrassed by the choices she had made, relative to what she now knew. She had made that gesture out of desperation, and out of a compulsion that she did not know whence it had come. Perhaps Yolk had been involved in that as well.

"So, we need to continue expanding your knowledge base. Sart is going to assign a variety of tutors for you, on a wide range of topics from history to magical lore, to mathematics, sciences, court etiquette, current politics, physical fitness, and so forth. You will need a well-rounded education. One never knows what will come in handy when facing a difficult or desperate situation. From now on, the bulk of your time will be spent on non-magical pursuits. Keep in mind, if you feel like this becomes too pedantic, that all these studies will enhance your knowledge and broaden your base of support for what you accomplish as a mage. Sometimes, understanding political intrigue or knowing the formal way to greet a foreign dignitary are worth far more than being able to cast a powerful spell.

"I gave you considerable freedom this past month because I wanted to see what you could accomplish. Now you must also learn to focus your intelligence across a span of areas, including magic, and continue to develop in each. Do you understand the importance of this?"

"Yes, ma'am. I do love to learn. It's just that growing up in the western villages, after all the chores, we had so little time or energy to spend with books."

"Well...that is good. Keep in mind that balance in life is essential. You will probably want to do more with your magic. If you really learn to focus when you practice the art, what time you spend will help you progress more satisfyingly.

"For now, I want you to take your current practice in another direction. Keep in mind that whatever tasks I give you, your inner control and focus are what you need to continue to develop. You have done well, quite well; but it gets harder from here.

"I am going to share with you something that I have never told anyone else. It is not anything awe-inspiring, nevertheless it gives one a perspective of one's advancement in the Art. I have not divulged this hierarchy to others because far too often such things are used to raise one's status above another. I don't think that will be a problem with you; however, remember that I am telling you this for a purpose. It will help you see where you were, how far you have come, and where you need to get.

"When I reached the beginning of my maturity as a magic-user, I tried to think back on all I had learned. I also made an effort to compare that to the focus and control I saw in my fellow mages. Ultimately, I devised a system of five levels. The first level – where you were when I met you – is where a mage has little or no control of the powers within. Until I showed you how to feel that power, you had little knowledge or conscious control of the energy that you described as 'stomach sickness.'" Meligance smiled, a slight upturning of her lips, before continuing.

"Over the past five weeks, you have moved rapidly through Level I and Level II, and are moving into Level III. You have made amazing progress, child.

"These levels are based on the types of things one can control and how one uses that control. Your demonstration of using the sphere to communicate, with enough control as to move it through the ether, is a solid Level III. It is a complex and focused manipulation of outside energy. All the other things you demonstrated are Level II, or in the case of simple movements of the orb, Level I control."

"Sorry to interrupt," Thistle said shyly. "Could I ask a question, mum?"

"Of course, what do you want to know?"

"When I send Blinkie through the ether, I sort of feel my way to do that. I'm not sure what actually happens."

"What do you think happens?" Meligance asked.

"Well, the ball is pure energy; at least that is how it feels to me. When I compress it and send it, I am sending energy, not substance. For whatever reason, it moves very quickly from one point to another. Having it return to form is simply letting go of the 'compression,' letting it return to its original shape where I wish it to be."

"Excellent! The truth is, Thistle, we don't know exactly what happens. Two truths about the nature of our world are suggested by this. One is that the ether, perhaps all matter, is mostly empty space. As you have already noted, pure energy can 'go through' objects. 'Form' is an organization of energy in some way, different for each substance in the world. We really don't know how that actually works. Thus, what appears solid and whole is, on an energy level, not. The other truth is that pure energy travels at an incredibly fast speed; it is almost instantaneous. Thus, sending energy over even a long distance appears to be immediate. This is an excellent query, and it is a question we will ponder again and again. Good.

"You will garner, as you work more and more with pure energy, other understandings. I could tell you, but it is often best to discover these things yourself – then you will have more control of that which you learn to manipulate.

"For now," Meligance stood, placing her fingers lightly on the desk before her, "I want to get you more firmly rooted into Level III control. You will begin to use the magical energy of the sphere in new ways, and as you do, you will need to develop the inner focus and control to maintain and direct energy *you* gather. Know this, at Level III you have entered into a long and arduous study. It takes a deep personal concentration to reach Level IV, when you can easily garner energies from without and learn to control them. If you don't have it, you will likely hurt yourself and others. Only the best magic-users learn to have a solid Level IV control."

The White Wizardess paused, continuing even more seriously. "Level V, now that is another thing altogether. That is learning to control the ether of this plane of existence, which you are not ready to begin to understand. It also encompasses the ability to develop the focus and power to control that which comes from other planes. I have only known two mages, ever, who had such control – true control – I am one of them. The other was my teacher." Meligance stated this casually, without any hint that she placed herself above others because of her ability.

"Also, should you ever reach a Level V control, understand that this type of magic is quite dangerous. We do not fully understand it and we never may. It is one of the things I pursue when I have the time. As Sart likes to say, 'at best our control is suspect.' While some users of magic don't like to admit it, he is right. Of course, those mages rarely live long enough to reach anything close to Level V control." Meligance smiled again, that wisp of a smile that showed her true beauty and elegance and spoke to a keen mind behind.

"Note especially, that when I talk of these levels, I focus on the concept of being in direct command of all you do. There are numerous mages who have delved into the magic of the higher levels. Unfortunately, most of them did not establish the firm foundation the need to be able manipulate such tremendous power. Often it results in harm to others -- and sometimes to themselves. You will only begin these levels of study when you have developed the command to ensure, as much as possible, true success in the uses of so much energy.

"To your tasks for the next months – watch this." Meligance, with a wave of her hand, opened the window that looked out over the palace grounds. She drew one of the floating spheres to her; with a flick of her hand, she sent it flying out of the building at an incredible speed. It smashed into the side of the stonework fifty paces across the way. There was a bright white explosion that expanded outward from its epicenter ten feet in every direction, raining sparks on the greensward below.

"Oh!" Thistle was surprised at the power of the explosion.

"Now take your sphere and do that," Meligance directed.

"But, I… Ah… Blink…"

"Do it! Now!" It was a stern command, brooking no exceptions.

"I…"

"Now!"

Thistle raised her right hand with Blinkie in it. In a blindingly fast mental and emotional focus, she drew upon her power, propelling the orb through the window and into the opposing wall. The purple sphere hit and exploded with so much force that the four-foot walls surrounding them shook with the reverberation. A thirty-foot-wide, white incandescence wiped the light from the sky for several seconds.

Meligance looked at Thistle with her eyebrows raised. "So, you see, there are things to be learned… Sit." She gestured toward a high oaken stool, directly across the long table from her.

Shocked and frightened, by both the power of the second explosion and Meligance's inflexible order, Thistle did as she was directed.

"First, never hesitate when you have to use magic. In this case, I forced you. There will be times, many times in the years to come, where a split second will mean your life and the lives of many others. Be willing to act and to act fast.

"Secondly, your sphere is nothing more or less than a ball of energy, controlled, as you have already fathomed, by other forces and by our inner power. We can manipulate this energy as we will with our power. It is not a plaything or a pet; it does not live. Life, as we understand it, is something more than this. If you want a philosophical discussion about life, souls, and a myriad of religions and perspectives thereof, ask Sart. Again, if you attribute life where there is none, you risk yourself and others. You will have much harder decisions to make in your life that *will* affect the life-force of others. You cannot hesitate. Understand?"

Thistle nodded, numbly.

"Thirdly," Meligance paused, noting both the embarrassed blush to Thistle's cheeks and her bowed head as she stared down at the floor. "Look at me, Thistle." The red-cheeked girl slowly looked up.

"I am not angry with you, child. I want you to learn. Sometimes a dramatic lesson teaches far better than words ever can. Your best educational experiences will eventually come out there," Meligance gestured expansively, "in the real world – the world of people and beasts, of good and evil, of all things great and small. For now, I will occasionally provide you with real lessons to help you learn.

"So, you noted, that during the past five weeks you added to the sphere. I can't say how you did that, because I was not with you. But you managed to draw some additional energy into the sphere. That explosion – that massive explosion -- was the result. This was not your personal energy, else the sphere would have changed in other ways. I had you throw that sphere, your 'Blinkie,' because I wanted you to experience first-hand what power can do. More importantly, what our inadvertent or uncontrolled, *unknowing* use of power can do. You may have noticed slight changes in your sphere over the past few weeks. That," Meligance pointed out the window, "is what even the slightest of unwitting manipulation of power can produce. So, now you know. And you can be ever more careful as you practice.

"Finally, this is your quest for the next few months: learning control of power garnered from without, the energy that is all around us, and understanding from where you draw it. As you work to develop this skill and knowledge, you will be forced to focus intently on your own power, and to gain command of it beyond anything you can now imagine.

"Thistle," Meligance caught the girl's eyes, "magic is always dangerous. Now you know that more directly and more personally than I could have told you or demonstrated myself. In the weeks and months to come, I will test you, sometimes daily, on what you are learning and on how your manipulation of that which is separate from you, and your control of that which is inside of you, is developing. Concentrate, understand, practice; find the center of your control."

"How?" Thistle began. Meligance waved her to silence.

"Your first task is to tap into the energy of the ether, to tap into that which is all around us. Watch." Meligance appeared to draw inward for only an instant. She reached out with her right hand, as if she was collecting the air itself. Finally, she drew her fingers inward toward her palm. When she opened them, an orb instantly expanded in the space above her hand. When she released it, it floated up to join the others about the room.

"I am not going to tell you any more than I already have. But! And this is critical – do not use your own power for anything except drawing energy to you from without and learning to manipulate it. Elsewise, you will drain yourself quickly. You can even hurt yourself. If you feel faint or nauseous, you will be drawing upon your own energy too much. Find the source outside yourself. You will find it is all around. To start with, you will expend a good bit of your own energy simply focusing enough to draw even a mote of energy from the ether, perhaps not even enough to make a speck of light. It might take you weeks or months to even get that far. Be patient.

"Most minor users of magic never learn this. The tricks and bits of magic they produce come from their personal reserves of power, and that power is quickly drained. Some few, the dangerous ones, do learn to tap into other sources. Unfortunately, they often do so without true control. A few develop control in other ways, by... well that is

73

another matter altogether.

"You have already touched the power without, inadvertently perhaps; but you drew energy from somewhere into your ball. Focus, practice, be patient. Know what you need; know what you use; know what its effect will be before you use it.

"Go, child. Sart will see you this afternoon to arrange for your other studies. I am off again for one week. After that, I plan to be here to help guide your work."

Thistle stood up and curtsied. She turned around, and without even thinking or making a conscious effort, she found herself striding away from the anteroom down the Hall of Magic.

Meligance watched from far above. Here was great potential worth her focus. The gods willing, they would both live to see it to fruition.

Of Elves and Other Things

"Tell me a bit more about Elanar, Simon-Nathan. I need to know as much as I can before I approach him."

"Approach him? Are you crazy? He'd as soon kill you."

"Yes, perhaps, however, the grandmaster said something about 'my other problem.' At first, I wasn't sure whether he was talking about Thistle, or... well, I'm fairly confident it wasn't about my not being able to spend time with my girlfriend. The elves are the only other thing I can think of that is really concerning right now."

"Did he say anything about what he wanted you to do?" Simon-Nathan asked.

"No, he was fairly cryptic. He said to face things head-on."

"So, you're going to jump right into the fire? The frying pan isn't hot enough?"

"Elanar?" Jared looked up, eyebrows raised.

"Yeah, well, I told you about his heritage – him having a bit of human, a smidge of dwarf, and many centuries after that of elven blood mixed in. The thing is with all the 'almost' elves, they feel shamed at having been barred... well, kicked out, from Moulanes, and you can't really blame them. The difficulty, for some of them, is that they have resisted giving up that insult. Elanar has failed to pass his Journeyman trials twice. His friends, the other 'almost elves,' only once. They are all back to study and prepare for going out again.

"The general rule for this, Jared, is that, if you do not succeed as a Journeyman, you are given a second chance after further study. If you don't succeed a second time, you have to return, and study and prepare for two to four additional years, or more, before going out one last time. It is actually a fairly generous policy; they don't want to lose talented prospects after years of training, because maybe there wasn't a good fit, or some other reason beyond one's control."

"Do you know why Elanar did not succeed?"

"Rumor has it, that it is his attitude. He places himself above others: his instructors, the Bards who oversaw his internships, the town elders, the people he works with and entertains, in general, I guess. It's not hard to imagine that when you see him in the yard."

"Yes, I can see that about him. Good, thank you Simon-Nathan, this will help."

"Be careful."

Jared shrugged.

Simon-Nathan looked away from Jared, down at his feet. He cleared his throat, and finally, "Ah... could I ask you something personal, Jared?"

"Hey, you're my best friend; ask me anything, always."

"Well..." he hesitated; finally he blurted it out, "Do you like Karenna?"

"Wow! That is a bit awkward. There is Thistle. There will always be Thistle, though..."

"She likes you, you know. I think Karenna really likes you."

"I know. Well, actually, I don't know, except for that kiss. I don't know what to do. She is really nice, and I won't be with Thistle for..." Jared's voice trailed off.

"I have an idea."

"About?"

"How you could see Thistle."

"Really?" Jared perked up.

"It's the Yule season soon, and we break for two weeks. I know you don't have anywhere to go; so I talked it over with my parents, and they said they would love to have you spend the holidays with us. I was thinking that if you could get a message to Thistle, she could come, too, at least for a day or more, as long as she likes."

"Are you positive they wouldn't mind?"

"Not at all. We have a large house, with lots of extra rooms. Do you think Thistle might send that ball-thing again? You could ask her if she does."

"Don't know. It sounded like it wasn't an easy thing to do. Why don't we send her a note by post? There's still time." Jared was thinking quickly. "Why don't you get a formal invitation from your parents that we can enclose; then I'll send it to her as soon as we get it. That way it will look proper for someone at the palace."

"Good idea. Tomorrow is Solisday, and I can get off campus to see them. Good. This will be fun."

"Wow! Thanks, Simon-Nathan."

Jared had all of Solisday alone to think of a strategy for approaching Elanar. He wasn't sure he would succeed at first; he hoped he could couch his proposal in such a way as to at least plant a seed. He was nervous, but the grandmaster had said, "head-on."

He was also thankful that Karenna was busy preparing for a presentation to the theory club. She was the president-elect, a true honor for a freshman, so she wanted to make a good impression. He had tried to be interested when she told him the title: "The Use of Ornamentation in the new Florid Style of Post-Revival Tonality as Exemplified in the Vocal Style of the Court Musicale." Luckily, they had not been alone since "the kiss." Jared was still quite confused about that. Thistle's kisses had always been light, even chaste, hinting of much more. Karenna's had been full, deep, her lips moist and sweet. It had stirred something in Jared's depths that he was afraid to admit.

He hoped to be able to find Elanar alone during their first hour in the yard away from the other elves. Often, he was assigned to help younger students with their long sword forms; but not infrequently he would be practicing first hour, as Jared did. Luckily, today he appeared to be getting ready to launch into the half hour forms warm-up. Jared walked quickly across the sward toward him.

He had considered a thousand ways to approach the elf the past few days; yet, so far he had never been confident any particular path would work. Ultimately, he decided to go with his gut. After his opening, he would have to follow through based on Elanar's reaction anyway. At least, he hoped he had thought about most of the possible ways that he might react.

Jared strode up to face him directly. "Elanar, I would thou grant me a boon." He said it in a prescribed manner. He felt that a formal request might be less likely to be ignored, or sneered at.

"What boon, half-elf?" There was a good bit of scorn to Elanar's return, yet also at least a hint of interest.

Jared bowed slightly, inclining his head and the upper part of his torso. "I was taught the high language by my mother in my youth, although I am far from expert. Since we don't have the opportunity to study it here until our third year, I was wondering if you might consent to tutoring me a few hours each week. In…"

Elanar looked Jared in the eyes, his lips curled in a sneer, "You want…"

Jared raised his hand palm outward. It was a formal request to stop, as well as to allow himself to speak. It was, also, as Elanar well knew, a form of rebuke, because he was interrupting the elf. Yet since he had interrupted Jared, the slight was highly debatable. "In return," Jared continued, his voice now more powerful, with an added edge to sternness, "I will help you with your swordplay. We both know I am the better swordsman." Which was, in this form of parlance not only a statement of fact, but a challenge to the elf to gainsay him. "I could help you challenge for the Long Sword Cup."

The Bard Hall Challenge Cup was the annual end-of-year challenge for all fourth-year students, as well as for those Apprentice and Journeyman Bards returning from the field. One could challenge in a wide variety of weapon groups. It was quite prestigious to win. One's name was formally entered into the Lists forever in Bard Hall annals. Jared had discovered that Elanar had been runner-up on his three previous attempts. Now that he was back from the field, he would be eligible to try again. This year the competition would be even tougher. There were several half-elves, and the one almost-elf who had beaten him the three previous times, who were better than Elanar.

"Go on." Elanar's reply was curt, but his position had changed. He had relaxed his posture slightly. Formally, this meant he was willing to listen.

"We could start today," Jared said. "I am free this hour. If we plan ahead, we could get two or three hours in each week. As to my working with you on High Elvish, we could pick a time in the evenings or on Solisday."

"Let's start today. After, if I think this might be valuable, we will make a pact. Agreed?"

"Agreed. I'll get my sword."

They both bowed to each other – the end to the formal proceedings. Now, the rest depended on what would transpire on the field of battle.

Ten minutes later, after they had both gone through some of the standard forms together to warm-up, Jared signaled Elanar to stop. "Set up for Attack Form II; go through it twice – first at normal speed, the second time at half speed. I will watch."

Elanar immediately launched into the form. He was a solid swordsman, knew the forms perfectly, and was quick. In addition, he had a wiry strength to his slim, tall frame. Jared could see no breaks in his rendition, either time.

"Good, perfect. Now watch what I do." Jared also launched into the identical form.

"It is the same, the standard form."

"Yes. Now, watch this, I am going to change something." Jared started the form once more; but during a left attack/parry combination, instead of following the attack with the parry, he flipped his wrist over, side-stepped slightly, and added a backhand right attack to the mix. He finished the form as designed.

"Can you show me what I did differently?"

Elanar shrugged. He started the form slowly. He managed to awkwardly recreate Jared's move.

"Good. To become the best swordsperson, my father always told us to think creatively in battle. I can tell you this, Elanar, Qa-ryks and gzks don't follow standard forms. They come at you and keep coming at you. You have to constantly create new moves to stay alive. You have to react to what they do."

"You have fought gzks? Qa-ryks? Truly?"

"Yes, and they are deadly."

This time, Elanar nodded a slight bow.

Jared bowed in return, in acceptance of the deference.

"What I want you to do now is the same form; however, somewhere within the standard moves change something. Do it quickly. Let it flow from whatever move you just made or into a move you are about to make. You want to reach a point where you don't really think about it, you react to what is coming at you. Understand?"

Elanar shrugged. He started the form again. About half way through, he swept out of a parry into a broad slashing attack, moving downward from left to right. It was awkward, and much too slow; but it was the right idea.

"Good. That's a start. What we want to do each day is expand your repertoire, change it in different ways until change feels right. It will take you a while; eventually you will start to do these variations without thinking. Once you get the knack to strike creatively, we can work on your reacting to moves that are a surprise. Let's try the same form, me attacking, you defending, and I will change one element. We'll do it half speed to start with, so you have time to react. Then we'll reverse positions."

For the next two weeks, until the Yule holiday, Jared and Elanar met on the field and in the library for their sessions. They weren't becoming friends, but the antagonism and personal challenge between them began to dissipate.

The Source of Energy

Thistle's new tutors were piling on the work; and though she loved to read and even tolerated math problems, she found she had little free time. To help, Sart changed their schedule of studying the old language from six days a week in the evenings to three. She still had to get up early, long before Alli stirred to bring her breakfast, to practice her magic.

For the past week, she had used the two hours before dawn to focus her attention on creating an orb of energy. From the start, she felt like she was floundering through the darkness of the ether. Meligance had said that she had already, in some way, taken energy from the ether and added it to the orb. She needed to recreate her prior actions, or else find another way. She discovered that even at her deepest focus, it was difficult to keep her own energy in control and separate from that which she strived to garner to her.

She tried recreating in her mind and body the sensations she had when working through all the different games and exercises she had done with Blinkie. She had a good memory, but that effort appeared to be using her own personal energy to control what was already in the ball. She had not, as far as she could fathom, added to the sphere's energy that way.

Next, Thistle tried to focus on everything she had done using her own power to send the sphere to another locale. She envisioned collapsing the energy, and then visualized moving it through the ether to another space. Still, she saw no way that any other power was involved, only what she used of her core and what the orb already possessed.

Standing still, going deep within, and studying the energy of the sphere gave her more focus. She practiced this each day for several hours. The deeper she got, the more she was able to separate herself, her personal energy, and the energy that was the orb.

. It was six days since she had seen Meligance. With still no success, she tried to recreate what she had seen Meligance do, when she drew energy from the ether. Frustrated with herself, she sat on the edge of the bed cradling Yolk. Slowly, she went deep within to focus on her own energy. She sank deeper and deeper until she felt like she had passed some threshold or blockage within. All at once, her whole being seemed to be collapsing into a dark, extremely dense center. Using that as a catalyst, she was able to create an intense white orb of light right in her core. She used that energy and focus to reach out with her hand, or so it appeared in her mind's eye. Suddenly, she saw the ether beyond, sparkling with a million-billion minuscule lights. It was as if they were each turning on and off rapidly. Reaching out with her own energy, she focused in on one of the brightest sparkles, speeding toward it in her mind. She touched it with her power.

She woke with a pounding headache, the light of the bright winter sun streaming in her window. She forced her eyes open and found herself staring into the big yellow eyes of Yolk. He was sitting curled up on her upper chest, looking down at her as she lay on the bed.

"Milady, breakfast is ready. Are you up?"

Thistle groaned.

It was a start, albeit a dangerous one. Thistle felt she had finally really seen the difference between the energy she had within herself and what was "out there." Whatever she had done had certainly not been controlled. She took a day off from her practice. Then, since Meligance had not yet called for her, she tried to go back into the deep state she had felt she was in before "the incident."

Once deep within, she focused only on the energy closest to her. Very carefully this time, Thistle reached out and began to gather the specks of intensity she saw around her. She used her own energy, drawing thousands upon thousands of the energy dots toward a single point, trying to form them into a sphere. It felt like her energy was a powerful thread that could draw, almost like a magnet, the energy of the ether. It took tremendous concentration. And though she felt quite inept, she kept at it. When she opened her eyes after what seemed a long time, she saw she had created a tiny orb the size of the head of a pin. She was completely drained, as was Yolk, who had supported her own energy in the effort; but it was a start.

Over the next few days she was able to recreate the orb many times, slowly learning to gather more of the "dots of energy" ever more quickly, while using less of her own power in the process. It took her five more days before she was able to create a weakly glowing sphere the size of her thumb. It would have to do. Meligance had summoned her.

Thistle was anxious about seeing Meligance because she felt compelled to tell her about the incident that had caused her to lose half a day. However, she was also excited. She had gotten a fancy green envelope addressed to her from Bard Hall. When she had opened it, she had seen the invite from Simon-Nathan's parents for the Yule with Jared's neat handwriting added at the bottom, telling her he would be there. She hoped Meligance and Sart would let her go.

"What did you do, child?" Meligance asked as soon as she saw Thistle.

Thistle looked at her questioningly.

Meligance responded by handing her a mirror. She pointed toward the left side of Thistle's head. Thistle looked into the mirror. By tilting it slightly, she could see a long, thin streak of white hair on her left side, embedded in her light brown locks. "I… I don't know. I…" Alli brushed Thistle's hair twice a day. She insisted on doing it, as she said she loved to feel it in her hands. Thistle indulged her because she loved the sense of being taken care of and of being coddled a bit. Alli hadn't said anything about the streak, and otherwise Thistle rarely used a mirror. She never indulged in the vanities of the other women at court who wore lipstick and thick makeup.

"Tell me."

Thistle related the story of how she had first touched the tiny spark of distant energy, and what had happened. Meligance listened quietly, at first saying nothing about what Thistle had done. Instead, she directed her to demonstrate bringing the energy ball into existence. She smiled when Thistle created her thumb-sized ball.

"My child, you continue to astound me; and there is not much I haven't witnessed or done in my day. What happened," she pointed to Thistle's hair, "is that you seem to have touched what I call, 'the other side.' The opposite of our world, the inverse, perhaps? It is hard to describe. I have been there several times myself, but to get there I went to... well, the furthest reaches of Level Five focus and control. I never imagined you could come close to such a depth at this stage of your development, else I would have warned you. It appears you had enough control to choose to go there or not. That is good. I should not try to recreate what you described to me. This is a power far beyond what we can control, you or I, at this point in time." Meligance smiled slightly. She wanted Thistle to take in what she had revealed; everyone had limits.

"For now, you need to focus on what you have demonstrated to me – controlling and using the energy from without. As you have discovered, it is not easy to learn to draw it to you. You are beginning to understand how to use your core energy so as to manipulate what you connect with in the ether. For months to come, as you practice, you will learn to garner more and more energy with less and less effort. Once your inner focus is in control, keep expanding your understanding outward. You will find that this will become far easier, but it will take some time to achieve the ability you will need for an instantaneous focusing of large amounts of energy.

"You are on the right track. When in doubt, back off. What you touched was an impulse, a minute fraction of the power inherent in that speck of inverse matter. Had you actually managed to bring it into this realm, you might have destroyed yourself. I don't think any mage I have ever heard of could contain this form of energy or power. Be careful, my child."

They talked for some time about Thistle's other studies. Meligance was chatty this day. Thistle took the opportunity to ask her many questions. Eventually, she got around to broaching the subject of the Yule.

After thinking about it for a minute, Meligance acquiesced to her spending a few days away from the palace and her work. "I had considered sending you home for a month; however, that would have been too soon to interrupt what we are working on. This is a good second choice. You can take a couple of days and return to your work after. I will tell Sart to give you a break from your other tutors for the next three weeks. Keep up with your studies and focus on garnering energy from without. Do what you will with your maid servant. I should give her a few days to visit her home as well."

Thistle thanked Meligance profusely. She was going to see Jared much sooner than she had anticipated. She felt like she had made so much progress that they might be able to be together...

***

"Milady?" Sart bowed as he approached Meligance. Strangely, she had summoned him to meet her in one of the many courtyards about the expansive palace. This one, below her suite of rooms in the northwest tower, was specifically reserved for her uses. Still, he couldn't remember another time when she had asked to meet him outside.

"Ah, my dear cleric. You are well?" Meligance laughed lightly upon seeing him. She reached out with both her hands as he rose from his bow.

Sart bent again, this time to kiss her right hand. His smile broadened as he straightened. Looking into her eyes, he drew her up. She laughed again. He responded by wrapping his massive arms about her and drawing her into a big bear hug.

Meligance laughed once more as he let her go and helped her back to her seat. "I have missed you, my ursine friend, your hugs especially. It is a beautiful early winter day to be out, is it not? Here, sit beside me."

Sart glanced up at the bright sunlight, as if just noticing its warmth; he sat where she had patted the stone bench.

"How is the boy?" Meligance asked.

"He does well. It was a rough go at the start. He was late to term and had no formal musical training. But he is bright and has caught up in most subjects. Theory is testing him; however, Leonis feels he will catch on."

"That is good. Very good."

"He excels at weaponry. Selim considers him the best archer the Hall has seen since the elves retreated into Moulanes. His father was Manfred, you know?"

Meligance nodded. "We will need him and others like him."

"The girl's studies?"

"She is remarkable, Sart. Unbelievable, actually." Meligance turned to face him more directly, taking one of his big tanned hands in hers. "I have never seen her like. In three months, she is years past where I was at her age – years, my good cleric."

"We will have need of her, too... and others."

"Her time comes. It will be difficult for her."

"I will help where I may, though as you know, there are no cures for womanly difficulties – only mixtures of herbs and tinctures for treatment."

"I know; it was torture for me the first year or so. As you know, for those with magic, it takes longer, too. She may have it even harder. Her inner power is extraordinary."

"We must keep a close watch."

"Truly." Meligance caressed Sart's hand. Even the memories of what she had been through were painful. She chose to shift the focus. "The west?"

"Is quiet, except for rumors."

"And?"

Sart shook his head. "I don't know. Something is happening beyond our reach. I can sense it. There has been naught of Aberon since the breaking of the Altar. Yet there is tension in the far west that bodes of changes, dark changes."

"Do you think he perished when the altar broke?"

"Nay, good lady, I wish it were so. Something happened. He has gone into seclusion deep in the west. His mark is still felt; my men afield have sensed it. And it has changed. He has changed. His power is... well, for want of a better word, 'developing.'"

"A calm before the storm? Will we be ready in time?"

"The gods willing. It is the focus of all I and my fellow brethren do."

"We need all the time we can get, my dear friend – years, a decade or two. I can bring her along no faster than her gift allows."

"Pray that we can hold the west at bay that long."

"Shall we repair up?"

"I am yours to command," Sart stood as he spoke.

At that, Meligance laughed again, more heartily this time. She took his arm.

Holiday Magic

Jared was rolling on his bed, holding his gut, trying unsuccessfully to control his laughter. Simon-Nathan was doing his best to mimic the grandmaster while reciting a Christmas poem. They had returned from the Yuletide banquet at which grandmaster Leonis had presided. He had told jokes, given out awards – one, which surprised the three of them, went to Jared for mentoring young students in weaponry – and had spoken briefly about the ideals of Bard Hall. It had been an extravagant repast. Stuffed, and a bit tipsy from the mulled wine, the three friends were now gathered in Room 456 to exchange gifts and to say their goodbyes.

Although he would have liked to have done better, Jared had managed a middling "fair" grade on his theory exam; still, he had passed. In all other subjects, he had done well. With Simon-Nathan's last-minute tutoring, he had scratched out an "Excellent" in history. As expected, Karenna had excelled at all her subjects. Simon-Nathan, who received top honors in history and lore, managed to only squeak by in weaponry in spite of all of Jared's coaching. He had received "Very Good" marks in all his other subjects.

The past week had been highly stressful. Simon-Nathan had assured them that the spring exams would be even harder. Now they wanted to relax and enjoy.

Karenna was heading out of town for their break. Her carriage was due in half an hour. As soon as Jared managed to get up following Simon's rendition, she pushed him back onto his bed, grabbing the medal from his chest. "Come on, Karenna, it's just a medal. It's not a big deal."

"You are so naïve, Jared. It *is* a big deal." She examined the medal as she spoke; then she handed it to Simon-Nathan. "This was a special award. The grandmaster is taking notice of you, and... Well, he should, you are talented."

Me?" Jared laughed again, "You're twice as smart as I am. You're good at everything. You'd make a top-notch Bard."

"If they ever let women be Bards." She snorted, spun around, and plopped down in the chair at Jared's desk.

"Crum! I'm sorry, Karenna. They will, some day. I know they will." After that slip, Jared sobered up quickly. Karenna desperately wanted to be a Bard. Unfortunately, as of the current state of things, women could only become court musicians, directors, and teachers. The old school Bards were even fighting to keep them from becoming masters of a given field. Right now, the highest honor a woman could receive was the designation, "Professor."

"Look," Jared pulled her to her feet, whirling her about the small floor space in a fast reel. "When I'm grandmaster, I'll make it a priority. I'll make you the first Bardess."

"Bardess? Yuck." Karenna pushed him back. He lost his balance, grabbing for her as he fell back toward the bed. She landed full on top of him. This time, though later he would blame the impulse on the wine, he planted a solid kiss on her mouth.

"Hey, you two, enough. We have ten minutes to give each other our presents and get downstairs," Simon-Nathan said, tugging on one of Karenna's bright orange braids.

Karenna pulled back, blushing a deep crimson. She straightened her skirt and blouse; then she sat, a bit too primly, on the edge of the desk chair.

"Me first," said Simon-Nathan. "You're both going to love my gifts. And don't tell me they're too much; remember my dad is rich, and I like to spend for my friends." He walked over to his closet and drew out two large bundles he had hidden amongst the piles of clothes there.

"Karenna, you first." Simon-Nathan handed her a large box wrapped in a vibrant green silk scarf from the south.

Eagerly, she unwrapped the package, taking a moment to rub the soft cloth against her cheek. Inside was a gorgeous mahogany box with two gold clasps. Opening it gingerly, Karenna lifted the lid. "Oh my!" she exclaimed. "Simon, they're so beautiful." She turned the box so Jared could see.

Inside was a complete grooming set of carved jade and silver. Brushes, combs, a gilded mirror, hair pins, the finest scissors, and more. "Thank you, thank you, thank you." She jumped up, set the box on the desk, and pulled Simon-Nathan into a bear hug. kissing him soundly on his cheek. He flushed a bright red.

"You're next, Jared." He managed to squeak out, when Karenna let him go. "Here." He handed Jared a large oblong box wrapped in simple brown paper.

"Hey, how come I don't get a scarf?" Jared gibed, as he carefully removed the wrapping and set it aside. Inside he found a finely wrought wooden case of polished dark walnut. With some hesitation, he moved each of the three brass slides to the side. He opened the lid slowly. "By-the-gods, Simon-Nathan, I... I can't accept this. Really, it *is* too much."

"It's yours, Jared," his roommate beamed. "You're my best friend, and I want you to have it. That settles it by my accounting."

Jared was stunned. Inside the case was one of the most beautiful lutes he had ever seen. The carving on the sounding box was a rich dark walnut that matched the case. It contrasted with the bright yellow-white spruce of the instrument top. The whole thing was a work of art, made by a master luthier.

Simon-Nathan went on talking, but his words were lost to Jared as he continued to stare at the instrument. "...you will play it beautifully."

Jared set the case aside on his bed. Then he stood up. He took Simon-Nathan's wrist and drew his roommate into a hug. "I will accept it; truly, Simon-Nathan, it is too much. I...Thank you, good friend."

"I'm next," Karenna bubbled, after Jared sat back down. "Here, Simon-Nathan, I had my father send this up from the south. He found it in an old shop. I...I hope you like it." She handed him a brightly wrapped package that was obviously a large tome.

Simon-Nathan unwrapped the book carefully. "Oh, my. Yes! Thank you! I have looked for this in all the stores here. You remembered," he beamed. It was a rare, illustrated original, *History of Music of the Second Age – The Masters of Polyphony.*

"Thank you, Karenna, I'm in heaven." He sat down on his bed and immediately opened the tome to peruse it.

"Jared." Karenna handed Jared a smaller package, also a book by its size, shape, and weight. Jared smiled. It was Karenna being Karenna. "Go on, open it."

Untying the bow, Jared opened the wrapping. Inside was a leather-bound book with a picture of a unicorn lying in a meadow on the cover; a lass was sitting next to the magical beast with her head resting on his side. Jared read the title, *Minstrel and*

Jongleur Tunes of the Early Revival: Scored for the Lute and Portative Harp.

"I knew what Simon-Nathan got you, so I wanted to get you something you could use forever."

"It's wonderful, Karenna. I've never had anything so perfect, from both of you." Jared had tears in his eyes. "Thank you both. I am overwhelmed." He stopped, flushing slightly. "I'm sorry, but I have little money. Only what Sart gave me when he dropped me off, in case I needed things. I... well, I made you both something."

Sitting back down, Jared drew two packages from underneath his bed. The smallest he handed to Karenna; he gave a long, thin one to Simon-Nathan. "This is from my heart. I hope you both know that. You have been the best friends anyone could have."

Karenna eagerly tore the gossamer wrapping from her present. "It is only a trifle..." Jared began.

Since winters in the north country run long and cold, a common hobby is carving. Jared had become skilled at working the hard ironwood from the far south that was brought north for various uses. In his youth, he had been able to scrounge miscellaneous cast-off pieces in the woodpiles at home. He had learned to carve them into animal shapes. The wood had been much easier to find here in Borea. He had asked Simon-Nathan to find him some small blocks, knowing that his roommate's father imported the wood in one of his many warehouses. Simon-the-Elder let his son pick whatever he wanted. Jared had made Karenna an otter, a bear, and his favorite animal, an eagle.

"Jared, they are so beautiful," she cried, kneeling in front of him. She leaned in, touched her nose to his and gave him a soft lingering kiss. "I love them. I..." her voice trailed off. She drew back slowly, her hand brushing his lightly as she pulled away.

"Simon-Na..." Jared had a lump in his throat and could barely speak.

Jared's roommate nodded. He pulled off the tie that held the coarse cloth wrapping around his gift. Folding back the material, he revealed eight perfect target arrows that Jared had painstakingly formed to fit his draw length. "Now you won't have any excuse for missing," Jared laughed.

"They're wonderful, Jared, though I'm afraid I still won't be a great archer. Thank you! I'll try harder next term."

"I figured it was time you had something proper to shoot. Those yard arrows are pretty basic."

A few minutes later, after hastily putting their presents away and hugging each other goodbye, they were down at the gates climbing into waiting carriages. Karenna had tears in her eyes when she gave Jared a quick buss on the cheek.

Jared heard from Thistle later that day. It was another sending, with a much smaller sphere. She seemed tired, unable to hold it for long. He heard her say, "I'm coming, Yuletide evening for two days. See you soon..." Her voice trailed off as the orb disappeared. He was anxious to see her, yet a bit worried that she was overdoing things. Unfortunately, they still had several days until the Yule.

Jared spent the first few days away from school helping Simon-Nathan's father at one of his stores. The elder Simon – Simon-Nathan the Tenth – needed all the help he could get preceding the Yule. Jared took advantage of this new knowledge by calling his roommate "Eleventh" for a day.

The two "Bardlings" spent ten hours each of the first two days unloading goods from the south for Simon-the-Elder's specialty shops. Jared was fascinated by the exotic crafts, foodstuffs, clothing, and other strange wares they were unpacking. As busy as they were, the days went by quickly. On the third day, the last before Yuletide eve, they only worked a half-day. On the morrow, there would be religious celebrations and all the stores would be closed. On Yuletide, a grand festival was held across the city. Both days were decreed holidays by the king, but the elder Simon had given his workers a full week off. Only his food and staple stores would be open following the Yule until after the New Year.

***

Leona was very excited about the festive season. She had been working extra hard to make Ge-or and her father gifts. She had been especially busy the last few days baking special breads, cakes, pies, and other good things from the fall harvest.

Ge-or and Aldred donned snowshoes and made a difficult, and rewarding, trip up out of the valley into the evergreens to gather sweet smelling boughs and a small tree that Leona insisted upon. Aldred grumbled most of the way, but Ge-or could tell he was as fond of keeping his wife's old traditions as his daughter was.

Except for the rough going, Ge-or enjoyed the trek immensely. Having to spend a good bit of time inside the past few days, he had started to become restless. A few days earlier, he had decided enough was enough. He had gone out in a light goat skin coat and with one of the robbers' swords had furiously attacked the hardwood posts he had set in the earth a month earlier. For two hours he worked: first a half hour of warm-up going through the standard sword forms; the rest of the time he spent using the almost dull blade to hack at the posts.

Leona watched him for a long time from the window. She marveled at both the fluidity of his movements and his muscles rippling under the jacket. She understood his restlessness had driven him outdoors. It was a reminder that she would eventually lose him. As he had told her, it was in his blood. She smiled, because for now she was happy, far happier than she thought she might ever be. As she turned away from the window, she pledged to herself that she would remember these moments for the rest of her life.

***

Jared joined Simon-Nathan's family for their religious observances at a nearby cathedral. Then, after a light luncheon, he anxiously awaited Thistle's arrival. When he wasn't pacing, he sat at the front bay window of the large mansion looking out at the street. After over an hour, a gilded palace carriage finally drew up to the front of the fence. Before the footman could open the door, Jared was halfway to the gate. As he ran down the gravel walkway, a large figure, clad in voluminous brown robes, emerged from the cab, extending his hand to someone within.

"Sart!" Jared exclaimed in surprise and joy at seeing his friend. He bounded forward, grabbing the cleric around the shoulders as Thistle stepped out onto the cobblestones.

"Jared, my boy, so good to see you." Sart released Thistle's hand. He pulled them both in toward his bosom with his massive arms. "I have heard good things from Leonis about you, my lad. Good things, indeed. Well... here is your little lady. I suppose she is not so little anymore, heh!" He raised his eyebrows and laughed his usual boisterous laugh. "Take her hand, you dolt, and give her a kiss. I'm not a prude."

Jared and Thistle both laughed. When Sart released them, they shyly came together, nuzzling each other's cheeks; they kissed lightly, before stepping back. "Good, good, come, let's go inside and have a chat. I must be off anon; religious duties – Tis the season."

It was good to see Sart. It had been a while since he had last stopped by at Bard Hall to check in. He quickly filled Jared in on what he had been up to. "In spite of my best efforts, I have naught to tell you about your... ah... the stone." He half-whispered, "It is safe?"

Jared nodded, fingering the rough oblong object under his tunic.

"Good, good. I'm afraid I will need to take my research south to some of the old winter palaces. Well, that will come soon enough.

"Thistle, you need to know that I will be departing shortly after the New Year on several months of travel."

"What?"

"Do not worry, child. You are in good hands, and you are ready for Meligance to take over your language study. She can verse you far better than I on the use of high elvish for magic."

"I..." Thistle looked shocked.

"Come, child. I am an old codger. Well, perhaps not quite old yet, but the other term certainly applies," Sart chuckled. "I will be back soon enough. And I am sure I will be further amazed at your progress. It is time to get you out into the court anyway, where you will meet many others. Perhaps not so intelligent or suave as myself." He laughed again. "You will do fine, my dear." He patted her arm.

"So, I must be off, though I wish I could stay. The bishop has requested my service for the evening ceremonies. Godspeed, both of you."

Sart stood and walked toward the door, drawing both of them close under his arms as he went. "Stay safe, think before you act, and above all be true to who you are... and to who you wish to become," he added as he opened the door. "Merry Yuletide to all. I wish you a blessed night."

The evening festivities were the most wonderful Jared ever remembered. Thistle was by his side the whole time. They were hardly ever not touching or holding hands. Spiced-rum eggnog flowed liberally. After a sumptuous meal of varied and exotic roast fowl, Simon-Nathan, Jared, and Simon-the-Elder performed, Jared played his new lute, Simon Senior was a competent recordist, and Simon-Nathan sat to the virginal. After nearly an hour of joyful melodies, they all began to sing carols with lute and keyboard accompaniment. Just past midnight, with busses all around and many a "Merry Yule," they went upstairs to their respective rooms.

Jared reluctantly kissed Thistle good night. He said simply, "My love," as she drew away from his arms and went down the hall to her own chamber.

As Jared was about to blow out his bedside candle, there was a soft scraping at the door. "Yes?" he whispered.

Thistle opened the door and stepped through. She put her finger to her lips. "Sh-h-h."

She was dressed in a lacy white shift, with a medium-heavy blue robe over. Her light-brown hair tumbled about her shoulders. Stepping toward the bed, she said, "Br-r-r, move over."

Jared swept back the covers, letting her settle in next to him. They faced each other, at first simply breathing in each other's essence. Jared stroked her face and hair. He felt that he must be dreaming. She is so beautiful, he thought. He also knew, in spite of everything Sart had said about the dangers, that he was becoming aroused.

He cradled the back of her head in his hand and pulled her in to his lips. They kissed, lightly at first, but after a minute or so, more fervently and more passionately. Jared moaned as he felt himself respond physically. Thistle moaned, too, deep in her throat, then more loudly, almost as if she were in pain.

Suddenly, she pushed Jared on the chest hard, shoving him to the far side of the feather bed. "Stop! Gods, I'm sorry... I'm so sorry," she exclaimed. She scrambled frantically out of the bed.

Jared looked at her in shock. It was as if her whole body was shaking, vibrating. Tiny sparks, at least that was what he believed he saw at the time, were shooting from her hair in all directions. She stood by the bedside, half bent over, holding her middle.

"Thistle, I'm sorry. Did I... are you hurt? What can I do?"

"No, no, Jared. It's me. It's...it's the magic. I believed I had control of it, but not... not when...We can't; I'm sorry. I'll be all right. I...I can't stay here." With that, she turned, flung open the door, and ran down the hallway.

***

Leona decorated the main room of the cabin gaily. She used the boughs the two men had brought back, adding ribbons and bows from the many bits of fabrics left over from the bounty of the robbers' wagon. She placed beeswax candles about to add to the atmosphere. The main room, with the fire built up in the stove, was cozy and comfortably pleasant.

Though none of them were particularly religious, Leona made her father offer thanks for the year and their many blessings. They had a festive dinner, capped by more than a couple of tonics, as Aldred liked to refer to the sweet liquor he had distilled that fall from honey and corn.

With a promise of more food and presents in the morning, Leona kissed her father goodnight, and shortly thereafter, drew Ge-or into their bed.

***

Jared got no sleep. He was incredibly tense, both because of the unrequited arousal, and because he was deeply worried about Thistle. He dared not go to her. She was right... until they... No! Until *she* could maintain control, they would of needs remain aloof from each other. He was not even sure they would be able to kiss again with any degree of safety. Her obvious distress, and the circumstances of her leaving, had shaken him.

The next morning Jared waited in his room until he heard Thistle's door open and her steps come down the hall. He opened his door, gesturing for her to enter. She shook her head; nevertheless, he reached out, took her arm, and drew her, somewhat forcefully, in. He said as calmly as he could, "We have to talk."

Tears formed in her already red and swollen eyes. "I'm sorry, Jared. I don't know what to say."

"Say you love me, Thistle. You know I love you, and that hasn't changed. We will get through this. You were right. It is hard. I do want you; I want to be with you so much… we have to learn what we can and can't do. Last night we crossed a line we shouldn't have." He gently raised her bowed head so she was looking at him.

"It wasn't all your fault. I am as complicit as you are, maybe more so." He drew her to him in a hug. But he only held her for a second – pushing her away gently. Touching her face lightly, he brushed away her tears. She kept her arms up against her chest so that he could not bring her closer. He understood why.

Tears shining anew on her cheeks, Thistle took a small step further back, to establish even more distance between them. "I do love you, Jared, so much. Sometimes I wish I had never heard of magic. I wish…"

"Thistle, I know this is hard for you; yet, it is not something you could have refused. It is who you are. We have to find our way through this. Sart said you have made amazing progress. Keep working, keep learning, you…we will find our way."

He wanted to draw her to him again, but he could see she was struggling with herself. "Go back to your room, my love. Wash up. I will go down first. Let us enjoy this day as we may, together with friends."

She nodded, wiping at the tears that continued to flow. She turned and left him. The hurt he felt in his gut and chest, more for her and her inner pain than his own, cut deeply. Somehow, he knew that they would survive this. He loved her too much to let anything stand in the way of their feelings for each other.

Simon-the-Elder presided over the day's festivities. Everyone enjoyed a lightly spiked punch while they all opened presents. Thistle and Jared both received gifts from the family, though Jared protested that it was too much. He received two sets of doublets and trousers with a nice pair of shoes, to, as Simon-Nathan said, "have something to wear besides your school uniform." Jared had to admit that wearing bright yellow out in the town had been a bit embarrassing. Thistle received a lovely bouquet of flowers from the family and a large basket of delectable southern treats from Simon-Nathan.

Thistle had brought a writ from the court, honoring Simon-Nathan the Tenth for his community service. It had been Sart's idea; she had begged the boon of the Lord

89

Chancellor. After due investigation, it was agreed that it was well deserved. Simon-the-Elder was beside himself. He immediately proclaimed Thistle an official member of the household "now and forever after." For the family, she created a small ball of light to set upon the top of the Yule tree. She promised a new one each year if she were able. She explained that it would, without magical care, dissipate into the ether over a month's time.

Jared had carved a life-size, dark walnut falcon for an arched cavity in the foyer. Simon-Nathan had told Jared that the family once had a small alabaster statue of a parrot there; unfortunately, the cat had broken it several years before. Jared felt it was a poor substitute for some well-known artist's work, yet they said they loved it and immediately placed it in the alcove.

It was over a massive banquet, with roast beef as the highlight, that Thistle and Jared met Simon-Nathan's sister. She had not been feeling well and had begged off the previous day's festivities. Jared noted that she was a bit pale, though she was a lovely young lady, a couple of years Simon-Nathan's junior. Athena's light blond hair stood out amongst the crowd at the table. She was affable and poised for so young an age. Jared could not help glancing in her direction throughout the meal. There was something about her that troubled him.

Simon-the-Elder had invited many important guests, and Jared was amazed at how they deferred to Thistle. Of all the people at the Yule dinner, she was accorded the seat of honor on the left of their host. Jared was sitting next to her. He felt lost in comparison. Everyone appeared to value her opinion on this or that.

Afterward, he asked her, "How do you do that? Command such respect?"

"They fear me," she answered frankly, smiling for the first time since the evening before. "I am the White Wizardess's apprentice. For some reason, they equate me with Meligance. She is amazing, Jared. I have seen dukes, courtiers, countesses, and visiting Wizards bow almost to the ground when she passes. She disdains all that, avoids it if she can; on occasion she must venture forth and deal with affairs of the kingdom. She has begun to take me with her. I am to learn courtly ways," she sniffed. "Gods, Jared, you should see all the affectation. It makes me feel slimy to watch."

"I guess I am lucky. Things are much more straightforward at Bard Hall. Though I must admit, it is a man's world. Women are only beginning to make footholds into that bastion."

"Maybe that is something we can change." She smiled again and winked at Jared. It was good to see her mood had improved.

The truth was that Thistle had been terribly frightened the night before. As soon as she had given into the passion, the energy within her had risen to the surface. It had taken all her control to do what she had done – to keep it from flowing out of herself into Jared and into the room. When she had left, it had taken her most of the night to bring herself back to focus. Bursts of energy appeared to escape in every direction. If she hadn't known better, she would have sworn she had burnt holes in the sheets and bedding. When she had finally felt she was at last calm and in complete control, too exhausted to even sleep, she had wept bitterly.

She now knew she had much more to learn about control. She had deluded herself into thinking that she was well in command of her inner powers. She only hoped that Jared would understand. She knew that he had been upset and... and frustrated.

The next morning, when he had forced her into his room, she had been both afraid and relieved. He still loved her, he was concerned about her, and he understood that they would have to back off. It was so hard to think about not being able to be together. She knew, too, they had weathered a make or break situation regarding their feelings for each other. At least, she could feel good about that.

Thistle left later that day, just as the light was failing in the west. They all gathered outside to say goodbye, so she and Jared did not have the privacy for an intimate goodbye. It was probably for the best. He bussed her on the cheek and squeezed her hand tightly. She knew that it would be a long time before they would see each other again. As hard as that was, she also knew it would be for the best.

***

Goat Haven, as Ge-or had come to think of the hidden vale, received another heavy dusting of snow Yuletide night. Leona and Ge-or woke late to an idyllic scene from the bedroom window. They lay snuggling in bed a long time. He laid his hand on her belly and pressed his face into her sweet-smelling curls. For now, it was perfect; he had nowhere else he wished to be.

Leona finally pulled away when she heard Aldred shuffling about in the kitchen. "I must get some tea brewing, or he'll be a grouch all day," she whispered, leaning over the bed to give Ge-or a kiss on the cheek.

"I'll be along when you get the stove warmed up," Ge-or said sleepily, still groggy from the effects of too much of Aldred's brew.

"Lazy!" Leona retorted. She smiled, drawing the blankets up over his shoulder again. "Hmmm," he groaned as he snuggled further into the warmth.

They spent the day indoors. The night before, Aldred had seen that the goats and mules were well-supplied with hay and with an additional Yule gift of molasses-infused grain; so except for necessary runs outside, they relaxed.

After a hearty breakfast of venison sausage, eggs, corn-meal biscuits, slatherings of fresh butter, fried onions and potatoes, and Aldred's favorite -- hotcakes and honey -- they all sat around the stove enjoying the warmth and comforts of a wilderness cabin. For Ge-or, it was good to feel safe. This was a place he could come back to.

A bit later, after hot kaffa with a touch of rum in it, they gave each other gifts. Leona had knitted Ge-or a beautiful, heavy, alpaca sweater with the best of the wool she had carded and spun this year. She gave Aldred a thick pair of mittens made from one of the cured pelts of the timber wolves Ge-or had killed. The outside leather she had worked to a smooth, pliable feel, and the warm inner fur would provide protection under the cruelest winter conditions.

Ge-or presented Leona with her first bow -- a practice bow carved from a single piece of ash with which she could begin her training. She could use it until her crafted bow was ready. He had also made a dozen birch arrows with blunt tips. He told her that on the morrow she would have her first lesson. He had also, secretly in Aldred's shop, built a beautiful oak cradle for the baby. When she saw it, she began to cry and took his hands and kissed him all over his face.

Aldred gave his daughter a set of movable figures, animal and human, that

91

were "for the babe when he or she's old enough." They all shared a laugh. Ge-or and Leona wondered when he had taken the time to craft them, because when he was whittling by the stove, it never looked like he finished anything of any definitive form.

Ge-or gave Aldred one of his prized throwing knives. "If you can't shoot, this will serve as a good second," Ge-or told him. "I will help you to hone your skill".

Aldred kept saying he couldn't accept one of Ge-or's own knives, The big man insisted, and Aldred finally gave in.

Hemming and hawing a bit, Aldred gave Ge-or something he had purchased on his last trip to the trading post. It was a basic, serviceable, helm of quality steel. "To protect that head of yours that isn't quite as hard as you might think." Both men laughed, and Ge-or accepted the gift gratefully. It was not the best armor available, but Aldred had a good eye. Ge-or knew it would serve him well.

The rest of the day they spent playing drafts, cards, and other games that one or the other remembered from their youth. As the light was failing outside, they celebrated with a fine dinner of goose comfit, ham steaks, and "No goat for once," Leona had laughed. They ended the perfect day nibbling on the breads, cakes, and sweets that Leona had made while sitting and chatting about this or that, mostly about the baby to come.

Something Lost; Something Gained

In spite of Jared's vehement protestations, Simon-the-Elder insisted on paying him for his work at his warehouse and store, both before and the week after Yuletide. Simon-Nathan's father was still all-aglow over the court homage, and it was well-deserved. He was indeed a generous man. Unlike some of his pinch-penny competitors, his big-hearted approach to business had earned him many loyal customers. He had the document placed in an ornate gilt frame, which he hung proudly in his largest store. Jared was thus indirectly the beneficiary of Sart and Thistle's gift. Though the wages were only those of an average workman, this was the first time in his life that he had ever earned real money. It felt good, he had to admit, to have something that jingled in his purse. He planned to save the money for presents for his friends and for Thistle.

Jared and Simon-Nathan enjoyed their time together. The work had been invigorating, and his roommate proved to be quite a storyteller. They had been so busy at school that almost everything had been focused on study and practice. This chance to work together and talk of many other things was greatly appreciated. Jared also found time to ask Simon-Nathan about his sister.

"Yes, she is sick, Jared, more than my father is willing to let on. He is stubborn about some things. He had a bad experience with a healer once, so he won't let any of them in the house. He keeps trying herbal remedies brought up from the south."

"Sart would help; I know he would. He is a powerful cleric and healer, Simon-Nathan."

"You saw how cool my father was to him when he met him. No, I am positive he wouldn't let him in the door again. He only let him in the first time because he was with Thistle, and you, of course."

Jared knew not to push it any further, yet he was concerned. Athena had not looked well at all when they had left for school. Even with make-up, she had looked thin and wan.

Second term

The term started in full force the second day after the New Year; and though Jared's classes remained the same, the pace was more frenetic. They already felt the pressure of passing level exams, of auditioning for next year's large ensembles, trying out for masters, and the like. Even Elanar, who was usually staid and focused, was anxious about stepping up practices for the Long Sword Cup. He asked Jared to add another couple of hours to their practice schedule.

"I would love to oblige, Elanar, except I don't want to give up any more of my free time during our weaponry classes. I need to spend some time on what the masters give me during my lessons."

After thinking about it, he did come up with an idea. "Do you think they would let us practice in the yard on Solisday afternoons before dinner?" Jared was doing well in the instrumental area. He felt he could afford the time during the study/practice period required from four to six. Simon-Nathan was visiting home at that time, and Karenna had her theory club meetings. It was a time he usually reserved for making up tunes and polishing the exercises he had been assigned for instrumental class.

"It is an unusual request," Elanar answered, "but I think the masters might agree. Let's ask."

Elanar was so enthusiastic about the extended practice that Jared decided they should both broach the subject with the master who monitored the hallways. He in turn directed them to the music master, who oversaw all lessons, ensembles, composition, and performance. After checking with both Jared and Elanar's music professors, they received the go ahead to ask Elwind, Master of the Yard. He also agreed, provided they kept up with their responsibilities in their classes and lessons.

That Solisday found the two of them in the Yard out of breath after working out for an hour and a half. "We're out of shape," Jared wheezed. "I've gotten soft. My father used to make us do two or three sessions like this a day."

Elanar, who was leaning heavily on his sword, point stuck in the ground, nodded in agreement as he sucked the cold January air into his lungs.

"I think we need to find time to exercise –running and working out. It will make a major difference in how you hold up through the Long Sword Cup challenge. I'm told it is held over only three days?"

Elanar took in another deep breath and answered. "Yes. It can be quite brutal, especially with the heavier weapons. The long sword is the hardest because it is the most prestigious. There are many rounds, as almost everyone wants to see if they can place."

"What about early? Before breakfast?"

"That would be excellent, but cold."

Jared smiled, patting the elf on the shoulder. "You'll get used to it!"

The elves had concentrated far to the south in and around Moulanes, even before Kan's evil had spread. With their light frames and thin bodies, they were more comfortable in a warmer clime. Unfortunately, their enclave, which was enclosed by mountains, had also set their race apart from the others in the Borean world. The one entrance, up a long narrow gorge, allowed them the peace of trees and nature as they preferred, but also isolation. Northern-bred, as Jared was, Borea's weather was almost balmy for mid-winter. By now, Thiele would be surrounded with ice at sea; and there would be huge drifts of snow built up all around their stockade.

The next morning found the two of them running around the Bard Hall enclave. Within three weeks they were able to raise their pace and endurance to complete three circuits of the slightly more than half a league route, though not without a good bit of soreness as a result. They started and finished with careful stretching exercises that Manfred had taught his sons. Elanar suggested that they alternate days working with weights in the Yard, which suited Jared as well. He was finding his maturing body was increasing in height, mass, and strength.

For several weeks, Karenna and Jared managed to avoid each other, or have Simon-Nathan present whenever they were together. They both sensed a tension in their relationship that had not been there before.

Jared was also dealing with the angst he felt over his parting with Thistle. They had reaffirmed their love for each other, yet there had been far too much not said about what had happened. Thistle had made no effort to contact him with her colored sphere, and Jared felt at a loss as to whether he should attempt to connect with her. He didn't want a letter he sent opened by some lackey at court, which he surmised was probably the procedure for any communications that came addressed to the Borean Palace; so he hadn't tried to write either.

Finally, tired of the avoidance game they seemed to be playing, and desperate for assistance with a theory conundrum, Jared asked Karenna for help. They got together the first Solisday of February during study hours in Jared's room. Elanar and his friends had taken the day to meet with an elven Journeyman Bard who had returned from his four years in the field, so they had deferred their practice.

"Hi, Karenna, come in, come in. It's good to see you. You look great!" Jared tried to sound natural, but he was really nervous about this meeting.

She *did* look great. She had taken off her unappealing first year yellow tunic, belt, and skirt and put on "townie" clothes: a light green blouse, matching skirt, and a flowery red sash about her thin waist. Her beautiful long red hair flowed down her back, held in place by two clasps from Simon-Nathan's Yule gift set. Jared would have sworn that she had used some light make-up to enhance her lips and cheeks. When she slid past him to plop herself on Simon-Nathan's bed, he caught a whiff of perfume that almost made him groan. Pulling her legs up under her, she set her books aside. She smiled sweetly at him as he settled to face her on his own bed.

"I..." Jared started, after an awkward silence. Karenna interrupted.

"We need to talk, Jared." She held his gaze, waited a second, and then went on. "I want to be with you." She stated matter-of-factly, placing both her hands primly on her thighs. "There, I've said it and... and I don't care about what anyone else thinks. Let's do it and see where it takes us."

Jared's eyes opened wide. He sat and stared at Karenna. Thoughts tumbled through his head, one on top of another: Be with me? What? Thistle? Do it? What? What! By-the-gods, I... Are all women like this here? In Thiele no one would...

"Jared? I just offered myself to you. You could say something." Tears formed in Karenna's eyes and one leaked down her cheek.

"I'm sorry, Karenna. I... You..." Jared finally reached out and took her hands
95

in his. An instant later, at least that is how he remembered it; they were in each other's arms kissing passionately.

Jared woke to the sweet smell of flowers and the softness of bare skin touching his. Karenna lay asleep, half draped over him and half on the bed, her left arm curled around his neck. He reached up with his free arm and caressed her cheek.

It had been awkward since neither of them was experienced, but it had also been wonderful in so many ways. He was relaxed for the first time in weeks, probably months. In spite of something nagging in the back of his head, he felt good. Really good.

He lay there for several minutes, drinking in the scent and feel of Karenna. Jared was taking another deep breath of her essence when he heard footsteps – the doorknob turned. By-the-gods!

"Simon-Nathan, don't... don't come in," he whispered loudly. It was too late. Karenna shifted as his roommate pushed the door in; the blanket fell away from her shoulders revealing too much in the candlelight.

Jared saw Simon-Nathan's eyes widen, while a deep crimson flush rose in his cheeks. His roommate gasped in shock. Jared heard him groan as he slammed the door.

"Oh, no!" Jared and Karenna exclaimed together as Simon-Nathan's running steps echoed down the hallway.

Later that evening, Jared sat alone at his desk, his head in his hands. For several hours, he had been going over again and again what had happened – Karenna, Thistle, Simon-Nathan – all of it. Karenna had left hurriedly, immediately after Simon-Nathan had dashed away. She had dressed, given Jared a long kiss suggesting to him that, though she was embarrassed by the situation, she was not ashamed or bothered by what they had done together.

He went back and forth, thinking of Thistle. About what she had said to him, and about her sincerity at the time. He wondered whether or not she truly, in her innocence, knew what that meant. Now, having crossed that line, Jared felt like he had betrayed her.

Karenna? He did like her, and in a way, he supposed he loved her. She was intelligent, beautiful in a far different way than Thistle – more what he would call desirable -- where Thistle was a classic beauty, exquisite, but almost untouchable. And what of Karenna? She knew about Thistle; she knew Jared's feelings. Now that they had... what would she do? Would she accept that Jared still loved another woman?

What really made his head hurt was that Simon-Nathan had caught them, virtually in the act. Somewhere deep down, Jared knew that his roommate fancied Karenna. It had been little things in his expression and actions when the three of them were together. He would have sworn that Simon-Nathan wished she was his girlfriend. Jared groaned, then hit his head on his desk. It didn't help.

Sometime later his roommate tentatively opened the door and said, "Jared? Can I come in?"

"Yeah, it's just me," Jared answered. He watched as Simon-Nathan entered, crossed to his bed, threw his books on the desk, and lay down with his face to the wall.

"I'm sorry. I'm so sorry, Simon-Nathan. It... it happened. I... she, damn it. It happened, that's all."

It was a minute before Simon-Nathan turned around. His eyes were wet. "It's not your fault, Jared. She's wanted... well, she told me she liked you. She wanted you to notice her. It's kind of shocking to come back and..."

"Yeah, I know."

It took Jared a second to realize what his roommate had said. "You mean you knew that she wanted... That..."

"Of course. Didn't you? She's thrown herself at you again and again. She... Heck, it doesn't matter, really. We're still friends, right?"

"Of course, best friends. I didn't want... well, it shouldn't have happened the way it did, that's all."

"Hey, Jared, you didn't do anything wrong. I came back early. Well, we need to work out some system if... well, you know."

Jared blushed.

The next Solisday, following his sparring session with Elanar and a long hot soak in the baths, Jared dressed for a rendezvous with Karenna. They had planned a long after-dinner walk down to the fount/statuary complex at the northern end of the Hall. Jared had discovered that it was an unspoken and unofficial trysting place for couples in the evenings. It was far enough away to not disturb others; and it had enough corners and alcoves to have a bit of privacy. It had surprised him the first time he had wandered by late one evening to see men as duos, as well. Each to his own, he thought. It was not unheard of in the northern villages, but it was never so obvious.

Jared began to dress back into his bright yellow uniform, musing, Why not wear townies? He felt Karenna might like that, and he would feel more comfortable.

They had only had a few, brief meetings together since their tryst in Jared's room. They had kissed, held each other, but not spoken at any length. Jared was a bit anxious about what they might talk about this evening. He needed to find out what she was thinking; he wanted to know how she really felt.

Absentmindedly, he put on his tunic, reaching into the little secret door on the desk to retrieve the pendant. He always stashed it there when he went down to the baths, as he didn't want others to ask questions about it. He had kept it as secret as possible. Otherwise, he wore it underneath his clothes at all other times.

Coming out of his reverie when he didn't feel the stone under his fingers, he pulled the drawer completely out and looked inside. There was nothing there. He stopped. Yes, he remembered putting it in there as he usually did. Yet, as he thought more about it, maybe he was remembering the previous day. He began rummaging amongst the papers and books strewn on the desk and finally in all the alcoves and drawers. Beginning to panic a bit, he dashed out the door and down to the baths. No one was in the pools. They were usually quiet during the late afternoons on Solisday, because many of the students were off campus or still in study hours by the time Jared and Elanar finished their sparring.

He searched all around the area he had been, and finally the whole large hot springs pool. Nothing. The one lone towel boy on duty told him he had not found anything, and that no one had been there since Jared had left fifteen minutes before. Starting back up toward the main hall, Jared remembered that he definitely had not had the pendant when he entered the pool. He had double-checked. He couldn't think of any other place he might have put it, except the drawer.

The dinner bell rang as he was hurrying back to the main hall. As he approached the sets of doors to the dining hall, Karenna hailed him from behind. "Jared, wait. Sorry, I am a bit behind schedule. I wanted to look nice for you." She blushed lightly, her color enhancing the redness of her hair and deep blue of her eyes.

Jared caught his breath. By-the-gods, she is gorgeous, he thought. He swept her up into his arms, lifting her off the floor as they kissed. "I've missed you," he said, completely forgetting his dilemma. Releasing her to the ground, he took her hand and they walked together into the dining room.

Dinner was informal on Solisdays with so many away. For one thing, they were allowed to sit anywhere. The food was served on the tables closest to the front of the hall, nearest to the masters' table. Karenna whispered to Jared as they moved forward. "Let's grab some wine, cheese, and bread, and have a picnic. I know just the spot. It's protected from the wind, and we'll have some privacy, too."

Jared almost didn't respond; his focus had returned to the missing pendant. He did smile and gave Karenna's hand a squeeze as they walked up to the front.

Instead of going to Karenna's planned spot, they ended up going back up to Jared's room for their picnic. When Jared told Karenna about the missing pendant – she being one of the few who knew about it – she insisted they look for it again. "Maybe you put it in your purse or one of your pockets," she had suggested. Jared had not considered looking in his clothes because he had been positive he had placed it in the drawer.

They searched everywhere, with no luck. Jared was at a loss as what to do next.

"I'm sorry to upset our plans, Karenna; this is vital. Not so much to me, personally, but Sart said it was an important artifact."

"You searched the baths thoroughly?"

He nodded. "I talked with the towel boy, too. Unless he was lying, it isn't – wasn't there. I definitely didn't have it when I got into the bath, and I'm fairly confident

I placed it in the drawer like I usually do." He smiled and leaned forward to kiss Karenna. "Though I may have been distracted by thoughts of being with you."

Karenna returned the kiss, suggestively, then backed away. "We should talk about us, Jared, about our relationship." She pulled her hands away, brushed a lock of hair from her face, and took a long drink of the white wine in her mug. She spoke hesitatingly. "I care about you, Jared, too much, probably. I do understand about Thistle, or I think I do. I don't really want to come between you both, I…" Tears came to her eyes as she started to say more.

Jared raised his hand and touched her lips, silencing her. "I care about you, so much, Karenna; but I don't want to lie to you either. With Thistle, I don't know, it is like we belong together. We fit." He stopped for a minute, wondering how much to tell Karenna. He decided he had to be truthful. "There is something else you need to know. It is hard to say because you may feel hurt by it. First, I want you to understand that what happened, what we did last Solisday, was spontaneous. It just happened. I needed you; I wanted you. I didn't plan for it at all. Do you understand?"

"Yes, for me, too. Well, mostly. I guess you could say I did have ideas about us, and I did ask. It did seem to happen all of a sudden." She blushed, remembering.

"Karenna, you need to know that Thistle and I can't be together, not like you and I have been together, not for a long time. Her magic is really dangerous; as much as she has learned, she still cannot control it. We discovered this at Simon-Nathan's house this Yule. We cannot be passionate together at all.

"Do you remember a while ago when she came to visit here, a few weeks before the Yule?"

Karenna nodded. "I remember. I was… well, a bit jealous, I suppose."

"That eve, Karenna, before Thistle left, she told me that I should see others, be with others. She explained about all of this magic stuff and how it meant we couldn't be together physically. She said she didn't want me to hold myself to any promises of fidelity. I don't think she truly understood what she was saying; but after we were together at Simon-Nathan's, it struck home. I…" Jared choked back sadness and some irritation. "I haven't heard from her since."

Karenna sat still, looking intently at Jared. Her mind was whirring at a frenetic speed, trying to keep up with the whirlwind of emotions that were flowing through her. She understood what Jared had told her, though it wasn't easy to grasp the full implications.

"So, in a sense, she granted us leave to be together, to love each other?" she finally said.

"Yes," Jared replied. "That wasn't why... She didn't know that you…"

"I know; but it does feel a bit that way, doesn't it?" Karenna pushed back slightly.

"Karenna." Jared took her hands in his. "I do care for you, deeply, both as a friend, and now as a lover. I don't want you to have the wrong impression about Thistle and my feelings for her. I still love her. I think I will always love her, whatever happens." He drew her over to his bed, and put his arm around her, cradling her to his chest as she sobbed.

"Oh, Jared," she finally managed to gasp out, "we are some pair."

They cuddled and kissed lightly until Simon-Nathan returned.

"I don't know, Jared," Simon-Nathan said, flushed from the cold. "I've been out all afternoon. I just got back. You both looked all over here?"

Jared and Karenna nodded. "I don't know what to do next," Jared said. "I have to get a message to Sart, and the fastest way to do that might be through the Grandmaster."

"I think that is what you have to do," Karenna said, "if it is as important an artifact as he indicated. You know that if you do, the whole school will know? They don't abide thievery or dishonor in Bard Hall."

"Maybe there is a way to keep it quiet," Jared said. He stood up, bringing Karenna with him. "I'll go to see him tomorrow; he will know how to handle this."

Control, Control, Control

After returning from what she considered a disastrous Yule, it took Thistle nearly a week to feel comfortable enough to continue her magical work. Since Meligance had been called away, she took the time to focus on all her other studies. She discovered that she enjoyed delving into the history and language of magic in the Borean library and its archives.

As a result, she made considerable progress in translating the pile of parchments Meligance had given to her. Most of it turned out to be memoirs, replete with little asides about meals the Wizard had enjoyed, places he had visited, and tricks he had pulled on his fellows. There appeared to be little of a true magical nature within them, though Thistle still could not decipher some of the stranger text. She discovered that Sart had been right – he knew little of the specialized language of magic.

Finally, she returned to her magical work. Thistle found that by carefully practicing everything she had done, she regained enough confidence to continue her work coalescing energy from without. Soon, she was able to produce an orb about half the size of Blinkie. Once she had accumulated the energy for that, she could manipulate it as she had learned previously.

Thistle was well aware that the effort she was expending was much too draining. She needed to learn how to garner more energy without having to waste so much of her own focusing and gathering. She decided to add another dimension to her practice. While she was working one day when Alli called her to dinner, it occurred to her that outside distractions interrupted her ability to maintain focus and control. Rather than do all of her magical practice during periods of quietude, she would reverse that and learn to focus when she was likely to be interrupted.

By the end of the second week of this new form of focus, she had Alli purposefully try to interrupt her: by talking to her, banging on pots and pans, and even touching her or trying to tickle her. She felt she was improving, but her progress felt naggingly slow.

Immediately after returning, Meligance called. She put Thistle through her paces. When Thistle was done, the Wizardess asked, "Are you all right?"

Thistle had done well, demonstrating to her mentor how far she had come in drawing the energy into the ball. The White Wizardess was satisfied and told her so; however, something was missing. The girl was focused, serious, and adamant about her work; yet there appeared to be little personal involvement in what she did. She was going through the motions.

"I'm fine, ma'am. I do get too tired, I feel, for the progress I am making."

"No, it is something else. Something happened?"

Thistle blinked; she didn't offer anything more.

"Did something happen with Jared over the Yule?"

Thistle bent her head; the tears began to trickle down her cheeks.

"Explain, child. You will feel better, and it is best that I know."

Thistle related the incident in Jared's bedroom. She glossed over the details yet explained how scared she had been.

"How long were you lying next to him?"

"Less than a minute, maybe only seconds. I'm not really sure. It happened so quickly."

"That's good, actually. You saw the signs, and you decided to get out. Else you may have hurt him, or yourself, or both. You did fine. You said you struggled most of the night to regain your control."

"Yes, mum."

Meligance knew this was hard for her protégé; but she also knew that the girl needed to deal with it, so she pressed ahead, cajoling her to open up about the incident. "In the end you felt like you had regained your focus enough to meet with him, to talk to him the next day?"

"Yes, though..."

"Did you touch... after, I mean."

"Yes, several times. He drew me into his room in the morning. He told me he understood. We held each other for a minute, just standing."

"Good." Meligance relaxed back into her seat, realizing she had been tense, too. "I'm sorry that you had to go through that, Thistle, but it was inevitable. You handled it as best as can be expected. No one got hurt; and you were able to regain control, which is important. Remember what I said about experience being our best teacher?"

Thistle nodded.

"This is an experience that you created for yourself; a hard one to live through, no doubt, but useful. You now know how difficult your task is going to be over the next few years. You will need to have control of your energy within before you can be with your lover. You also know what to watch for should this type of thing ever happen again."

"It won't..." Thistle said firmly.

"Child, child, don't be so hard on yourself. Love is a reason to live; maybe *the* reason to live. There is nothing wrong in what you did, nor in what you desired. It is the most natural thing in the world. You have learned that your gift has to be controlled; that is an important lesson for you."

"I... I could have killed him. He..." she broke down sobbing.

"Yes, you could have, and that is important to understand. Yet, you did not; and now, it is unlikely that you will. You can set parameters from here on for your relationship. It will be hard, believe me; I know this from personal experience. If you persevere, you will come out on the other side much stronger as a mage and also as a person.

"Perhaps I shouldn't tell you this, Thistle; but when the time comes where you can control the magic... Well, let me say this – your love-making will reach heights others only imagine." Meligance smiled that wisp of a smile of hers.

"Now," Meligance purposefully and abruptly changed the subject, "I want to demonstrate something for you and explain what your next focus needs to be. Watch carefully."

Meligance opened the window with a flick of her finger. A cold gush of air rushed through the room, sending all the orbs dancing about. With a gesture of her hand, she drew energy from the ether into her palm. In an instant, she formed it into a bright white ball, slightly smaller than the spheres floating about. Then, in one swift motion, she sent the concentrated energy flying out the window to crash into the far wall, where it burst into a flaming ball five feet across. The entire process took less than two seconds.

"Now, again." Meligance repeated the process with as little effort as she had with the previous orb.

"So, Thistle, what you have been doing is trying to corral the energy you see in your mind's eye when you go into a deep focus. That is good, but not nearly enough. If you are to be useful as a mage, you need to be able to garner much more energy, almost instantaneously; and then be ready to do it again and again – all without expending much of your own power. That," she pointed out the window, "I have done for hours at a time in a pitched battle."

"How?"

Meligance waved her question off. "In order to command a great deal of energy, Thistle, you need to learn to draw it to you. Your focus and control are coming along fine. Granted, there is much to learn and practice." She raised her right eyebrow and looked quizzically at Thistle. "If I am not mistaken, you are gathering infinitesimal dots of energy within your range when you are focused inward. From all I have learned about our world and magic, what you are 'seeing' is the energy produced by the tiniest motes of matter.

"For the next few days, start to bring the energy to you. Imagine the flow of millions of those sparks coming together at your will, by your power, under your control. Do not gather them, use your energy to draw them toward you. It will take a while to gain the knack. Be patient and be careful, it will come.

"In addition, the one thing else you must learn immediately is when to cut the flow of power. You always need to maintain control. Pull in only what you need. Eventually, you will have a precise feel of how much energy you require for any given spell or effect. Any questions?"

"No, ma'am."

"Go then. We will meet often now. It is time to learn the language of magic, and it is also time for me to guide your work more closely."

Thistle turned to leave. As she was beginning to step forward, she heard her mentor say, "Contact Jared, when you will, if you will. You will feel better."

The next month began with Thistle seeing Meligance almost every other day. As her mentor had suggested, it took time to learn to garner more power and to control it while maintaining her concentration. She found the balance critical. It was frustrating when she couldn't move ahead more rapidly.

She was improving, slowly: her orbs of power were intensifying; she was less distracted by outside disturbances; and she found she could quickly settle into a space mentally and physically where she could begin her efforts.

Her understanding of the relationship between the high elvish language and magic was also expanding rapidly. As Meligance had repeatedly told her, magic did not need language; yet language could facilitate the focus needed to acquire and wield power. The uniqueness of the elven language was such that the flow of words, inflection, rhythm, and tone that prose and poetry created, helped a magician bring a complex garnering of energy, molded by his or her own power, into a finite form for an express purpose.

Thus, while a competent mage, as Meligance most assuredly was, could create

103

fire from the ether, using a word or phrase associated with producing it helped her focus. In actuality, she didn't need to use any words or gestures at all. Meligance freely admitted that when she did create fire, she instinctively thought of the appropriate elven phrase, depending on what type of fire she desired to produce. It set in her mind her purpose, as well as the method she had learned to put that purpose into a physical reality. Verbalizing externally, she explained, was for effect only: to impress, terrify, or confound any within hearing distance, and importantly, at times, to draw attention to oneself and away from others.

Such had been the "spell" Thistle had learned and "cast" upon Sart deep in Kan's dungeons. The words had drawn her own and Yolk's power into focus, though she had no ken of it herself. Having done it once with the aid of Meligance in the sending, she was able to reproduce the effect – the sensation of garnering that power for a specific use. Unfortunately, it did not immediately translate to her being able to do the same for other uses, or even for the basic task of garnering energy. There was no shortcut to what she needed to learn and practice.

Thistle loved the high language. Her favorite time of day was when she was able to spend time with it, either reading, translating, or working with Meligance to become familiar with all things magical. She quickly learned the words and short phrases that made up the standard repertoire of most competent magic-users. As she worked on her magical abilities, she found that she loved to caress in her mind a particular word or phrase. When she worked with the energy that she associated with it, the words became a part of the whole experience.

Cabin Fever

By mid-winter, Ge-or was getting seriously restless. Even on the worst of days, he had taken to spending long hours outside practicing his weaponry at the blocks. On better days, he would bundle a hefty lunch from Leona into his backpack and head up out of the vale to hunt. Several times he had been caught out by a sudden storm and spent a night or two amongst the heavy firs on the side of the hills to the south. He was more than thankful for the food she had provided and the warm clothing she had insisted he pack.

Leona was always a bit sad when the weather turned better. She knew Ge-or would be off again on a trek. Since he was always so ebullient when he returned, no matter the hardships he had encountered, she knew it was for the best. Still, when he swept her into his strong arms and kissed her soundly, it reinforced her understanding of his wanderlust nature. She knew he would not be completely happy if he felt obliged to stay. She tried not to think on it. Leona tried to enjoy him for who he was, thanking the gods and blessing all the moments they shared together.

If he was gone more than a couple of days, she would start to worry. He assured her, however, that he was an excellent backwoodsman. True to his word, he was always back before the third day had passed. Then he would be extra loving and attentive for days to come, until once again his yearn to roam would send him back up the hilly path into the wilds.

Ge-or was a superb hunter. His treks were always productive. The first few times he went out he was able to thin the local wolf population to such an extent that Aldred was able to idle his traps. The pelts began to pile up in one of the sheds. On the days when the cold or snow kept them predominantly indoors, the three would spend time treating and working the skins so that they would bring a better price at market.

Ge-or would frequently return with fresh game for the hearth and larder. Rabbits and squirrel were especially plentiful. One trip out he felled two nice-sized doe that he brought back quartered and nestled between a pile of pelts on the pull sled that he had designed, and Aldred had helped him build.

Leona was thrilled to have the soft rabbit pelts for working into warm clothing, as well as the deer skins for the fine leather they would provide. She set to work making a warm snuggle for the baby.

A Solution to a Problem

Jared stood in front of Grandmaster Leonis' studio pausing to say goodbye to his friends. He, Simon-Nathan, and Karenna had stayed up most of the night discussing possible solutions for dealing with the loss of the pendant. Jared, however, was always cognizant of Sart's warning relative to the significance of the stone. He was anxious about the furor that might result if someone was found to have stolen it from their room. *Honor* was one of the key ideals of Bard Hall; it was first on the list. It was why doors did not have locks – even the masters' studios were open to all. Honor was implied in all they did and how they did it. You were expected to live it.

"Leonis is very wise, Jared. He will know what to do." Karenna gave him a gentle push toward the door. Simon-Nathan was standing off to the side, his eyes downcast. During the long night, he had been unusually quiet and had not come up with any ideas either.

Jared took her hands in his. "I'm not frightened, Karenna, just nervous that this will explode into something that hurts a lot of people. I'll see you soon in class." He bent down to give her a quick kiss and waved to Simon-Nathan; finally he reached up to knock on the door.

The familiar booming voice reverberated through the wood. "Come in." Jared turned the handle and pushed.

"Ah, Jared, to what do I owe this honor so early on the morrow?"

"I'm afraid, sir, that a valuable has gone missing from my room."

"Missing?" The grandmasters mustache turned down in a frown.

"Perhaps stolen, sir."

Leonis quizzed Jared over and over until his head was spinning. In the end, he still had to admit to himself, and to the grandmaster, that he was positive he had placed the pendant in the drawer. Leonis' face deepened by the minute into a sad heaviness. It made Jared want to hide from the knowledge that he had somehow brought Bard Hall such embarrassment. He kept thinking he should have insisted that Sart take the stone. The cleric, though, had been adamant that when powerful items passed from one owner to another, it was with purpose. Until Sart knew more about the artifact, he did not want to deny that possibility.

Leonis told Jared that since he was already planning on coming to the dining hall that evening for dinner, he would make some kind of general announcement. He also promised to contact Sart at the Borean Palace immediately.

As Jared walked toward theory, he wondered both what Leonis would say about the theft, as well as what reason the grandmaster would have to break with tradition and attend a meal in the middle of the term.

Jared let Karenna know in theory class, and Simon-Nathan during lunch, what had transpired. The rest of the day he fidgeted through all his classes, only able to settle down a little in his performance classes and weaponry.

Elanar immediately remarked on his mood. "You seem lost in your own thoughts today, Jared. Do you want to be alone?"

"Yes, I do, but really, no. The spar will help me forget my concerns. I have a new trick I want to show you. I acknowledge and appreciate your asking, Elanar. You have become a friend. I hope you know that."

The elf blushed, one of his more human-acquired traits. "Perhaps we have. There is something I have wanted to say for some time. It is selfish, as it weighs on me and not you. Please know that I say this sincerely." He cleared his throat nervously; then said in the more formal approach to a better, flushing brightly, "I must of needs apologize for my behavior, my arrogance, in striking you that first day. It has shamed me, and I wish thou would let me make recompense." Elanar bowed his head, dipping his sword tip to the ground.

Jared, having had blade protocol drilled into him by his father, set his sword tip under Elanar's and lifted it up to eye level. "Your honor is my recompense." He added, "Friend."

They crossed swords and bowed. Following which, Jared yelled, "To Point!" He put the Elanar through a brutal workout so that the almost elf could partially feel he had paid his debt.

Jared and Simon-Nathan nibbled at the roast duck and goose platters that had been laid for the evening meal. Karenna was far down their line of tables, with the other first year women, so they could not see how she was faring. They had been nervously chatting as they walked to dinner, trying not to think about what was to come.

At the bell, the Grandmaster walked in and sat at the center of the masters' table. A hush fell over the room when he appeared. Tradition at Bard Hall was duly respected; anything that broke it created a stir. It was not, however, until platters were cleared and dessert served that Leonis stood to speak, a large heavy wooden staff-mace in hand. He struck the brass end on the floor thrice. It rang through the hall.

"Masters and students," his voice boomed, "today is a momentous occasion for Bard Hall." His deep baritone carried throughout the large room so that none had to strain to hear him. "As you know, we hold tightly to our traditions here; but the world is changing, has changed. In order for us to maintain a proper position in which to serve the people and the kingdom, we must also be willing to revolutionize our thought, as well as our processes and procedures.

"Therefore," Leonis paused for effect, "from this time forward we, the Masters Council of Bard Hall, have decided to open the Bard Hall Challenge Cup matches to all students." There was a collective sharp intake of breath. This *was* a big surprise. "As you know, until this decision, only seniors and post-graduate students in situ have been eligible. We now feel, because of the dangers currently facing the Borean world, especially in outlying villages and towns, that a new emphasis on weaponry study is of paramount importance for all our students, especially the Apprentices, Journeymen, and Bards entering the field. We feel that this change will encourage all to participate further in our challenge matches. Levels and other details will be available in the Yard on the morrow. Best of luck."

An immediate buzz followed the announcement. Jared and Simon-Nathan, watching carefully, knew the grandmaster was not done.

"Furthermore! Furthermore!" Leonis' voice boomed out again. The room quieted immediately. "A concern, a deeply troubling concern, has arisen. Yesterday, in the late afternoon, a valuable item was taken from one of our student rooms." A murmur, followed by a deadly hush, fell in a wave across the huge chamber as the implications of this sped through the crowd of students and masters alike. "As is our policy in matters of honor, we expect the transgressor to come forward voluntarily. This matter *will* be resolved." The grandmaster raised the staff and struck the floor hard once more, adding finality to his words. The dining hall erupted into immediate chaos.

Before he could even rise from his seat, Jared was jostled by students climbing over benches and through the small spaces between sets of tables. It seemed like everyone needed to reach some friend or another to talk about these two incredible revelations. When he was able to wedge his way out of the bench, he noticed that Simon-Nathan had already left. His roommate was pushing his way through the crowd some twenty paces ahead. After a few seconds, Jared gave up trying to catch him through the crush of bodies. He knew that Simon-Nathan would head for their room. Karenna was likely to follow.

When Jared opened the door, he found Simon-Nathan sitting on the end of the bed with his head in his hands. Jared went to his bed and sat down opposite his roommate. Simon-Nathan raised his head. His eyes were red and swollen from crying. He met Jared's eyes, barely, and said, "I'm sorry. I'm so sorry, Jared. I… I wanted to help her get well. She's dying. I know she's dying, and Father won't do anything. I didn't know what else to do. I'm so sorry." Tears streamed down his face.

"Sorry about wh…? By-the-gods!" Jared suddenly put it all together: Simon-Nathan's sister, the healing stone, opportunity, motive…

The door was still partially ajar, and at that instant Karenna arrived. She began to push it open. Jared leapt up and yelled, a bit too loudly and harshly, "No! Wait! Not now, Karenna." He reached out and grabbed the door, blocking her from entering the room.

She looked at him, her eyes flashing; but then she saw Simon-Nathan. Her mouth opened in surprise. She started to ask a question, "Wha…"

"Give me a couple of more minutes, please." Jared's eyes searched her face. She relaxed her stance, nodding. "I'll be out here?"

"Yes, please wait."

Karenna pulled the door shut as Jared turned back to his roommate. "You took the pendant?"

Simon-Nathan nodded. "She's so sick, Jared. I didn't know what else to do. I wanted to ask you, but… I was afraid you would insist on Sart coming. My father would have… I don't know. I didn't think. I panicked, and… it's not working. She's getting worse. I put it around her neck Solisday evening. She should be getting better, only she's getting worse."

"Simon… Simon, it doesn't work that way. Artifacts like this often only work for the owner, or if it is willfully given to another." Jared put his hand on his roommate's shoulder to comfort him. "This is bad; I don't know what we can do. By-the-gods, Simon, why didn't you tell me before I went to the grandmaster?"

"I don't know. I guess… I guess I was buying time; hoping it would work overnight. I'm sorry… really sorry, Jared. It's my fault. I will have to pay the consequences. I don't care. All I want is for Athena to get well." He began to sob again.

***

Jared, Karenna, and Simon-Nathan sat quietly looking at each other. They had been there for hours. They had not been able to find any solution that would save Simon-Nathan from expulsion from Bard Hall. It was nearing midnight.

Since Simon-Nathan, as a second-year, could get off campus, Jared had convinced him to send word to Sart. The cleric was due to arrive at seven in the morning. Now, actually retrieving the stone seemed of little importance. The one thing that they had finally agreed upon was that Sart should go to Simon-the-Elder's house, force his way in if necessary, to see if he could help Athena. Jared hoped that they would be allowed to go as well.

With nothing more to be said, and too exhausted to continue, Jared took Karenna's hand and pulled her up. "Come. I'll walk you down the hall. We are agreed to meet at Leonis' door at seven. Mayhap we will come up with something before that. Certainly, there are extenuating circumstances; and your motive was more than honorable, Simon-Nathan."

"It won't matter; they will be forced to punish me. I'm so sorry, Jared." He turned toward the wall and curled up on his bed, weeping softly.

As light was beginning to show through the high cathedral windows of the main hall, the three of them gathered outside Leonis' door. None of them had slept much. Jared stayed awake the whole night tossing and turning, nagged by a feeling that there was a way to resolve this that he hadn't considered.

They didn't have long to wait; they had been there only a few minutes when Leonis walked toward them down the hallway. Sart was alongside the grandmaster. They approached quickly, followed by several of the members of the Council of Masters. Simon-Nathan's head fell to his chest. His knew his fate was sealed.

The two held hands and waited. Karenna had to forcefully keep Jared from pacing. Finally, she gave up and let go of his hand. "What? What can we do?" she asked.

"I don't know," said Jared, exasperated, "There must be something I haven't thought of, I know it. I feel it. If I could think of what it is; something is nagging at me."

"Well, I hope you think of it soon. That is, if these masters ever let us in to have a word. Bards really can be stuffy and frustrating at times."

"What...? That's it. I..."

The door opened and Jared wasn't able to finish his idea. Master Hagaman, the venerable historian, poked his head out. He looked grave. "You may come in," he said ominously.

Jared leaned toward Karenna, and whispered, "Let me handle this... please." He pushed her ahead through the door.

Once they were in the room, Jared immediately went to Simon-Nathan, who sat at the far end of a long oaken table, facing his six inquisitors. He bent over to whisper in his friend's ear, "Follow my lead. I may be able to help you stay in school."

Simon-Nathan looked up at Jared, then lowered his head again as his roommate went on into the chamber.

Leonis gestured for Karenna and Jared to stand at the side of the table. "I understand you wish to say something in Simon-Nathan's behalf. I will allow you to do so; however, know this, the charges are serious, very serious. In spite of his reasons, your friend made several grave mistakes. Proceed." He indicated that Karenna should speak first.

She bowed to Leonis and the council members. "I defer to Jared, who knows more of this affair than I. I ask only for leniency for my friend; his intentions were

109

honorable. He is an excellent student, the best I know of in history." She inclined her head toward Master Hagaman. She saw his mouth tighten, for Simon-Nathan had been his protégé.

"Jared?"

"Grandmaster, learned Cleric, Honorable Council Members..." Jared cleared his throat, trying to put his thoughts together quickly. "I believe I may have a solution to this problem, which while not being completely satisfactory, will allow honor and justice to prevail." He paused again to let those words sink in before continuing. "My roommate and friend has dedicated his time here to becoming a Bard. It is his wish in life. Because of the Honor of this Hall, this deed cannot go unpunished; yet, would you all wish to see Bard Hall lose an honor student, an exceptional student? A student who excels in History and Lore, and may be able to make many contributions to both fields?"

Jared stopped again, as much for emphasis as to swallow. His mouth felt parched, and he was incredibly nervous. He knew Simon-Nathan's future life depended on whether they would buy into his ploy. "I propose that as punishment, a fair and definitive punishment for his transgressions, that Simon-Nathan be banned forever from becoming a Bard." Simon-Nathan emitted a low groan and Karenna gasped. Jared pressed ahead, "That he be allowed to remain at Bard Hall as a student to pursue a more sedentary and studious position as a Master of History and Lore."

Simon Nathan's head rose ever so slowly as Jared spoke; he was staring at him when he finished. Jared prayed fervently, Look sad, cry, do something to make them think this is bad.

Luckily, Simon-Nathan was in shock. He looked like he had been shot in the chest with an arrow, or several. He continued to stare at Jared, his mouth moving wordlessly.

Leonis looked to the other masters; then at Simon-Nathan. "Would you be willing to accept this punishment and stay at Bard Hall under these conditions, young man?"

Tears began to flow down Simon-Nathan's cheeks. They were not tears of distress or sadness; they were of relief. He did manage to stay alert enough not to smile. In one of their late-night conversations, the two roommates had discussed their ambitions. Jared had been surprised to learn that only one in fifty students, or fewer, studying at Bard Hall had designs to actually become Bards. Many were simply sent there by wealthy parents to study for four years, before moving into the family business, or joining the military ranks as officers, or going into other professions. Others, like Simon-Nathan and Karenna, wanted to excel in the more mundane areas of Theory, History, Lore, Music Composition, Orchestration, and the like. Simon-Nathan had confided to Jared that his ultimate goal was to become a Master of History and Lore someday. Although few of the Barding students made a full career decision until after a year in the field as an Apprentice, Simon-Nathan really had no designs of becoming a Bard.

Tears streaking his face, Simon-Nathan stood up, bowed to the head of the table, took a deep breath, and said, "I will accept any punishment if it means I may continue to study here. I am dreadfully sorry for what I have done – for shaming my friends and the Hall." He bowed his head and looked down.

"We shall discuss this amongst ourselves and make a final decision. Please retire with your friends." Leonis gestured toward the door.

Karenna and Simon-Nathan mobbed Jared when they were outside. "Brilliant, absolutely brilliant. By-the-gods, Jared, I hope they agree. Do you think they really bought it? Do you think Leonis bought it?" Karenna was overjoyed.

"We'll know soon enough," Jared replied. He saw the door swinging outward.

With the Council members having departed, Sart led the subdued Simon-Nathan toward the outside gates where a carriage stood waiting to take them to see Athena. Jared and Karenna stood by the conference room door, completely drained. "I don't think I can handle classes this morning. Perhaps we should go to the infirmary and get passes until this afternoon," Karenna suggested. "I…"

At that moment, Leonis opened the door. She stopped. The grandmaster gestured for the two of them to enter.

"You have both done something extraordinary for a friend," the grandmaster began, looking first at Jared and Karenna. "That is what Honor truly is, and I admire you for showing such courage and for your willingness to risk your own positions here. *But*, and you both should remember this, I am not so old as to have the cotton pulled over my eyes just yet. Your solution satisfies because it creates the illusion of punishment in a difficult situation – a situation in which honor resides on both sides." Leonis paused to wipe what Jared could have sworn was a tear from the side of his eye. "Know this, also – love, true caring for another – is the greatest of all ideals, and often at the root of Honor. I would it were one of Bard Hall's principles; unfortunately, too often the word itself is misinterpreted and misrepresented. You have lived it today.

"Now, both of you, I imagine have been up all night. I have written a pass for this morning's classes. Go to the kitchens and eat something, rest, make your afternoon responsibilities… and Jared."

"Yes, Grandmaster?"

"I think we have gotten to know each other enough for one year, don't you?" He raised his eyebrows and gave him the merest hint of a smile as he shooed them out the door.

Piling On

Jared was still tired when he got to the Yard for his afternoon session with Elanar. He was more than a little surprised when he saw the four elves squared off at the eastern edge of the enclosure. Typically, he and Elanar worked in one of the sparring pits more to the north the first hour. He strode quickly toward the group; but as he approached, Elanar turned his back on him, engaging his friends.

"Elanar?"

"What?" There was an edge to his voice; he remained facing away.

"I thought we had practice today. Was I mistaken?"

The elf spun around, his face an impassive mask. "I figured you would not want to continue our bargain, since you are now open to challenge for the Long Sword Cup."

Jared fought down a compulsion to respond angrily. "Yes, I do plan to enter the challenge, since it is now open to me, to all of us. I…"

"I knew that is what you would do, half-elf." Elanar began to turn to face the other way again.

Having had enough the past couple of days, Jared shouted at his back, "Though you may not realize it, all things do not revolve around you, or the elves, for that matter. Just so you know, I plan to challenge in shortbow and short sword. I have no interest in challenging for the long sword." He turned about on his heel and started back across the Yard.

"Jared!"

He spun back around at his name, ready for a challenge. Elanar was standing with his head bowed. He spoke slowly and deliberately. "I am sorry, friend; this is my great failing. Our…" he turned his head slightly toward the other four elves, who also stood with their heads bowed as well, "great shame. It has proven our bane here. Our shaming by the elders is… is…" His voice trailed off.

Jared took a few steps back toward the group, until he was close enough for all of them to hear him clearly. He placed his right hand on Elanar's chest and shoulder, a gesture of peace and acceptance. "Perhaps the great shame is theirs." He let the comment hang in the air. The elves all looked up and stared at him.

Jared raised his practice sword and saluted them. "Come, let us all spar together this day." They saluted him back, each bowing low in turn.

Karenna and Jared met after dinner in the entrance hall, hoping to hear something from Sart or Simon-Nathan. Leonis had said it was best that the two not go with Sart to Simon-the-Elder's house. He deemed, and was probably correct, that the situation would be difficult enough without the added confusion of more people. Sart would need to focus his powers if Athena's condition was as bad as Simon-Nathan had suggested. The cleric had asked for, and received, Jared's permission to use the stone. He had felt strongly that it would be of no avail to him elsewhere.

They paced slowly back and forth across the marble floor whispering about various school activities and studies, trying to keep from constantly worrying. It was past nine when the cleric finally came through the door, looking disheveled and weary.

"How…" both Karenna and Jared asked at once as Sart approached.

He held up his hands, palm outward. "Hold, let me catch my breath." He stopped, set his hands on his knees, leaned forward, and closed his eyes, breathing deeply.

A minute later, he straightened. "There, that's better. My, I should have rested before I came back; but I knew you would want to hear. Healing is difficult; often-times we clerics drive ourselves too far.

"There..." he took one more deep breath. "Athena is better. She had a tumor. It was very bad. It had spread quite far. It is a frightful illness at any time; they should have called someone in much sooner. There is damage. I am afraid she will never be completely vital. She should live a whole life, or near to one; however, it is likely she will be frail.

"I managed to kill the worm and remove its vestiges. Without the stone, I don't think I would have succeeded. It is a remarkable item, Jared. We need to ensure that it remains safe; that is something we should discuss later."

"For now," he took in several more deep breaths, "she is resting. I left the pendant about her neck. I believe it will help speed her recovery. Simon-the-Elder will return it in a week. He is a good man, who unfortunately had a bad experience in his youth with a charlatan. It cost him his mother's life.

"Now, let us take our discussion to another location. Leonis promised me victuals and wine. I imagine that neither of you ate much at this eve's meal. Am I correct?"

They both nodded. "Good. Come. I am told that the grandmaster sets an exquisite and exotic table, and his wines come from a private cellar." Sart's color was returning and with it his joy of life.

Anyone Can Make a Mistake

Thistle was making slow, steady progress. And though Meligance was pleased with her efforts and the successes she consistently made, her apprentice never appeared to be satisfied. The Wizardess could tell that she was beginning to drive herself too hard. Magic was focus, control, *and* patience. They had just run through a series of basic exercises; Thistle obviously wanted to push ahead.

"Thistle!" Meligance's tone demanded immediate attention.

"Yes, ma'am."

"I am disappointed; you are losing sight of what is most important."

Thistle opened her mouth, surprised at Meligance's stern demeanor and at the sharp timbre of her voice.

The Wizardess softened her tone slightly before going on. "You have made amazing progress, child. However, you will likely hurt yourself and lose your confidence, if you keep pushing. If that happens, it is a long, long road back. Do you understand what I am trying to say?"

Thistle blinked, then shook her head "Yes," and "No."

"You have begun to garner more and more power through your work. That is good, to a point. What I am not seeing, what you are not spending nearly enough time on, is manipulating the power so you know precisely how much does what."

"But…"

"I know, child, you feel if you gather even more energy, you will be able to do more. That having 'X' will give you the power to do 'Y'. And while that is true in one sense, there is a greater rule of thumb here that is much more important – you must learn to use the least power for the greatest effect. That takes personal power, focus, control, creativity, and work – lots and lots of practice.

"Someday you will find yourself in a situation, perhaps a great battle or a conundrum, that requires all your intelligence, power, and creativity. The end result will not depend on the mass of energy you can bring to bear, but on your ability to manipulate what energy you can, control it as expediently as possible, and with finesse.

"Right now, and for many months to come, your focus should be on ever-expanding the wealth of things you can do with the energy you can garner right now. As you develop these types of skills, you will slowly, inexorably, find that the energy you need will be there."

Meligance paused, almost afraid to bring up the next point. She knew there was something else behind Thistle's focus and drive.

"There is something more that is diverting your attention, or perhaps more accurately, is underlying your drive to excel, to move ahead without due caution. I know that in one sense this is not my business; however, your training and your welfare are." She paused, making sure Thistle was focusing on what she was about to say.

"You have not contacted Jared, have you?"

Tears immediately came to Thistle's eyes. She bowed her head, blinking rapidly to try to disperse them. She answered hesitantly, "No, mum."

"This, one way or another, is something with which you must deal. I know as your teacher and mentor, Thistle, that stepping across this line into your personal life is not entirely appropriate. Remember this – with magic, everything matters. While there is unresolved stress in your life, it will affect what you accomplish. Do you ken what I am trying to say to you?"

"Yes, ma'am, but... but I don't know what to say to him. I don't know what to do. I feel so lost." Then, she did break down and began to cry, putting her hands to her face.

To be sixteen, and feel such things again, Meligance thought, understanding both the pain and joy of young love.

"Come, child; talk with Sart when you can, He should be back within a few days. He can give you guidance better than I. He is wise in the ways of the world. Find a way to resolve this for both you and the boy. From all you have shared with me, Jared still loves you. He is likely anxious that you have not tried to reconnect."

"Yes, milady."

Thistle was so happy to see Sart that when the big man enfolded her in his massive arms, she broke down immediately. True to his nature as a priest and healer, he spent several hours with her over the next few days talking about her work, Jared, her feelings, and her choices. Finally, she resolved to use an orb to reconnect with Jared on her next day of rest from her studies. She had considered sending a gift or card, but decided, and Sart concurred, that personal communications might facilitate things.

As part of Thistle's well-rounded education, Meligance began to introduce her apprentice to courtly ways. Whenever feasible she would have the girl, decked out in appropriate regalia, accompany her to relatively benign court functions such as luncheons, dinners, and light evening entertainments. This evening they were scheduled to attend a soiree for some visiting dignitaries from the south.

Thistle found these events quite boring and rather ludicrous. She felt she had nothing in common with the dandies at court. The ladies, while courteous enough to her when she was on Meligance's arm, tended to avoid her completely when the Wizardess was engaged elsewhere. Though they were frightened of Meligance, she was at least a known factor. They were terrified of Thistle, because she was, after all, the great Wizardess's apprentice – the only one she had ever accepted – and because they did not know her.

More often than not, Thistle would find herself in some corner talking banality with some overly-costumed and made-up princeling, who fancied himself a brave and dashing fellow with his rapier slapping his side. Thistle doubted whether the man-boy ever had taken the weapon from its scabbard to defend himself or another. She had found a way to smile, nod, and pretend interest while practicing her focus and concentration. Before long, the fellow or fellows would depart, when they realized she was not really even in the room with them.

Unfortunately, as Meligance was often fond of reminding her, experience was the mother of all teachers.

Strangely, Meligance insisted that Thistle return to her studio immediately following this particular outing, not giving either of them the opportunity to change from their gowns to more appropriate work attire. As soon as they had teleported up, Meligance turned toward Thistle.

"You have been practicing your focus and control while there are other

115

distractions about?" she asked innocently.

"Yes, Ma'am. I think I have made good progress. I am able to keep my focus centered in spite of what is happening about me. Alli helps me with this type of practice."

"Hm-m-m.... Yet, when you practice this, you go deep enough that you don't really know what is happening around you?"

"Well, yes, I guess that is the case. I have been trying to find a completely calm center where nothing gets in."

"Ah, well, that explains something. I'm assuming that you have no recollection of meeting our illustrious crown prince this evening?"

"Wha-a-a... By-the-gods, I didn't?"

"Yes," Meligance smiled, "I'm afraid you did. He was a bit nonplussed after you failed to respond to several questions. I assured him you were in a trance, and that I had brought you to the soiree to see how long you could maintain it."

"Oh, my!" Thistle blushed. "Was he angry?"

"No, not really, at least not after his initial irritation at being ignored. He does not ken magic nor even have much sense as to what it can do for him. I am afraid he is a bit of a weakling and dolt. Perhaps someday we will discuss these things. For now, be thankful his father is still in good health. He at least has some sense."

"Did... did I do anything?" Thistle asked, feeling quite self-conscious now, though they were both alone in Meligance's studio.

"Yes, interestingly enough, you smiled and nodded as if you were listening. It even took me few seconds to realize you weren't 'in the room.'

"This is an important lesson to be learned, Thistle. What you are practicing is essential to being successful with magic. You do need to learn not to be distracted by noise, horror, death, anything that happens near, around, or even sometimes to you as you are working with power. But! You must learn to do this while being completely aware of what *is* happening around you. Else you and others will die before you can react to something that *does* need your attention." Meligance stopped and raised her eyebrows.

"Yes, ma'am, I understand. I'll work on it."

"Please do so." Smiling, she waved for Thistle to go.

Three's a Crowd

Elanar was making good progress in learning to be inventive in his attacks and defenses. The problem was that he still wasn't fast enough in making decisions during a spar to really bring that to bear in a tournament setting. Jared had an idea to force the elf into a more realistic tempo while fighting. It had taken him a few minutes to convince his friend that this new approach would work.

"The short sword is not my weapon, Jared. I'll feel even more awkward."

"I know; try, just this once." Jared tossed the blade over to Elanar, and said, "To Point."

Initially, Jared kept to a moderate pace because Elanar was obviously not used to the capabilities of the weapon; however, he was game once they were engaged.

Twenty-five minutes later and Elanar was gasping for breath. "I see what you mean. You can switch directions much faster. It gives your body more maneuverability as well. I feel so out of place with this in my hand." Elanar held up the blade.

"Take your own sword now, and let's try it again." Jared saluted him, then got set.

"You're going to still use that?" Elanar gestured toward Jared's short sword.

"Yes, my friend. Today you learn to react and react and react. You wondered what it would be like to fight a gzk or a Qa-ryk. Today you get a taste of that."

Jared kept his tempo controlled and steady, so Elanar had some chance to respond; he still overmatched the elf easily. There were two advantages to a long sword – length and weight. But if the wielder was imaginatively skilled with a short sword, and fast, he almost always had the advantage. Typically used one-handed, and often with a small buckler or a shield, the twenty-nine to thirty-two-inch blade was deadly in close quarters fighting. The long sword, typically used one-handed or one-and a half-handed in this era, as opposed to the two-handed, more knightly cousin of the previous age, was much longer with a blade of forty to as much as forty-five inches. It was also considerably heavier. The concept in using the longer blade was of overwhelming one's opponent. With the short sword, quickness played a more important role.

Their session produced benefits for both of them. Jared got to work with his preferred weapon, and Elanar was forced to respond ever more quickly to attacks. The workout also taxed them beyond anything they had done to that point.

Jared was tired and excited. He and Karenna hadn't been together for two weeks. They had set the late afternoon and evening aside for a room picnic, followed by love-making. Because of the earlier spar with Elanar, he was more tired than he would have liked. It would be great to be with Karenna; he had missed her softness.

Karenna rolled back on top of Jared. "I've missed you and," she smiled, kissing him on the lips, "it seems you have missed me." He moaned pleasurably and kissed her in return, suggestively.

"Jared? Jared."

His eyes closed, Jared was not at first aware of the change in the lighting of the room. Responding to his suggestive kiss, Karenna had begun to move slowly against him. When the voice penetrated her consciousness, she gasped.

"Jared?"

"By-the-gods, no!" Jared said under his breath, suddenly realizing what was happening. "Thistle?"

"Who? What? Jared? What's that light?" Karenna cried, turning around toward the purple ball that now floated above the bed. "Oh, no!"

There was a choking sound followed by a sharp cry. The purple orb flickered out.

Thistle had been really nervous for several days before her attempt to reconnect with Jared. When she finally got up enough courage to do so, it took her three tries before she could concentrate enough to send the ball she had created. Completely focused and anxious to talk with him, she had swallowed hard and sent the energy sphere.

It had been a disaster. She had heard some high-pitched moans, a gasp, Jared's exclamation, her name, and finally a girl's voice. Devastated, her focus had shattered. The orb, released from her control, simply dissipated in the ether.

"I'm leaving, Jared... Wha...! Could she hear us? Could she see us? How long was that thing there? Jared... why didn't you tell me? I have to go. I have to go."

"Karenna, wait, please... Please." He reached out and grasped her hand, which stopped her from continuing to dress. "Please sit. No, she couldn't see us. The light orb must have just arrived. I'm sorry, Karenna. I didn't know anything about this. We haven't spoken since the Yule. I don't know what to say. Things haven't changed. I..."

"They have changed." Karenna hit him on the chest with her small fists. "Jared, I'm a fool; we're both fools. I love you. I don't know if I can do this. It's too hard to share you. She... I..."

"Karenna, I love you, too, more than I knew; but... I don't know what more I can say. I haven't lied to you about how I feel. It's all so confusing right now."

"Let me go, Jared. I need to think, to be alone for a little while. I'll... I'll see you tomorrow. I'm sorry, I love you so much. It's just how I feel." With tears coming to her eyes and a deep, strangled sob, she gave him a quick buss on the lips; then she pulled away from his arms. She threw on her school tunic and rushed out the door.

Thistle was beyond distraught. Alli could do nothing for her mistress except sit by her side as she cried far into the night.

"I'm so angry with myself. I can't believe I was so stupid. I wanted to be noble and not silly like other women, so I let him go. I told him he was free to be with other girls, and now... now he's gone. I've lost him." Thistle's eyes filled with tears.

"Child, dear child." Sart cuddled the distraught girl in toward his chest. "I know how badly you feel. Perhaps you were right in a sense. It will be years before you can be with a man in a loving relationship. You didn't do a noble thing for Jared, but you may have done the right thing. And, from all you have related to me, I do not believe you are giving the young man a chance. Perhaps this incident you sort of witnessed was simply a momentary tryst. Even if it was, or is, more than that, it does not say he does not still love you."

118

Thistle pulled up and looked at the cleric. "Oh, Sart, then why does it hurt so much?" Tears were now trickling down her cheeks, though she had thought she had cried herself out over the past two weeks.

Sart took her hand in his large callused ones and replied, "Because you are young, and your tender heart has so much to learn and experience. I wish that I could say some words to ease your troubles, my child; alas, with the affairs of the heart, we often have to work through them ourselves. I will always be a person you can talk to about anything. For now, try to immerse yourself in your work and studies. Time will heal, and in ways you cannot imagine right now.

"Come, let us focus on other things for a while. You will heal from this, although it may not seem so right now. Trust me in this."

Thistle nodded; tears still trickled from the sides of her eyes. It took her a few more minutes to compose herself fully. Somehow, Sart always managed to help her through the worst of times.

"There, that's better." Sart smiled up at Thistle, as she returned from washing her face and hands. "Just so you know, child, I met recently with Meligance. She is pleased with your progress. She has given me permission to take you about town one day each week to... well, ostensibly to show you the sights. As you know, there is always method to her ways. She wants us to visit museums, factories, shops, historical sites – whatever strikes your interest. You will learn a great deal, and for the most part it should be fun."

Thistle managed a smile. She asked, "Can Alli come with us?"

"Of course," Sart replied jovially, trying to bring her further out of her upset. "Someone needs to keep you out of mischief."

Wanderlust

Though it was early spring, the cold, snow, and ice still held the high hills in sway. Ge-or had taken to longer and longer treks in search of late season pelts, and to "stretch his legs." Leona knew that her time with him was drawing to a close. With her belly now swelling noticeably, she grew ever more comfort from the child growing within. She would spend hours singing light tunes and humming while she worked about the house. She was preparing as best she could for two eventualities – Ge-or's leaving and the baby's arrival.

On this particular trek, Ge-or set out heading almost due south from the vale, toward the high foothills. His goal was to see if any wolf packs remained on the edge of the hills in the heavy pine woods. He had mostly wandered west during the winter months, since the going was easier that way, and there was less chance of encountering gzks in the forests to the south, or goblins near the mountains in the southwest. Luckily, Qa-ryks tended to be much less active during the cold. They preferred to stay near or within their stockades, almost hibernating like bears and other creatures of the woods and hills during the coldest periods. He had not been overly worried he would run into wandering patrols or an ambush.

He pushed hard the first day, covering a good bit of ground in the wet snow. By nightfall, he was well within the lower range of the evergreens. He picked a large fir with heavy drooping branches as his camp site. It would be dry and comfortable underneath its boughs. His hardwood fire would provide needed warmth; what smoke there was would vent through the thick needles. The fire would help keep the wolves at bay should they wander near.

The next day he went deeper into the trees, finally picking up tracks of a large wolf pack that had passed to the east in the night. Paralleling the track westward, Ge-or hoped to find their den so he could set an ambush. Wolves were cunning, but their almost constant need for food would drive them to follow his scent once they picked it up.

When the sun was high in the sky, Ge-or came to a well-hidden den, situated under an outcropping along the rocky slope of a large hill. Tossing an old shirt into the opening, Ge-or hid his sled further up the incline. He found an opening that overlooked the cave and waited. If he was right, the wolves would return from their hunt sometime in the evening hours. Though they were predominantly nocturnal, preferring to hunt in the wee hours, by the signs, this pack was so large that hunting during the day in the thick, dark pine forest would give them an advantage in bringing large game to bay.

The first of the pack, several younger wolves, appeared out of the tree-line at early dusk. Ge-or drew his bow partially back, testing the string. He waited and watched as more and more appeared sniffing at his trail. Several paused and looked hesitatingly up toward the den. They looked hungry, which meant they were less likely to be cautious when they figured out where he was. He set his unsheathed sword next to him and had his knives handy on a rock shelf to his fore. He knew he could drop several before they reached him; after that, depending on how hungry they were, he figured they would attack. He also knew that large timber wolves could easily bound up the rocks to his position. His primary advantage was that they could not get behind him. He was protected at his back by a solid rock wall with a slight overhang above.

Ge-or waited until six of the younger wolves had entered the den and had torn at the shirt he had tossed inside. As they began to emerge, he raised up and shot the nearest wolf when it quartered away looking for its quarry. The beast went down yelping. The other wolves almost immediately caught his scent leading up and around the den. As Ge-or released a second arrow, they began to yip and howl excitedly, running up the slope, nose to the ground.

With a second wolf down in the snow, red blood splattering the white surface as it writhed, Ge-or set another arrow. He aimed at the lead wolf heading toward him. A head-on shot wasn't ideal, but he wanted to get at least two more of the beasts before he was forced into a close-quarter defense. His arrow whistled directly into the wolf's chest, just as the pack spotted him.

Quickly nocking another arrow, Ge-or fired once more as the next wolf coming up the slope leapt right at him. The arrow penetrated the animal's throat. The wolf landed at Ge-or's feet. Grabbing his sword and long knife, Ge-or braced himself as the next two beasts launched themselves through the air. One skewered itself on his sword as he thrust upward; the other dove into his left side, its cruel teeth snapping fiercely. Ge-or drove the long knife into its belly. Still, the wolf managed to get its teeth into his well-padded shoulder. He had to rip the knife up through the guts all the way to the chest plate before it released and fell. Spinning sideways and to the right, Ge-or raised his sword. With a flashing upward stroke, he almost decapitated another of the beasts when it came in from the side. A lightning swipe with his knife caught another of the wolves across the side. It leapt out of the battle zone and went whining down the slope.

The death of the pack leaders and almost half the pack resulted in the younger wolves retreating. He switched back to his bow and was able to kill one more before they slunk off in defeat. It was unlikely that they would attack again. Still, Ge-or stayed alert with his weapons close to hand while he skinned the dead wolves. Fortunately, the moon came up early, and with the blanket of snow, there was plenty of light for the bloody task.

Several hours later, tired, but pleased with the results, Ge-or built a fire at the entrance to the wolf den. He ate a cold meal from Leona's caringly packed food bundle and settled into the comfortable space for the night.

In the morning, Ge-or used the well-protected cave as a base. Setting a slow-burning fire at the mouth of the lair, he left the pelt bundle inside with some of his other gear. He headed back into the forest for game or, if he were lucky, a stray wolf or badger. Setting some snap snares for rabbits around several active breeding warrens in the area, he wended his way further south, near the edge of the forest and around the side of the mountain. His plan was to turn around before mid-day, so that he could return to the camp no later than late evening if he were packing meat or skins, and so he would still have enough light to check his snares.

He would have liked to continue further south to explore around a few more bends; but the hillside slope had turned rocky, and the tree line was thickening. Passage became difficult on the slick incline in the twilight. As he was about to turn back, he kicked two small deer from a hollow where they were bedded down. They jumped out, ran a few steps, and stopped, sniffing the air. Setting himself for a shot, Ge-or suddenly sensed something that caused his skin to tingle. Turning his head from the deer and the easy shot, he scanned the area around him, trying to see what was troubling him. He could see nothing out of the ordinary, so he slowly came back to focus on the deer.

They were young – two bucks, probably twins and in their second year – each had long forked spikes. They stood fidgeting slightly, wondering what sound had disturbed their rest. Ge-or refocused onto his clear line of sight, took a deep breath, holding it at the top; then he released the arrow.

In that instant, he realized that it had been his nose that had alerted him. There was the faintest hint of something different in the air. As the arrow accurately sped toward the deer's vitals, Ge-or moved in one fluid motion from his shot position, spinning upslope away. He nocked another arrow as he went.

He knew the smell. Once he recognized it, he didn't need another clue to respond to the danger. He hadn't gone more than a dozen paces upward when they began to emerge from the woods, arrayed in a semi-circle around his position on the slope. Gzks, he thought. I've been asleep.

He knew he was in their territory. Most of the pine forests this far south were home to wandering bands, yet this was the first time he had encountered any in his many excursions from Goat Haven.

Their aroma was not an unpleasant one. The gzks ate, actually craved, the sap from evergreens. Spring was just around the corner, so they were likely active tapping trees and reaping the first rewards of the season.

They were aggressive by nature, but only when they felt the odds were well in their favor. Luckily for Ge-or, they were far less numerous than goblins. Gzks typically roamed in small groups about their favored territory. Ge-or counted ten, no eleven, of the creatures as they started upward after him.

All except two, the smallest of the grey-green humanoids, had shortbows. Generally, their bows and arrows were of poor quality and useful only at close quarters, so in that sense, Ge-or held an advantage. They were close enough at forty paces to shoot him where they now stood. Their shots at that distance, however, would be inaccurate at best and not likely have the force to penetrate deeply. He knew he could down several of them before they could rush him. In addition to their bows, four of the creatures carried rough-looking short swords, three had crude clubs, and the others had no separate weapons other than their sharp yellow claws and three to four-inch fangs.

Drawing back and releasing as his bow came to his eye, Ge-or shot the largest of the beasts as it tried to circle closer to his left. His arrow caught the gzk full in the chest. It was flung backward down the slope by the impact. The others stopped. When Ge-or's second arrow struck another through the throat, those with bows pulled back and released their shafts. Following the flight of arrows, the gzks charged up the slope.

The shower of arrows fell all around Ge-or, only three hitting their target. One glanced off his right side; another hit him full in the chest but did not penetrate fully through his heavy leather jacket and undergarments; and the third stuck in his thigh, mid-way up from the knee. Jerking the arrow out of his leg, Ge-or immediately set it to his string and fired it back down the slope at another gzk. Poorly made of inferior wood, the stick flew badly out of the more powerful bow. It struck a half-foot wide of where it had been aimed, hitting the gzk in the upper arm.

Scrabbling quickly upward on their long limbs, the remaining beasts were upon Ge-or before he could set another arrow. He tossed the bow aside and drew his blade as the first gzk swung at his head with its ugly, heavy club. Ge-or ducked under the swing and swiftly brought his blade up, thrusting it into the gzk's stomach. He ripped it out with an upward pull as the creature clawed at him. Taking a step to his left onto a flat sandy area, Ge-or swung into full motion with his blade. The gzks, thinking he was a lone trapper, rudimentarily skilled in weapons, now experienced, albeit briefly, a well-trained half-elven fighter unleashed in an almost ideal battle environment.

With both feet planted firmly on solid ground, Ge-or wove an intricate pattern with his blade, cleaving through the weapons, guards, flesh, and sinew of the beasts as they came at him. If the destruction of life could be considered an art, a type of beauty, it was certainly represented in how Ge-or handled his sword. Nothing short of a well-timed and well-executed stroke, or a lucky one, could have penetrated his flashing blade. In the time it would take to breathe deeply thrice, he had laid out all except two of the gzks. These were now fleeing as quickly as they had attacked, back into the forest.

For several minutes after the last of the creatures had fled into the woods, Ge-or stood and took deep breaths. He wasn't actually winded. His hours at the blocks had paid off many-fold in that respect. He was simply relishing the feeling of power as it drained from his body. He had been in gzk fights before, none where he had stood alone against a band of them with no other blade or person to be wary of. Most skirmishes and battles were in close confines where one had to maintain awareness of not only the enemy, but also of one's compatriots. Here, he had been able to unleash his full potential as a swordsman as well as his full power. It had been devastating.

Ge-or knelt and bowed his head. Though he didn't follow any particular god, his father had taught him to respect all living things, even those of evil temperament. He did not enjoy killing; he did recognize its necessity. Reluctantly he acknowledged that there was something almost addictive about the frenzy and power of battle.

Finally, he stood and scanned the battleground. There was nothing he could do for the beasts that had attacked him. Had any lived, he would have dispatched them mercifully – he had been thorough. As for himself, he had a wound to tend, and a deer to gut and prepare for the sled journey back.

It was well past midnight, when he finally pulled the small sled up the slope to the wolf den. His thigh wound had been deep enough to cause some concern, so he had cleaned it carefully, put on a bandage with a salve of herbs, and finally splinted it to minimize movement. Still, he knew he could not walk through the forest for hours dragging a sled without irritating a muscle wound. He was happy to draw into the cave, spike the almost dead coals with new wood, and roast one of the rabbits from his snares while he dozed fitfully.

Ge-or awoke fully at dawn. He ate the well-roasted rabbit and some dried fruits and bread before stiffly rising to face the trek back to the vale.

Refusing to leave his pelts, the deer, and the coneys, Ge-or packed the sled as well as he could and set off to the north. The going was slow because his thigh pained him. In spite of his best efforts, he had to stop several times to re-bandage the steadily seeping wound. By nightfall he was still at least a day's slow hike from succor.

Leona was worried when Ge-or didn't return by nightfall of the third day. He had told her that he planned to go further south than he had ventured previously, but she couldn't help being a little concerned. She sat up past midnight knitting and fretting.

She was finally coaxed to go to bed by her father, who had been slumbering in his rocking chair next to where she was knitting.

By mid-day following, she was beginning to worry in earnest; and by evening, with no sign of Ge-or returning, she asked Aldred to go up to the back entrance to the vale and shout. He returned a half hour later shaking his head.

Leona continued to fret throughout dinner. She had a difficult time staying with her knitting as evening wore on. As midnight drew near, she again asked her father to go up the vale. Reluctantly, he got up from his snooze. "Peace, Daughter. He's a big fella, and there's not much out there gonna give him trouble." Yet Leona detected an edge of concern in his tone, too, as he struggled into his warm wool over-jacket.

Forty-five minutes later, Leona leapt to her feet when she saw her father's torchlight through the window. Opening the cabin door, she stepped out into the cold and saw two figures in the distance. One was limping and leaning heavily on an oaken staff. Her father's shoulders were bowed, pulling a laden sled behind with the torch in hand.

"Ge-or? Ge-or!" Leona rushed from the porch through the slush of the melting snow. He dropped his staff as she ran up. Grinning broadly, Ge-or swept her up in his strong arms, kissing her unreservedly on the lips while Aldred harrumphed and looked away.

"You're hurt."

"It's nothing. Healing, a bit stiff and sore. A minor arrow wound I got from a scuffle with some gzks."

"Scuffle? I was worried."

"I'm home now. How about some of those scrambled eggs of yours and a hunk of sausage for your wounded hero?"

"Ge-or!"

Leaving

The second week after the spring equinox saw a major warm-up. By the end of the week, most of the snow had receded from the vale. Trying to be discreet, Ge-or began his preparations for leaving. Pelts had to be re-baled, weapons honed, mules reshod, the wagon checked, and wheels greased. He did all of this out of Leona's sight; still, she knew their time together was short.

She tried not to show him how badly she wanted him to stay. During lovemaking, she would wrap her arms about him as if to keep him there forever.

Finally, sitting by the stove one night, he drew her into his arms after Aldred had gone to bed. "I will leave anon, my love," he said, as he cradled her in his lap stroking her swollen belly lightly.

"I know, my knight," she said.

"I will return as I have promised. Perhaps by summer's end. If not then, before the first snows. Mayhap I can spend another winter; I cannot promise, though."

Leona drew up from his shoulder and smiled slightly, touching his lips with her fingertips. "Truly? You might stay again?"

"If it works out. I would love to spend time with you and the child."

"Oh, Ge-or, I know you must go. I can't help loving you, but I also understand the needs you have. I see it in everything you do, and I would not have it otherwise. It is who you are. Come back to me when you can. That is all I ask."

"I promise." He whispered in her ear. He lifted her easily and carried her into their room.

Two days later, early on a chilly morn, the three stood in front of the house as Ge-or was set to leave. He gave Aldred another large handful of the coppers, "For the child." The previous eve he had pressed the two gems he had taken from Harky's boot into Leona's hand saying, "These are for an emergency. They are not of great value. They should bring enough to set you up in comfort in a small community for some years should you ever need to." Leona had accepted them, knowing that Ge-or gave them from his heart.

Aldred shook Ge-or's hand firmly and gave him a hearty clap on his shoulder. "You have become like a son to me. I regret ever having mistrusted you. Go and get that dragon of yours, and come back for the child and... well, ahem," he stammered. "I have some work to do in the barn. Birthings are starting, so I'll leave ye. Good travels, Ge-or."

Ge-or held Leona close for a long time before releasing her. He said goodbye with a final kiss. He had a large lump in his throat and was unable to speak. Leona could not contain her tears; she smiled up at him and waved as he hied the mules forward. The last he saw before he turned up out of the gate was her standing on the porch and waving, her cheeks shining with tears.

The Bard Hall Challenge

End-of-year exams had been tough, really tough, but Jared had gotten through them successfully. He hadn't received any academic or performance awards at the school convocation, yet he was happy with how he had done. Theory was only a "Good-minus," though his grades had steadily improved throughout the year; and he actually received a solid 'Good' on his exam. History and Lore were "Good-plusses," and he had received "Excellents" in all his performance classes.

Jared cheered and cheered when Simon-Nathan won the top honors medals in History and for Lore for second years. He cheered even louder when Karenna walked off with four medals for Theory, History, Lore, and Composition for first years.

The focus for the next week would be on the annual tournament. Jared was the hands-down favorite to take the top prize at the highest level in Advanced Shortbow, and one of the favorites for the advanced Long Sword Cup. He didn't want to leave anything to chance, so he stepped up his practices and workouts. Karenna and Simon-Nathan volunteered to help him with his fitness routines and his practices where they could. Neither was making any effort to try out at any level, so they had lots of free time.

Jared and Karenna had spent a good bit of time together since the "sphere debacle." Mostly they talked, held hands, and tried to pick up the pieces of their relationship. Jared tried to be as open as he could with Karenna. He had not forgotten about Thistle. Yet things were so different that he did not really know how he felt about her.

Karenna tried to convince Jared and herself that what mattered most were the moments that they were able to have together. They enjoyed being with each other, and very much loved being close and intimate. On a daily basis, they continued to share the ups and downs of school with each other and with Simon-Nathan.

The next year promised to be a mixed bag for the trio. Karenna received advance placement in all the academic subjects, which meant she and Jared would not be in morning classes together. However, since she, Jared, and Simon-Nathan all chose string instruments as their major focus, they would have advanced instrumental class and ensemble together.

Bard Freeburg, the lute master, approached Jared, Karenna, and Simon-Nathan to join a newly formed "orchestra" of fiddles. The instrument, an outgrowth of the rebec and other early stringed instruments, had become popular in the southlands. The more-rounded, carved form had excellent tonal properties and resonance. It was an instrument well suited to the new music with its elaborate frills and ornamentation. Jared was to lead one of the upper fiddle sections; and Simon-Nathan, whose father had been approached to donate some instruments to the school, was to lead the tenor fiddles.

Jared also received an honor rarely given even graduate students – he was asked to be an assistant instructor to Selim in archery. He would likely be Simon-Nathan's instructor, and quite possibly Karenna's as well, since a rumor was circulating that girls would now be allowed to take archery in addition to knife work in the Yard.

Tournament week started with three days of practice; then, on Thorinsday, the bouts began.

Jared moved easily through the early rounds. By the afternoon he had captured top prize for first years in both shortbow and the short sword. On subsequent days, he knew he would follow a tougher schedule to make all his required times for both disciplines in the finals, as well as to try to catch some of Elanar's bouts in the long sword.

Fridasday proved to be much the same. Jared moved steadily through the trials, maintaining his position as the premier archer and winning his short sword bouts. He would be in the advanced finals with both weapons.

Sammesday dawned warm and bright. It was a perfect day for archery. Yet Jared knew that by mid-afternoon it would be a demanding day for the sword play. Those who were not participating or who were no longer in the trials were asked to standby to provide refreshments and assistance to those who were.

As Jared stepped to the line for the first archery round, all the first and second year students cheered for him. He had helped so many of them with their skills, that he was the popular choice, as well as the favorite, to win the Challenge Archery Shortbow Cup. He did not disappoint. By the end of the third line, set to thirty paces, he was seven points ahead of the nearest archer, a fourth year. It was deemed an all but insurmountable lead. At the break and end of the fourth line, he was thirteen ahead. Following that, he had to rush over for his first short sword bout.

By mid-day, Jared had nearly secured the Shortbow Cup with only one line left to shoot. He had also won all of his early sword bouts, even though his opponents had been formidable. The field of thirty-two blades-men, the four best from each year, eight graduate students, and eight returning Apprentice or Journeymen Bards, was now narrowed to four. Jared was familiar with all except one, a huge fellow recently back from the wilds after his final year of Apprenticeship. First, however, he had to shoot his final archery line.

There were only four boys left in this final shoot. The slate was wiped clean. They were all to shoot thirty-six arrows: six at twenty paces; six at twenty-five; six at thirty; six at forty; six at the running deer, and finally the mobile. There was one point scored for each bulls-eye, no points if outside the line. No student had ever gotten a perfect score. The number to shoot for was thirty-two if you wanted your name etched in the lore of Bard Hall.

Jared shot easily and quickly. He had tuned his bow carefully, selecting his best gut and his best arrows for the match. Luckily, it was now warming; and it was not humid, which would affect the bowstring as the match went on. By the end of the third line, he still had a perfect score; and now the boys surrounding the archery field were beginning to get excited. Others were wandering over as the shooters set up for the fourth line.

Once again, Jared shot quickly and effortlessly. He did not try any tricks. He just wanted to place the arrows in the yellow and move on. At each shot the field of spectators, respectively silent for the shooters, would take a breath as the arrows sped toward the targets. Four lines, twenty-four points, Jared was ahead by three and still perfect.

To make the deer target a bit more difficult, the four archers had to shoot their arrows in sequence as the deer "ran" across the target area. Jared was furthest to the left; so he would shoot last on the first line, since the deer came from the right. Then they would each shift position, with Jared moving further to the right, and each archer shifting down one spot. Arrows were removed after each run.

Since there were already three arrows in the deer's vital/scoring section when the target went by, Jared had to plan to avoid the others, or risk his arrow being diverted or broken. He took an extra split second to find his aim; his arrow sailed true. After five arrows, he was still perfect. There was electricity in the arena each time he raised his bow. Placing his final shot dead center in the deer's vitals, Jared stepped back from the line. A few minutes later, after the last archer's shot, the place erupted in cheers.

With a five-point lead, the others conceded the match to let Jared shoot for score on the mobile. As efficiently as he had done the first time, Jared nocked, drew, aimed, and fired. When the sixth plate fell in sequence, a massive roar shook the Yard. He found himself swarmed over by first and second years, who patted him on the back and yelled their congratulations. With a short sword bout set for thirty minutes, Jared finally managed to extricate himself from the mob with Simon-Nathan's and Karenna's help.

Jared's next round with the short sword was a challenging one. His opponent was small and quick – a fourth year who had won the Long Sword Cup two years running. Jared, however, had real combat experience, which proved to be invaluable. By the tenth minute of the twelve-minute bout, he was up by two touches.

Their swords were not corked, but were required to be blunted and dull. One could certainly inflict some pain and damage, depending on the stroke used and by how well it was defended. One boy had his arm broken in an earlier bout. Jared managed to avoid all except light touches and few enough of those.

The final minutes of the match, the upper-class student pressed his attack. Jared whirled, twisted, parried, and ducked under the flurry of blows. When the bell rang, both boys were gasping for breath. Jared had managed to stay clean. He had won. Now, with only forty-five minutes until the final bout, he needed to rest.

The short sword final was the next to last bout of the day, followed by the long sword final. As Jared entered the ring, he sized up his opponent. The fellow, Markus of Aelfric, was big, even larger than Ge-or; and he was well-muscled. He was quick enough, too. Jared had caught the tail-end of one of his earlier rounds on his way over to shoot the third shortbow line. The big lad had overwhelmed his opponent. If he was to defeat the man, Jared knew he would have to rely on his quickness and get ahead right away.

He had fought many similar matches with his brother. Ge-or had always had the advantage in the longer, heavier blades; yet Jared could give him a fair fight with the short sword. He had learned to use his agility against his brother's power. But back then he was in the best shape of his life. Not only did the two of them spar and work out with weapons throughout the week, they also worked the fields, traps, cut wood, hauled loads, and generally worked almost every minute of every day.

Jared, afraid he would not measure up academically and musically, had let his fitness go the first term. Second term, though he had tried, he had not had the time to dedicate himself to regaining all he had lost physically. Plus, his opponent had spent the last five years as an Apprentice Bard in and around Aelfric, a border town where survival meant staying fit and maintaining one's prowess with weapons. The man was well-toned, hard, and looked determined.

After the formal salute and the ringing of the bell to commence the match, Jared went immediately on the offensive. He did not want to give Markus any time to learn what he was capable of, nor how tired he was. Jared spun, twisted, thrust, swung, and blocked. By the middle of the first period he had gained three touches and managed to stay clean himself. He knew he was tiring, and the brute in front of him just kept coming. Over the next three minutes, Jared was able to maintain his score, yet had not been able to penetrate Markus's defenses again. It was obvious to Jared that Markus had also been in real fights, because he learned rapidly from his opponent's attacks. He was also imaginative in closing previous gaps in his own defenses.

At the end of the first period, Jared sank to one knee, gasping for breath. He almost didn't hear the excited cheers of those encouraging him on. Karenna knew how the match had turned. She was worried when he sat down on a stool provided at the sidelines. "Jared," she said, "you are exhausted, and this guy looks like he will keep coming and coming. Perhaps you should concede; you have done so much today already."

Jared shook his head. "I won't quit, Karenna, that is something that is not part of my nature or upbringing, though I don't know if I can hold him off much longer." She offered him more water and he took a long swallow as she mopped his brow for the tenth time. He stood up, looked at her and smiled. "For you," he said, touching her lightly on the brow. In some way, it was the most loving gesture he had ever given her.

This time Markus charged forward, right away pressing the offensive. Jared parried his attacks smartly; yet, even with all his will focused on the fight, his body couldn't keep up any longer with his mind. One powerful attack, in which Markus kept up a flurry of hard driving blows from above, drove him back toward the edge of the ring. He met each with a sharp block, but he missed the penultimate move that led to a sharp thrust to his side. The ring referee yelled "Point!"

A half-minute later, the two combatants met again in center ring. A few seconds after that, and Jared had been touched again. This time he had been slow responding to an upward slash. Markus had twisted his blade sideways, changed directions in a flash, and brought the blade down hard on Jared's left thigh. He had gone down. He was asked if he could continue when he hobbled back to the line.

The leg was badly bruised. With it now cramping, it left him with little maneuverability. He gamely continued, yet was touched again, and then again, within seconds of starting each time. Struggling to the line again, Jared saw concern on his opponent's face; however, it was not Markus's place to ask for concession. Knowing he was overmatched, Jared raised his blade, saluted Markus and the referee, and finally lowered it to the ground. He was done.

Jared stayed to watch the long sword bout. Elanar and his elven comrade were once again in the final. It proved to be a close match. Joelin scored early; however, Elanar surprised his opponent by learning from the attack. He adjusted, and the next time Joelin used the same maneuver, Elanar responded with a new twist, and he gained the touch back.

The rest of the first period and through the second, no one scored. In the third period, it was a slip of the foot in the sand that caused Elanar to miss a block. Joelin scored a second point with less than a minute to go. Elanar was now breathing heavily, and his sword was drooping; yet, Jared could have sworn that his friend winked at him during one twisting turn he made to avoid a stroke. When his opponent had appeared to recover first after a flurry of exchanged strokes, Elanar suddenly came to life. He whirled on his toes, brought his sword up in a slashing block, and snap-flipped it over the top of his opponent's blade. He caught Joelin full in the chest with a nice thrust. The bell rang; the bout ended in a tie.

The referee announced that the match would be decided by the next touch. After two minutes rest, Elanar and Joelin met in center ring. Jared had never seen him so confident. He was smiling broadly, a rarity amongst the almost elves since they were ever stoic in dealing with others; and he was holding his blade lightly as if ready to pounce, while Joelin gripped his tightly, obviously anxious at the turn of events.

The match lasted only a few more seconds. Immediately at the bell, Elanar attacked. He touched Joelin with a quick upward parry-attack combination.

Elanar saluted his opponent, the referee, and turned and saluted Jared with his blade, saying in the old language, "Tu honara me." Jared bowed in return, accepting the honor.

***

Thistle, Sart, and Alli had spent the relatively warm late-spring day at a textile museum. They were now enjoying a light dinner next to the river before heading back to the palace. Alli had been fascinated by the many fabrics, the different types of spinning wheels and looms, and the myriad of ways that cotton, wool, flax, and many other natural materials were made into cloth. Since she had been involved at all levels of production of wool and linen in their western village, Thistle shared some of her personal experiences with handling such materials with Alli as they ate.

She and Alli spent the longest part of the day being shuffled from one section of the museum to another by the curator. He was more than willing to answer all their questions, and even allowed them to work any of the machines whenever they wished. Sart had politely bowed out after the first hour. He had returned late in the afternoon to escort them back.

As they sat on the grassy bank, Thistle asked Sart something that had been troubling her for some time. "Why don't I get to mix and work with the magic-users in the great hall?"

"Ah, well, I would have a guess at that; but I think you should ask Meligance. Your education is her choice and I, as you are, am simply part of the game plan. Keep in mind that she doesn't do anything lightly."

When Thistle asked the same question of Meligance, her mentor answered the question bluntly. "What you see as you pass by on your way here are mostly tricks and illusions meant to tease and entertain. Perhaps a few of those apprentices below will someday learn enough to enter the formal magic school; that is not here, Thistle.

"Magic is an individual, private acquisition. You will, my child, eventually reach a stage where you can, if you choose, combine forces with other magic-users to create more powerful effects. That will not be for a while. This use of magic can be effective, especially in a defensive sense; but most of that type of learning and practice is best left to when you have reached a high level of control.

"The kingdom's magic school, which is to the south, outside the city's walls, is in a small manor. It is run not unlike what you and I do together here. The instructors are higher-level mages, and they work almost exclusively with students one-on-one. It is a master-apprentice relationship, although it is not unusual for a mage to have two or more apprentices. Unfortunately, there are few enough of either masters or students

130

these days. The proclivity for talent in the Art appears to be waning in humankind.

"Know this, Thistle, you are more talented than any of the lot at that school, masters included."

Thistle was quite surprised by that matter-of-fact statement from her mentor.

Meligance continued, "I have been considering something to expand your education in a new direction. Perhaps this summer and into the fall, I will have you enroll in some classes at the University. You certainly could benefit from a broader understanding of history, mathematics, and the like. Would this please you? It is not necessary."

"Yes, I would like that very much. I get lonely for others, that is, to meet others my own age."

"Well, yes, I can understand that, certainly. Most of these students will be several years your senior. Still, you now have enough background to fit in intellectually." Meligance paused, judging Thistle's resolve about taking more on.

Looking up, she said, "Good, it is decided. I may have Sart sign you up for a couple of courses this summer; then we will see about next year."

Karenna was crying and holding tight to Jared. Bard Hall effectively shut down during the summer, allowing time to clean and refurbish the rooms and renovate any areas that had been damaged or fallen into disrepair. A skeleton group of masters and graduate students stayed on to do research. Almost all the students were expected to go home or go to work during the warm months. Karenna was heading down the coast to her home in Panterra. She would fish with her father and work in the family garden. Her carriage was due any minute; and though she and Jared had spent the night together, Simon-Nathan having already departed, she still did not want to let go.

"I will miss you so much, Jared. Can you come? Please, please?"

"I hope I can. You know what Simon-Nathan said. If we can head out with one of his father's wagon trains, mayhap we can visit, but it will be briefly; and, well, from what you have said, we will not have much privacy."

"I know... just to see you, so we could go for walks for a day or two." She raised up and kissed him lightly. "You've grown taller, half-elf." She darted down the path to her carriage as it came to the gate and waved frantically to him as it pulled away. When it disappeared in the distance, Jared turned down the street to head for Simon-the-Elder's mansion.

Simon-Nathan's father had generously offered Jared a job for the summer. Jared had accepted on the condition that he could work in the warehouses most of the time. He wanted to get back in shape, and standing behind a counter or restocking shelves did not appeal to him. His roommate had groaned when he heard the request, because he planned to work with Jared. He had hoped to spend the summer in a cool open-air shop, not in the heat of the covered storage centers. In the end, he had conceded, because he knew he needed the physical work as well; else he would grow as rotund as his father.

Aelfric

It took Ge-or almost three weeks to reach the gates of the frontier town of Aelfric. Travel had been slow on the muddy roads; and a spring storm had blown in from the east, causing him to hole up in a dry canyon for two-and-a-half-days. He hadn't encountered any other travelers until he was well south, which reinforced Aldred's perspective that many homesteaders had left the rich foothills because of the trouble to the west. After camping for a week by himself, and one night spent in a lonely outpost set to the east of the road he travelled, Ge-or did begin to pass a few others – mostly people heading south as he was.

Ge-or spent one half-day helping a family fix their wagon's broken wheel. A day after that, he invited a lone trapper, hauling his heavy winter bounty of skins on a sled drawn by an old mule, to join him for the few days left to the town. As luck would have it, the fellow was wise in the ways of the border city. Once they arrived, he led Ge-or to a warehouse where they could get top prices for their furs. He also knew the best livestock traders. Joshua willingly gave Ge-or a brief run-down of what to look for and what to avoid in the city. His advice was so valuable that Ge-or refused any offer of payment for helping him bring his hides to the town in his wagon.

Finally, with the hides and wagon sold, and the mules billeted until he could do some horse-trading, Ge-or deposited all his coin with a moneylender for safekeeping until he was in need of it. He didn't get much of an interest rate, but it was enough to pay for the better part of his lodging each week while he got acquainted with the city. Ge-or sought out the Druid's Hut that Stradryk, the half-gzk he had met the past fall, had recommended. When he stepped through the door, it hit him – now, he was an adventurer.

The Druid's Hut was akin to many a tavern in almost any town of any size in western Borea. The lighting was low, the tables were rough, and the clientele rougher. There was a bar in the large main room that was nearly the length of the back wall. A fireplace, filled with a roaring blaze of logs, was set in the western wall. There was something different – a certain feel that Ge-or recognized for what it was, although it was the first time he had ever experienced it. There was something in the atmosphere that spoke of solitude, the open road, yet also of a kinship and the camaraderie of resilience. He had been in several such places before with his father, but not as an adventurer. He had changed.

From where Ge-or stood in the doorway, he could see an odd mixture of humanoids scattered about the place. Two dwarves and a gnome sat at the bar whispering quietly; they did not even turn to see who had come in. They looked hearty, yet worn with age and hardship. A grimy, battered-looking knight, or perhaps an uncouth paladin of some offshoot religion, was slumped over in a booth. His head was resting on his vambrace as he snored loudly, several empty mugs resting near. A couple of seedy characters in ragged robes were playing draughts at a far table near the fire. These two did look up as the evening light drew their attention to the open door; just as quickly they looked back to their game, wary of the large figure bracing the doorway.

Other than the heavy darkness of the wood of the place, there was little to adorn it. Above the bar there was a large stuffed deer head showing signs of decay. Its antlers, however, were impressive, rising above the partially exposed skull. Ceramic, leather, and pewter mugs of a wide variety of shapes were hanging from pegs all along the back wall. Above the bar, a sign boldly displayed on the wall stated, "No fighting." Below that, carved in a stained blank board, "All others welcome."

Ge-or did not see a proprietor; he did notice a stairway to his left leading up to, as he figured, what lodging the place offered. Feeling no threat from any of the current occupants, Ge-or stepped forward to the bar. A minute later, a heavyset, mostly bald man came out from what Ge-or could now see was a shabby curtain that was nailed on the back wall under the deer head.

The beefy man spoke gruffly in greeting. "What ye be needin', friend?"

"A room, a bath if you have it, and after, ale and food," Ge-or replied. He stood at least a head taller than the inn-keeper, so he had to look down to meet his gaze.

"Coin?"

"Aye," Ge-or assured him. "What are the charges?"

"Room and board is trey-copper a day; fifteen for a week. That includes bread, butter, jam, and tea in mornings, and stew at night. Ale, drinks, and roast meat and fixins are extra, pay as you go. Rooms are up to six were we busy; but the spring crowd is thin so far, so take your choice. Jus don' take someone's head off in the middle of the night iffen they come in. A bath here is five-pence, though you can go down the street to the stable and get a wash for two pennies, iffen you don't mind the cold hosing you get at the end. Your choice.

"Name's Halbert, inn-keep. Where ye be from?" The man stuck out his large hand.

Ge-or took the man's wrist, appreciating the proprietor's candor. "Ge-or, from the coastline, north and west. Many thanks... I'll be back." He counted out seventeen coppers, and slapped them onto the bar. "I'd appreciate the stew, and a tall ale when I return. Run me a tab for the drink."

Halbert placed his hand over the coin, picking up the extra two coppers. He ran them through his fingers, looking at the big man quizzically. Ge-or nodded; Halbert grunted. Money was money in these times, and tips were rare. Ge-or wanted information, lots of information, and he was willing to pay. He didn't need anything now, but he would soon. He knew money helped loosen tongues. A few coppers here and there would not affect his equipment purchases, and might actually save him a good bit of time and money in the long run. Inn-keeps were the best source of any kind of information you needed. His dad had taught him that early on.

Ge-or spent the next three weeks getting to know Aelfric. For a man who had never been in a town larger than Thiele or Permis, this sprawling small city was filled with many wonders. At first, he simply wandered about the better parts of town examining the wide variety of shops and establishments. Both the trapper he had helped and the barkeep at the Druid's Hut had warned him about certain areas and taverns, those prone to thievery and violence, so initially he avoided them. He figured that if he ever needed to enter the darker parts of the town, he would seek additional advice. He also knew, from the many stories his father had told him and his brother, that often the best deals were made in places off of the beaten path.

Through his efforts, he discovered there was a wide diversity of people and goods in Aelfric, far different from the basic, solid folk of the western villages. There was a section of the town, raying out from the center square that boasted grand houses of two and three stories, all owned by the noble class and wealthy merchants. Surrounding this area were the best shops, if one considered gaudy, overdone, and expensive the best. Ge-or was amused to see that the "upscale" armories in this district catered to a clientele that preferred beauty and ornateness over practicality. After visiting one such shop, he was shaking his head in disbelief. A single breastplate with silver and gold mounting was priced at more than all the money he had accumulated. And the piece would have been virtually useless in a real fight. He could have crushed it with his bare hands.

If one looked carefully there were some quality goods amongst the trifles. He also discovered that there were shops that catered to all tastes and desires. Some of the food shops and inns served those with refined tastes; these had exotic fare. Other establishments had good, simple, hearty food – akin to what the Druid's Hut served. Clothiers had everything from the ornate and gaudy to the heavy, practical clothing needed by those who actually worked for a living. Here and there, even amongst the armorers that catered to the well-born, one could find a decent weapon or pair of bracers hidden in the recesses of an otherwise worthless pile of overindulgence. If you were partial to fine dishware, fine wines, fancy clothing, and similar expensive things, some of the shops carried things of quality from throughout the kingdom. It was a cornucopia of nearly anything anyone could possibly want if they had the price.

Much to Ge-or's amusement, those who primarily peopled the better district closest to the center of the town seemed to exemplify the wares he had seen in the shops. Fops, or "gentlemen of leisure," strolled about in gaudy finery with light rapiers strapped to their belts. Ge-or could not imagine that many of these fine fellows had ever actually had to use their weapon in a pitched fight. Halbert, the Druid Hut inn-keep, did warn him that a few were actually well-trained in the use of their weapons and were very quick in a duel. This did not concern Ge-or too much. His father had taught him and Jared the use of all weapons, "in case they might ever have to use one, or defend against one."

The ladies of the upper-class district, or "the snoots" as Halbert referred to them, wore bright, gaudy gowns of fine materials, with even more elaborate hats perched on their heads on the rare occasions they could be seen out and about. On certain early evenings, they tended to promenade about in tiny bright shoes, with strange, large circular sunshades on a stick, something Ge-or had never seen before. These devices were ostensibly to block the glaring spring sun from their delicate eyes and skin. The inn-keeper also told Ge-or that he would never see any of these "*fine* fellows" or "*fine* ladies," (he always emphasized the first word when referring to them), in the other parts of Aelfric, nor out past dusk when things often got "down-right nasty" in some sectors.

To the north and east of town center were the more down-to-earth establishments that promised to hold the types and quality equipment that Ge-or would need and could afford to purchase to complete his quest. He spent a good bit of time visiting the armor and weapon shops, talking with the proprietors, examining their wares, and generally getting to know them and what they had. He also visited the tanners, the bakers, fishmongers and butchers, the tack shops, used-item merchants, and so on. Each day, he built upon the knowledge he had gathered on previous treks about the town. Soon he was familiar with all except the south-central, the roughest section of Aelfric.

In the evenings, he returned to the Druid's hut for a late dinner, sat and drank ale or rum, and listened. On occasion, he would buy a particularly useful chap a drink or two to ply information from him. By "useful", Ge-or meant someone who might have information on anything that would help him understand the town, the inhabitants, the culture, and the general ways of not only this community, but also the world in general. He knew, because he had paid careful attention to his father's tales, that he was woefully undereducated about a broad perspective of the Borean world. He did not want to repeat anything like the mistake he had made in trusting his fellow travelers without a thorough exploration of the potentialities of any given situation.

He also waited this night, as he had waited every night since arriving, in the tavern's main room. He hoped that Stradryk would eventually show up, because he felt the fellow would be a trusted source of not only local information, but the gathering of information that might be useful on his quest. Ge-or hadn't made many inroads into learning about dragons, yet he at least knew that the half-gzk had seen the one he was after. Perhaps the fellow knew of other adventurers who might also have more information about the beasts.

In spite of his efforts and fortune, Ge-or discovered that he did not have nearly enough money to get the equipment he would need. Prices for good armor and weapons were high, yet not unexpectedly so. And, he did not have enough information about fighting the beasts to fully understand what he needed. Stradryk had suggested that he might be able to help Ge-or make adventuring connections which might prove fruitful. Therefore, each night he sat, talked, drank, and watched the front door. So far, after more than three weeks in Aelfric, he had not seen the half-gzk. He grunted, downed his last swallow of ale, and headed for the loft, which was now shared, as the town's populace continued to swell with the spring weather, with three other wayfarers. All, thankfully, appeared to be willing to mind their own business.

A Quest

It wasn't until the beginning of his fifth week in the border town, when Ge-or began to think he would be on his own in pursuing his revenge, that the half-gzk showed up. Stradryk strode into the Druid's hut one evening as Ge-or was finishing his stew. He waved him over, relieved to see the fellow. He had begun to doubt his ability to pursue something so monumental on his own. He ordered a tall mug of ale for his friend from the passing serving wench and another for himself.

"Well met, Stradryk. I was worried the great beast had found you a tasty morsel."

"Nay, the roads were muddy and the going slow. I had to trade for a mule at an outpost to get my sleigh here."

"Good trapping?"

"A good year for mink and muskrat, which bring the best prices. It was a decent haul. I found a new spot upstream of where I had been working my traps. You should come with me this winter next. You can see your beast and the obstacles you will face soon enough. That is, if you wish to persist in your quest."

The bar wench returned with their ale. Ge-or kept her from leaving with a raised finger. "I forget my manners, friend, are you hungry?"

"Desperately, it's been a long day. For the past two hours, I've been haggling with a stubborn fur trader; but I did well enough."

"Stew or Roast?"

"Stew is best after a wet trek. Perhaps we can celebrate on the morrow and have a roast and trimmings in a private room upstairs."

"I am in one of the common rooms." Ge-or gestured toward the stairway. "You are welcome to join me there."

Stradryk smiled a toothy smile. "I would if I could; my kind are frowned upon. It might be possible in this place, yet some would be, shall we say, uncomfortable. I usually get a single. If you would share a room with me, it would help defray some cost."

"I would be happy to stay with you. What is the cost?" Ge-or asked

"Forty coppers a week. It's a bit pricey, but I will pay twenty-five," Stradryk offered, "and you can cover the fifteen you are already paying."

"Nay, I will pay half. I will enjoy being out of the common room, so I will think it a bargain. I intend to bend your ear a bit. I am new to all of this." Ge-or gestured with his right hand in a big circle. "Your insight will be invaluable."

"Give me a day or so to get back on my feet, Ge-or. After that, you can ask what you will. I feel like I could sleep a year." Stradryk raised his mug and clinked it against Ge-or's. "I am well-pleased that we met, and that you waited here for me. When you are such as I, it is hard to make friends."

"I see naught about you except a friend."

"Then you are a rare person."

Ge-or and Stradryk were making the rounds of the tavern posting boards in search of a potentially lucrative adventure. The half-gzk was showing Ge-or the ropes of seeking out quests. He told Ge-or about the well-paid, generally boring jobs serving

136

as protection for the merchants travelling south through chatt territory along the edge of the Great Desert. He also spoke about the dangerous, and only occasionally successful, lode-finding missions of dwarf or gnome-led mining parties to their old digs in the west, well into the Qa-ryk and goblin lands.

There were also various adventures leaving to explore an old dungeon, ruined castle, or to seek buried treasure to the south and west. These were led by stout fighters, magic-users, or clerics of some repute, and could be quite lucrative. Success of these ventures varied, and one generally had to deal with gzks, goblins, the occasional mountain ogre, and other beasts, depending on where the ruin was located. Stradryk was inclined to seek the latter type of adventure. They were more interesting, and potentially could result in a "significant find in treasure," shared by all.

Over the week spent with Stradryk, Ge-or learned much more about Aelfric than he had been able to glean on his own. The half-gzk was a wealth of information. He knew enough to be able to take Ge-or about the sordid regions of the city, pointing out establishments and shops that were worth exploring, while informing the big fighter what precautions to take, what to avoid, and advising him to stay away from these disreputable areas after dusk. He was even able to introduce Ge-or to several old fighters, who at least knew about dragon hunting, though it had been their forebears that had actually gone on dragon quests.

He did not learn much from these beaten down old men; what little he learned had reinforced the cleric's admonitions. Ge-or was ill-prepared for such a quest. The beasts were devilishly hard to kill because they had few weak spots in their armor. Those, as Ge-or guessed correctly when he had seen the beast turn on its tail, were the lighter shadings of their scales. Even these areas took a great force to penetrate: a superior longbow, or tremendous power behind the thrust of a sword, preferably a dwarf or elven-made sword, and magical, if one could get so fine a blade these days.

Dealing with their liquid-fire was something else entirely. Powerful fire-resistant potions could be purchased at extraordinary cost, which could help. And some type of fire-resistant leather armor was essential. Unfortunately, the best of this armor came from the dragons themselves, and it had been over a hundred years since a red dragon had been killed. The old leather under-garments made from these beasts had long since lost their efficacy. No one knew of any way to acquire well-toned and well-cared for dragon leather garments today, except perhaps the elves, who may have kept their old garments in good repair. In addition, once the heat was at least partially defended against, one needed to have high quality armor to be able to withstand strikes from the beast's claws, tail, and teeth.

Even then, great skill, intelligence, subterfuge, and luck were also needed. Hunting a dragon alone was considered suicide. Contrary to popular notions and tales, most dragon hunters had travelled in packs. Ge-or found out he would need considerably more money and much more information to have any chance at succeeding.

Each day after their rounds, Stradryk and Ge-or met to discuss what they had turned up. To date they had found little that had tweaked the half-gzk's interest. He quickly dismissed many adventures as "being poorly led," "too dangerous," "potentially little chance for success," and so on. He seemed to know what he was looking for. Ge-or patiently learned all he could from his friend's approach.

After this day's turn about the town's taverns, they met back at the Druid's Hut at dinner time. Ge-or could tell right away that his friend had found something of more interest. "Tell me," he said, as they swung into an open side table to order their dinner and ale.

"A cleric... I've worked with him before. While he's not the most powerful I have known, he is good, both as a healer and a leader. It is always good to have a healer along on treks."

"What is the goal?"

"An old castle, out to the west on the edge of the Beze range. It was an old magic-user's place. Sart wants to..."

"Did you say, 'Sart?'"

"You know of him?"

"He saved my life after our village was destroyed. I had been whacked on the head by a Qa-ryk. I'm not sure I would have made it otherwise. He appeared to be forthright and wise, though he did trick me with a sleeping potion."

"Yes, that sounds like Sart. He can be wily, as well as kind. On this trek, he is after old scrolls and other documents. The man is always seeking information. Still, there is a good chance there is treasure amongst the ruins. Mages, powerful ones, tended to hoard valuables and magical things. We might do well, except there are drawbacks."

"Like?"

"We will be on the edge of Qa-ryk country and in the heart of the goblin range. It is possible, nay, likely, that the dirty grovelers will have taken over the old mage's digs and dungeon. We might even encounter an ogre or two. They tend to cohabitate with the cavern dwellers. The larger beasts often take the upper levels of dungeons and leave the deeper places to the grey vermin."

"Big party? Magic-users?"

"Notice calls for six to ten, so not too big, probably adequate. Didn't mention any mages, but he might hire one or two. They can be useful in some circumstances. Meeting is scheduled for a week from today. Want to give it a try?"

"Sounds like what we have been looking for. I am getting antsy sitting around."

"I know what you mean. It is time to get back on the road."

As their stew arrived, this night loaded with pork and vegetables, Ge-or and Stradryk lapsed into silence and ate. They didn't talk again until they were enjoying an after-dinner mug of hot-spiced rum. A cold wind from the north had blown through during the previous night; and the tavern was cold, in spite of the roaring fire in the corner.

Ge-or cleared his throat, looking Stradryk in the eyes as he looked up. "I would ask you another question, an awkward one; as you know I am new to all of this."

"Ask, friend. I will answer if I may."

"I would know about... ahem... about women, companionship, if you know what I mean."

"Aye, I know of such, even though for me it is a difficult thing being... Well, enough of that, I will tell you what I know, and give you what advice I can give."

Ge-or nodded. He felt really uncomfortable. He had become more than a little lonely for Leona's softness and caresses over the past weeks. He had been tempted to buy a steed and ride back to visit her. Yet he knew that would make things even more difficult for both of them. He knew nothing about women outside of the mores of a wilderness village. He had seen many women about Aelfric that were obviously selling themselves; however, he had no conception about how to approach them, nor what might be safe or not safe in pursuing these types of liaisons. Still, he had become used to being with a woman. He had to be honest with himself; he missed it mightily. And though he was not bound by any particular beliefs, or even mores associated with such, Ge-or knew Leona would be upset if she knew he looked elsewhere for companionship. It would be something he would need to think about.

Stradryk, looking a bit uncomfortable himself, said, "There be ladies-of-the-night, whores, and wenches, take your pick. The important thing is to bed those that don't have some disease you can catch. You can get this or that remedy from the hags or soothsayers, ...well, the truth is, if you catch the clap or worse, you'll need a good cleric to get rid of it. That can get pricey. Nothing is free these days, leastwise not in a town like this.

"The trouble is – and this might be your main concern, Ge-or – how do you know? To start with, pick the right establishment. Sometimes the wenches in a place like the Druid's Hut are available for a price. They are fairly picky, so often they are as safe as any. The high-priced ladies-of-the-night in the center of town take herbs and other precautions. They're generally as safe as can be expected from what I've been told. As to the streetwalkers and others of the red-district, stay away. You're asking for trouble if you bed them, and it is likely you'd get robbed in the bargain."

Stradryk paused, looking down, avoiding Ge-or's eyes. "Most wenches who are good, and relatively safe, will… well… they will check you over, which is a might embarrassing. And… you should check them over, too. Here's what to look for..."

For the next half hour, Ge-or's education took a new, wide-eyed turn. For saying he had trouble getting a woman, the half-gzk seemed to know a great deal about a much-maligned profession. Ge-or paid attention. He took mental notes of all Stradryk told him. He learned of diseases, rates, giveaways, or "freesies" in the local parlance – and the tendency for the upper-class woman to offer themselves by enticing young men off the streets, especially strong, broad-shouldered young men like Ge-or.

There were also rampant sexual games often played by the wealthiest in Aelfric – things like group orgies, mate-swapping, and other frolics. It took him the next week to think about everything Stradryk offered and to compare those notes with the ladies he ran into throughout the border town. Their glances and coquetry had a whole different meaning than before.

A week after their talk, Ge-or found himself standing with Stradryk in the courtyard of the Dancing Pony tavern with several dozen other potential adventurers, all waiting for Sart to turn up.

A loud 'Hoy!' from the back announced the cleric's arrival. As the large fellow pushed his way through the crowd, he nodded to those he knew. He clapped Stradryk on the back, as he drew nearer the front. "Well met, Stradryk; I was hoping you would be here, and who is... Well, by-the-gods, Ge-or? From Thiele?"

Ge-or grinned. "And I have much to thank you for, my good cleric," he said, grasping arms with the priest.

"Well, well, perhaps you can do me a favor and join my little band in return. Well met, indeed, well met!"

Sart pushed his way to the front of the crowd. He stood on a wooden box to see over the massed adventure seekers. "Thanks for coming. Please take note that this will be a long trek, probably taking most of the summer. I plan to root about in the old boy's castle for a while. You know me, anything for something to read."

There were several laughs and a few groans. Some members of the small crowd were already beginning to melt away, not wishing to spend so much time on a venture. "While I would like to promise you grand treasure, the truth is I don't know what we will find. The place has been left to the birds, and likely the goblins, for almost a century. General pay is two silver pieces per month plus victuals. All treasure except scrolls and books to be divided equally amongst the group. You will have to provide your own gear, steed, and pack animals. We have a great cook along, Tyron, the gnome." Murmurs followed that announcement. Stradryk nudged Ge-or and whispered, "Sart never stints on the food. Tyron's one of the best trail cooks around."

"If you are still interested, stay around. I'll talk with each of you in the meeting room." Sart pointed to a side door of the tavern. "Line forms there."

More souls drifted away from the courtyard as Sart made his way through the door into the tavern's meeting room. Stradryk led Ge-or over to the line now forming at the open doorway.

Two hours later, the two adventurers sat on hard benches with six other souls listening to Sart detail the trip. He had picked a sturdy lot: Ge-or and Stradryk, plus a short, strong looking fellow; a skinny, wiry young man, and his massive associate who stood a hand taller than Ge-or and was at least several stone heavier. Two magic-users – a young man and an even younger woman – and Tyron completed the party.

"We leave in two days at dawn. I recommend a pack mule and a mountain-trained horse, pony, or mule for riding. Light armor will be best in confined spaces, otherwise choose what you will. We have several experienced adventurers in the party.

Stradryk and I have been on several treks together, and Motuk..." the shorter, sturdy-looking fighter stood up and bowed to the group, "is also well-versed in dungeon fighting. Seek them out for additional advice. Tyron has prepared a detailed list of supplies that will be useful to pack out.

"Unless you have particular food needs, we will have a fine larder, which we hope some of you hunters will help augment along the way with fresh game. Talk with Tyron about anything you might require. I can't promise you we can haul everything you want, but we will eat well. Note my ample belly," Sart laughed. His voluminous robes hid what was obviously a massive, though not distinctly overweight, constitution.

"Now, as to drink – we will have ale, and a keg or two of rum, which will be doled out carefully. If you wish to bring your own libations, please be judicious. As some of you know, I am as fond of drink as the next fellow; however, our lives depend on each other, and I will quickly dismiss anyone who gets out of hand. I hope this is understood." Sart paused, looking over the group. They all nodded.

"Good. Go and prepare. I have had a long day, so we will spend time getting to know each other better on the road. If you need me or Tyron in the next two days, we are staying here at the Prancing Pony. Otherwise, I will see you in the early morn, two days from now. Do not be late."

Preparations

Over the past week, Ge-or and Stradryk had talked at length about adventuring, the types of equipment Ge-or would need to get, the best suppliers and armorers, and much more. The half-gzk had been an invaluable source. He reinforced much of what Ge-or had learned from the trapper, the inn-keepers, and from his own wanderings about Aelfric.

His first order of business was to go back and mule-trade with the stable owner where he had boarded his animals. Ge-or knew that the bargaining would be difficult. Good animals were hard to come by.

Stradryk didn't ride, so he couldn't offer Ge-or much advice on what breed of horse to buy, or on what qualities would be best for their trek into the mountains. Gzks were built for scrambling over the worst terrain, and they had incredible endurance. As a half-gzk, he had found out the hard way that horses didn't often abide his kind. Perhaps, he had mused, that was because gzks were quite fond of horse meat. He told Ge-or that it had taken him some time to find a mule that would tolerate him leading it.

Ge-or, however, was knowledgeable enough about horses. His father had owned several mountain-bred mares. They had used them about the farm or to ride to the closest towns for trading purposes. He and Jared had often ridden them simply for pleasure through the fields and foothills of Thiele. Mountain-bred stock tended to be slightly smaller than the large stallions of the plains, a bit broader for their weight, and therefore sturdier. They had adapted to the rough terrain through many years of carefully breeding for traits that made them more tolerant of the cold and surer afoot.

He spent the better part of a day looking through those animals of any interest that the stable master had in his corrals. Finally, Ge-or settled on a well-built, tough-looking mare who had seen a good many years. He figured she still had several more seasons of work in her. There were some mountain stallions that might have proved stronger over the long-term; but Ge-or knew they would be expensive and, being considerably younger, less well-trained. He wanted an animal that would serve him well on his first expedition, without having to worry too much about it learning commands or reacting well in a fight.

When he brought his choice forward to the stable master, the big fellow grunted, "Good animal. Well-trained. Older, you know that?"

Ge-or nodded.

"She's a good 'un. Can't let her go cheap."

The bargaining began. Ge-or had watched his father and other villagers bargain at length. He knew that in the best of hands, it was an art form. The stable master obviously knew what he was about, yet Ge-or had a stubborn streak. It was a good hour before they came to a compromise. Ge-or had to give the man three of his "fine" mules (the horse-trader had described them as "fair"), plus one silver piece and six coppers. Ge-or had insisted on picking the best of his mules to use as his pack animal. In the end, the stable master agreed to toss in a much-used, quality saddle, and other used tack in the bargain. Finally, they shook hands. Ge-or paid the man an additional five coppers to house the animals until he left.

It was a steep price to pay for a steed as old as the mare; but Ge-or had put her through all the paces he knew, and she had responded well. She also had a personality that suited him. She didn't back away from any of the other animals in the stable, yet was temperate enough when he worked with her. He visited her later that night. She already recognized him when he came up to her stall and gave her several carrots.

Armor was another important consideration for Ge-or. Stradryk, though he only wore reinforced leather himself, recommended two shops for the best quality equipment and price. These were two of the three establishments that Ge-or had settled on, so he was pleased that at least he had recognized quality workmanship and had a sense of what pricing might be reasonable.

During their wanderings about town, the two of them discussed what might be the best accoutrements for Ge-or for this trek, and what was within his budgetary limits. Fortunately, Ge-or had the helm that Aldred had given him. With Stradryk's input, he decided that a good coif and byrnie of chainmail, worn over high-quality, reinforced, hardened leather, would be all he could afford and still have some money left for other supplies.

They started at the leather armorer's where Stradryk had purchased his own gear. Ge-or bought what the half-gzk recommended: a leather jerkin, heavy and stiff in the torso, with medium weight long sleeves that left good flexibility in the arms. The shoulders were doubly thick for extra protection. Stradryk explained to Ge-or that they would purchase some formed steel plates. Once they had loosened the top piece of the shoulder pads of the leather tunic, they could slip these under. The plates would provide added protection at vulnerable spots. Ge-or decided on a small wood and leather buckler; the formed metal ones at the armorer were quite pricey. He needed to save his money for the chain mail.

Stradryk told him that goblins would often scrabble at a man's legs with their sharp claws while one was otherwise engaged fighting with blades and shield; so Ge-or bought some medium weight, leather pants with a stiff extra layer at the thighs for added protection. He also bought a pair of heavy calf-length boots that he felt were much more expensive than necessary. The half-gzk convinced him they were well worth the price. Well-fitted, comfortable footwear that would stand up well in a fight was essential. Studded leather gauntlets completed the ensemble.

Next the two headed to the armorer. It took Ge-or two hours to haggle the price of the chainmail shirt and coif down to a point where he would have enough money left to buy everything he wanted to purchase. The short, massive armorer kept grumbling that Ge-or was a "big un," and thus he should have to pay more for the extra links. Ge-or finally convinced him otherwise.

All-in-all, Ge-or felt good about his purchases. As he and Stradryk headed back to the Druid's Hut for a late supper, he thanked the half-gzk for his help. Stradryk waved him off. "Back to Back, Ge-or. It's the most important rule on a trek. What remains to be seen is whether the other fellows along understand what that means."

The next morning Ge-or went to check on Sandy – a name that befit the mare's predominantly light tan coat. She also appeared to have a fair amount of grit, because most of the other animals gave her a wide berth. She was only tolerant of one of the younger stallions.

After seeing to Sandy, Ge-or worked out in his new armor for two hours in an empty stall at the stables. He felt awkward at first, having rarely worn anything except light leather protection during the treks with his father and brother. He got used to the feel and weight fairly quickly and was pleased he could move as freely as he would wish.

In the afternoon, he and Stradryk went out to make their final purchases. Ge-or didn't need much, since he had left Goat Haven as well-provisioned as he might be. He added some heavy gauge steel spikes to his pack on the half-gzk's recommendation. "One never knows when you might need to nail a door open or shut," Stradryk said. He also bought some extra strong rope, several water skins, nose bags for the horse and mule, and a variety of miscellaneous items, including more soap, a better-quality straight razor, and grooming supplies.

Ge-or had spent considerable time at weapons shops since he had arrived in Aelfric looking at weapons, yet he did not have the wherewithal to purchase a better sword. Thankfully, Ge-or's own blade, though not much to look at, was a strong, resilient steel that would continue to serve him until he could afford a high quality dwarven-made weapon. He did have enough coin left to buy one extra throwing knife to replace the one he had given to Aldred. Finally, he doubled his arrow supply when he found a fletcher that made shafts to his liking and draw-length.

By nightfall, the two felt ready. Over mugs of rum they sat quietly before the great fireplace at the Druid's Hut contemplating private thoughts. Ge-or's soon drifted to Leona. He wondered how she was doing. Finally, with an ache in his heart, he headed up to their room to try to sleep.

***

Leona was getting heavy, and it was frustrating to her that she couldn't get around as well as she was used to. It was even more bothersome that she had to give up doing some of the lifting and more difficult work that she had often helped Aldred with.

She kept busy. If she paused long enough to really think about it, tears would spring to her eyes; and she would ache throughout her body. She missed Ge-or desperately. Though she carried his child, it was ever so lonely at night when she crawled into "their" bed alone. After he had been gone several days, she had taken to holding his goose-down pillow in her arms all through the night. It might have been her imagination, but she felt she could still smell his scent on the cover.

Aldred knew she was suffering. He tried his best to fill the gap by being a bit more attentive and talkative than he had ever been. The two of them had been alone so long that they had gotten used to limited communication, content to know the other was around working somewhere on the farm. He knew that his daughter could use a bit more companionship; so he would play draughts with her at night, and talk about this goat or that and his toils of the day. Even to him, there was now a gap in their lives. They had gotten used to the strong, likeable man. At night, after Leona had gone to bed, Aldred would whittle, and wonder how the babe would change their lives. Then he would smile, sit back, and often doze off for half the night in his rocking chair.

144

Adventuring

Stradryk and Ge-or arrived at the Prancing Pony about a half hour before dawn. Tyron and Motuk were already there. They were rechecking the packing of the six mules and the cart that held all the food and whatever equipment Sart and the gnome were bringing along. Another large mule and a rugged mountain pony stood to the side, which Ge-or assumed were Sart and Tyron's rides, respectively.

Within minutes, the others began to arrive. Each person acknowledged the others with a nod, turning away to silently recheck their own packing. The sun was rising above the horizon to the east when Sart stepped out from the tavern. He gestured for Ge-or to follow him inside.

The cleric shut the door behind them. He clapped Ge-or on the shoulder. "My friend, I must apologize to you, for I have waited far too long to tell you this. My excuse is that the trek has been on my mind, and it wasn't until late last night that I remembered that you didn't know."

Ge-or stared at Sart with a puzzled look. "Know what?"

"Your brother, he is alive."

"Jared?"

"Aye. I came across him soon after I left you in Thiele. We had quite an adventure together that was..." Sart noticed the strange look of surprise and disbelief on Ge-or's face. He stopped in mid-sentence – continuing a second later, understanding that this would take the half-elf some time to digest, "...well, a tale I will relate to you as we travel."

"My brother, Jared is alive? Well?"

"Quite so, I left him at Bard Hall late last fall. He is doing very well."

"Bard Hall? My brother?"

"Another part of the tale... Come, let us rejoin the others and get on our way. We will have all the time we need to talk anon."

"By-the-gods!" Ge-or slapped both his hands down on Sart's shoulders, almost causing the big cleric's knees to buckle. Then he grabbed the cleric in a huge bear hug, lifting the large man off the ground.

"Yes," Sart said grinning, after he was back on the earth. "By-the-gods is right."

The party headed west along the main road out of Aelfric. They rode easily, with Stradryk loping ahead to serve as scout. Sart was on Crunch, his broad-backed mule. The others were on mountain-bred horses, similar in breed to Ge-or's mare.

Early on, the cleric eased up next to Ge-or and proceeded to tell him all about the adventure he had with his brother. He told him how they had met, of Thistle, and of how Jared had ended up in Bard Hall. Ge-or kept interrupting him with numerous, "By-the-gods," or with questions. He wanted to know as many details as the cleric could remember.

When the tale was done, Ge-or was stunned. "I am amazed, Sart... I should have put the first part of this together. When you told me you had not seen any half-elves amongst the dead, and thereafter I saw for myself the truth of it when I sent all the bodies into the sea, I should have been suspicious. When I made out the markings along

145

the trail to the south into the hills, I did not ken whose they might be. I knew that there was something there that I had missed. I could tell someone had passed that way and managed to kill a Qa-ryk while escaping. I never put the two things together. Even though the heavy-footed beasts had tramped over everything, I should have recognized my brother's footprints. I think that I did not dare hope it was he.

"Jared alive and well, and in Bard Hall. By-the-gods, Sart, you have filled my heart with joy this day."

"He was badly wounded, Ge-or. When he saw you fall and was chased by the Qa-ryk leader, he had no choice except to flee. The battle, as you saw, was lost."

"Nay, I would not think such a thing of him. I know my brother. He is no coward. The tale you have told shows that. An adventure, not unlike ones we used to dream of, with a fair maiden to boot!" Ge-or's eyes shone and he laughed heartily. "It is good to hear all that you have told me."

"And of you, Ge-or? How have you passed the year since I left you with…" Sart paused, reddening slightly. "I must apologize again to you. It was devious of me to give you the sleeping potion, but you were in need of rest."

"Nay, my good cleric, you were in the right. I was not thinking straight, and it was to my honor that you took that step. I needed to take care of my brethren and friends, though the task tore at my soul. As to my story since? Well, I have had a bit of an adventure myself and would appreciate your advice on a point."

"I am at your service."

For much of the rest of the morning, Ge-or told Sart of his meeting Stradryk, his near death at the hands of the robbers, and the miracle of finding Goat Haven. He did feel awkward talking about the whole situation with Leona and Aldred as it had evolved; yet once he had gotten it all out, he asked the cleric, "I wonder if I have done wrong. Whether I should go back and marry the lady to live the life my father wished me to lead, or so I felt for a long time. Truly, Sart, something else calls to me, at me. I…" His voice trailed off.

"My son," Sart looked Ge-or in the eyes, "you have made many choices for yourself and others. From what you have told me, these have all come from your heart. There is no foul in that. Above all, you have been open and honest with Leona and her father about who you are, without shirking responsibility. You are a good man, Ge-or. Follow your heart in all things, and you cannot go too far wrong. Yes, sometimes the choices are difficult for us to make. Still, I can see no fault in your decisions and actions." Sart paused, assessing Ge-or's mood.

He continued a few seconds later in a more serious tone. "I can see your heart is heavy, and that your soul has been hurt deeply by what you have seen and experienced at Thiele. Revenge, hate, anger, grief, and other negative emotions can eat at us. It will take time, but try to release what is tied up tight within you. I can feel the burden that you carry; it is a part of my training to help ease these types of burdens in my fellows."

Ge-or grimaced. His own tale had reminded him all too much of his repressed feelings and his desire for revenge on the dragon and the Qa-ryks. Although he felt half his heart was filled with joy at knowing his brother was well and starting a new life, his mood had been affected by his own inner struggles.

"Ride ahead," Sart gestured, knowing that action would be the best salve for what currently troubled Ge-or. "Find Stradryk and ask him to seek a campsite about two hours from here. If you can find us a nice deer on your way, Tyron would be pleased to serve fresh meat this first night."

Ge-or saluted Sart with a wave of his hand; he nudged the mare. The breeze caught in his hair, and joy erupted anew in his heart. He grinned as he rode ahead.

After a hearty meal of spiced roast venison, campfire bread, skillet potatoes with onions and dried sharp peppers, and new spring spinach, Sart drew the party together around the campfire to make more formal introductions.

"As you all know, I am a Cleric of the Earth. I will do all in my power to care for you and to treat any injuries that may occur. I would prefer that we all remain whole and sound throughout this adventure. Please note, also, that while there is much I can do for you, I cannot bring you back from the dead."

There were a couple of laughs as some believed Sart was making a joke; however, when they saw that he was actually serious, they caught themselves. Some priests do claim such powers; Sart was letting them know that he did not.

"I would like each of you to stand, introduce yourself, let everyone know a bit about your experience and whatever else you might wish to share. We will be working, sleeping, and riding together for the next two months or more. I trust we can all get to know each other and get along. There is really only one code out here –Back to Back." Sart scanned the group. All nodded to acknowledge they knew what he meant.

"So, you have all met Tyron." Sart gestured toward the gnome, who was now busy cleaning up after their meal. The small fellow waved at them with the pan he had in his hand. "Our good gnome is not only an accomplished cook, as you just found out; he is also a novice in the Order of the Earth. He can help with minor wounds, bindings, herbal treatments, and salves. If I am otherwise engaged, seek his help. He is quite knowledgeable and will be a great help to all.

"Motuk, would you start?"

The short, solidly-built man stood and acknowledged Sart with a low bow. "I am Motuk, fighter. I prefer a good axe, club, or mace, and have some skill with blades and bow as well. I have been on many a trek like this and ken dungeon fighting. If ye wish, I will be happy to give what guidance I may. Goblins, like gzks, are nasty creatures." Motuk spit in the direction of Stradryk.

Ge-or tensed immediately, wondering if the half-gzk would take offense. But Motuk grinned. "Stradryk and I have been in many a tight brawl together. He is quick in a fight, so if ye get in trouble, look to either of us for aid." He bowed toward the center of the circle, and added as an afterthought, "I have a wee bit of dwarf in me, if ye are curious. I'm comfortable down in the depths and have better than average vision in the dark. I'll take the lead in the dungeons, if that suits?" He looked at Sart. The cleric nodded back.

The reed-thin, tall, but wiry-muscled fighter stood next. "I'm Stevin, blade-fighter and scrapper. Most of my experience is in street brawls and the like. Me and me brother – that's Brand," he gestured at the massive figure sitting on his right, "we've also done a fair bit of goblin-bashing."

Brand stood pounding his fists together. He said forcefully, "Kill goblins; crush goblins." He sat down again, staring straight into the heart of the fire.

Stevin continued. "My brother's a bit different, but he can tear the devils apart with his bare hands. I... well, our family and many friends were killed by a horde of goblins on our way to settle in the west some years ago. We have something of a grudge against them, you might say. We're both good in a close fight. Be aware that you won't get much out of Brand as far as talkin'. He's kind of singular-focused, if you know what I mean. He ain't slow. It's just since our parents were killed, he doesn't seem to care about much except killing goblins." He slapped his brother on the back as he sat back down.

"Kill goblins!"

"Yes, we're going to kill goblins, Brand. Lots of goblins."

Stradryk looked at Ge-or and raised his eyebrows. Stradryk didn't say anything; however, he obviously didn't feel comfortable having these two on the trek.

Sart, if he saw Stradryk's expression, did not react. He looked toward the young magic-users. The lad stood first. "I'm Ardan, recently of Borea, where I received my training with my sister, Katelyn, at the palace." He nodded toward the young lady sitting next to him. "I wish I could say I was a powerful Wizard, capable of great feats of magical prowess; the truth is, my skill is in the manipulation of objects. To a degree I can move objects and also assist with a variety of tasks that may require force. Though not a thief, I can also use magic to open locks, chests, doors, and other obstacles. This is our first trek under the auspices of the kingdom. We will appreciate any assistance and protection you might afford us." He bowed, taking his sister's hand to help her stand.

"I am Katelyn," the young, brown-haired maiden said. "I am an illusionist by training, which means I can create a wide-variety of imaginary, quite realistic images." She gestured dramatically to her fore. An instant later, a very real looking unicorn danced across the fire and leapt over Stevin's head. He ducked and then laughed as the image faded into the early evening mist. "I hope that I will be of service to this quest as well." She also bowed to the group and sat.

Ge-or noted that she was lithe and slim, as well as quite fair. Her eyes played about the group while she spoke. He could have sworn that she winked at him; still, the

148

twilight and dancing flames made it difficult for him to tell for sure. Since she was only an arm's length to his left, he didn't know if she was even looking at him.

"Ge-or?" Sart said, gesturing to him when Ge-or didn't rise.

"Ah, sorry." Ge-or stood, blushing slightly, though no-one could tell in the light. "I am Ge-or, recently of Thiele. This is my first dungeon adventure, yet I have had some experience fighting gzks, goblins, and recently Qa-ryks. I have fair training in all weapons. I am at your service and look forward to learning from all of you." He began to sit.

"Hold, Ge-or, stay standing," Sart directed. "Our young half-elf is too modest. He was trained by his father, Manfred of Borea, recently of Thiele, the renowned fighter."

Several of the group sitting around the fire drew in their breath. Stradryk looked up with renewed interest at his friend. Manfred of Borea was an almost universally known name throughout the north kingdom and beyond.

Sart continued, "If you wish to know about weapons, I would be willing to bet that Ge-or could teach us all, even an old mace wielder like me." Sart gestured for Ge-or to sit.

Stradryk stood next and bowed low toward Ge-or. "I am honored to be in this company." He grinned. "I am a scrapper, too," he looked toward Stevin, "and a scrabbler in a fight, quick on my feet and with my hands. I can serve as scout and also take the lead in the dungeons with Motuk. Half-gzk is my heritage, not half-goblin. I have gotten used to being in holes in the ground after many such adventures." He started to sit, but rose again. "I suppose of some interest is that I seem to have a nose for treasure. Hah!"

Sart stood again. "Hah, is right. Stradryk does appear to be able to ferret out much that others might miss.

"So, we are a good, well-balanced group. I believe we will do well together. Use your strengths; get help when needed from any and all. Keep in mind that our primary mission is for me to gather information, scrolls, books, and other items that are relevant to my studies. I will not otherwise take a share of any treasure. All of you will share equally, including our cook, regardless of who finds what. You are welcome to anything we find that is of value.

"We will ride easily to the west and south for the next two weeks. I want to arrive in good shape and ready for adventure. Get to know each other, help out around camp, that is all I ask for now. The Gods rest ye well."

Stradryk nudged Ge-or as they were setting out their sleeping rolls, "Manfred?"

Ge-or shrugged, as if to say, "it is nothing; not important to discuss."

As Sart had suggested, they kept an easy pace, free to intermingle and get to know each other as they rode. Ge-or found Ardan to be quite loquacious, rambling on about all things Borean and modern. His sister was more subdued, gracious and graceful to all when she did join in their chatter.

Ge-or saw her as an extremely attractive maiden, innocent and charming, yet there was something more under the surface. He wasn't sure what it was. He found himself feeling protective toward her. Still, he had no reason to suspect that any of the others thought of her as other than one of the party.

The big fellow, Brand, was quiet. He always seemed to have his attention locked on something. Sometimes he would be entranced by what they were talking about; just as often, he might be humming to himself or watching a butterfly flit about amongst the spring flowers by the side of the trail. They included him in all their conversations and doings, assigning him tasks about camp, which he always diligently accomplished. Before long, though he rarely spoke or engaged anyone, he was simply one of the group. His brother was a bit more talkative, yet still reserved, preferring to listen to everyone else tell their tales.

Motuk turned out to be quite the storyteller. They all enjoyed his yarns about other adventures, the good old days, or his extended family – mostly the dwarfish side. As dwarves and gnomes were closely allied, Tyron would needle him about this or that point regarding lineages. The two obviously had worked together before and enjoyed baiting each other on points of "family history."

Stradryk spent most of the days scouting ahead of the column, so he didn't interact with the group much. The usually talkative half-gzk was strangely silent when he was back with the main group. He only grunted when Ge-or asked him what was bothering him.

Finally, late one afternoon, Ge-or corralled Sart. The two went ahead of the main party on the pretense of finding a possible camping site. When they finally caught up to Stradryk, they drew him off the trail into a grove of trees to talk.

Once they were unhorsed, Sart went right to the point. "Stradryk, there is something troubling you; we have both noted on it. It is best to get it out now, before there is more trouble to deal with."

The half-gzk grimaced. "I am uncomfortable with having Brand on this quest. He is not right… mayhap here." He pointed to his head.

Ge-or waited to see what Sart would say. He had believed it strange that Sart would have hired the two brothers. They looked to be capable fighters, yet something did not feel quite right about having a man who was so different, who appeared not completely right in the head, along on a potentially dangerous quest. He had figured Sart's judgment was better than his on such matters, so he had left it alone.

"I ken what troubles you, Stradryk," Sart said. "I felt the same when they came forward. Stevin told me their tale, and it is a sad and difficult situation he finds himself in. It seems Brand has a singular focus and has had it since their parents were killed by goblins. They had been planning on settling in the west, but made the mistake of camping in an old goblin-infested ruin on a rainy night. The goblins poured up from below when the moon went down. Caught off guard, two-thirds of their party was wiped out, and the rest barely managed to escape by fighting their way to the east. Stevin said Brand's size and power was one of the reasons the survivors got away. He stood in the center of the narrow entrance to the ruins, keeping the horde at bay long enough for the others to escape.

"Since then, he has been… how should I put this? …fixated on killing goblins. Every year in the late spring, about the time they had their misadventure, he starts getting anxious and insists that Stevin take him to where he can kill goblins. He cannot be dissuaded and would go wandering west on his own if his brother didn't promise to find a trek.

"When they first approached me, I said 'No,' yet after telling me his story..."

Sart shrugged. "He begged me to take them on."

"Cannot this illness, this fixation, as you called it, be cured?" Ge-or asked.

"Not through any means I am aware of. Illness of the mind is one thing we clerics have yet to understand or be able to heal. Unfortunately, these types of illnesses are not uncommon." He turned toward Stradryk. "Stradryk, I am still not altogether comfortable with this either, but I have spoken at length with both Stevin and his brother. It is how he spoke the other day – Brand kens much. He can answer most questions and will respond if you ask him things directly – usually only with nods or shakes of the head. He certainly understands what is happening, what our purpose is, and so on. As you have seen, he does what he is asked and contributes where he may. He is no slouch. He has a singular mental focus."

"How will he be if we encounter Qa-ryks or other beasts or fiends? Will he help or hinder?" Stradryk asked.

"Stevin says he will do what he is told. He is monstrously strong, and he fights with his bare hands. His brother says he can even crush plate armor between them. I am sorry, Stradryk. I considered this for a while before giving in and taking them on. I know this troubles you more than others and with good reason.

"I do hope I have made the right decision. The only part that assuages me a little is that Stevin assures me that Brand would find a way westward to goblin lairs with or without a party to join. Perhaps we are as good a choice as any."

Stradryk shrugged; he stood from his crouch. "I will try to engage him. Perhaps over time it will make a difference if he thinks on other things. Thank you for explaining. I apologize for being out-of-sorts."

"It is always best to talk through things when they do not seem right," Sart said, clapping Stradryk on the shoulder. "Your concerns are appropriate. Let us all pay more attention to Brand in the days ahead. Perhaps, as you have said, it will help draw him out more. I wish no ill to befall any of us."

It took most of them several days to get acclimated to so much time in the saddle. Only Stradryk, who did not ride, was not saddle sore. Ge-or, who had never spent days on end a-horse, found out that he had muscles that he rarely used and soft spots on parts of his anatomy that were now covered with sores.

Sart, noticing their discomfort, gave each small jars of salve to use. It helped.

On the eve of their fourth day out from Aelfric, as Ge-or was setting out his bedroll on a soft piece of earth and moss some distance from the dying campfire, he was surprised to see Katelyn emerge from the darkness. She was coming toward him with her bedroll in her arms.

"Ge-or?" She said, smiling up at him. She stood barely to his shoulder, and her expression appeared guileless with the moonlight shining over her right side.

"Milady?"

"I would like to be your companion for the trek. Are you willing?"

Ge-or looked at her agape, completely floored by what she had asked him. He blinked thrice, shut his mouth, and opened it again.

Katelyn reddened. "It is a simple question, half-elf. A gentleman would give a lady an answer."

"Ah... I am sorry, milady, ah Katelyn. You have surprised me, and I am at a loss – both as to what is acceptable, appropriate, and, well... I must apologize, for this is my first quest."

"Yes, I know. Let me try another approach. Do you find me attractive?"

"You are beautiful, milady," Ge-or murmured.

"Are you married or committed in some way to another?"

Ge-or thought for a minute about his recent conversation with Sart; he shook his head, "No."

"Well?"

Ge-or glanced over past the fire toward where Ardan was already abed.

"Don't mind my brother. He doesn't approve, but I am old enough to make my own choices. May I join you this night?" Her voice had begun to take on an edge to it. She was obviously starting to feel more uncomfortable by the minute.

Ge-or gestured at the ground next to his bedroll. He was still in shock at her boldness; however, after so many weeks away from Leona, he was already partly aroused by Katelyn's sweet scent. As she moved yet closer to him, a small groan escaped his lips. She took his rough hand in hers, then suggested, with a gesture of her chin, for them to move even further away. He followed.

He had a very pleasing night, with little sleep. His head was still spinning in the morning when Katelyn got up, gathered her things, kissed him on his forehead, and left for a nearby mountain pond. She said over her shoulder as she departed, "At least you are experienced. I was worried that I would have to teach you everything." She swung her hips seductively and went around the brush at the edge of the stream that fed the mere.

Following his first night with Katelyn, Ge-or asked Stradryk whether his behavior, his trysting with Katelyn, was appropriate on a quest. The half-gzk laughed, punching Ge-or in the shoulder. "Woman or man, we each do what is in our best interest as long as it does not interfere with the mission or the safety of others." He added. "Enjoy yourself, my friend. Sometimes, on longer treks, it is wise to hook up with a partner before signing on. Each to his own."

Though he continued to wonder in the days ahead, Ge-or was pleased with the arrangement with the young illusionist. Yet he was also a bit uncomfortable when he considered Leona. He had made no promises to her that he would remain true. Eventually he understood that this new relationship with Katelyn was as much a part of his desire for freedom as was his deep-rooted need to explore the world without constraints.

Unfortunately, Ge-or realized much faster that Katelyn's brother was not of the same mind. He was obviously quite uncomfortable with his sister's choices. After that first night, Ardan stayed far from Ge-or and would ride to the rear whenever his sister and Ge-or rode close together. This made Ge-or more uncomfortable than his concerns about Leona.

On the seventh day out from Aelfric, as they were starting to climb along a well-worn path into the foothills of the southern mountains, Sart told them they would spend the next day resting in the comfortable grove that Stradryk had found for them to camp in. "We should loosen up, spar a bit, take care of the animals, and let them rest.

Elsewise, we will prepare for the week ahead. We will be climbing steadily most of the time from now on, and more often than not we will have to lead the animals through narrow, winding pathways. We should redistribute provisions and gear accordingly.

"Ge-or has agreed to lead weapons practice tomorrow. Do not be afraid to ask him whatever you need to know. I urge all of you to set a time with him. He has much he can teach us all."

Ge-or was up early to practice the standard forms alone. It felt good to swing his sword. Throughout the day he sparred with those who sought him out: Stradryk, Tyron, and Stevin with swords; Motuk with hammer, axe, and club; Sart with his mace. On a suggestion from Stevin, he spent a vigorous half hour wrestling with Brand, who laughed the whole while he grappled with the faster, but not stronger, half-elf.

He even gave pointers to an unwilling Ardan on knife-work. Following the less than satisfactory half hour with Ardan, Ge-or drew him aside. "I know you are upset with me. I would know how we can put this aside. I did not encourage your sister; I promise you that, though I do enjoy her company now. Is there anything I can say to you?"

"Nay, Ge-or," Ardan flushed, "it is me. I am over-protective. I know she has a mind of her own, and that her wish is to be open and free. Still, it is difficult for me to accept this side of her."

"Aye, she does have a mind of her own. I was shocked when she came up to me. I am not used to such... such brazenness in women, and she..."

"...looks so young and innocent. Yes, I know," Ardan said, a smile crossing his lips. "It is probably one reason it is hard for me to accept this side of her."

"Can we be friends?"

"Aye. I am a fool. Forgive me my moodiness. Just be kind to her, and if you will, keep as far away from me at night as is feasible."

"It is done." Ge-or reached out and clasped Ardan's arm. "Back to Back."

"Aye."

153

Destination

On the fifteenth day out from Aelfric, as they spiraled further up the easternmost peak of the Beze Range, they got their first glimpse of the old mage's mountain fortress. The place was in better shape than Sart had expected. One of the three towers remained relatively intact, and though there was crumbling of masonry all along the outer wall, the place had obviously held up well despite a hundred years lying empty of "constructive habitation," as Sart put it.

It was dusk by the time they neared the last of the twisting paths that led to the main gate, so Sart called a halt. They settled in for the night almost under the rampart walls. The mage, Randaul the Recluse, had spent much of his life holed up in this minor fortress. Theoretically, according to Sart, he was studying ancient scrolls and tomes, trying to find the key to understanding "the Heart of the World."

At their campfire that night, Sart related what little he knew about the great diamond. "It was reputedly a large, perfectly clear diamond that was dug from deep within the earth by the dwarves. This was during the first age of the Borean world, when elves, dragons, dwarves, and gnomes held sway, and the race of man was beginning to spread across the land. The gem was supposedly wondrous to behold. While the dwarves and gnomes occasionally put it on display for everyone to see, for the most part it was kept secreted away. Those who saw it and were allowed to handle it, came away changed. It was admired by all and coveted by many.

"When the elven mage, Mangor, absconded with "The Heart" and later split it in twain, much changed in Borea. The riving marked the end of the first age of the Borean world -- the beginning of the decline of the elves. The two separated halves – one that radiated good, the other evil – created an imbalance to the world. Rifts grew between the elves, dwarves, gnomes, dragons, and the other inhabitants of the earth. Open war resulted, and all the races were diminished, except men.

"It was also at the splitting of the Heart that the bowels of the earth opened, and many of the evils that the Kingdom of Borea has long striven against came up from the depths in great numbers – ogres, trolls, goblins, and their kind, as well as other horrors. After many centuries of strife against these and worse, the races came together again for a brief time to defeat Mangor and his evil minions. Thus was formed the first and last alliance – that of the elves, dwarves, gnomes, *and* men." Sart's eyes lowered during the telling. A weight appeared to come upon him that was difficult for him to support. His shoulders drooped.

He continued, tiredly. "I ken not why, but the two halves of the Heart of the World were never brought back together and were eventually moved far apart. Since then, unfortunately, most of the lore of both the halves seems to have been lost to us. Following Mangor's defeat, the races drifted apart once more; and men began to hold sway in Borea. Thus began the second age of our world.

"Though Mangor was no more, the horrors from the depths remained as a scourge, to remind all that the world is not whole." Sart raised his head, and they saw a bit of the old twinkle in his eye. "Those like Randaul and myself have sought, and ever seek, information about the two stones that made up the Heart of the World."

"It is the reason I have come here – to see what Randaul may have discovered. Perhaps, if we are lucky, we may find evidence within the Recluse's library of what became of the two halves. I also hope to learn more about their influence. Evil presses ever eastward. The more we can understand what we are fighting, and anything we can find to use on our side of the effort, the better."

"Do you think the pieces of the Heart of the World might be here?" asked Stevin.

"Nay, to all the information I have, they have long been lost to the world. There are many stories: thrown in the ocean's depths; buried separately deep within the earth; destroyed by dragon fire, though I believe it to be impossible for the Heart to be destroyed; and so on."

"You said, 'When Mangor was destroyed with the first and last alliance.' What did you mean by that?" Ge-or asked.

"Both refer to the war with Mangor. The first alliance is when men fought with the other races of the Borean world against his evil reign. The last alliance describes the same time – when the elves, dwarves, gnomes, and dragons fought together for the last time. After Mangor was destroyed, the races drifted yet further apart and began to fight amongst themselves. This eventually led to the dragon wars. Randaul believed that the division of the Heart of the World was to blame."

"What would happen if the two halves were discovered again?" Katelyn asked.

"Hah! That is indeed a question for the ages," Sart snorted. "There are many ideas and concerns about that eventuality. Separated, the stones are said to represent the greatest evil and the greatest good. We do not know whether reuniting them, should it be possible, would heal the rift in our world or not. Some of the wise speculate that the damage is irreversible, and we will always have blatant evil in the world forever. Others believe that the two stones, if placed together, would merge. Then, over time, true evil would no longer be part of this world; though the potential for evil or good would still be in all of us, as it was before the gem was split.

"The truth is we do not know. It is a moot point anyway, since we do not know the whereabouts of either of the stones. Nor, from what I gather, did Randaul, though he likely knew much more than he let on to the Borean council. His studies seem to have focused more on the influence of the two stones deep in the past – good and evil, evil and good.

"We do know that Kan, a powerful elven mage, stole the dark half some hundred or more years ago. From what I have learned, he was the last to have the evil piece. By all accounts, he wielded great malevolent power. Well, that is, until he was destroyed by his own creations, the Qa-ryks, or so it has been suggested. Since he was destroyed from within, the dark stone has been lost, too.

"Some of the wise, including myself, my young illusionist," Sart smiled grimly at her, "believe that the evil forces coming from the west may be influenced in some way by this dread artifact. We do not know if the dark half of the Heart of the World has been put into play or not. It was only recently that Kan's former fortress was found, and his altar of dark power destroyed. The depths of that evil bastion have yet to be explored. It is a task that I may face in the years to come. I have hopes that Randaul may have information that will help direct my further efforts. I do not like going into deep, dark holes without as much knowledge as I can glean as to my purpose."

"Of the 'good' stone, the other half, virtually nothing is known. Some supposed the elves to have had it last. Some speculate that they still have it, though it is unlikely, because one would suppose that they would have used it to counteract Kan's treachery. There are no records of it that I can find in the kingdom's libraries. It seems lost to all memory. We do not even know its properties. For example, does it emanate goodness as the dark stone reputably radiates evil?

"With the elves isolating themselves in Moulanes, much lore has been lost to us. And over years of strife amongst men, the annals of Borea have also been misplaced, buried in dark vaults, or never scribed in the first place."

"Why didn't the elves try to merge the two stones after the defeat of Mangor? Why did they keep them apart?" Katelyn asked.

"I cannot answer that either," Sart said. "Kan's treachery created a rift between the high elves and rest of the Borean Kingdom. What happened before that is lost to us. Their further seclusion since has left many questions unanswered. We do not have access to their lore or their memories. I have tried to gain entrance to their stronghold, but their doors are shut. Few, except the pure-bred, have been allowed into Moulanes in the past century.

"Though not much time has passed since Kan's power collapsed from within – only a hundred years of this era – unfortunately, during that time of strife, much information has been lost.

"The first Qa-ryk invasion, which over-ran the western settlements and Beze range, kept the kingdom focused on other things. Now, with the renewed expansion of the beasts, driven by dark druids and some evil force they wield...Well, let us say that history and lore are of interest only to the wise. The power of the throne focuses most of its efforts on self-preservation. If we are to eventually answer such questions, it will be through the effort of others like me, who work tirelessly behind the scenes. I am but an acolyte of the wise and their quest for knowledge.

"Well," Sart straightened from his slouched seat on the log, "enough of speculation. Tomorrow we will start exploring. Rest well. I plan a month here; there is much ground to cover. The Recluse's dungeons were reputedly dug deep -- deep enough to hide his secrets."

That night Ge-or and Katelyn settled down behind a boulder discreetly away from the main camp. They snuggled for a long time before making love. Afterward, he stayed awake, enjoying her aliveness and her warmth.

He felt very tender toward her. She was an experienced lover, and he was an avid pupil. Yet, there was something else – something perhaps about the power she wielded that made their love-making especially intense and quite different from the silent strength of Leona.

At this point on the trek, Ge-or did not feel guilty about these "companion trysts" with the illusionist. At first, he had felt that he was cheating on Leona. He guessed that she would be upset that he had found another to love, albeit it was mostly a physical attraction with Katelyn. Yet, he had reinforced his own truth – he was an adventurer at heart. He needed to be free of the constraints of deep emotional attachments. What he and Katelyn were sharing felt perfectly natural to him. She was just what he needed to keep the nightmarish recent past at bay. Their love-making kept him from focusing on the horrors of the recent past before he fell asleep. This eve he drifted off with both women in his thoughts and in his heart.

156

Randaul's Keep

The party moved cautiously into the old citadel early the next morning. The place was overgrown with scrubs, mosses, and lichens; but overall it was in remarkably good shape. Being on the leeward side of the mountains and virtually atop the Great Desert, the elements had not done as much damage as one might suppose. Two of the three towers had partially collapsed, and the wooden and slate roofs of most of the outer rooms had caved in. Many of the walls, however, were still intact.

As they moved slowly up through the open gate, Sart explained that Randaul had been protective of his immediate environs, using whatever means at his disposal to ensure his work was undisturbed. Except for a small staff of servants and mercenaries, others were kept out. Sart speculated that the place might still have some of its magical wards, which would have discouraged most random exploration. He cautioned them that even now older magical shielding could still be active, if no creature had stumbled into it and set it off.

The castle itself was not large. They divided into two groups, one led by Sart and the other by Tyron. Each moved carefully through the ground level rooms, discovering nothing except mold, rot, and rust.

Next, they directed their attention to the towers. These had been built so Randaul's men could watch afar to see if any dared approach. The north tower, the one that was still relatively intact, had contained one of his studies. This is where Sart intended to start his search, though he felt that the most important scrolls and tomes in the mage's library would lie deep within the dungeons. It had been long rumored that Randaul had delved far deeper under the mountain than he had built above it.

Sart gathered them in the large central entry chamber to plan their further exploration. "Remain alert for anything. There is only a small chance that we will encounter any really dangerous creatures within the upper citadel; still, I don't want anyone to take unnecessary risks. Be especially cautious of traps, closed doors, and anything that could be hazardous. Call for Ardan if there are any concerns. He can disarm most mechanisms, as well as remove magical traps and warding incantations.

"As long as we are in the upper levels, in order to cover more ground, we will break into three groups. Motuk and I will take the north tower, which was Randaul's main study; Katelyn, Ge-or, and Stradryk, take the southern tower; and Ardan, Stevin, and Brand, the east tower. While we search these, Tyron will see that our animals are fed and stabled in the courtyard. After that, he will endeavor to bring the kitchen back to life. Find what ye may; do be cautious of loose stonework. Gather any tomes or scrolls; or if you find a large stash of such documents, mark it on your map, and I will search through it later.

"Call if you have any trouble. The place is small enough that we all should be within shouting distance. Let your mages lead, as they both have experience detecting residual magic that could indicate a trap or ward. We will all gather back here before dark." Sart gestured about him, indicating the great central room that had served for whatever few gatherings the Recluse had ever had. "We will eat and spend our nights in here unless we find better accommodations during our explorations. Bring your gear in and store it in there…" Sart gestured toward a large open doorway that led to an anteroom that had no other entrance.

"Katelyn, if you will," Sart looked toward the illusionist, "when all is placed within, throw an illusion that shows the entrance to be a solid wall."

"I will, but be careful," she said. Smiling somewhat wickedly, Ge-or thought. "Once I set the spell, I will cast it to last while we are here. Make sure you remember where the entrance is, else you may bonk your head on another wall. You can walk through the illusion unhindered, and it will remain as I have placed it."

"Good, let's get started," Sart directed.

A half-hour later saw the three groups scrabbling over rubble toward their respective towers. Sart and Motuk had an easy passage into the lowest level of their tower, as little rubble had fallen. Soon they were climbing steadily upward on the spiral stonework steps. The towers were like needles growing up out of the ground. Except for platforms with viewing slots, some stone benches, and rotted wood, there was little to explore. When they had climbed almost a hundred feet without discovering anything of interest, they came to an empty platform was divided in half by a solid wall. A mostly rotted door lay on the floor, leaving an opening through the masonry to the other side.

Sart moved cautiously into the opening, gesturing for Motuk to hold back. Sensing no charms, he continued into the half-circular room. From what he could see, there had been an old pulley system here that ran through the ceiling upward so that Randaul could call for things to be delivered when he wished. Anything in the room that had been of any value looked to have long rotted away. Where part of the tower had collapsed, they could see out to the east and the citadel below.

Sart gestured for Motuk to enter. The two of them poked about amongst the rotted clutter to see if anything of interest had survived. They eventually discovered several crevices in the wall that had been hidden behind rotted material of some sort. These proved to be empty, and neither could find any devices that suggested secret hiding places.

Meanwhile, Katelyn led her group to the south, where they discovered the tower entrance had been almost completely blocked by rubble. Stradryk and Ge-or set to work clearing a space big enough they could easily pass through, while the illusionist scanned the immediate area for magical wards.

Likewise, Ardan's group came across a massive pile of crumbled stonework before the entrance to the eastern tower. Deciding that physical labor would take far too long, the young mage created a shimmering square of energy in front of him. As he sent the wall of force into the large pile, it drove the top layer off and to the side. Doing the same "trick" several times resulted in the doorway being clear of debris, except for some residual stone piled inside the opening. Brand and Stevin quickly tossed what remained aside.

As they climbed, Ardan's party discovered that the eastern tower, which over-looked the castle entrance, had been constructed for defense. They came upon regular platforms every twenty steps up. Each was set with archery slots overlooking the ramparts. There also appeared to have been other mechanisms, now rotted and rusted into unidentifiable lumps of decay, which they assumed had been designed for warding off an assault.

Having climbed to the apex of their tower, Ardan cautiously entered what appeared to have once been a large circular watchtower. Unfortunately, fully two-thirds of the structure had crumbled below. The remaining floor space was strong enough to stand on, but they could see without further exploration that there was nothing of value in the empty room.

Ardan turned to the others, "Nothing. Nor have I sensed any magical wards. We should head back down, rechecking all as we go; this appears to have been a defensive tower and nothing more. Stevin, lead the way, please be cautious. As we saw coming up, the stonework is questionable at best. Brand, follow your brother closely. I will sweep each area with a light magical aura as I come behind. If we have passed anything unnoticed, I should be able to detect it."

Sart and Motuk arrived at the large upper room of the mage's tower at about the same time that Ardan's party had turned about to head down. They had to maneuver through a hole in the floor via a steep stone stairway leading to where a trapdoor had once been set. Climbing carefully up and into the room, he and Motuk did a visual sweep of all they could see. The chamber was connected via a short passageway to the mountainside due west of their position. Sart stepped into the tunnel, sweeping the area with his power as he went toward the broad side of the mountain ahead. Motuk followed close behind, his double-bladed axe now in hand.

Katelyn's group, having finally cleared enough of the rubble, started upward. Throughout their climb they kept encountering more debris, pausing frequently to push or lift larger stones aside. They, too, found little of interest until they came to the hundred-foot level. Here a large platform had been formed with the tower fixed to the mountain behind.

Ge-or took a small torch from his backpack and knelt to light the reed and pitch bundle with his flint. However, before he could dig the stone from his backpack, Katelyn stepped forward, and with a flick of her finger set it on fire. Impressed, Ge-or grinned at her. He had little experience with magic. The illusions she had created – the unicorn by the fire, and the wall to hide the belongings – had amazed him. In all their training, his father had rarely spoken of powers other than those physical. He was wary of anything beyond what he could understand and manipulate.

Katelyn smiled back, gesturing toward Stradryk. Turning, Ge-or could see that his friend also had a torch in hand. He set it ablaze with his. Passing her hand over the doorway, Katelyn checked it for an aura. Not sensing any magic present, she gestured for Ge-or to lead the way.

On their way back down, Ardan, Stevin, and Brand stopped at a large defensive platform. The mage, wanting to check the area more thoroughly, asked the others to stand back. He passed his hands over the walls searching for magical signatures.

Sensing something almost immediately on the far western wall, Ardan paused twice at the same spot. Moving closer to the wall, he noticed a one-foot-wide block of granite that did not appear to match the other stones in age and carving. After further study, he reached out, and pushed slightly on the center of the block. A mechanism released, and the partial block pushed outward and flipped open and down on a set of brass hinges. Inside the cavity, Ardan saw an ornate dagger lying on a partially decomposed, dark-red, velvet cloth.

Unfortunately, Stevin had a clear view of the block as it opened. Upon seeing the dagger, he rushed forward. Excited at the prospect of treasure, he elbowed Ardan aside and reached into the cavity for the dagger's handle.

"Don't..." Ardan shouted... There was a bright flash, followed by a shriek from Stevin as the blade fell to the stone at their feet.

"Agggghhh, I'm burnt."

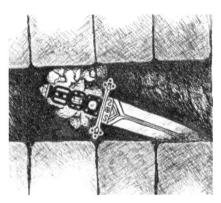

"You bloody fool!" Ardan grabbed Stevin by the shoulders and drew him back. "Sart warned us... By-the-gods, man, that's bad."

The gangly man's hand was burnt, blistering and reddened by the blast. He was writhing in agony now, trying to twist out of Ardan's grasp.

"Brand! Brand? Call for Sart."

Stevin's brother was standing nearby, looking down at Stevin with a pained look on his face.

"Brand, yell for Sart. We need him," Ardan said again forcefully, trying to maintain some control of Stevin as he flailed about.

Suddenly, the big fellow's voice boomed out from the tower, echoing within the citadel and beyond. Ardan was surprised at the power of the giant man's voice. They had rarely heard Brand speak in any way except a soft-spoken manner.

"SART! SART! SART, SART, SAR..."

"That's good!" Ardan yelled. Giving up on trying to control Stevin's writhing, he released him. Stevin fell to the granite blocks, still screaming, clutching at his wrist as if to strangle the pain from his hand.

"Coming!" They heard Motuk's voice echo across the courtyard.

"Brand, can you carry your brother down the stairs?"

Brand shrugged, and, despite Stevin's protests, he slung his brother over his shoulder and started stoically marching down the spiral steps.

Sart and Motuk had entered a doorway leading into the side of the mountain when they heard Brand's call. They could see that the room beyond, though narrow and long, encompassed four separate doorways along the mountainside. The study was filled with scrolls, manuscripts, tomes, and smaller bound volumes, still resting on

160

heavy wooden shelves or on a massive oaken table that ran nearly the length of the room. Most of the materials appeared to be in decent condition, except that they were covered with a thick coat of dust. They did not have time to explore further. Sart immediately turned around when he heard the shout. He hastened back to the steps and down, followed closely by Motuk.

The chamber Ge-or had entered was narrow and long, with only a bit of rotted wood and other debris near the entrance. They followed it cautiously back, barely able to stay three abreast. After about fifty paces, it ended at a heavy oaken door, which was still intact and showed little sign of wear. Katelyn passed her hands over the surface but did not detect any sign of magic. It appeared to open inward, so she gestured to Ge-or. "Try it."

He placed his hand on the handle and pulled it down; it was frozen in place. There was no lock on the door, yet it would not budge for all his efforts. "Try your shoulder," Katelyn suggested.

Ge-or set himself, pressing into the door; then he heaved. It didn't budge. He stepped back and swung forward into the door with more force. There was a sudden release, and the door swung in reluctantly, grinding on its hinges.

"Oy, what's that smell?" Ge-or coughed, backing up quickly; he almost retched. A strong odor of decay effused from the interior out into the corridor. They all covered their noses, Katelyn taking out a lace kerchief from the pocket of her cape.

Stradryk, less bothered by the fumes, stepped forward with his torch. Poking it into the chamber beyond, he looked inside. He quickly withdrew, closing the door. He waved for them to follow him down the hallway toward the tower proper, explaining as they went. "It's a small armory. Not much to speak of from what I could see: studded clubs, rusted swords, bins of bolts and arrows, and the like."

"What's the smell coming from?" Ge-or asked, grimacing.

"They must have locked some poor fella in there. Long decayed bones, but the stench has been bottled up for a long time. Didn't see anything of interest. We could go back?" He looked inquiringly at Katelyn.

"Not now. Let's press further up. If Sart thinks it is of any interest we, or he, can return."

Five minutes later they had gone as far as they could upward. Though they were only about seventy feet above the ground, the walls of the tower above had collapsed inward, and the stairway was completely choked with rubble. From what they could tell by leaning out the nearest opening, not much of the tower remained above.

"Let's head back down and report to Sart. This appears to have been a guard tow…" The booming of Brand's voice cut Katelyn's sentence short. She immediately gestured for them to head downward.

They all met up at nearly the same time in the central great room. Stevin was in bad shape. His eyes were glazed in shock, his horribly burnt hand obviously causing him great pain. Sart dosed him with a strong painkiller from his bag, then carefully looked at the wound. He waved all the others to leave except for Brand. "Go, search the outbuildings along the walls. Let's make sure there are no surprises before we settle in for the night. I can help with this; but he will not be able to use it for at least a week, perhaps more. The damage is deep, and I will have to expend considerable energy in the healing. Give me an hour. "Brand?"

The big man looked expectantly at Sart.

"I need you to hold him very still. This will be painful, I'm afraid. Can you do that? Do you understand?"

The big fellow nodded. "I ken."

"Hold him like this…"

Tyron cooked them an elaborate dinner. Having the uses of a large oven and spit, he roasted the second half of a small boar that Ge-or had shot the previous day. He also dug out some of the better crocks of preserves for their first repast at the citadel. They ate on the large stone table and benches set at one end of the hall. There was little conversation. As in all adventures, injury and loss had swiftly driven home the hazardous nature of such treks. They had been lucky to this point not to have had any encounters with the dangerous beasts that thrived in this part of the world.

As dinner wound down and they were enjoying a touch of rum from their meager stores of libations, Sart updated them on Stevin's condition. "He will need to rest for several days. He can assist Tyron in making our camp here more comfortable, and in helping provide some additional protection for what we leave here while we further explore the immediate environs of the citadel. He said he can fight left-handed, but not as effectively as with his right. I think it better that he remains behind for now. After that, we will see how he fares. It was a nasty, deep burn. I have healed the major damage, though time is still the great healer.

"For this... I further caution you all. Call one of us," he gestured to Ardan and Katelyn to include them, "if magic is suspected, else we will have more accidents of this nature.

"Now, show me this dagger."

Ardan passed the ornate weapon to Sart.

The cleric turned it over slowly several times, studying the designs, stones, and workmanship. Finally, he straightened up from his perusal. He gave it to Ge-or to pass around to the others. "It is of fine quality – worth a bit, certainly, not a fortune, mostly for its gemstones and blade. It is also lightly magicked. My guess, without spending further energy to explore it, is that it has a minor spell set in one of the stones, likely the ruby. It can empower the wielder and might prove of some use against magical creatures or perhaps the more formidable undead, such as wraiths and ghosts. Ardan, why don't you keep it while we are here? It is safe to use. When we return to Aelfric, we should get a good price for it.

"Now, for the morrow," Sart raised his bushy eyebrows, "we will start early, so get some rest. I would like Motuk and Katelyn with me to explore the Wizard's study. The rest, go with Ardan. Stay close enough together to aid each other if trouble arises. Begin to explore the second level chambers and those that were built into the mountain behind. Go cautiously; there is no need for haste."

Worried on the Farm

Leona moaned and rocked back and forth in Aldred's chair. The pains were intermittent, but strong enough to warrant some concern. Her father had gotten a midwife to stop in several weeks before. The old lady had said all was well. She had assured them she would return about the time the baby was due and stay a few days to see her through the birth. This was too soon, much too soon. Leona was worried.

Aldred came back to the house at dinner time. He found his daughter lying abed groaning. He sat next to her and stroked her forehead. "It is alright, my child. These are likely false contractions. It was so with Cilia before you were ready to come. Overly protective man that I am, I flew out the door and after the midwife, only to be told that I was a bloody fool and to wait for them to pass."

Leona groaned as another spasm swept through her. As it subsided, she moved to get up.

"Nay, Daughter. I'll be fixing the victuals tonight. Perhaps some oatmeal and honey, and if you feel better, some eggs. Rest awhile. With Cilia, the pains lasted only a day or so, as I remember. She was right as rain when I got back from my visit to the midwife's.

Later that night the pains indeed slowly dissipated. Leona was "right as rain," except for the typical aches associated with carrying a babe that was a month or so from being born.

Delving Deep

For three days, Sart, Katelyn, and Ardan alternated shifts in the tower study, going through the vast array of scrolls and tomes piled everywhere. The others searched the rest of the upper citadel. There was little of value in the study: miscellaneous notes, copies of manuscripts that were readily available in Borea, and a few older historical volumes of good quality, which would bring a good price at the market. They did find some writings of Randaul that reflected on his long obsession with the Heart of the World, and a few leather-bound books that related parts of its known history. These Sart carefully wrapped in layers of cloth and finally in oilskin to preserve them from the elements. They warranted further study once he was back in Borea.

The others also found little of interest: a few pieces of ancient armor of decent quality that might draw a price at an auction of antiques; some ornately-wrought baubles of silver, ivory, and teak, not of great value; and many items of little worth that had somehow survived the hundred years of slow decay. Mostly they found dust, rot, rust, and piles of indeterminate "stuff" that had been eaten away by layers of mold and mildew. They took to wearing linen masks as they moved from room to room, stirring up clouds of dust.

On their last day above ground, they discovered a chamber hidden behind a heavy, decaying tapestry. Ardan disarmed the trap guarding the door; then Ge-or shouldered it inward, revealing an undisturbed, and fortuitously little-changed, wine cellar. Several hundred bottles were set neatly on wooden shelves, with layers of dust to indicate that they had been stored in this small cool room, untouched, for over a hundred years.

When Sart came down later that evening, he was surprised to find that the bottles and corks were in pristine condition. As he studied various labels, he knew they had indeed made a fortuitous find. "These are fine wines and vintages, my friends, from many years ago. If they are still drinkable, they could be worth a fair amount on the auction market in Borea. These we will not want to sell in Aelfric. We will get twice the amount in the capital. I imagine they will be coveted by the rich and famous.

"Come, let us sample a few bottles this eve to test a few out. I believe Tyron has prepared us a rich venison stew." His eyes twinkled as he selected several bottles and passed them out to Katelyn and Motuk. "We might as well enjoy them while we are here, for we will be able to transport only the best bottles with us on the mules and in the cart."

Indeed, all except one of the four bottles Sart had withdrawn from the collection proved to be in fine flavor. The other had turned to a fine vinegar, which Tyron said he could use in his cooking. From that day on, they enjoyed a bottle or two each eve with their dinner, carefully resealing the room after each entry, so as not further disturb the wines that remained.

Satisfied that all that was of any value had been gleaned from the citadel proper, Sart announced at dinner that they would prepare to go down into the cellars and dungeons of the palace the next day. During their explorations, they had discovered two stairways leading below: one at the east side of the Great Hall, and the other in a chamber near the edge of the west wall, toward the back of the citadel. He chose to explore the passage leading down from the Great Room first. The heavy oaken door

164

there had survived the intervening years.

The cleric knew they had been lucky so far. The citadel had been devoid of any malevolent creatures. Except for large rats, equally large spiders, and an occasional lost bird, they had not encountered anything alive during their search. He expected that would change once they started downward.

As they stood ready to un-spike the doors to go below, Sart cautioned them once again. "Stay alert at all times. Be sure you know exactly where your comrades are at any given moment. We rely on each other.

"I do not doubt we will encounter dark creatures below. Though they live and breed beneath the earth and rarely surface except at night, ogres and goblins have little love for digging if they have a choice. They often take over the depths of such places and make them their homes.

"Since this place was sparsely populated throughout Randaul's life, I do not expect to encounter the undead; yet it is possible we may cross paths with a lonely wraith, ghost, or shadow. If you see anything you expect is of this nature, call me. I can handle apparitions much more readily with my powers. Since they are often unaffected by non-magical weapons, you may not be able to harm them anyway. If you are cornered, use the holy water vials I have given you. It will burn them as fire burns our bodies. Most of the undead will draw back or even flee the area when attacked with blessed items."

Sart paused, noting they were all listening intently. Stevin's injury had served to heighten their sense of self-preservation. "Dungeon fighting is often close quarters. If a large force of goblins or the like should attack us, let the fighters to the fore and give them some room to work. Motuk, Ge-or, and Stradryk will alternate with me, Katelyn, and Ardan at point.

"Brand?" Sart turned toward the big man.

The big fellow was standing behind Ge-or. Towering over all, he was following Sart's every word and movement.

"Stay to the rear with Stevin, Brand; protect him unless we need you. Until your brother is whole, I would prefer you stay back behind the main group to watch over him."

Brand nodded, yet he did turn back. Ge-or could have sworn he saw disappointment cross the man's face. Stevin patted his brother on the back and whispered, "We'll get you some goblins, I promise."

Sart motioned ahead, "Go on, Ge-or."

Ge-or set his spike puller and began withdrawing the large nails that Stradryk had placed there days before as a precautionary measure. Minutes later, with torches in hand, the half-elf and Sart led the way into the depths.

The first cellar below the main citadel was smaller than they had expected. They were able to move quickly from one empty room to another. Whatever had been in these chambers had either been taken away or used up. Except for dust and a minimum of debris, the whole level of small adjoining rooms was empty.

Following a break to eat dried meats and fruits that Tyron had provided, they pressed ahead, down a wide stairway to the second level. Here they discovered another storage room. They were now deeper under the mountain, yet it was still dry. Most of the shelving and containers had been destroyed, and they found themselves shuffling through piles of detritus. After finding nothing of value, they met at the far side where they faced another wide staircase leading down.

Some fifty steps further into the depths brought them to a round flat area with two large doors ahead, separated by ten feet of wall. They could tell by the many scrapes and claw marks on the stone of the platform that the doors had been recently used. Here the dust of the ages had been disturbed.

Ge-or stepped back, brought his shortbow forward, and nocked an arrow. When the half-elf was set, Ardan addressed each of the doors with his power. Finding no magical wards or traps, the mage moved back and gestured for Motuk to open the right-hand door.

Pulling it toward him to the right, the stout warrior held his torch so its light would shine into the space beyond. The ten-foot radius illuminated by the torch was empty. They could see from where they stood that the other door led into the same wide space. Motuk went in, his torch in his left hand. The dwarf-man had a small buckler strapped to the wrist and his short sword was in his right. Ge-or eased behind him with his bow and an arrow still nocked, but with the string relaxed. The others followed him slowly, Katelyn carrying another torch. Ardan, the ornate dagger now in his left hand, paused while the others filed past.

The chamber they entered was massive and rough-hewn. The light from the party's three torches did not extend to the far reaches, so they only moved about a quarter of the way into the room and waited. Sart nodded to Ardan, "Light."

Ardan gestured with his right hand. Instantly, a sphere of white light appeared and grew from his right hand. It slowly expanded in size and intensity until it was about a foot in diameter. He flicked his wrist, releasing it so that it floated up toward the ceiling. As it moved slowly upward toward the far side of the chamber, they all began to distinguish forms at the other end of the room.

Fortunately, Stradryk had taken the time to open the other door behind them as an extra means of egress. At the far end of the room, they could see arrayed a mass of goblins, with two large mountain ogres to their fore. The creatures had obviously known someone was entering their domain; they were gathered to drive the intruders out. As they watched, more of the grey and black-mottled creatures, many clad in black leather armor, streamed from holes in the floor and side walls.

"Back!" Sart shouted. "Back to the doors. They are too many to fight in the open. Ge-or, Motuk, stay forward until we are behind."

Ge-or immediately understood the concept of fighting in a dungeon, In the doorways, he and Motuk could fend off the goblins for a long time. The two fighters would be able to inflict considerable damage to the beasts' ranks from such a defensive position. The goblins would not be able to come at them more than three or four at a time, so their ability to engage effectively would be limited.

As large as they were, the ogres would not have much room to use their strength either. Since the ceiling was low by the doors, he correctly reasoned that only one of the massive beasts would be able to engage them readily. Even then, it would be discomfited by the space. In addition, Katelyn, Ardan, and Sart could use their powers to thwart or confuse the huge beasts while standing behind the two fighters.

Though it took Brand a second to react, his mind seemed to focus on one detail – those were goblins in front of him: goblins hurt; goblins kill; goblins took his family from him. Instead of falling back with the others, the large man suddenly broke into a lumbering run. He charged into the center of the rocky chamber yelling in his booming voice, "Kill goblins. Kill goblins. Brand kill goblins."

At least three voices from the party yelled, "Brand, no!"

The goblins, seeing him running forward alone, rushed forward and quickly swarmed around and over his massive form, fangs bared and claws ripping.

His massive arms moving about amongst the press of grey bodies, Brand was literally pulling apart the goblins he could get a grip on. But there were far too many. From the start of the one-sided battle, they were inflicting serious wounds. Brand didn't seem to notice; he kept tearing at the creatures about him.

"Brand!" An anguished cry came from Stevin as he ran forward to go to his brother's rescue.

Ge-or reacted quickly. He released his arrow at one of the ogres spearing it in the neck. Dropping his bow, he ran forward shoving Stevin to the side as he went by. He yelled as he ran toward the beleaguered Brand. "Stradryk, your sword! Motuk, with me! Everyone else stay back." He caught Stradryk's short sword in his left hand, as the half-gzk tossed it to him. With his own blade now in his right, he swept directly into the mass of goblins at Brand's left. Motuk came into the fray on the large man's right, battle-axe now in hand.

Ge-or swept into the fight with the two swords slicing rhythmically in practiced deadly arcs. He cleaved through a dozen or more of the wiry creatures before they had time to react to the half-elven warrior in their midst. His skill with the two swords, working in parallel to each side, scattered hands, arms, heads, and other pieces of the goblins in a gory dark profusion about the floor, ceiling, and southern wall of the room.

On the right, Motuk charged almost as effectively into the creatures' flank with the two-handed battle axe swirling in great arcs about him.

The fierceness of their assault caused the attack on Brand to completely wither away, with the goblins scrabbling backward to avoid almost certain death from the two expert weapons-men. By this time, Brand had fallen to his knees, bleeding profusely from many wounds. Even so, he was still ripping limbs and flesh from the creatures he was able to grasp in his hands.

Hoping that they could keep the swarm of goblins at bay long enough to extract the big man, Sart gestured for Katelyn and Ardan to use their powers in whatever way they figured best to help stem the tide. Sart knew that Ge-or and Motuk's furious attack would only bring them a couple of seconds. He ran forward with Stradryk and Stevin to help extricate Brand from the battle.

As Stradryk came up, he dispatched the few goblins still clinging to Brand with his long knife. Sart managed to bash the heads of several others who were intent on coming into the fray regardless of the danger. Stevin grabbed his brother's arms from behind and tried to draw him back toward the doors. But Brand proved too heavy and too strong. He shook them off, yelling again, "Kill goblins. Brand kill goblins."

Meanwhile, Ge-or and Motuk pressed a few paces ahead to give the others some clearance from the goblins, though they risked being swarmed over. The wiry creatures were now reorganizing in the far reaches of the room for another attack. The ogres were also pushing forward, brushing goblins aside as they came at the two fighters.

Knowing that they could only stand against such a massed attack for a few more minutes at best, Ge-or shouted again. "Get him out now! We cannot hold much longer."

Seconds later the mass of goblins was upon the two fighters again. This time they did not swarm ahead haphazardly; they darted in and out trying to find openings between the slashing blades.

Katelyn, directly behind Ge-or, was preparing to cast an illusion, while Ardan on the other side had already created a wall of energy that covered about a thirty-foot space the goblins could not pass through. This energy wall gave Motuk enough of a window on that side of the chamber, so he could help Sart and Stevin with Brand. The big fellow continued to resist their dragging him from the fight. With the aid of the blood-slippery floor and his weakened condition, the three of them were able to slowly draw him back.

With his flashing blades, Ge-or managed to keep the goblins back; but one of the massive ogres, the broken arrow shaft sticking from its thick neck, pressed through the goblins. As he came up, the beast took a swipe at Ge-or with its huge club. It was at that instant that Katelyn finished her incantation. As Ge-or stepped sideways and back to avoid the blow from the club, a stone wall suddenly appeared across the entire room, crossing behind where the ogre stood face to face with the half-elf.

The ogre's first blow missed because Ge-or was quick enough to duck while he finished off a goblin that had dared to come within range. The second swing of the massive club he was only able to parry with Stradryk's sword. The fire-hardened wood slammed into the blade, breaking it in two. The force of the blow brought Ge-or almost to his knees.

Katelyn's illusion had worked well enough to keep the goblins at bay. Though there was a good bit of howling coming from behind the false wall, none of the slow-witted creatures beyond thought to see if it was real.

Free of any other attack now, Ge-or turned his full attention to the beast in front of him. Mountain ogres were thick-skinned, heavily muscled, and outweighed even the largest of men by two-fold. They were slow of mind and of foot, yet were fierce fighters who would give no quarter. Human and elven flesh were a delicacy to them. This one scented blood. Ge-or, however, had no intention of letting this beast survive now that he had the advantage. He parried one more blow with the half-blade in his left hand, then started carving at the ogre with the sword in his right.

His sword was not a magical or power-imbued weapon, but the quality steel blade was still ultra-sharp from Ge-or's regular tending of it with his whetstone. As skilled a swordsman as he was, it did the beast damage at each stroke. Ge-or's flurry of blows cut here and there about the ogre's head, shoulders and torso making shallow cuts in its tough flesh while he sought an opening that would allow him a killing thrust. That opportunity came when the ogre bellowed angrily, raising its club for a smashing blow. Ge-or spun, ducked, and thrust upward under the falling club. His blade bit deep into the beast's throat. A flood of blackish blood erupted as he pulled back. Following up the thrust, he swung again, in an arc that clove half-way through the beast's neck. The ogre fell to its knees, before collapsing heavily to the stonework pavement. Ge-or turned, swept the room with his eyes, and being currently free from the goblins, he loped back to help the others who were with the stricken Brand.

Ge-or was only halfway back, when goblins began erupting through the illusion. The creatures could climb almost any surface, and once they had determined that the wall did not reach to the ceiling, they decided to scamper over it. Of course, the minute they touched it, the goblins fell through the illusion. It took the rest little time to understand and follow.

Sart knelt to check Brand's pulse as Ge-or, Motuk and Stradryk fanned out to meet the goblins that were now past the illusionary wall and reorganizing for another attack. Stradryk had taken a wicked-looking mace out to replace the blade he had tossed to Ge-or. The three of them braced for the assault as the goblins rushed forward.

Sart's voice boomed out above the chattering of the goblins. "Back! Back to the doors! Brand is gone. We must see to ourselves. Move, now!"

The three fighters eased slowly back to where Sart stood over Brand's bloody corpse. "Go! Get behind me through the doors and get ready to slam them shut. Tell Ardan to lock them quickly once I am through. I will take care of this." Sart waved his hand toward the horde of goblins as they rushed forward.

Uncomfortable with leaving the cleric alone, Ge-or picked up his bow and hung back in front of the doorway to see what developed. Meanwhile, Sart reached into the folds of his voluminous robes and retrieved a large vial of what looked like a greenish liquid in the light from the still brightly glowing white sphere above their heads. Backing himself closer to the doors, he raised the vial above his head. He took aim at a spot on the stone floor some five paces in front of the charging goblins. "Now," he yelled, throwing the vial hard at the floor. He turned about and ran straight into Ge-or, who did not have time to move out of the way. Sart hit him mid-chest; Ge-or fell sideways and back. Sart managed to keep his feet by twisting awkwardly to the other side. He righted himself and stumbled through the doorway. Ge-or hit the wall, spun up, and followed the cleric. Just before Stradryk and Ardan slammed the door shut, they saw a billowing cloud of yellowish-green smoke erupt from the floor where the vial had struck.

Sart gasped out, "Up, up. It is possible the poison may seep underneath the lintel. We must get away from here."

"What of my brother?" Stevin wailed.

"He will rest there until we return. None will be able to survive in that room for several days. Come, let us tend to our wounds and to our sorrows." Sart led them up and out of the dungeons. They all collapsed in the citadel great room. Ge-or didn't know if he had ever been so tired. From the looks of most of the others, they had spent themselves as well in the frenzy of the attack and defense.

The fight in the dungeon and death of their comrade sapped their will for several days. Ge-or, who for the first time in his life had put to use full range of the outstanding training he had received in weaponry from his father, was both exhilarated and sick from the experience. He had felt a power and intensity during the battle the like of which he had never experienced. The few skirmishes he had with gzks and others seemed as nothing compared to the all-out frenzy of this brawl. But the aftermath of the killing – the sense of having ended so much life – had him feeling nauseous and empty. He had experienced these feelings before with his father and brother, but this fight brought out how capable he was at killing.

Ge-or spent much of the first two days of their recovery out in the nearby woods, hiking and hunting, trying to deal with the swirl of thoughts and emotions that came flooding up. Toward the end of the second day, Stradryk joined him. Though they did not speak of it, Ge-or received the understanding and support he needed from the more experienced fighter's presence.

It was four days before Sart would let anyone approach the dungeon chamber where Brand's body lay. During that period, the cleric spoke to them, both individually and collectively, about their loss, the battle, and their feelings. Brand's death had hit all of them hard, especially considering the situation. Sart took the big man's loss personally, second-guessing his reasoning for including him and his brother on the trek.

Stevin, surprisingly, became the one person who finally brought them out of their self-castigation. On the second night following the battle below, he stood to address them after their somber dinner.

"He were my brother, and I will miss him greatly. Yet there was nothing I could do about his obsession and… I tried. I tried healings and herbs, brought him to clerics, and even paid for a spell or two to be cast on him. Please don't blame yourselves. I begged our good cleric to take us on. I did not see another choice, for Brand were a stubborn one. If there is fault here, it is with me. The real blame rests with the beasts that destroyed our family and friends." He stopped, blinking back tears.

After swiping at his tears with his sleeve, he continued hesitatingly. "Brand appreciated all of you and your kindness to him. It wasn't like him to put such into words, but I could see it in his eyes and manner. Too often on treks we have been on, he was treated as an outcast, and yet, each of you accepted him for who he was."

"It is the way of adventurers," Motuk whispered. "Or it should be."

"Aye, 'Back to Back,' and 'each to his own.' I ken the code… this was more. I believe he felt you treated him like a part of a family. I am in your debt for that. I also appreciate your efforts to save him from his own single-mindedness. I wish…" Stevin paused again, wiping tears from his eyes with a dirty rag this time.

"I know this may be hard to see; but I think he died as he might have wished, fighting the beasts that took so much from both of us." Stevin's voice finally trailed off. He sat down heavily on the stone bench, laid his head on his arms, and sobbed. Katelyn went over to comfort him.

Later, each in turn thanked him for what he had said with a hand to his shoulder or a pat on the back.

Sart brought them all back to focus the next morning. While he felt it was still too dangerous to head back to the dungeon where Brand's body lay, he had them all help with sorting through manuscripts and scrolls that they had brought down from Randaul's tower study. He was still trying to weed out what might prove useful, and it helped draw their focus away from the heaviness of their feelings.

On the fourth day after the dungeon battle, Sart led them below to recover Brand's body. The poison seemed to have fully dissipated; however, Sart insisted they take precautions. He had them all wear leather gloves soaked in oil that they discarded after bringing the body up and out.

While below, they saw that many goblins had perished from the poison. Their brethren, who would often eat their own kind, had known enough to leave them where they had fallen. Only one ogre was amongst the dead. Sart supposed the other had perhaps survived the toxic cloud's effects; yet if it had breathed in any of the poison, it would likely have weakened its lungs. They had no compulsion to do anything with the many bodies; time would take its due course.

Brand was buried in a cairn on a small hillock overlooking a beautiful mountain stream. Sart led a short ceremony in which they all said goodbye to their fallen comrade. After, they took another full day to mourn before they prepared to resume their search in the dungeons below the keep.

It was late that evening, after Sart had let them pass around an extra bottle of fine wine, that Stevin announced to the group that he would be heading back to Aelfric the next day. "I canna bear to fight such creatures again. It was one thing when Brand was so set on his revenge. But now the life of it is gone from me. I wish for nothing more except to settle down to work in a shop if I can find such a place. Mayhap someday I will own a wee grocery of me own. Our Dad having been a farmer, I guess food is in me blood, though I never took to turning the soil.

"I hope this does not put ye all out; I think I would do more harm than good if I stayed." He got red-faced and hemmed and hawed, then sat down with a definitive, "So be it."

The others began to protest, yet they could see Stevin's face was set. Sart waved his hand for quiet. "You are welcome to stay and assist Tyron and still share in what we find. You would not be required to go below. Would this suit?"

"Nay, good Father, I would be away. I'm set on it. I canna stay in this place more."

"Well, we shall fill your saddle bags with some of the finest wines so you can have your shop. If you would sell them in Aelfric, go to Harman the wine merchant on Arevekal Street. Tell him I said to give you a proper price. He knows I will roast his toes if he doesn't. You won't get as much as if you sold them at auction in Borea; yet he will be fair, and the sum should set you up nicely if you are careful with your money."

"Nay, Father, I have done nothing to earn... I..."

"You must," said Katelyn.

"Yes." "Certainly" "Please." The others chimed in.

Stevin reddened again. "Well, I am obliged. If it is my fate to keep a few bottles from Tyron's lips, so be it."

They all laughed, though there was little merriment in their hearts.

Stevin left the next morn at dawn, loaded down with ten bottles of the best from the cellar and a few of the trinkets they had found elsewhere. His hand had healed well enough now that he could hold his sword. Sart hoped that with his blessing and good weather Stevin would be able to make it back to Aelfric without incident. They last saw him kneeling at the rise of ground where Brand's cairn lay stark against the rising sun.

Moving on

Rather than have to deal with the many rotting corpses in the room where Brand had died, Sart decided that they would explore the other passageway that led below. They hoped they would be able to progress deeper down into the Recluse's dungeons from there. Ardan, who had nominated himself as mapmaker, suggested that it was more than likely that the two passageways would connect at some point. They should eventually be able to explore back up to the death room from below. If not, Sart would decide later whether to brave that way down again.

They soon discovered that the western stairwell led far down into the bowels of the earth, with only occasional short platforms to mark the way. They finally came to a larger flat area and a locked door. According to Ardan's count, they were over three hundred steps below the main castle level. Here the air was close and warm, not cool like they would have expected.

Sart cautioned them again that his poison, as devastating as it had been to the goblins in the large hall, had certainly not killed all the creatures in the dungeons below the citadel. He did hope that it had done their ranks serious damage, as he did not have any more vials of such a powerful alchemical concoction to use again. Arraying themselves in battle order facing the door, they felt they were prepared for almost anything.

The door swung inward at Ge-or's push. With torch in one hand and his sword in the other, he and Motuk moved into the widening space of a natural cavern. It was not a huge cave. In the torchlight reflecting off crystalline structures high above, they could see several additional caves stretching off in front of them in various directions. The effect of the multi-colored reflective surface, which covered virtually the entire ceiling and much of the walls, was breathtaking. Ge-or had never seen anything like it, though he and his brother had explored many a cave around the vicinity of their childhood home.

"Are they gems?" Motuk gasped, finally taking a breath.

"Nay, dwarf-kin; it is quartz, feldspar, and other lower quality gemstones; pretty, yet of no great value," Sart answered. "That is, unless we find large samples, as large as your hand or even bigger. Some artisans carve quartz into beautiful detailed sculptures for the wealthy. Alas, for that we would have to become miners. It has never been in my best interest to do physical labor, or so I have maintained." Sart's eyes twinkled.

"I think the dwarves would be interested in these digs," Motuk said.

"True," Sart mused, "however, the memories of being driven from these mountains by the Qa-ryks are still too close. Mayhap, if this evil is overcome, they will return to their digs here and westward. Where there is quartz, there is often gold."

"Gold!"

"Avarice becomes you, Motuk," Sart laughed. "You have more dwarf in you than you might think. I'm afraid you would have to dig far deeper to find rich veins of it. Perhaps you can sell maps to some of your friends when we return to Aelfric. Just be sure to mark this spot with a big 'X.'"

"Harumph," grunted Motuk, reddening slightly.

172

"Come. Let us see what lies ahead."

They spent the next week exploring the caverns through long twisted pathways that went deep into the mountain. Except for the extraordinary displays of the varied crystalline structures on the ceilings and walls, the caves were empty. They seemed to have simply been used by Randaul as a place to come to admire their beauty, for he had done nothing to disturb what was naturally there.

On the fourth day exploring the interconnected string of caverns, they discovered another doorway set in one wall that appeared to lead up in the vicinity of the dungeons they had explored before. They spiked it shut, so they could continue to follow the caves without threat from that quarter.

Each fork they took usually ended in a gap too narrow to explore further. Though they searched carefully they saw no sign of goblin, ogre, troll, or any other creatures of the depths. Disappointingly, they found no treasure or anything of value either.

One night, as they were sitting in the great room in front of the embers in the fireplace, Katelyn asked why they had not encountered any goblins in the natural caverns. "These caves look like ideal places for underground creatures to dwell. They are mostly dry, the crystals reflect light, and there are dozens of chambers that could be used for many purposes."

Sart did not know why they were uninhabited, but he hazarded a guess. "The forests of minor gemstones that blanket the walls and ceilings of these many caverns are not the typical dank, rotten environs that such creatures prefer. When they can't get flesh, goblins eat lichens, moss, molds, and the creepy, crawling things of the moist earth. There would be little in these caverns that would interest them. Also, they do not cherish bright things, as all except the dimmest light hurts their eyes. Ogres and trolls have been known to horde things as gems, coin, armor, weapons, and other items they have taken from those they have killed; but I have never heard of them mining gemstones or gold.

"In addition, my young illusionist, you are attributing human characteristics to these beasts. They do not live as we do in small family groups with separate environs. Goblins swarm together like bees. The goblin horde is almost a thing alive unto itself. The hobgoblins, those of greater size and who have more cunning, are like the head, the underlings the body; and there is a constant flux to the whole thing."

173

"Are the chatts of the desert the same?"

"Nay, I think not. I have rarely encountered them," Sart said. "Their desert environs, as the forest is to their cousins the gzks, dictates much of what they are like. Hence, chatts are colored more like the desert sands -- yellow and brown hues. And though they are numerous, they are quite clannish. Water is their lifeblood, and each clan protects its source."

"Gzks are typically grey-green with some brownish tints, because they are of the forest," Stradryk added, pulling his leather sleeve up to show more of his mottled skin. "They travel in bands like hunters or wolves in independent, extended family groups. They rarely fight each other; they respect each other's territories."

"What did Randaul use the caverns for?"

"Likely, he enjoyed walking through them with a torch," Sart said. "By all reports he was fascinated with gemstones. Mayhap he built his castle in this place because he had found these caves."

"They are beautiful," Katelyn said, snuggling closer under Ge-or's arm. "But I am not fond of deep places and the dark. I will be happy when we have finished our exploring. Do you know why some of these deep caverns are warm and not cold or cool?"

"We have not come upon anything to tell us for sure; my guess is there are warm springs somewhere in the vicinity. Perhaps below where we stand. That is sometimes the case. There is a place like this west and north of here that I visited recently," Sart said, remembering his sojourn at Xur. "Well," he added, "we should rest so we can start early on the morrow. It is time to find out what else Randaul may have secreted in his dungeons. We will take the doorway up in the morn."

Beyond the heavy oaken door that led out of the crystal caverns, they found a narrow passageway leading up. With Motuk ahead, they soon came to steps going ever higher. Ardan, mapping as they went, counted sixty-five steps before they came to another door. This door was barred from the inside; and though Ge-or and Motuk put their shoulders to it together, it would not budge. Ardan finally stepped ahead and used his power to slide the bar on the other side up and out. The two fighters were able, with great effort, to push in the heavy panel as the old rusted hinges complained mightily. The door opened into a wide, much cooler corridor with many doors and openings on either side.

They spent half the day exploring the many small chambers that branched off the main corridor. What they found was largely refuse from what must have been a storage area for those items that would have benefited from being held in the coolness deep beneath the earth. All the casks, barrels, boxes, and cabinets they found had either rotted or been breached by other creatures. What had been within had been eaten, scattered, rotted, or taken away. They found nothing of value despite their diligent efforts stirring through the rubbish.

The main corridor ended at another door whose hinges had rusted to such an extent that a blow from Sart's mace crumbled them. Ge-or was then able to shift the heavy wood to the side. More steps led up to another door, and yet another corridor and series of adjoining rooms.

The chambers on this next level appeared to have been enlarged from natural caves. In the first room they entered, they heard a scurrying of claws on rock and saw

174

grey creatures at the far end scramble out of sight into holes in the floor and ceiling.

"Goblins," Motuk spat. "Stay together and stay alert. They may not attack all of us in these close confines, but they won't hesitate to try to overwhelm anyone who gets separated from the main group."

Ge-or drew his sword and led the way into the room with the shorter warrior to his right.

As below, the chambers were empty except for the leavings of the goblins. The stench of their less-than-clean living environs was strong, so they hurried their search. After only an hour they took another stairway which led up to a spacious platform, extending to both sides of where they entered. There were two large openings on each wall and two doors ahead, spaced about twenty paces apart. Sart gestured for Ge-or, Ardan, and Stradryk to check out the opening to the left, and for Katelyn and Motuk to follow him to the right.

Ge-or, sword and buckler in hand, had taken only a few steps to the left when a mighty roar erupted from the opening in front of him. A moment later, the head and shoulders of a huge ogre came into view. Ge-or braced for a charge, feeling for a solid purchase on the rough rock surface. Stradryk followed suit on his right. Ardan, behind the two, backed a bit more, allowing them plenty of room. He began gathering energy. This beast had to mass twice the two they had seen over a week before. As it emerged, Ge-or reset his feet again, trying to find something to brace his back foot against.

Sart gestured for Motuk to watch the other opening; then he moved back toward Ge-or's small group, bringing his mace out from under his robe as he went back to help.

The ogre was armed with a gigantic club in its right hand. It had a circular leather and wood buckler that had to be three feet across in its left, yet the device looked small held against the beast's body. It lumbered toward Ge-or, obviously not happy with them being there.

Sart yelled a warning as the beast took a swipe at Ge-or with its club. "It's the mother of the other two. Stay away if possible. Engage only when you have a clear stroke. That thing can smash through any armor we have."

Ge-or didn't have to be warned. He could see with his own eyes how powerful this she-beast was. He ducked under the club, spun, and gave a terrific blow to the shield with his blade, hoping he might dislodge it so he would have a better entrance for his next swing.

Unfortunately, the shield was well-constructed, and for an instant his blade stuck. The ogre, looking like it had not even noticed the powerful blow, ripped the shield back, almost tearing the sword from Ge-or's grip. He managed to hold on and the blade dislodged, but he had to duck back from another swipe of the club. This beast is fast – faster than her cubs, that is certain, Ge-or thought, as he spun away again, looking for an opening.

Stradryk, seeing he would be of better use from afar while leaving Ge-or room to maneuver, switched to his bow. Standing to the side, he sent an arrow flying into the ogre's throat, just as she swung again at the ducking half-elf. This time Ge-or had to take the strike on his own shield. He felt the force of the blow shiver up through his arm; but he also noted as his knees buckled slightly, that the beast raised its shield high while making the swing.

As Ge-or maneuvered for another strike, the she-beast ripped the arrow from the side of its neck with its shield hand and roared again.

This gave Ge-or a brief opening. He let his knees continue to fold downward until he was low enough to push off strongly. As he launched himself up, he aimed a penetrating thrust at the ogre's thigh. The blade sank in about four inches until the ogre slammed the shield downward. Ge-or was shocked again by the force of the blow as his blade was forced down and out by the buckler's edge. Thankfully, the tempered steel held. He dove for the floor under another swing of the club, rolling back and to the side before regaining his knees and finally his feet.

As the battle continued, Ge-or found himself being inexorably pushed back despite his best efforts.

Meanwhile, Stradryk had fired two more times. Each arrow found a target in the unprotected side of the ogre, yet the huge creature simply brushed the arrows off as if they were merely pins and lumbered ever ahead, swinging the club in wide arcs.

Ardan, knowing that anything he could do would only interfere with what was happening, watched for any opening in which he might use his power to frustrate or hamper the beast.

Deciding that any damage to the massive creature was better than none, Ge-or suddenly plunged ahead with a flurry of strikes. He swung his sword in a blur of swift swipes and jabs that began to frustrate the huge beast. The shield and club and the ogre's tough skin prevented him from inflicting any serious damage, but he kept looking for any opening that would present a better stroke.

Frustrated, the ogre drove ahead, using the shield almost as a battering ram. Ge-or was again forced back. This giving and taking of small amounts of ground in the center of the cavern continued for several minutes, until Ge-or heard Katelyn yell above the clash of the weapons and the beast's roaring. "Look for an opening soon. I 'm going to try to draw its attention."

Ge-or slowed the pace of his swings slightly, continuing to keep the beast busy. A minute later, as he drew his weapon back for another swing, he saw three large fierce-looking dogs suddenly appear in his peripheral vision. They leapt toward the ogre. Though Ge-or knew they were an illusion, they were so real he almost ducked himself. The she-beast, reacting to this new threat, turned sideways, exposing her right side to Ge-or. Taking advantage of the opening, he stabbed upward. The sharp blade penetrated into the ogre's armpit as she raised her shield and club to block the dogs' assault.

Of course, the illusion vaporized as soon as it passed the ogre; but Ge-or's thrust had gone deep, stopping only when it hit bone. The ogre dropped her club and roared even louder. Still, far from being incapacitated, she brought her right arm back and up. With a vicious swipe, she caught Ge-or full in the shoulder and buckler as he was withdrawing his blade. The blow threw him across the room. He hit the far wall without touching the ground and crumbled to the floor.

"Motuk," Sart yelled, as he and Stradryk entered the fray with mace and long knife. The dwarven warrior left his post where he was still watching the other opening, gesturing for Ardan to keep his eye on it as he passed him with his axe raised high. The three encircled the furious ogre, who was now swinging with its fist at anything that moved close enough to be hit. Katelyn ran over to see to Ge-or.

He was beginning to move as she knelt next to him. "Ge-or?"

"Whuff! By-the-gods, that thing is strong." He pushed himself up to a sitting position and shook his head. "Dizzy a bit... Fine. I'm Fine. Help me up."

176

Katelyn grasped him under his shoulder as he pushed with his sword arm, looking about for his blade as he rose. "Ge-or?"

"I'm good. Where's my sword? Ah!" He saw it lying on the ground next to the wall where he had fallen. He bent, picked it up. The movement caused him to reach out with his left arm for balance. Suddenly he felt the damage of the beast's smashing blow and he groaned. He stood there regaining his equilibrium, glancing over to where the battle was still being fought.

The ogre had been able to keep its three enemies at bay; but the wounds in its thigh and side, under the armpit, were steadily weeping thick blackish blood. Occasionally, one of the fighters would get in a blow to an exposed part of its body, and for now they successfully stayed away from the flailing arm.

Ge-or shifted his left arm with the buckler still in his hand, grimacing as he brought it to the fore. "Back at it, Kate," he said grimly; and he strode quickly toward the milling group.

The ogre had slowed considerably by the time Ge-or re-entered the fray. Sart stepped to the side to give the big half-elf room to maneuver.

It took Ge-or only a second to calculate the ogre's frantic swings. With a fast stab to the chest, followed by a slice upward across its arm, Ge-or spun inward, driving his sword up through the under-jaw of the beast almost to the hilt. It straightened, shuddered, and finally collapsed backward, pulling off the blade as it fell.

They all stood back panting, admiring the tremendous size of the ogre. Though its burlap tunic was now soaked in black blood, the mottled-green beast was no less impressive laid out. It was fully eight feet from head to toe and more than three and a half feet broad at the shoulders. Its muscles were almost as hard as a rock when Stradryk poked it with his long-knife to be sure it was dead.

Ge-or, sword and shield drooping at his side, wandered over to one of the walls where he sat down heavily. Sart followed close behind to minister to his hurts. After a few minutes, the cleric assured Ge-or and the worried Katelyn that the big fighter had not broken anything. He gave Ge-or a mild draught of a pain killer. "Drink this. It will ease most of the discomfort. I have done a mild healing, but you will be bruised and sore for several days. It is good you had the chain and well-padded leather. That saved your shoulder from being crushed.

"Come. Let us take a respite and eat; after we shall see if this beast was protecting anything."

After a meal of fruits, cheese, dried meats, and fried bread leftover from their morning repast, they all felt well enough to continue their explorations.

The opening from which the ogre had charged was her lair. It was filled with shredded leather and clothes that she had used for a bed. In one corner, she had amassed an impressive collection of bones and paraphernalia that she had obviously collected from her victims. There were pieces of armor, most of little value, bracelets and other minor pieces of jewelry, cups, plate-ware, knives and swords, and other knickknacks, a few of minor value. Motuk was charged with sorting through the mess to pick out what might be worth selling. The rest of the party went over to investigate the other opening.

This turned out to be the den of the two smaller ogres, the cubs of the dame. The second, the one Ge-or had wounded, was lying dead on a bed of refuse. The poison had acted, but it had been slow enough in the big beast's system that the cub had been able to return to its lair. A thorough search of this large chamber yielded only some shiny stones, lots of gnawed humanoid bones, and rusting weapons.

When they had finished with the dens, the party met back by the doors. Motuk joined them carrying a filled pack slung on his back. Opening the left door, which was not locked, they entered a large chamber empty of life. As they spread out on the one side of the room, Ardan spiked the two doors behind them. Katelyn and Stradryk held their torches high and moved to the left and right as the others moved down the center of the room. There were goblin holes in the floor and ceiling, and doors spaced along both walls, so they went cautiously, fearing an attack akin to the one that had caught them over a week before.

On the far side of the chamber, a long table made of heavy timber stretched the length of the wall. Sconces for holding torches were set in the stone every few feet, and several candelabra of bronze hung at intervals over the table. Sart began to think that this may have been where Randaul had come to study his more valuable papers; and though they found nothing of interest on or around the table, he hoped the side rooms might hold more of import to his quest.

There were three doors on each of the long side walls of the chamber; Sart and Motuk took them one at a time while Stradryk and Ge-or stood guard. The two doors closest to the table were protected by glyphs. These they left untouched while they searched further. The other rooms opened easily and looked to have been storage.

One had obviously been a small armory. Unfortunately, the weapons and armor had been of inferior quality, all of which had rusted beyond repair. Another had housed crates and barrels that they supposed contained victuals and libations to sustain Randaul and whatever staff joined him here in the depths. These had all been staved in and the contents taken. Of the two remaining chambers, one was empty; the other held a locked chest of a moderate size set in the center of the room.

Sart took Katelyn and Ge-or with him to address the magical wards on the other two rooms, leaving Ardan to examine the room with the chest. The cleric was skilled at neutralizing such glyph protections. He asked Katelyn to use her power to help illuminate the elaborate designs. They turned out to be traced symbols that the cleric was able to reverse by following them back along the paths in which they had been drawn. It took him several minutes to unwind the patterns.

When he was done, the doors opened readily to his touch. Inside they found what Sart had been seeking: piles of scrolls and tomes scattered throughout on shelves and in wooden chests. Thankfully, due to the wards, these two chambers had kept dry and undisturbed over the many years since Randaul had last been in them.

Meanwhile, Arden spent a long time working his hands over the surface of the chest in an effort to understand how the device was protected. Once he felt comfortable, he removed the ward, much as Sart had dealt with the wards on the doors. Then he concentrated on carefully moving the five tumblers that comprised the locking mechanism. He used his power to move each tumbler one at a time until it clicked into place. When he had finally shifted the last, a loud click resounded through the small room and the lid of the chest sprang partially up. By this time, Ardan was drenched with sweat from his concentrated effort. He took a step back, gesturing for Motuk to come in.

Given the go-ahead by the mage, the dwarf-man picked the chest up and moved it out into the main room so they all could witness its opening. Even Sart and

Katelyn interrupted their work to see what they had found.

Disappointingly, the chest held only a small amount of gold and silver, a few gemstones of high enough quality to be of interest, and a plethora of minor gems that Sart guessed Randaul had found interesting because of their odd shapes and sizes. Of more import to the cleric was a large leather-bound tome, in perfect condition, that was entitled, "Diary of My Search for the Heart of the World."

For the next two weeks Sart, Ardan, and Katelyn returned each day to Randaul's library and poured over the materials there, removing those that were of any interest to Sart's quest or to the kingdom in general. Stradryk, Motuk, and Ge-or provided protection for the three as they worked. In pairs, they also alternated making short excursions into the rest of the dungeon levels, searching for anything else that might be of interest.

They discovered two more levels above the library room before they reencountered the goblin death chamber above that. Those two levels were of several small rooms each. Here there was nothing of interest amongst the rubble either.

Though they occasionally heard scrapings, the goblins that remained did not disturb their work. By the end of the first week, the fighters standing guard were starting to get bored, so Sart began letting them individually spend what time they could outdoors hunting or exploring.

Ge-or had found everything up to that point on their quest to be quite interesting. He enjoyed the light tension associated with exploring new environs, and he did not seem to mind too much being down in the depths; yet he was glad to get out-of-doors once the true exploration had ended.

On the days he was able to be free of the dungeon to explore the environs around the castle, he found himself considering the whole experience of the trek. He was surprised at his reaction to the fighting and killing. He had some experience fighting gzks, wolves, and finally the Qa-ryks that had attacked his village; yet he had never believed that he would become so callous so quickly about killing another creature. When he or another was in danger, he acted. It turned out he was quite good at killing. His father had taught him well.

Yet, it was not something he relished. Deep within, Ge-or believed that life was special. Killing a creature, no matter how aggressive or evil, left a hole inside oneself when the deed was done. In some measure, he had experienced this when hunting. He vividly remembered the first time he had killed a deer. His father had him acknowledge those difficult feelings and also made him offer a quick prayer in reverence for the animal slain for their table.

With humanoids, he found that the killing left yet a bigger void. However, remote the relationship, there was a kinship somehow with all creatures. When he stood over the beasts he had killed, he did not feel proud, exultant, powerful, or triumphant; he felt shame, emptiness, and sadness.

Though Sart tried to explain the malevolent nature of the beasts they had slain, it didn't matter one way or the other to him. When he was assailed, when those he was with were in danger, he became a killing machine. When he was called upon to act, he barely gave it another thought. Even the killing of the ogre dame had been something he had done "of the moment." He had focused solely on his skills to ensure their survival. Only when she was stretched on the cold stone floor had he considered how sad it was that she had to experience her cubs' death.

The piles of the slain goblins had also given him pause when they had retrieved Brand's body. It was somehow wrong to him that so much life had been taken in such a way. Yet, he did ken loyalty to his comrades. Sart had made a quick decision to save all of them. It was something else his father had drilled into them -- you can't hesitate in battle. Your life and others were in the balance. The deeper emptiness that remained following death and destruction, he knew he would have to learn to live with.

Now that the fighting was done, and the discovering of new things and new places over, Ge-or was becoming restless. Even at night, he found that Katelyn did not completely satisfy his edginess. So, at those opportunities Sart allowed him, he took long jaunts outside the citadel, ostensibly looking for game for Tyron's pot.

His restlessness paid off. Nearing the time when Sart and the mages were completing their work, Ge-or took a long excursion into the west across the high foothills of the mountain range. Then, before he was about to head back, he discovered the crumbling ruins of an old watchtower set alongside the rocky expanse. From its original height, it would have commanded a wide view to the east, north, and west.

Fully half of the old tower had collapsed in upon itself; however, Ge-or was able to scramble up the rock-clogged steps to the third level. There he found a skeleton of a large man clad in full plate armor with a broadsword resting between its knees. For whatever reason, the man must have crawled into the tower to die.

Ge-or searched carefully but could find nothing about the skeleton that would help identify him. Nor were there any indications that the man had died violently or from any wounds. The armor was plain and unadorned, and clearly of a fine quality steel alloy. Deciding that the man's armor was of no use to him anymore, Ge-or removed it carefully, trying not to disturb the bones too much in the process.

When he had all the pieces set aside, he took stones from about the tower and built a cairn over the dead warrior's final resting place.

At the last, he packaged all the armor and the sword into a layered bundle and tied it securely, hoisting it onto his back for the trek back to the citadel.

***

Leona groaned. This was for real now. The contractions were less than three minutes apart and the midwife had begun to heat water on the stove to prepare for the birth. When she wasn't trying to get through the pains, Leona almost laughed. Her father, had he been willing to stay anywhere near the house during the birthing, would have been shocked to hear her swearing at the gods, Ge-or, and him, in that order, for getting her into this condition. Still, she knew she was strong and would get through this.

Return

Jared worked hard for Simon-the-Elder. In mid-summer, he was promoted to work foreman of one of the warehouses. At the same time, Simon-Nathan was moved inside to oversee one of the larger shops nearby. They still saw each other during breaks and for a mid-day meal; but unfortunately, because of his new responsibilities, Jared had not been able to visit Karenna.

He had taken the initiative to send her a note on her birthday, and thereafter they had written each other once a week. The mail service between the coastal cities was excellent, with regular couriers riding each way several times a day and night. Still, it took almost two weeks for a letter sent by one to reach the other. Jared enjoyed receiving the long notes from Karenna detailing her own work and family life written in her perfect flowing script.

It was a good summer, a connection with Thistle the only thing missing. He was surprised how much he missed her and how often he thought of her, but he still couldn't get up the courage to reconnect. In the late evenings, not infrequently, he found himself sitting and staring at a blank piece of parchment wondering what he could say that would make a difference, so as to lessen the rift between them.

***

Two days after Ge-or returned from his trek to the west, Sart announced that he had gleaned all he could from Randaul's library. It took them another two days to pack to Sart's satisfaction for the trip back. Special care was given to all the writings he had taken from the Recluse's libraries: scrolls were rolled together to save space, and books and tomes were carefully wrapped against any exigency during their trip back to Aelfric.

As the sun rose on their last day, the wagon was carefully loaded with many of the items they had found. Hides preserved by Tyron from the animals they had killed for food were laid on the bottom. This was followed with a layer of moist leaves and loam from the forest, upon which the best bottles of wine, individually wrapped in leather, were laid. These were topped with more hides, another layer of wines, and finally books, tomes, and scrolls were piled atop. The most valuable documents were placed in packs or saddlebags that they carried on their own steeds.

Thankfully, most of their journey would be in the cooler upper foothills of the mountains; however, Sart was concerned that the wine would suffer if it were not well protected once they reached the flats. Any bottles that remained and would not fit in the protected confines of the cart were placed in large padded saddlebags lined with moss on two of the mules. They were all instructed to help keep the cloth they were wrapped in moist whenever they passed streams and ponds. Some of these bottles they would indulge in on their trip back.

The rest of the miscellaneous treasure and the plate mail and sword that Ge-or had found were packed out on the other mules, along with, and often amidst, whatever food stuffs and gear Tyron was still hauling.

They made much better time on the return journey – partially because they were heading downhill for most of the trek, and also because Sart urged them forward from dawn until dusk. Now that summer was waning, he had pressing business in Borea.

He was also anxious to begin his study of the many writings and gathered works of the Recluse.

They pushed ahead with no incidents to mar their trip. Though Ge-or was a bit surprised they didn't run into wandering parties of gzks or a patrol of Qa-ryks out to be blooded, he was content to hurry back with the others. He often thought of Leona. He knew that her time had likely come or was near. That responsibility had begun to settle on his shoulders again. There was something about the realization that he was to be a father that added to his underlying excitement. He resolved to see her and the baby as soon as was feasible.

He and Katelyn also knew that their time together was coming to an end. Ge-or had thoroughly enjoyed the many differences between the sturdy nature and shy approach of Leona, and the energetic, willful, and direct desire of Katelyn. In some ways, the two women complimented each other. He was pleasantly surprised by all that he had learned and experienced from both.

What he did not fully understand, because part of him was still closed to those deeper feelings, was the deep need that both these women seemed to have to hold on to him. As had Leona, Katelyn manifested this by grasping him tight throughout the night and staying close during the day as they traveled back. Several times, she said things that alluded to her not wanting the relationship to end.

With Katelyn, Ge-or was at a loss. She had come to him, and in such a way that he understood that their relationship would be only for the duration of the trek. From their first night together, he had accepted that as fundamental and had been fine with that arrangement. He had even told Katelyn of his time with Leona and of the child she would soon bear. He had spoken to her at some length about how he felt a responsibility toward the child. She had agreed with him, at least in principle. She had also let him know that she had protected herself magically from getting pregnant, so that he would have no concerns about that with her. Yet, as their adventure wound down, she did not want to let go or move on. Finally, worried that he would hurt yet another woman, Ge-or decided to talk with Sart again.

Only two days out from Aelfric, Ge-or got some time alone with the cleric while Katelyn was refreshing herself in a stream. "Ah, my friend, my good half-elf," Sart slapped him upon the back, "women are ever like that. Most of them, those that do care, put themselves wholly into a relationship. It is a good thing, too, for we need caring; yet, it is hard in the end, because one does not wish to release what has become close to one's heart. I myself have also experienced this type of deep caring several times over the years.

"Take this advice with you, my son. Care as you will, enjoy that they care for you, and don't read more into it than there is. Be sure to let the women you are with know that you care, too, and what that means to you. That is a generous and compassionate way to be with people. Young Katelyn will move on; she will remember you and this time together with you, as you will remember her. Yes, your feelings are likely different; but this is true of most relationships, despite what we might wish. For whatever reasons, often men tend to be able to move from such relationships more easily than women. Perhaps that is the sexual nature of the beast, so to speak. Hah!"

Sart grew a bit more serious. "Truly, the important thing is that you care and that you have been honest with yourself and with her. You will both survive the morrow. Enjoy what you have now and remember the joy in it forever; for what we cherish does not diminish with time."

Ge-or thanked the cleric. With the time that remained for them, he tried to pay even more attention to Katelyn.

The group arrived back in Aelfric on their twelfth day following their departure from the citadel. Sart spent the rest of the day haggling with various merchants, with Ge-or and Motuk judiciously standing behind looking grim and formidable in their armor. He got good prices for all the items they had found. In some ways Ge-or was reluctant to part with the quality armor, as it fit him with only minor adjustments; yet he had no real need for full plate, and he did not like its restrictive feel. So instead of taking it as his share of the loot, he put it in with the rest to be sold.

The next day, they all met back at the Prancing Pony – including Stevin, to whom Sart had sent a message – to divvy up the proceeds and to say their goodbyes. Sart spoke briefly, giving homage to their fallen comrade and thanking them for their commitment to the success of the quest. When all had been distributed – with another allotment being held back for Stevin in remembrance of Brand, which had been agreed to by all – Sart wished them well. He encouraged them to seek him out in the future for further adventures. "I am always up and about seeking this or that. The kingdom ever calls for me to delve into whatever is needed. Check the bulletin boards here in the spring, or if ye are ever in the capital, look me up at the palace or at our monastery. If I have the means and the foreknowledge of what I am about, I may send a message to each of you.

"You have all comported yourselves well, and I sincerely appreciate your efforts. I know this wasn't a greatly lucrative venture, but I have added your pay to the pile. I promise to send, hopefully within the next few weeks, additional monies should the auction of the wines do better than the appraisal we received here from Harlan. I believe it will; the wines appeared to have survived the journey in good form." He raised a glass to all of them. They saluted him back with theirs. "Say farewell to this rare treat. Back to back, my friends."

"Back to back," they echoed.

"Ah, Sart."

"Ge-or?"

"Would you do me a favor?"

"Anything, Ge-or. You have proved a stalwart friend and warrior. I would have you on any quest in the future. What can I help you with?"

"Well, as you may have noticed, I am a quiet sort and not the best at communicating, but... Well, I have written a note to Jared. Would you get it to him when you are in the capital?"

Sart flushed. "Aye, Ge-or. It is the least I can do. I plan to stop in to see him soon after I return to Borea."

"My thanks, good friend."

Ge-or and Katelyn spent one last night together. She and Ardan were traveling with Sart to Borea. The two magic-users also had to report in and see what lay ahead for them for the fall. Katelyn held Ge-or in a long, tight embrace the next morn. She whispered in his ear, "I loved being with you. I... I love you, my brave half-elf." She turned and leapt aboard her mare, wheeling the animal around quickly so that he could not see her reddening face and the tears in her eyes.

Perplexed, Ge-or stared after her for a long time before returning to his bed. He decided that a good day's rest was perhaps in order before he tried to figure women out.

Ge-or's share of the treasure was more money than he had ever seen in his life, yet he had hoped they would have garnered much more. The tales Motuk and Stradryk had shared at their campfires during the first days of the quest had told of finding treasure rooms with piles of gold, silver, and jewelry, even hordes of top-quality weapons and armor. From what he could gather, there was likely a good bit of exaggeration to the tales. Yet there also seemed much to be had, for those willing to make the effort.

Though anxious to head north to Goat Haven to see Leona, her father, and the babe, Ge-or stuck around Aelfric hoping they would hear from Sart soon. He wanted to get the additional monies due from the wine auction in Borea. Then he would have enough to buy some of the equipment he wanted, as well as have a bit extra to help them through the fall and winter.

For several weeks, he and Stradryk visited the equipment shops and smithies, seeking the best way to spend some of Ge-or's earnings. Stradryk had placed most of his with a moneylender and was cryptic about how he meant to spend it. Ge-or didn't feel a need to push him on the point.

After trying out almost every blade in Aelfric, Ge-or settled on spending almost all he had garnered from the quest, except for a few silver coins for living expenses, on the best sword he could find. Though he was fond of the blade he had made, and it had served him well, he knew that if he were to fight Qa-ryk's and dragons he would need a blade of the finest quality. The sword he chose was medium in length, of a good heft and weight, dwarven-made and elven-finished. It was not magical, yet it was as good a blade as he would find anywhere that was not so imbued. It suited him well. He dubbed it Kate, for it was sharp, but had an easy feel.

Stradryk invited him to spend the winter months with him in the west fur-trapping. Ge-or appreciated the offer, but he was leaning toward spending that time with Leona and the child in the hidden vale. It seemed like a pleasant prospect. He felt that for at least a few winters he could spend some time with the child and influence its upbringing. He liked the image of teaching the lad or lass weaponry at a young age, as his own father had with him and Jared. If he got a fair amount from Sart, and he did as well as he had the previous winter with the wolves, he might have enough in the spring to head out after the great beast he sought.

It took a bit longer than any of them would have wished; but as the first whiff of fall was in the air, a courier from Sart arrived in Aelfric with a note for one of the local moneylenders. Since Katelyn, Ardan, and Tyron were in Borea, they had received their share directly from Sart. Stradryk, Motuk, and Ge-or gathered together once more at the bank and received a pleasant surprise. The wines had done quite well. The money Sart had sent was more than what they had already received from their adventure to Randaul's fortress.

Along with the bank note, Sart had enclosed a letter from Jared for Ge-or. In it his brother had given him a brief summary of his work at Bard Hall, ending with the hope that they could get together as soon as may be.

Ge-or immediately set about his final preparations for the ride north and west, hoping that he and Jared might find a way to meet during his time at Goat Haven.

He considered buying a beautiful dress for Leona as a gift, yet he finally settled on several bolts of cloth that were both of a sturdy weave and a flowery pattern that he felt she would enjoy. With saddlebags loaded and mule in tow, he said goodbye to Stradryk at the western gate. "Next spring," he called as he waved.

Stradryk waved as his half-elven friend trotted away. "Back to back!" The half-gzk turned away. Fall was in the air, and it was time to think about packing his sled.

Second Year

Reunited

It was late in the summer, as Jared and Simon-Nathan were preparing to go back to school, that a serendipitous event occurred. The two young men were in one of Simon-the-Elder's shops helping with sales, as well as selecting items for their room, when Thistle and Sart walked in through the front door.

"Jared!" Simon-Nathan poked him in the ribs.

Jared looked up from the sale he was completing for another student. He stood for an instant in shock. A thousand times he had wanted to go to the palace to try to get in to see her; but he had always talked himself out of it, telling himself things like: "They wouldn't let me in," "She wouldn't want to see me," "Meligance would turn me away…" He ended up each time hoping she would send her sphere. Now, here she was in front of him, chatting amiably with Sart and glancing about at the wares.

By-the-gods, she is beautiful, he thought. She had matured, gaining in height, and looked ever more a lady. He couldn't tell, perhaps a touch of makeup added to her beauty and bearing. And albeit she was wearing a simple summer frock of light blue adorned with yellow flowers, she still looked somehow regal and stately. Or perhaps it was merely her confident manner.

Thistle had not yet seen Jared or Simon-Nathan. She appeared to be more interested in her conversation with the cleric than in actually examining the merchandise in the aisles. Simon-Nathan swung around the counter and gave Jared a push. "Go," he whispered. "I'll finish up here." When Jared hesitated, he gave him a harder shove. "Come on, you've been moping around all summer about finding a way to talk with her. Go. I won't tell Karenna."

Jared gave his roommate an annoyed glance. The issue was not Karenna; it was his embarrassment – bred more from the failure to reengage, than the incident that had kept them apart. Simon-Nathan was right, though; Jared wanted, nay, needed, to talk with Thistle. He had to admit to himself, he really missed her.

Finally, he decided to press ahead despite his chagrin. He nodded at Simon-Nathan, gritted his teeth, and headed down the aisle toward her.

He was only a few paces away when she turned from Sart and looked in his direction. He said immediately, "Thistle."

"Jared?" She said smiling. "What a wonderful surprise." However, her tone of voice and inflection seemed to say something more akin to, "What are you doing here? This is awkward."

"Thistle, I…" Jared decided to tell the truth. "I've meant to… I've so wanted to come to you. I'm sorry. I lacked the courage. I've been afraid you would reject me."

"Oh, Jared, I would never do that." Thistle's tone was stilted, as if she wanted to maintain a distance.

"Harrrmmm." Sart cleared his throat loudly. "Well met, young Bardling. I have heard good things from Leonis – winning the Archery Cup, setting a new record. You even made it through theory, I'm told."

Jared flushed. "Hail, Sart, and well met, too. It is good to see you." He extended his arm and gripped the cleric's wrist. "Actually, it is wonderful to see you both." He turned back to Thistle wanting her to know that he was sincere.

"Well, it is indeed well met," the cleric rejoined, "because I have things I should do; and if you are willing, you can show our young lady here about the shop and district. I presume that Simon would give you leave for a couple of hours?"

"That's fine," Simon-Nathan shouted from the back. "It is a slow day anyway." Which was not really true; the two weeks before school started were one of their busiest seasons, but Jared appreciated the gesture.

Thistle glanced up with an angry flash at Sart. Unfazed, he propelled her forward with a push on the elbow. "Come, come. I will return in a couple of hours. Enjoy yourselves." With that, he turned quickly and strode out the door.

The two stood about a pace apart, waiting for the other to speak. Thistle felt very awkward and embarrassed; Jared thought she was angry with him. Finally, he said the one thing that leapt into his head. "Did Sart plan this meeting?"

At that, Thistle seemed to let go of something she was holding onto. She laughed lightly, "I imagine he did. Well, at least I wouldn't put it past him." She flushed and took a slight step back.

"I'm sorry, Jared. It's been such a long time and..."

"It was an embarrassing parting the last time," Jared jumped in. "Well, the last time we sort of spoke... I'm sorry, Thistle, I... I care about Karenna. We... we enjoy being together. But you are still here." He touched his heart.

A tear came to Thistle's eyes; she started to turn away.

"Please don't leave, Thistle. Please. We need to talk."

She turned back around, tears now trickling down her cheeks. "Not here," she whispered, looking over Jared's shoulder at the many people in the shop.

"Come," he said. "There is a fount down the street. With everyone shopping, it should be relatively quiet."

They walked slowly, neither touching nor speaking, until they came to the small fount. Jared laid a kerchief on the marble for Thistle to sit on; she kept standing and turned to him.

"It's not your fault, Jared. It's all mine. I shouldn't have... Well, it goes back further than my sending the sphere to your room at... at that time. The truth is I shouldn't have come to you that night at Simon's. It set off so many things for me... in me. Now I understand the work I must do, the control I have to have, as well as the pain and denial that I will have to accept, perhaps for years to come."

"Thistle..."

"No, let me finish, please. I released you, Jared. And it was the right thing to do. I know that deep inside... It was so hard when I heard you... when I knew you were with someone else. Karenna?" Thistle asked.

"Yes, she is a student. You met her the day you came."

"The redhead!" Thistle flushed. "Yes, I remember; she is beautiful. I..." She paused again, tried to smile up at him; instead, more tears came. She swiped at them angrily, taking a kerchief from her pocket to wipe them away.

"Jared, I'm not angry at you. I'm upset with myself for being so weak, so... so stupid. I wanted to be noble and strong, but it hurt. It still hurts."

"What do we do, Thistle?"

"Do you love her?"

187

"I suppose I do in a way. She knows about you, about us. How I feel about you. She tries to understand. I… I know that this hurts her, too. I struggle with this, Thistle. I don't know what is right, or if there is a right or wrong here. I only know that I do still care, very much, for you. I have missed you. I have missed you a great deal. Perhaps for now, we are friends, until a time that..."

"Can we do that? Can I do that?" Thistle sounded almost angry again. "Why are relationships so complicated, Jared? It wasn't so long ago that I was facing engagement to a man I knew nothing about, only that he was a good man from a solid family. I had accepted my fate, and I hoped to make him a good wife. Suddenly you and I were thrust together, seemingly by a whim of the world; and we came to love each other. I know that. When I think on it, I still feel that way. But..."

"But things have changed, and we've changed, too."

"Yes, we have." Thistle placed her hand on his chest, touching him for the first time. "You are a man now, Jared, and I am becoming a woman."

"A lady, a beautiful lady."

"Perhaps, yet I am still a girl in many ways. Yes, it is best, for now, that we try to accept who we are and where we are. If we struggle against this, it will only make our lives much more difficult. How do we stay friends? How can we be together and not? Even now, when I see you, I want to be close to you; and I can't... I just can't." Her tears started flowing in earnest.

Jared waited until she regained control, wanting so much to reach out and take her hand, knowing he shouldn't. It was incredibly frustrating that he couldn't simply comfort her in his arms. Finally, her crying stopped. She looked back up at him and tried to smile.

"I am allowed off campus on Solisday afternoons now, Thistle. We could meet, once a week, maybe?"

"No, that would be unfair to Karenna. Perhaps once a month… to talk. Can we do that? Will she be able to accept that?"

"I will talk with her. I have tried to be honest with her. She understands, but…"

"It is hard for her. I do understand that."

"No spheres?"

Thistle smiled, reaching up to touch his face lightly. "Yes, no magic. Can you forgive me, Jared?"

"There was never anything to forgive. It was a mistake, that you could not have anticipated. You have to forgive yourself, Thistle."

"Yes, that is what Sart tells me. Come, let us walk together."

Back to the Grind

Almost immediately, they found themselves in full swing in the new school term. Jared was surprised to find mathematics on his morning schedule, a course which he had not made any effort to prepare for. He had garnered Simon-Nathan's second year books and notes for all his other classes. These he perused during the slow periods at the warehouse. He had also read and taken notes on all the books required for the whole year in History and Lore, a study skill that his roommate had taught him. Now he could focus on his performance and whatever else that came up. Theory, he had decided, he would tackle day to day.

With his new responsibilities at the archery range, Jared had much less time to devote to sparring with Elanar. Nonetheless that had worked out better for both of them. Elanar had also been asked to assume new duties as an assistant instructor for the long sword. They still ran almost every morning and worked out with weights twice a week together. Surprisingly, both Simon-Nathan and Karenna, as well as several other students, joined them in their early morning workouts.

Karenna and Jared had renewed their relationship two days before school began. She came up from the south early to purchase books and materials for the new term. Simon-Nathan had asked his parents, and she had been able to stay at his family's home until Bard Hall opened. The first night she snuck into Jared's room. They spent that eve making up for the long summer apart.

Music theory, after an initial review, became a daily grind of analyzing pieces of new music. Jared quickly gave up on the purely analytical, mental exercise of it all. He would take the work back to their room, play through it on his lute or portative harp, and label all the non-key chords and material as "X." While playing each section slowly, he would figure out what possible keys or relationships these had to the whole. He found the process quite enjoyable. It gave him ideas for harmonizing the music he had in his lessons on lyre and lute.

Karenna, on the other hand, tried to convince him that learning how to analyze music "properly" would save him considerable time and effort. She challenged him to analyze any piece of his choosing, to see which method was faster: his practical performance, or her mental-intellectual approach. He declined. "Karenna, you would kick my butt. I wouldn't stand a chance. You are way past what I am doing in my classes. You know this stuff, and you understand it better than most graduate students."

She smiled. She told him she would love to kick his butt because it was so cute.

He flushed deeply red at that; and Simon-Nathan decided, with several "Harumphs" for emphasis, that it was time to leave the discussion and the room.

Jared had auditioned for Therin at the end of the previous term. While the master of the strings had been impressed with his accomplishments without his having had any previous formal instruction, he had assigned Jared to one of his assistants.

Initially, private instrument study was a struggle for Jared. He was used to doing things the way he had taught himself. Changing his hand position, finger technique, plucking and strumming techniques and so forth, proved quite difficult to accept. Eventually, he did see the logic in approaching performance in a more efficient and controlled manner. It took him a long time to make some of the adjustments. He kept at it; and by mid-term he was beginning to gain facility with the new techniques.

What he did excel at instrumentally was improvising on a tune – both polyphonically, the old style, and in the form of the new music, creating a harmonization for it. Often, he would mix elements of the old and new styles together, which was a bit perplexing to both his instructor and to Karenna. The music sounded so expressive and powerful that they would leave him to his inspiration.

There was no doubt that they were all busy with their studies, practicing, and weaponry. Even Karenna found herself swamped with homework. Her advanced classes focused on analysis and research, and the masters "piled it on" – an expression that they all became quite fond of using. She ended up spending much of her free time in the Hall library.

Jared and Karenna did find time to be alone, though it was far less than they would have wished. Occasionally, they would find moments to kiss and hold each other, yet time alone for lovemaking was at a premium. Luckily, Simon-Nathan, as a third year, had permission to not only go home on Solisday afternoons; he could stay overnight as long as he was back in time for classes on Lunesday. Karenna would then come to their room and spend the night.

This was Jared's favorite time. He loved waking up in the early morning with Karenna's red tresses flowing about his face and her soft warm body pressed against his. Sometimes he would lay there waiting for first light to come through the window, while he gently caressed her cheek or arms. Simon-Nathan would wait patiently for them to show up outside for the start of their exercise routine.

Jared spent time when he could with Simon-Nathan, coaching him on the intricacies of fighting with a short sword. He convinced his roommate that when he went on his apprenticeship, it would be the most useful weapon to use in a brawl. Simon-Nathan doubted he would ever find himself in such a situation, yet he found he actually liked the heft of the weapon. He slowly began to improve his skills and his creativity with the blade.

Karenna and his roommate were both working with Jared in archery. When Leonis made the announcement that women would be allowed to learn the shortbow, Karenna had signed up immediately for the next term, ever jumping on the latest opportunity for women.

Neither of Jared's two friends was a natural, but they both worked hard. Simon-Nathan confessed to Jared that he was, like his father, not much interested in physical or weaponry pursuits. He did understand their importance in this day and age; therefore, he was determined to get himself in shape. Though he believed he would never grow much taller than his current five feet-eight inches, he felt he should at least do what he could to have what he called "a respectable physique."

Jared found Karenna to be focused and intense as an archer. She calculated everything. While this helped in some ways, she did not have the spontaneity to respond quickly to small cues in the environment around her. She tended to hold on the target too long, and as a result, her aim would drift. Instead of developing a flow to her preparation, she would try to control it all the more. Simon-Nathan, on the other hand, was much more relaxed with a bow. He had gotten the idea and technique of nocking, aiming, and releasing all in one fluid motion. He still lacked the physical strength to shoot well, but he was improving.

As a teacher, Jared enjoyed having them in his stable. He got to see better how they approached things, how they thought, and their differing, yet profound determination.

Karenna had also been willing to go along with his once monthly sojourns into town to meet with Thistle. They talked openly about it at some length during the first few weeks of the term. Karenna had accepted that it was important to him. However, she didn't feel that talking about how he, she, and Thistle felt about each other was going to be of benefit to any of them; so they had agreed to leave it as it was. She did become a bit distant and slightly grumpy the few days following the monthly get-togethers; however, Jared was always able to draw her mind away from her moodiness by making an effort to be even more attentive during those few days.

All in all, things were going well. Lessons were learned, papers written, analyses completed, and muscles and flexibility were being developed. It was a good time for all of them, with little to mar their enjoyment of life as dedicated students in the Hall of the Bards.

The Power of Magic

It was all about energy. Thistle finally felt she was beginning to understand some of the power she could grasp to use as *she* willed. Over the past few months, she had really begun to learn what she could accomplish with the power that she drew in from the ether. Meligance had given her access to the courtyard below her window to practice her magic. The space had long been considered a testing ground for the White Wizardess's incantations, as she would often open her window and hurl a spell toward the far wall. No one else had dared to use it in decades. Now, Thistle could be found there at least once a day.

Meligance had shown her apprentice that energy in its purest form, a white-pulsing intensity, was most effective in magic if used for a specific purpose molded by the magic-user. A ball of intense energy hurled at an object would do a certain amount of shocking and percussive damage. It could effectively kill creatures or people depending on the force used. It could be a much more effective weapon, capable of killing on a massive scale, if it was used in a specific form, like fire; or, depending upon the creature or creatures one was facing, even water or air could be most damaging.

Thistle learned that her use of energy meant finding the simplest, most effective means to produce what she needed. "Making" water from energy was tedious and extremely difficult. She learned, however, that there was water readily available all around: in founts, ponds, the sea, and most usefully, in the air. She just had to use energy to gather it.

Thistle also learned she could manipulate that which she drew to her. She and Alli had great fun experimenting. One such practice led to her chambers being suffused with steam; and another, hours spent giggling and cleaning up after she had fooled around with "earth" and "water."

"Unsculpted" energy was the descriptor Meligance used to refer to any force, any incantation, that was not completely in the control of the magic-user. Thistle spent many hours facing the courtyard wall, practicing: learning to mold her grasp of power into specific uses, as well as learning to control the amount, dimensions, and impact of

192

the "spells" she "threw."

As in all learning, practical experience was often the best. She learned that a blast of fire or a bolt of force could as easily damage one's friends, as well as one's enemies, if it were not controlled precisely. After singeing her hair several times, Thistle sculpted her fireballs ever more carefully.

The work, at times, *was* tedious. She had to practice over and over the same mechanics, watching carefully as to how any variation in what she did, how she focused, changed the result. It was also often exciting. As she worked, she could feel her control improving. She could sense that she was beginning to compartmentalize the process. Her personal power remained separate from the power drawn from without. At the same time, her mind became more and more aware of everything around her that might impact what she was doing, as well as what she was about to do.

By early December, Meligance had begun to set impediments in Thistle's way. Friendly forces, in the form of ghost knights, might appear to one side, while another threat appeared to her fore. Or the Wizardess might throw an offensive or defensive spell while Thistle was gathering energy for another strike.

It did not take Thistle long to realize how much she didn't know and how much she couldn't control. They had yet to do much work on defensive spells, an arena that Meligance assured her apprentice was even more difficult to learn and control well. There were other uses of magic that they had not touched on at all: sendings; conjurations or summonings; the production of objects from pure energy, which was at the highest level of magic, and though rarely used, could be life-saving; and many other uses, fringe and otherwise.

Mentor and apprentice began to meet almost daily. A favorite time was early in the evening, before dinner, when they would sit at Meligance's desk and discuss the day's practice, most often directed at the ramifications of what Thistle had felt she learned.

One evening, feeling particularly overwhelmed after a hard day of study and work at the wall, Thistle asked her mentor a question that had been troubling her. "The more I work, the more I realize how much I don't know. It seems that it will be years, maybe decades before I know enough to be truly effective as a mage, to really understand what I need to…"

"To fully control the power you feel?"

"Yes, that and… Well, I keep thinking of Jared, and whether there is any hope for us in the future."

Meligance laughed that light laugh of hers that usually made Thistle feel better instantly, but right now the angst she felt ran deep.

The White Wizardess understood. "I'm sorry, child, I don't mean to make light of your concern. You are confusing a number of issues. First, it is well that you appreciate how little you know, how little you control, and how long it will take to gain even a modicum of understanding of magic, of the uses of energy and power.

"The truth is, it will take you a lifetime and more. *Never...*" Meligance became serious and lowered her voice, "Never assume you are completely in control. Far too many mages have died because of that error. What you strive for daily is control of yourself, your inner power. *That* you can fine tune. And you are doing so rapidly, far more rapidly than I expected. The power we never completely ken or control is that which comes from without. Always think of it as if you were a small girl playing near a dangerous fire, for we don't wholly understand what we deal with. We must remember that it can change in an instant. A million factors we don't ken, and don't completely control, can impinge on what we do. That is why I introduce such distractions while you work.

"Secondly, as to your love life…" Meligance smiled again. "There are some factors you are not fully aware of. As I said, you have been moving along quite quickly. In some ways that raises concern in my mind. But as you know, I regularly test you to be certain that your focus and control are as they appear on the surface. You have done remarkably well.

"There is still more work to do. There are several things to add to your understanding now; things that I did not want to reveal earlier. Have you felt an intensifying of your power within recently?"

Thistle nodded, hanging her head. She had been afraid to tell Meligance. She thought she might be somehow leaking energy from without into her core.

"Child, do not worry that you are taking energy from without and using it in your core. That I have been watching very carefully. You would know in an instant, because it would harm you. What is happening is called maturation. And though you have had early signs of it for over a year, you are at long last becoming a woman. There is nothing you or I can really do about that without being quite drastic.

"Understand this – you will continue to grow in power, and your inner energy will build further until you are in your late thirties or early forties; then it will level off. There is a benefit to this, which brings me to the all-important point in regard to your love." Meligance raised her eyebrows, fixing her gaze on her student. "Those gifted, especially those gifted with the degree of power that you and I possess, naturally develop slowly. We mature less quickly.

"You may have noticed that you are a woman in all respects at this point…"

Thistle flushed, as this past fall Alli had to help her with all that was happening to her physically.

"…but in comparison, you are developing in certain areas much more slowly than your chambermaid, who is younger than you?"

This was true, too, and Thistle flushed even deeper. Alli's breasts were far bigger, her hips had filled out, and she constantly talked of this courtier or that page about the castle. Thistle was much less interested in boys or men in general.

"Well, child, or I should say, 'young woman,' this is a mage's curse, as well as blessing. You probably started puberty more or less on time, yet it has been slow and sporadic. Yes?"

Thistle nodded. She had bled the first time before she had even met Jared, then rarely thereafter, until this fall.

"Well, our curse is that we are not truly a woman, not fully, for some years later than normal. The urges of puberty come on even more slowly for us, and as you will find, more intensely. You have begun to experience some of that. It will intensify soon, and then you will have to move even more cautiously with your magical studies. The blessing is that those with true magical power, both men and women, continue to develop more slowly and therefore live longer lives. How old do you think I am, Thistle?"

Thistle hesitated, not feeling comfortable answering the question.

"Please, it is all right to answer me. I will not be offended, I assure you."

194

"Forty, maybe, mid-forties?"

Meligance was, if one was brave enough to observe her fully, stately, a classic beauty with a perfect body. She had few wrinkles – only some spider-webs about the eyes that gave her an air of wisdom and added to her presence of nobility and power.

"Child, and you really are a child to me, I am well over eighty. You may not live as long as your half-elf, but you might give him a run for his money. I assure you, if your love is true, you will have many years together.

"There is one other ramification of magic that is rather tragic in those that are as powerful as we both are, and you need to understand this as well. When the time comes and you can indulge in the joys of the physical, you probably won't be able to conceive, to have a child. It is not impossible, for it has been known to happen rarely; however, there is something about the power within that makes the womb unreceptive to fertilization. I am sorry, Thistle; it would have been so whether you studied magic or no."

Thistle stared at her mentor. So much she had wondered about suddenly clicked into place in her mind. Her marriage to Baldo would have been a sham. Her acceptance of her fate as a dutiful wife, making love to her husband, watching the homestead, and raising children, would have dissipated over the course of a year or two. She would have found herself outcast anyway, even if all this had not happened. The magic would have destroyed her "normalcy" at the cost of another, maybe even through his injury or death.

She also understood now how different she really was. Why all the people at court from the lowliest servant to the highest born looked askance at her, gave her wide berth when they could, and whispered behind her back after she passed. She would never be normal. She hadn't been born that way.

When she had first understood the feeling of her power within, and that her "indigestion" had been so much more, it had explained occurrences that no one had understood in her home. Little things: like shattered pottery, missing items found in odd places, and things she could do that others couldn't – like holding hot or cold items, working long hours after everyone else was exhausted, and so on. This made her difference from others even more profound. She was an outsider, albeit one with an extraordinary gift to use if she could make it work for herself and for others.

Meligance let her digest the news, watching her carefully. It was an important moment of acceptance of her fate, of who she was. It was something Meligance had gone through many years before; and she still remembered, very clearly, when she had learned these things.

Thistle seemed to ponder it for a while. After a minute, Meligance saw her back stiffen. Now she is on the path, Meligance knew.

"Thistle, to truthfully answer your implied question of when you will be able to 'be with' your young man – sooner than you might think. Certainly, within a few years, not decades, I would warrant, as long as you continue to progress as you have been."

Thistle felt quite joyous that evening, as if a great weight had been lifted from her shoulders. She was encouraged that she and Jared could be together sooner than she had expected. She ordered a fine wine for dinner that she shared with Alli. They talked of girlish things well into the next morning.

195

Something Lost

The dark figure slid across the ground, searching, searching. He had been there for two days and had magically searched each square foot of the land. Yet, he could not sense it. He had been a fool; he should have realized it was missing from the start, though he had much more pressing matters to attend to following the massacre here.

It was night, and Aberon welcomed the cold darkness. He had also searched during the day, though his power was greater at night. Former villagers or neighbors had obviously been here and done something with the remains. Had they been buried? He saw no cairns or mounds. Maybe all had been burned. There was evidence of fire about, especially in the square; but that could have simply been the dragon's work. Realizing that his effort was wasted, he sat on a nearby stone.

It had to be here, or... where? The boy with the lyre had the stone, that he knew. It was outside his reach, for now. Initially, its loss had weighed on Aberon. The loss of this ring more so, for it was meant to be a gift to the Great Druid – for some reason he coveted it.

The girl, he knew, did not have the ring either. He had searched them both carefully. Plus, he had been with them long enough to have felt it. There was one other he knew about from Thiele who had also survived the final slaughter – brother to the other. Unfortunately, he had not known this for some time following the disaster at Kan's Altar. This one, from reports of his spies, was in the south with a group of adventurers.

He had sensed it during the battle, before the dragon had struck for the last time. And he knew Fis did not have it. He had asked the beast. The dragon had come for the sword, nothing more. The sword was a treasure to the great beast far more than its value as a weapon. It was the blade that had killed his sire. At that time, it had been wielded by a great elven warrior. Aberon had let the fell beast have it. It was best that it was out of circulation. Supposedly now, this other scion of the great warrior had pledged to go after his father's sword. Well, he would let the fool die in his quest. The question he needed answered was, "Did he have the ring?"

Aberon's plans following the destruction of Thiele had all gone awry. Initially weakening him in the eyes of his compatriots, something had happened at Kan's Altar that he did not at first ken. Some power had surged through him as the Altar had broken; and though he had fled at that instant, it strangely stayed with him. It had become a part of his permanent strength, his inner force. Already that force was growing within; and soon he would be able to use that power to move up much more rapidly in the ranks of the Black Druids than he had ever felt possible, realizing his ambitions. Finding the ring now would simply be a bonus to his plans. And who knew? It might prove valuable to have, to keep it for himself, especially if he could understand its geas. The One had desired it for some reason.

It had taken a while for his brethren to accept, sometimes through forcible means, that he was far from diminished, that his failure had actually led to gain. Now, at long last, he *was* one of the Nine – the least of that elite group, but allowed access to the greatest secrets of their order. He had set his sights back on his true goal: the gathering of power, ever more power, until he would be the One.

There was something else that troubled him even more than having missed the ring. Besides the burying or burning of the dead, this place, Thiele, had been cleansed. The debris of the battle and the remaining structures had been cleared, sometime recently. For what reason? Were the Boreans foolish enough to rebuild this outpost village in the midst of the druids' planned expansion north and east? He would need to have his spies keep an eye on the site henceforth.

Aberon had recently discovered the pit where all the refuse had been burned from the buildings, yet there were no bone fragments within. What he sought was not there either. For certain, it was no longer here. He could think of no other who could have taken it except the sword-wielder's son. It was time to journey to the south, time to meet up with this half-elf to see if he had it or had knowledge of its whereabouts. He would be off in the morn.

At a Loss

The weather was perfect, with warm days and cool nights; so Ge-or pushed ahead, rising early and staying in the saddle until late evening. By his calculations, Leona would have had the babe over a month before, and depending on the day of conception, perhaps a bit later.

The closer he got to Goat Haven, the longer he rode each day, pushing himself well into the night. After ten days, he knew he was less than a day's ride out; so he decided to stay in the saddle until long after midnight, before taking a short rest and rising at dawn.

He eased his mare down the narrow path he had first taken into the vale. It seemed like a lifetime ago already, but it was less than a year.

It wasn't until he neared the gate that he sensed something was wrong. Though the gate was securely latched, there were no animals in sight; and there had always been geese and chickens about underfoot. Often, the mules were allowed to graze freely here as well, so as to keep the vegetation down near the house. Also, the garden, up the hill to the right, looked overgrown and untended. Leona had been meticulous in keeping it weed-free, even in the fall after much of the harvest had been taken in.

Worried, Ge-or leapt off his horse, drew her and the mule through the gate, and ran up the hill to the house and stopped. Aldred or Leona had nailed rough planks across the door and covered the large bedroom window as well. Running down the porch, Ge-or looked toward the tool shed and saw that its door had also been nailed shut.

"What happened?"

Many thoughts ran quickly through his head: Did Leona die in childbirth? The babe? Had some catastrophe fallen after he left? Wolves? Qa-ryks? Yet, someone had closed the place up, hoping to keep looters out. Who? And why?

He ran down to the barn. There the door was unbarred, so Ge-or heaved it open, only to find it completely empty with no hay stored above or in the enclosures. Something had caused them to leave before the harvest.

Ge-or took a long walk through the vale. Except for squirrels and other wild things scampering about, he found no sign of life. The few crops that Aldred typically planted were wasting overgrown in the untended and un-harvested fields. Finally, he trudged back to the house. He took a walk around the perimeter, trying to see if there was some clue as to what had happened.

As he walked up the slope toward the stream where he had accepted Leona's proposition, he noticed something had changed at the top of the rise next to Aldred's fishing hole. There was a fresh mound of dirt, beginning to sprout wild grasses and weeds. Ge-or's dread increased as he moved closer. His heart fell when he saw a large, blue-gray stone set back at the head of the mound.

He walked past the mound and stood silently staring at the letters roughly chiseled into the rock. He was alternately saddened, relieved, and gladdened as he read, Aldred, Husband, Father, Grandfather. She's alive! And with the babe!

He stood there, thinking through what might have happened. Aldred had died or been killed. Sometime, not long after the baby had come into the world, he guessed. Leona knew she could not tend to a large farm, the goats, and the other animals with a small babe to care for, so she had left.

Ge-or said a quick prayer to the gods for Aldred; then he hurried to the front door of the cabin and ripped the boards off with his bare hands. He hoped that Leona had left him some indication of where she had gone, perhaps a note explaining what had happened.

When he got inside, his search turned up nothing to indicate anything except that she was gone. The encouraging aspects to the whole situation were that the cradle had been taken, and the cabin obviously prepared for being empty for some time: all the linens and the mattresses had been removed, only the bed frames remained, and nothing that would attract mice, rats, or other creatures was left inside. Leona had left the place neat and clean.

Eventually, he also noticed that she had taken her bow and arrows with her. He felt good about that. She obviously had thought the situation through carefully.

Deciding there was nothing there that would help him find her and the babe, Ge-or left the house. When he reached his horse, he pulled a hammer from his tool kit, and went to rebar the door. On a whim, he went back down toward the barn. He smiled when he saw that the target he had set along the one side to practice her shooting had been well used. She was a practical, sensible woman, and that gave him hope.

Since there was nothing there for him, Ge-or chose to start out immediately in search of Leona and the baby. He guessed she would head due east to the trading post where she and Aldred had done much of their business. She would have had to sell the goats and whatever livestock she did not need or could not care for. Leona had taken the two-mule, covered cart that Ge-or had seen Aldred use the previous fall when he had gone to pick up more necessities for the winter.

Ge-or pushed his animals hard that day; and as dusk was falling, he saw the small tavern, the Last Outpost. Finding empty stalls for his horse and mule in the stables, Ge-or grabbed his saddlebags and entered the main building, looking for the proprietor.

The place was dark, lit only by a couple of candles and the glow from a single fireplace. Ge-or walked up to the small bar. A large woman, both in height and girth, came out from behind a curtain. "Hail stranger," she said, appearing put out by Ge-or's presence.

"I need a room for the night, food, and drink. I can pay."

A small smile creased her lips, but it did nothing to improve her tone of voice.

"Coin?"

"Aye, coin, and I need some information if you have it."

"Five coppers for room, board, and stabling. Information can be bought, too, if the price is right and I don't mind the givin'."

Ge-or groaned inwardly. Leona and Aldred must have had a time bargaining with this one; five coppers was outrageous for one night's lodging in such a place. He reached into his purse and took out a silver piece. "It's yours if you can help me. I am looking for Leona, daughter of Aldred, the goat-herder you have often done business with. She..."

"Who is that there, Matilda?" A voice, weak and gravelly, came from the back.

"Quiet, John, get your rest. Tis a customer with coin, someone as claims to know Leona and Aldred."

"Leona? I saw her... *cough*... back a pace... *cough*... maybe three - four weeks?" The voice croaked.

"Leona did come through here?" Ge-or said, frowning at the inn-keeper's wife. He drew the silver piece back when she reached for it.

"Aye," she said. "Leona was here, about a month ago. I didn't see her. I was out helping with a birth to the south. John dealt with her."

"Could I speak with him? Please, it is important."

"He's not well. Got the ague bad."

Ge-or held the silver piece up, twirled it in his fingers, finally laying it back down on the bar. Matilda quickly snatched it up. With a deep frown she gestured for Ge-or to follow her.

John was laying on a bed set against the far wall in what was the kitchen and pantry for the tavern. He was wan and yellowish. He coughed hoarsely as Ge-or came around the curtain. "The man wants to know about Leona and Aldred. You remember when she was here last."

The proprietor nodded, coughed again, wiped his lips with a heavily soiled rag and croaked out, "Aye, I remember it well. She came by a few weeks back. Had a good-sized herd of goats and a couple of mules to sell, and if I remember rightly, some geese and chickens, too. She was a bit put out because she said Aldred had passed.

"Sad thing. He was a good fella... *cough*. She didn't even bargain with me, and she was usually a haggler, that one." John laughed, which set off another coughing bout. "Gave her the best price I could considering the circumstances. Times ha' been tough, though."

Ge-or doubted Leona had been given a fair price; she would have likely been in a hurry and upset by what had happened. There was naught for it now. He wanted to find her.

"Do you know where she was headed? Which way she went?"

"She went east. Don-na know more than that. She took her money and left straight away. Was kinda in a rush. That was all for it." He coughed again.

"And the baby?" Ge-or asked, when he had recovered.

"Baby? Nay, I didna see any babe. She parked the wagon out front, herded the animals into the corral, left as soon as she was paid. Didna even have a bite to eat."

"You saw no sign of a baby? It would have been small, a month old."

"Nay. Not unless she had it swaddled in the cart. She weren't here long, so that's possible if it were asleep. She never mentioned a babe. Only about her da..." John

200

began to cough again. He tried to control it; his shoulders shook from the effort.

Ge-or waited for the fit to pass. "What did she say about Aldred?"

"Said she found him in the field one evening. He just up and fell over and that were the end of it. My guess is it were his heart. He were a hard fella, but the gods call us when they will."

"Leona didn't say anything about where she was going?"

"Nay. I was busy though with all the animals, and she wanted to get back on the trail. Wisht I could help more. She wasn't here more'n an hour; less, I warrant."

"My thanks... She was in good health?"

"Aye, she were sad, to be sure; but she was always a hard woman. Took after Aldred that way."

"My thanks again," Ge-or said. "I will stay the one night. I have some herbs, given me by a good cleric. They might help your cough and illness. You are welcome to half. Brew them as a tea and drink a couple of times each day for three days. I will get them for you."

Ge-or left early the next morning. He headed east. He was determined to find Leona and, he hoped, a healthy baby.

Two months later, Ge-or was no closer to finding Leona than he had been when he left the Last Outpost behind. The trail had gone cold immediately upon heading east. Try as he might, riding from one town and tavern to another throughout that part of the kingdom, no one could give him any definitive information. There were so many farmers and ranchers on the roads this time of year, trading and gathering things for the winter to come, that one lone woman in a cart with or without a babe, did not stand out in anyone's memory.

First, he had gone east up to and across the King's Wall. After that, he had backtracked and tried every road and trail north and south he could find, tracing each until they came to a town or outpost and another and another. He would continue until that path seemed futile; then he would try another.

By late in the fall, far to the north, his money was getting low. He knew he had to make a decision. Stradryk's offer was still on the table, though he might not make it that far to the west before the winter snows settled in. His other choice was to head back to Aelfric to find some other source of employment. Yet he loathed the thought of hiring on as a guard for the wine merchants heading south, or a group of miners heading into the west.

Finally, he decided to take the half-gzk up on his offer. He knew how to trap and hunt. It would be an active lifestyle in spite of the cold and ice, and he would at least feel closer to home. Plus, it would give him the opportunity to seek out and study the dragon near its lair.

Taking the coin he had remaining, he bought as much additional provisions as his mule and mare could carry; finally he started out across the northern road to the west. He figured that if the snows blocked him in early, he would be able to stay in one of the coastal villages for the winter, earning his keep through hard work.

If the weather held, he would head south at Permis; or if he could bear to go there, west to Thiele and beyond.

***

"I'm glad you waited before you shot!" Ge-or laughed, jumping off his horse and grabbing Stradryk in a bear hug. "I was worried the snows would keep me from finding you."

Stradryk grinned. "I had all but given up hope you would come. Trapping is picking up. I'm glad you are here. Tell me what you have been up to."

Ge-or caught Stradryk up on his travels and concerns. They sat in front of the fireplace of the comfortable one room cabin the half-gzk had built and sparsely furnished over the past three trapping seasons. It was good to see his friend. For the first time in months, Ge-or felt he was where he was supposed to be, at least for now.

End of Term and Beyond

Term exams and performance juries had taken virtually all their time the two weeks before Yuletide. The few minutes Jared and Karenna had been able to sneak aside had only allowed them a quick kiss and snuggle. Both of them had done well, or well enough. Jared was once again "Good-minus" at theory, and received an "Excellent" for history, "Good-plus" for lore, and "Good-plus" for mathematics – it ranked right up there with music theory, as far as his enjoying the class was concerned. He had received "Excellents" in his performance classes. He felt that was only because he had been tops at improvisation during the juried exams. Karenna had received all "Excellents" per usual, though Jared had never seen her study so hard. Her only "bad" mark, as she referred to it, was in archery, where she was still over-controlling her shots. Markings were different for weaponry; she had received an "Improving."

Simon-Nathan had also done well, excelling in History and Lore with "Good" or better in all his other subjects. His practical musicianship, string instrument performance, and lessons were only "Goods;" but he didn't complain, as he had never had any desire to be a performer. He un-judiciously stuck his tongue out at Karenna when she found out that he had received a "Marked Improvement" in archery. She was still, ostensibly, not talking to him.

***

Karenna stirred, and Jared stroked her hair. "Hmmm, I like that, is it light yet?"

"No, we still have time... Karenna?"

"Yes?"

"Have you ever worried about, ah... been concerned about getting... being with child?"

"Wha-a...? Jared!Just like a man to ask long after it would likely matter." She tickled him.

"Hey, stop that, I was only trying to show some concern."

Karenna pushed herself partially up. "I am fine. I have some herbs; and yes, they are safe, and they are pretty reliable."

"Pretty?"

"Jared! You really can be dense sometimes. No method of birth-control is one hundred percent reliable, and you are half-elven. Well, if you don't know by now, it is difficult for elves to have children even under the best of circumstances, even half-elves. No, I am not taking unnecessary chances. I want to finish my schooling first. Then... well 'then' is a long way off."

"I surrender, oh wise one. Now where were we before I asked the stupid question?"

***

Aberon was fuming. The damned half-elf had led him on a peripatetic chase all over the countryside, through dozens of towns, hamlets, and outposts. Somehow, Aberon had always been one or two steps behind. It had taken him several weeks to finally have the sense to ask someone what the big fellow was up to. A woman and a babe? Ge-or? Ge-or, formerly of Thiele, and son of Manfred the Bold? The big brute had been busy since he had escaped the carnage of his village.

Now he appeared to have left this single-minded pursuit and gone to ground way out west somewhere. Aberon was not interested in pursuing this further during the winter. He had power to consolidate, and he wanted his brethren to know it. Well, if the dragon didn't fry the idiot, he would have some of his minions track him down in the spring. Still, it would be good to know if he had the thing. Too bad he hadn't gotten anywhere close enough to sense whether he had it on him. Now, he had other fish to fry. Number Eight was not going to like the oil he cooked him in; and if his mood didn't improve, the idiot might wish for such an easy end.

***

It was mid-winter, and Jared and Thistle were sipping rum-laced hot chocolate at a tavern near Bard Hall. Their situation still felt odd to Jared, yet he was happy to be with her. It was not that Karenna was forgotten; a different, deeper need spoke to him when he was with Thistle. He had not been able to tell if she really enjoyed seeing him or not. They typically talked about what they had been studying or working on, interesting tidbits about the past month, or general things happening in and about the Borean capital. She was always pleasant, greeted him warmly with a gloved handshake; and afterward, they either took a walk, if the weather was good, or enjoyed the service of the tavern if not. Today there was a cold gray mist blowing in from the sea; and though it wasn't freezing yet on the cobblestones, the bitterness penetrated even the warmest of cloaks.

"Thistle?"

"Yes, Jared?"

There, that's the problem, he thought. It's as if everything we say is formal, polite... too polite. We're not being ourselves.

"I want to tell you something, share something with you that I have been thinking about related to... well, to us and Karenna. Is that all right with you?"

Thistle nodded.

"I know this isn't going to be easy for you; however, I think it is important. I love Karenna. I love being with her, and we enjoy each other. I..." He paused trying to assess Thistle's reaction; she seemed content to wait for him to continue.

"I want you to know that how I feel about her doesn't diminish in any way how I feel about you; about wanting to be with you – to... to love you. If anything," he hesitated, but finally reached out and brushed her cheek with the fingertips of his right hand, "I feel like I care for you even more. Maybe it doesn't make much sense; yet I feel like I have learned to open myself up to the possibilities of love – and that doesn't diminish it, it makes it blossom." He reached up to touch her cheek again; she caught his hand in her gloved one and pushed it down.

"No, not yet, Jared. I'm not ready." Tears formed in her eyes. "Oh, Jared, I'm sorry, I'm so sorry." She buried her face in her hands and sobbed. All he could do was sit and wait, not daring to reach out to her again.

After what seemed like a long time, her sobbing stopped; and she was able to straighten up and look at him. A few tears ran down her cheeks. She dabbed at them with a kerchief. "I'm sorry, Jared. I... I need to explain some things...

"First, please understand that this is not me. Well, it is, though not entirely. I am going through a good bit of emotional upheaval right now because... because I am still becoming a woman. Meligance explained that it is different for me – slower and more intense in some ways because of the magic, because of the energy within me.

"I cannot touch you, allow you to touch me, because it would make all of this

204

turmoil inside of me even worse. I cannot, though I would wish it, understand what you told me either.

"I do trust you, Jared. You have always been truthful with me; and while it does hurt to think of you with another, with your Karenna, I know you would not tell me something unless it was important to you, and you felt it was important for me to understand. I will try; please give me time." Thistle tried to smile; her lips barely managed an upturn.

Jared knew this was quite difficult for her, and he knew enough to sit and listen as she went on.

"I also realize that these meetings we have are little nothings in which we are polite to each other and share simple things. To me they mean much more than that; they remind me of what I am working toward. Whether we end up together or not, you are my lifeline to the real world. Someday, I hope to be able to rejoin that world with you, or not, as myself. I will be different by then, as you will be; and we will find each other, or we will move apart and be with others. For now, your representing that is enough for me.

"There are times, Jared, that I would throw this all away if I could, just to spend one day and night with you. But I can't. At other times, I understand this gift and my responsibility to it. I am dedicated to making it work for me, for us. Please, be who you must be. Make the right choices for yourself. I will be waiting for you up to a point. We will see who we are, and what each of us can accept of, and from, the other."

Thistle reached out with her gloved hands taking his in hers. She turned them over so she could see his calluses. She caressed the hard spots with her fingers. "I am so happy you are making music. Someday, I will hear you play again, perhaps for me." She released his hands, stood quickly, and was striding out the door to her carriage before he could say goodbye.

***

"I wondered whether you would find an excuse to cause me some type of distress this year, young Jared." Leonis peered over a pair of spectacles he had perched on the end of his nose. "To what do I owe the honor this time?"

"Distress, sir? Never. I do appreciate your taking the time to see me about a concern... ah, more of a question, I have been pondering."

"Sometimes one can ponder too much, you know."

"Yes, sir, if I was worried, I would take that advice; perhaps this is more of an imponderable than a ponderable."

"Well, it must be of some import. Out with it, lad, or I will miss my nap."

"Constitutional?"

"Yes, of course, much better – my constitutional rest."

Jared grinned. He and Leonis had developed a bit of repartee in the few times they had run into each other this year, sparring lightly in spite of the differences in their age and position. Jared knew that if he ever did have a serious problem, the grandmaster would make every effort to help. What he wanted to know today was a bit more global, and in some sense, closer to home.

"Women, sir."

"You are having trouble with women? Son, I don't believe I can help."

"No sir! I'm fine. Ah..." Jared blushed. "I mean, I was wondering why women can't become Bards. I don't understand the reasoning, although, I must admit I was

205

surprised when I first got to Bard Hall to find that there were girls studying here at all. I had never seen a woman minstrel or jongleur come through our village."

"Not even in the troupes?"

"Well, yes, now that you mention it, there were women who sang, danced, and did acrobatics; however, the dramas and plays with music were all men, even in the female roles. The only instruments I saw them play were percussive, and those were simple tambours, cymbals, and so forth."

"Yes; well, young Jared, you have raised a long pondered and discussed concern of this institution. The answer always comes back to one basic concept."

"And that is?"

"Tradition."

"How...?"

"Hold a minute, Jared. Let me try to explain – times change, things change, customs change, all, typically, in good time. While travelling troupes of entertainers certainly have women in some roles and varying capacities, and some let women, especially in the last few decades, take on some non-traditional roles, the trained musicians have always studied here. Well, I should say, those with formal training have studied here. Even those who play many of our traditional instruments in these wandering troupes have gotten part of their education here at Bard Hall.

"As you have probably noted, many do not succeed here. The curriculum is difficult and you either measure up, or you are asked to leave. We do not abide those who are not dedicated, and, as you know, we do not accept those who do not have talent.

"Traditionally, for many centuries, Bard Hall was completely closed to women. Only within the last twenty years have we opened our doors to them, and only as students of music, not to become Bards."

"But..."

"Yes, but! Things *are* changing, Jared; and you are in the midst of it, as is your young lady friend." Leonis raised his left eyebrow and smiled. "The announcements last spring were a small, but important step in that direction.

"Jared, you must understand that traditions such as we have here are exceedingly difficult to change. Witness the new music – it has been 'in the works' for over two centuries. Ask Simon-Nathan, I imagine he would be happy to guide you through that historical progression. Much of that time, the music was changing out there." Leonis waved to include the whole kingdom. "Where the people have made choices based on what pleases their ears and what is easier to perform. Here in The Hall? Well, I tell you, there is even today much resistance to the new 'tuning,' harmonization, and modulations, a more vertical sound, and so forth.

"You and others like you, Jared, are at the forefront of what is really happening out in the real world of music – what people listen to, sing, and attempt to duplicate. When you come here, you bring it with you. Your whole life you have been performing this 'new' music, which in the field is still a combination of the old and the new, yet always with an inexorable move forward."

Leonis chuckled. "I am glad you came today, because I had cause to talk with you as well. Therin has been concerned about your performance, your instrumental lessons. He considers you to be a radical, a maverick, because you are constantly adding new to the old and old to the new in your improvisations. Whereas young Julingo, who did his Apprenticeship and Journeymanship during the heart of these changes, thinks you are brilliant.

"Here is some sage advice, my young friend, learn from both and you will excel. The old has its place, as does the new. We are at our best if we can embrace both, and take the best of all of it and make it our own.

"I have gone on enough. I am old, Jared, and I am from the old school of thought; but I do see the value in change. I have been fighting for it ever since becoming grandmaster. These things take time, perseverance, and careful handling. The full Council of Bards still has many from the old school: men who hold to tradition -- men only, polyphony is the only true music, and so forth – those who resist change whenever they can. We have made progress. I always find it amusing when they call me a 'progressive.' Ah, well." Leonis paused, considering something before continuing.

"You will see more changes happening, Son, sooner than later, I trust. What you ask about is still down the road a pace. Remember this, tradition *is* important – it sets guidelines for our lore; it establishes tried and true practices; and it gives us a foundation upon which to build. It also can be stodgy and inflexible."

Leonis straightened and smiled. "I do have one surprise that you can tell your friend if you wish. I would beg a boon that neither of you share it with others, except perhaps young Simon-Nathan, before the spring exams. I have pushed through the Council a one-year apprenticeship for women who have completed four years of study here."

"Truly?" Jared was actually amazed. He had figured Leonis would kindly tell him that some things would never change. This was an interesting development. Karenna would be ecstatic.

"Truly. While it may not seem like much of a victory, it is one of the hardest battles I have ever fought. It is a huge leap, one that may presage the dawn of a new era at Bard Hall, though there are many more hurdles to overcome."

"Thank you, Grandmaster. I do understand the import of this, and I know Karenna will as well. Also, thank you for the advice. I will do my best, sir."

"Do you think you will capture the Short Sword Cup this year?"

"I'm going to try, sir."

Leonis watched Jared leave. *I am* feeling old, he thought. This boy and others like him are the future of Bard Hall, or we won't have one.

"Jared," Karenna squeaked, when he told her and Simon-Nathan about his decision to ask Leonis the question the three of them had often talked about into the wee hours. She was elated by the news of the apprentice year for women. "You are a fool. You are the only person I know who actually goes to see the grandmaster to ask him questions. That's like your average merchant requesting to attend an audience with the king. I think I would throw up if I had to talk with the grandmaster."

"He's nice, actually, and he likes me. Well, I think he does. And, what's this about me being 'average?'"

"I didn't mean…" Karenna saw he was joking, and she launched herself into his arms and began to tickle him. "Come on, Simon-Nathan, this half-elf needs to be taught a lesson."

***

"How far up?"

"About half-way from what I can tell. He emerges there." Stradryk pointed high up the side of the mountain. "See the rocky outcropping; almost looks like a gopher's head."

Ge-or squinted in the bright sunlight; he nodded. "How long does he stay out while hunting?"

"Three, maybe four hours, sometimes much longer. He heads east. I imagine he will be back any time. He left while I was first checking the traps this morning. Big. I swear he scares me each time, but I know he has no interest in me. He wants a big fat cow or two; usually will have one in his mouth when he comes back. He drops it in his lair, then flies in big circles about the mountain for a space. That's the best time to get a look at him."

"He doesn't care that we watch him."

"I reckon he doesn't see us as a threat. Come, let's check the traps south while we wait. From what I picked up to the west, it was a good night."

Growing Up

Thistle was in agony, doubled up on the floor, unable to reach the bell pull, much less call Alli with her magic. She moaned, clutching her abdomen, then tried to pull herself along the floor. She didn't even know what time of day it was. She had fallen asleep after a hot bath, which had helped ease the cramping; suddenly she woke in worse pain. She hadn't made it to the doorway before she had collapsed, fainted, and later woke. Mercifully, she fainted again.

"Come, child, drink a bit more. It will ease the discomfort." Thistle opened her eyes, but she could not focus through the haze of red-fire pain in her head. She recognized Sart's voice, which seemed as if it was coming from another dimension. She tried to obey, yet she did not know whether she had been able to swallow. A while later, the fire eased, and shortly thereafter she fell deeply asleep.

"I am worried." Meligance looked across the table at Sart, who was sitting on a high stool, his eyes lowered. He, too, was frowning deeply. "It was never this bad for me, and it *was* bad. Some days I felt as if I was going to die, or at the least I felt the need to destroy something to give me release from the agony."

Sart's mouth tightened into a straight line. "I have given her some medicine; it is only for the worst days. She could become reliant on it. She is determined; I have to admit that. She won't even ask me for it."

"There is a stubborn streak about her, more than that, too; she is brave. Such a thin, light thing, and yet she is not afraid to face anything. There is great power there, else she would not be having so bad a time of it right now.

"I am surprised she didn't sense the magic. 'Indigestion,' she called the sensation. Did I tell you that?"

"Yes," Sart chuckled. "Wilderness-bred, my dear Meligance. Oldest of five girls. You learn to survive and put up with many difficulties."

Meligance nodded wearily. "All true, my good cleric. I cannot relate to that part of her. I am a city girl from privilege. It still was not an easy road. Perhaps it is best she has this kind of practical strength. Do you worry she won't get through this?"

"Nay," Sart answered. "She is strong in ways we cannot even ken, you and I. My worry is that it will damage the best things about her – her innocence, joy, her curiosity."

"We all must grow up, Sart."

"Must we?" Sart's eyes twinkled. "I must have forgotten that step."

"Yes, I guess I wasn't thinking. Take care of her, as best you may, please! We're going to need her one day."

"I will be here until summer; however, things are pressing out west. Let us hope she is improving by then."

***

Thistle was tired, but at least she was up and about. Alli had been wonderful helping her through the horribleness of it all – she drew baths twice a day for her mistress; remained at her side, keeping her warm deep into the night when the pains were bad; and kept looking after her every need. She did all of this and put up with her bad moods as well.

They were both sitting quietly in the study room reading. Thistle was with her translations; and Alli, now graduated to adult books, was studying weaving -- something she had been fascinated with since their visit to the museum.

"Alli?"

"Yes, Thistle." Putting her finger on the page where she had stopped, she looked up, smiling.

"I have an idea. An exciting idea, I hope. If... well, if I am hale enough to travel. Would you like to come with me to my home in Permis this summer? Meligance has given me leave to go. She says it will be good for me to take a break. Maybe it will help me get through some of this, too – to be around my family, you know?"

"Wouldn't it be a long, long trip by carriage, milady?"

"Oh, no, we couldn't go by carriage. The roads out west are too rough, and the trip would take many weeks. We can go by boat. It will take a week if the winds are favorable, not more than two."

"Boat! That would be fun if... if I don't get sick."

"Sart told me he has some medicine for that. I may even need some myself; it is a while since I have been on fishing boats. These woman troubles may make me nauseous anyway. And..." Thistle leaned forward and took the girl's hands in hers. "You can be as a sister to me. We will work together; everyone pitches in there. You will meet my family, and I can teach you so many things. You need to know that some of the work will be hard: hoeing, lifting, scrapping hides, tanning, spinning, dyeing, and weaving – you'll like that – and so much more. We can ride horses together, and I can show you my favorite secret places.

"Alli, please say you will come. We'll have so much fun together. I can be home and not do this for a while." She gestured in a circle. "I need a break."

"I think it would be fun, Thistle. I hope we can go."

"Mayhap I will have to practice some, but only to keep my edge. Nothing new. I want to feel free, even if I'm not, at least for a little while."

Fur Trading

It had been another good winter. Stradryk went so far to the west that no one else trapped anywhere near. Because of that, it would be a long trek back, through some very difficult terrain.

They left the cabin and trapping grounds at the first hint of spring. Ge-or and Stradryk knew they would likely have to brave a late snowstorm or two, but it was far easier drawing the sleds across the snow than through mud and muck once it thawed.

Ge-or had enjoyed the winter; and though he missed both Leona and Katelyn and the intimacy they had shared, Stradryk proved to be a good companion. After dark, they drank a homemade brew that Stradryk had concocted from local tubers gathered in the fall. It was "god-awful-stuff" according to Ge-or – it served. They shared tales, and played draughts, knights, and other games. Ge-or spent some of the evening carving pieces for them, while Stradryk preferred sitting out on the stoop and smoking a pipe of some smelly weed. He said he had picked up the habit in the south. Ge-or had only seen others who "smoked" on rare occasions, when some wandering minstrel or tin-man would come through their village. No one in his village had ever gotten the habit, nor could most have afforded such an expensive luxury. Stradryk said it was his only vice – he didn't think of women and drink as vices.

The work had been hard. Setting and checking traps was cold, miserable work, yet it was nothing compared to skinning and preserving the furs for transport. As long as it was light, they worked hard. Their only respite was when the weather got bad enough to keep them cooped up while the snow and wind raged outside. Still, it was honest work that you could see the benefit from. And they had done well. Even after building a second sled, they still had to leave some of the less desirable furs behind.

They made good time on their trek east and north, following almost the exact route that Ge-or had taken late in the fall. As he had on his way westward, Ge-or stopped with Stradryk in Permis, where he said hello to those from his village who had now made the place their home. After two days there, they continued eastward along the coast. Three weeks out from their trapping spot, the spring thaw started in earnest. They traded some furs for a walk-by cart that the mules could pull; then they headed south on the same road that Stradryk had told Ge-or about over a year ago.

Six weeks after leaving the far west, the two trappers found themselves settling back into the Druid's Hut in Aelfric. Stradryk took Ge-or to the fur-trading center, introducing him to all the traders. Ge-or was surprised to learn that the dealers, if one knew them well enough and you had top quality furs like ermine, mink, beaver, and sable, were willing to bid against each other. His only experience had been in selling his wolf pelts to a single man; these dealers were interested in the best quality.

For a week straight, they went each day with a small bundle of their furs, separated as to type and quality; presenting their wares to the traders, they let the fun begin. Often it was a combination of bidding, bargaining, and swearing before a final deal was agreed on. Stradryk obviously knew what he was doing, because he drew the attention of the best dealers. Somehow, they always did a bit better than the day before. The half-gzk planned out the whole charade from the beginning to the end, and the fur traders knew how he worked. The best of the best would be saved for the last day, only the traders didn't know which day that might be.

With Stradryk's expertise, they did quite well. Ge-or had enough money to do what he would for several months. First, he needed new clothes to replace those worn and patched so much that he hardly recognized the original cloth. Even the quality wools from Goat Haven were beginning to wear.

Ge-or decided to make one last effort to find Leona. He told Stradryk that he would return in one month. If the half-gzk was still in Aelfric when he returned, they would try to find an adventure together.

A weary and discouraged Ge-or straggled into Aelfric exactly one month after setting out determined to find his lost love. He had travelled even further than the previous year and spent all his money cajoling information from barkeeps, innkeepers, and merchants within forty leagues of Goat Haven. He had not heard anything that gave him any hope of finding her and the babe. He had to admit that the only evidence he had that spoke to her ever having had a baby with her was that she had taken the cradle, the baby things she had woven, and the toys Aldred had made. From what he had seen, there had been no second grave. On a side trip, he stopped once more in the vale to look around, but nothing had changed since his visit the previous fall.

He spent two days there trying to find anything he might have missed that would have spoken to where she had gone, wracking his brain as to whether she had ever mentioned any relatives. He had come up empty.

Luckily, Stradryk was still in Aelfric when he returned to the border town; and he did have some good news, which helped Ge-or focus on other things. Sart had sent word from Borea that he was looking for both of them. He had what he hoped would be a fast, and possibly lucrative, trek out to the western mountains. It was deep into Qa-ryk lands; nevertheless, they could move along the foothills of the southern range, trying to stay out of harm's way. He planned a small party that could move quickly. The crypt they would enter was small.

"Crypt?" asked Ge-or.

"Aye," Stradryk answered. "They are common adventuring sites; they often hold quality treasure and magical items."

"We go as grave robbers?"

"Come, Ge-or, think on it. These well-to-dos think they can take their beloved baubles with them, yet... Well, Sart is a cleric, and he does not mind. He believes that the soul moves on from the body, and what remains is eventually only dust, unless..."

"Unless what?"

"Well, he says some souls remain behind, because they try to hold onto this life. That's where the undead come in."

"Undead? You mean skeletons and zombies, children's nightmares?"

"Aye, those and others. Skels are not true undead; they are animated remains brought back to 'life' by magical means. The true undead are those 'things,' beings, former humanoids, that have chosen unlife after life. Their soul remains in this plane of existence; but they cannot sustain their body, as the life-force is no longer connected to all that makes us alive – like wraiths, ghouls, and ghosts. Nasty things."

Ge-or was appalled. "And we might meet these things? Have to fight them?"

"Aye. Fear not, my friend, skels and other animated undead are not so dangerous. The others? They are certainly deadly. Even so, we will have Sart. Clerics specialize in sending lost souls into the void, where they should have gone in the first place. Or, as Sart would say, into their next incarnation."

"Truthfully?" Ge-or shook his head. "I believed they were only childish fears."

"I am not the one to tell you of them. Sart can explain far better than I. Trust me on this, though, crypts can be treasure troves; and from what you have said, you will need much more money to further your quest to kill that big beast out west."

Ge-or knew that what Stradryk said was true. He was not much closer to having the means to fight the dragon than he was when he began; and after seeing it again, he knew he was ill-prepared for the venture.

It was three weeks before Sart intended to arrive in Aelfric, so Stradryk took Ge-or to some shops where he hadn't been before. At a weapons merchant in one of the most expensive areas of town, they purchased several dozen silver-alloy arrowheads, which, the half-gzk explained, could be effective against many of the true undead. He also had Ge-or buy a long silver stiletto, for which he lent his partner the money. "You can pay me back from the loot we take, else when we trap again next winter."

Ge-or was loathe to owe anyone. His father had drummed many platitudes into his sons' heads. One that had stuck, and had been somewhat of a north-village code that had spread more universally, was "Borrow not; Lend not," which held in respect only to monies, not tools, food, or other necessities which were freely given or lent. Stradryk did convince him that he would need quality weapons for this quest.

Finally, they wended their way through some of the darker alleys of the border town, ending up in front of a decrepit door of a dilapidated establishment. "Let me do the talking, Ge-or. This fellow's a might touchy."

Ge-or shrugged, wondering what Stradryk was up to now.

The half-gzk knocked on the door, once, twice, thrice, in a repetitive pattern; and finally, after a long pause, a disembodied voice seemed to come out of the woodwork right above their heads. "Fine, fine. By-the-gods, Stradryk, must you bother me all the time. Didn't I do something for you a couple of years ago? Did it wear off? I think not. Well, you're here and I'm awake, come in, come in."

Stradryk pulled the door outward, ducking under the low lintel to enter. Ge-or almost had to double over to get in.

Ge-or followed his friend as they wound their way through a very odd shop, stuffed with strange items on shelves and in glass-fronted cabinets. Making the atmosphere more eerie were dozens of multicolored cloths and draperies hanging from the ceiling. They had to brush these aside as they moved through the room. Eventually, they ended up in front of a small counter. The half-gzk stood patiently waiting for the proprietor to emerge.

After several minutes, Ge-or heard some shuffling. A small, wizened old man came out from behind a curtain of what looked to be the finest silk. It was dyed in a moving pattern of reds, blues, purples, and greens that threatened to mesmerize one's eyes. The fellow himself was odd. He had on a tall, light blue hat, much worn and spotted with dirt, which had as decoration what looked to be yellow moons, stars, and other celestial bodies sewn on it. His torso and on down to his knees was covered with an equally dirty, clashing purple robe. Ge-or opened his mouth, shut it. He noticed that

Stradryk was bowing low at the waist, gesturing for Ge-or to do the same. He followed suit.

"Stupendous one. Great Ordrake, grant us a boon."

"Yes, yes, I know, you know, it's all good. Come, what do you want?" The little man waved his hands in the air; suddenly it sounded like a hundred bells all began to chime at once.

Stradryk had to shout above the din. He gestured again toward Ge-or, "Your knife, Ge-or. The stiletto."

Ge-or blinked; he handed the blade to Stradryk, who in turn handed it to Ordrake.

The little man studied it carefully, turning it over and over in his hands. "Nice blade, silver. You going out with Sart to that crypt he's been wanting to explore? Some good stuff there, I warrant. You'll probably have some nasties to take care of. That's what you want me to do right? Magic it up a bit for you?"

"Aye, most revered Ordrake, if you…"

"Stop with the crap, you two. I'm old, but not touched in the head. All right, come back in a week. I'll do what I can. What do you have for me?"

Though Ge-or did not think he could be much more surprised, Stradryk held out his hand. Laying in his palm were two good-sized gems – a bright red ruby and a lovely shimmering green opal.

"Ah, the ruby will do nicely." Ordrake plucked the gem from Stradryk's hand. "I love rubies; they are quite nice for holding fire. One week. It'll be in the door, as

214

usual. Don't knock. It's hard enough getting sleep these days with all this noise in my head."

"Stradryk, I can't pay you back for this stone."

"Ge-or, we have been through this. Peace. Take it as a gift, or wait and you will find better than this and more on one of our quests. It is not of importance to me. I have more than enough money put away."

One thing Ge-or had often wondered about was what Stradryk did with his coin. As far as he had seen, except for what he needed for basic necessities and occasional equipment, the half-gzk deposited all he got with the moneylenders. Finally, curiosity got the better of him.

"Are you saving for a rainy day?"

"Nay, I hold some in reserve to keep me, if I should be too injured to work; the rest, well, I gift much of it."

"Gift?"

"Aye, Ge-or, I am one of the lucky ones of… of my kind. It happens more than you ken, and often the result is a creature that is not capable of fending for himself. There are others as well – outcasts of society. Some are simply unwanted oddities or mental cases that the rich do not want to deal with. What do you think comes of these creatures?"

"I know not."

"Nor do most; or those that know, think not on it."

"And?"

"There are places, they call them sanitariums. Often, they are run by monks or priests, but they are ill-funded. The moneylender I use is a good man. He showed me how I can make a small difference; and as he does, I donate to those places that help as they can."

"I feel ashamed. I have never heard of such. In the north we take care of our own; it matters not whether they are physically or mentally whole. It is part of the code."

"Aye. Well the code here, and in the great cities even more, seems to be denial and avoidance."

"You are a good man, Stradryk."

"No, I am not – neither man, nor good; yet perhaps I can do something to help compensate for my sins. I would prefer you ask me no more on this, friend." With that Stradryk took out his pipe, got up, and headed for the door of the Druid's Hut to smoke. Ge-or knew well enough not to disturb him further.

Summer: A Magical Time

It was Solisday. Karenna, Jared, and Simon-Nathan were sitting in the Green Horse tavern just down the street from Bard Hall with tall ales in hand. The spring term was over, and they were each celebrating having made it through another year. They felt good, though Jared was a bit battered from his final match against Markus. This year he had prevailed, mostly because of his hard work getting in better shape. Both the Archery Shortbow and Short Sword Cups were his.

They had all done well. As usual, Karenna received honors medals in all her academic subjects. Simon-Nathan excelled in history and lore, and he also placed fourth in archery in Level II, which he was even prouder of than his two academic medals. Jared had gotten "Excellents" in all his subjects except theory, which had dipped once again to "Good-minus." He didn't mind; he had done the best he could. Karenna was a bit chagrined because she had tried so hard to help him "get it."

Karenna snuggled up close to Jared. Her carriage home was picking her up in less than an hour. She was reluctant to go.

Simon-Nathan stood to leave. "Look, I'm going to head over to the house and get settled. You two need some time alone, and it's probably best to let Dad and Mom fawn all over me before you get there. That way I won't be so embarrassed." Simon-Nathan had thinned out considerably the past year thanks to their early morning workouts. Now that his face was gaining maturity and had lost some of its roundness, he was a striking young man.

Karenna jumped up and kissed him soundly on his cheek. He blushed a deep red. "Take care of yourself, Simon. I'll miss you. See you next term."

Jared also stood and patted his roommate on the back. "I'll be along anon. Don't worry about sending the carriage back. I want to walk."

With Simon-Nathan gone, the two huddled together in the corner of their bench, trying to remember this feeling enough to get them through the summer. All too soon, Karenna had to go. Outside she kissed Jared long and passionately. "Stay safe, elf-kin. I love you." She quickly turned away so he couldn't see her start to cry

Jared stood watching her go. It had been a good year. He had worked hard and accomplished a great deal. It was good to be alive. He looked forward to his summer working for Simon-the-Elder again. It would be a good break from academics. He had already planned a ride south in mid-summer to visit Karenna for a week. After that, they would come back together, and she would help out in one of the shops. It would be nice to have her close for at least part of the summer.

***

Thistle laughed gaily for the first time in months. The fresh sea breeze was blowing through her hair, and the rolling of the boat against the waves was something she had missed. She had always enjoyed the early morning fishing trips with her father during the spring and summer. Poor Alli was suffering a bit from nausea, but Sart had given her a powdered root that appeared to be helping. Thistle was enjoying tending her as a reversal of their roles. Truthfully, Alli was mortified that her mistress should do so, yet she was too weak to protest much. They were boarded in the best cabin on the merchant vessel. Even so, it was small and cramped compared to what they were used to. When not tending Alli, Thistle spent most of her time on deck chatting with the crew, or even lending a hand when they shifted sails to tack.

They were ten days out when the boat turned toward the coast. Only a few hours after that, Thistle could see the mountains rising in the distance to the west, and soon thereafter she could make out the dock of Permis through the light mist.

When a boat came to dock from the east, it was always a time for celebration in the western villages. Permis was virtually self-sufficient, yet there were many things that came from Borea that were of better quality, finer manufacture, and more exotic than the locally-made wares. If it was a productive year either in the fields with their sheep and cattle or with trapping, the townspeople could splurge on niceties they otherwise could not produce themselves. This year the fields were green from consistent rains, and their warehouses were full of new wool bales and late winter furs. There would be a day of festivities following the unloading and reloading of the boat.

It was good to be home and to spend time with her family and friends, especially her sisters. Thistle quickly discovered how soft her life had become. For three weeks, she struggled with sore fingers, blisters, and fatigue until she began to get hardened again. Alli struggled a bit, too. Though she was used to her chores as a chambermaid, she had never worked in the fields, spun wool, scrapped hides, or many of the other common tasks in a wilderness community. For once they were treated as equals, and that made Thistle more comfortable in getting to know her chambermaid as a friend.

During their limited free time, Thistle would take Alli up into the hills. There she taught her all she knew about woodsmanship. Her maid-servant was especially keen to learn to use a throwing knife, so they would try to get some practice sessions in several days a week. It wasn't until near the end of the summer that Alli managed to bring down a coney with one of her throws. She was prouder than a peacock when the rabbit was served up for dinner the next day.

Thistle was true to her personal promise to refrain from returning to her magic. She did spend an hour early each morning working on her focus, but she did not attempt any energy work. Though she was constantly asked to demonstrate things she had learned, she begged off, saying that the magic she was learning was for serious pursuits only, which was actually only partly true.

She certainly could have put on a display of magical tricks for the villagers: controlling and moving objects, creating light shows, making things disappear and reappear, and so on; however, she knew these frivolities had little to do with the focus of her magical arts. She agreed with Meligance that they were distractions from her true purpose, and they would give people the wrong impression of who she was and what she was about.

Whether it was her return to a more physically demanding lifestyle, her refraining from practice, her being with family and friends, or simply the passage of time, Thistle's female episodes were milder. She didn't have to take any of the medicine Sart had given her, and she had been able to meditate through the worse of the symptoms when they came on.

A few weeks before she was due to sail back, Thistle announced that she wanted to ride with Alli to visit Thiele. She had learned that a small contingent of rangers had settled there. They were building an outpost that would serve as a supply depot for some of the other wilderness posts, including Xur. She also felt a need to visit the stone obelisk erected there by the survivors of Thiele and the people of Permis. She wanted to close out that part of her former life by acknowledging the death of her betrothed.

She thought to go alone. Thistle's father, Harem, would hear none of that and insisted that she should have protection on the road. Alli had learned to ride that summer and wouldn't allow her mistress to wander off into the wilds without her, either. So, on a late summer day, before the sun began to rise in the east, the three of them rode west. It would be a long day, but none of them wanted to stay the night along the way.

Alli, on a brown and white pony, was always ahead of the two working stallions that Thistle and her father were riding. They made good time as they kept a fair pace. The sun began to get close to the western horizon when they saw the tops of the new stockade as they crested a hill.

Riding down toward the unfinished walls, Thistle suddenly realized something was wrong. A second later, Alli, who was riding ahead, stopped. She turned her pony around and was soon dashing back up the hill toward Thistle and her father. As she galloped up, she said breathlessly, "There's fighting. I heard shouting and the wall to the south appears to be on fire. We better go back."

Thistle didn't even have to think of what choice to make; she put her spurs into her horse's flanks and urged it toward the redoubt. "Thistle!" her father cried after her, but she didn't waver in her resolve. She continued on, aiming her steed toward the unfinished opening on the eastern part of the stockade.

"Come," Harem said to Alli. "Stay behind me. If we can help, we will." With that, he kneed his horse forward, drawing his sword as he went.

Thistle rode hard around the corner of the unfinished wall and immediately took in what was happening. Along the battlements to the west and south, the small stockade was under attack by Qa-ryks. Something or someone had blasted an opening in the western wall. She could tell that the rangers were overmanned; she could also see that the contingent of Qa-ryks wasn't more than a small company. This was not like the massacre at Thiele, nor did she think a dragon had done the damage she saw ahead. The fiery hole in the fence was too small.

Swinging off her mount, she rushed toward the opening, drawing her hand up as she went as if to cup a handful of air. Almost instantly, she was holding a bright intense ball in her fist. With a flick of her wrist, she sent it flying toward a cluster of the beasts who had scaled the southern wall. The pure energy hit the closest Qa-ryk in the chest and exploded, blowing him to bits. It sent the others near him, and at least two sections of the stockade, to the ground.

Whoops, thought Thistle. Control!

Thistle's father came around the corner as she released the energy. He stared wide-eyed at the power his daughter commanded. Alli, behind, grabbed his arm and pulled him back. "Hold! She can take care of herself." He nodded and slid off his horse, deciding to use his shortbow if he were needed.

Thistle continued to run toward the western wall of the stockade where a dozen rangers were fighting desperately to keep the beasts from overwhelming them. Luckily, the commander of the rangers had swung around to see whence the blast had come. He saw Thistle sprinting toward the group. She gasped out, "Fall back, get them back. I will…"

The young ranger nodded. He barked orders to his men. "Retreat! Retreat in order, back to the dock. Now!"

Immediately, the men began to disengage, following what appeared to be a practiced plan. The Qa-ryks, with nothing to hold them back except the narrowness of the opening, crushed through the broken stockade, jostling each other in their frenzy to continue the attack. That gave the rangers enough time to clear some distance as they ran toward the water.

Thistle, now about twenty-five paces from the mass of beasts, stood her ground. Once again, she reached into the air and created another ball of energy. Focusing a bit more than her hurried first attack, she focused on a single word, which triggered her control and manipulation of what she now held in her hand. Flicking her wrist again, the orb sped toward the center of the target area, expanding as it flew forward. About two paces in front of the Qa-ryks, it exploded into a massive fireball that swept into their ranks.

The beasts that were caught flush with that fearsome blast were virtually incinerated on the spot. Those to the periphery had their hair and skin sloughed off by the heat, they were instantly blinded, and many took the searing heat into their lungs as they gasped for air.

Ignoring the dreadful havoc she had just created, Thistle continued her work, now using energy bolts to selectively kill any of the Qa-ryks still on or within the stockade. By the time the inner walls were clear of any living beasts, her father, Alli, and half a dozen rangers, including the young lieutenant, had come up close behind her.

Once the skirmish was over, for all the remaining beasts fled after Thistle's destruction of their primary assault, the lieutenant thanked her profusely for her assistance. He begged to offer her his sword for saving his platoon. She politely declined, but accepted a small, finely crafted throwing dagger instead, for the man could not be dissuaded.

As the soldiers began to deal with the aftermath of the skirmish, Thistle took the time to visit the monument set in the center of where the old square had been. There she wept honest tears for Baldo and the many others who had fallen.

Finally, with darkness falling, she accepted an invitation from the lieutenant for her and Alli to use his officer's tent for the night. Thistle's father was happy to share another tent with the officer once all had been settled.

The next morn Thistle, her father, and Alli rode out of the encampment. The lieutenant and his men saluted her with their swords as they wended their way back up the hill to the east.

"By-the-gods!" It was probably the twentieth time her father had used the oath on their way back to Permis. "Had I known, Thistle!"

"Peace, Father. None of us knew; well, not before Thiele was destroyed. For better or for worse, it has always been my destiny. I am glad I found out before I could have hurt any of you or my husband. I do hope he is at peace with all the others." Much of the rest of the ride, they were content to enjoy the wonderful late summer day; yet even Alli had a new respect for her mistress's power.

***

Aberon was pacing and fuming. The Black Priest before him had just brought the news about the defeat at Thiele. The coward had run, scared out of his wits by a young witch. At least, that is how he had described her. According to his account, she had blasted a whole section of the stockade to bits and vaporized a patrol of the filthy beasts with a massive fire attack. That didn't sound like anyone young, and not in any way someone he would describe as a witch. This person had power and could use it – a mage? A Wizardess? Well, it didn't really matter, did it? The idiot before him had failed, and now there was this thorn of an outpost stuck in his side again.

He spun about once more, and with as much physical force as he could muster, he swung, slapping the man across the side of his head. The priest fell sideways onto the floor and lay there mewing.

""Pitiful! Get up, you idiot! It's bad enough that you fail me; you don't have to look the part. I have wasted too much time on this distraction already. I have my own business I must get back to. Send another patrol of young beasts who are anxious to please into the hills nearby. Have them keep an eye on the place. No further attacks. I want to know what they are doing there."

"Yes, Master," groveled the insect at his feet.

When he was the One, his subjects would suffer far worse fates than this worm, Aberon promised to himself. True power meant he was to be obeyed.

The Dead

Sart had been late arriving in Aelfric. It was early summer by the time the small group of adventurers left for the west. This time the cleric aimed to move quickly, and there were only four of them – Ge-or, Stradryk, Erno, an acolyte of the Earth, and Sart. They all rode mountain-bred horses with sure feet. In addition, each led a mule piled high with provisions. Though they would gather what game they could on the way, Sart did not want to waste any time; so they carried large quantities of victuals and even some fodder for the animals.

The acolyte, Erno, had been appointed primary cook and clean-up, since this was often the lot of novice adventurers. However, after their first, virtually inedible meal, Ge-or volunteered to take over. He did not fancy himself a good cook, yet he knew the basics. He had a passing knowledge of herbs and savories that would enhance their stews and roasts and enough campfire experience to be able to provide edible meals. Sart had been wise enough to ensure that they had some essentials. In addition, Ge-or was able to find a wide variety of wild herbs, onions, and garlic along their route. Following their second meal, Erno was re-designated chief pan-washer and water bearer.

Sart pushed them hard. From dawn until well into the evening, they skirted the edge of the mountains, taking what paths they could find that hugged the slopes. They stayed as far from the Qa-ryk patrol range as was feasible considering the terrain. Even so, they had to be wary of goblins and ogres at night. For their camp, they typically chose a well-protected niche against the rising walls to the south, or a defensible position amongst the trees and rocks of the foothills.

In spite of their efforts, it took them seventeen days before they turned northward toward what Sart described as a hidden vale where the ancient crypt lay. That evening, camping in a comfortable grove of hardwoods near a sparkling stream, Sart reviewed with them all that he knew of the site.

"As you know, what information I have on the vale and grave site comes from our work last summer. It seems Randaul's relations were as odd as he was. For several generations they were interred far to the west 'so as not to be disturbed.' In his rambling notes and diary, he speaks of an artifact that belonged to a great, great uncle, a minor king, who had received the device because he had done a boon for some powerful prince.

"He did not ever let on what the item was, only that it was magical and that it was coveted by his uncle. From what I could decipher, the fellow took it with him to the grave, clasped in his hands when he died. The family buried him with it. This all took place almost a hundred and fifty years ago. Since that initial interment, this uncle's immediate family all wished to be buried around the old fool -- literally.

"Randaul speaks of visiting the site in his youth for the last burial – a long-lived great aunt. He notes that in the crypt the one large sarcophagus of his great uncle is surrounded in an oval by lesser caskets. He said he felt a strange force radiating from the center of the center tomb, and there was 'a malevolency present that gave him a great fright.' He was only a young lad at the time, six or seven. He never went back; he did say he thought he should retrieve the item at some point.

"That, I'm afraid, is all we know. Good, evil, or neutral, a powerful device should not be left available to the forces that threaten the kingdom. It is remotely possible that it might have some bearing on Randaul's own quest for the Heart of the World, though that is completely supposition on my part.

"There is the possibility, even the likelihood, that the evil that Randaul felt present in the crypt was, and yet is, the spirits of the dead keeping watch on what lies buried there.

"We should reach the vale by nightfall tomorrow. We will camp outside and only enter during the day. Dark things are most powerful at night. Whatever lurks in the vale and in the tomb will be weakest when the sun is high. On the morrow, bring out your silvered and magicked weapons. I will bless all, and Erno will give each of you several vials of holy water, which burns the spirits of the dead like fire burns the living.

"If you have a choice, stay back should we be assailed by wraiths or other ethereal forms. These powerful undead spirits can drain your energy and life-force with their touch, which will make them even more powerful. I will handle them, with Erno's aid if needed. If you are cornered, stay out of range and use your arrows and vials first. Only resort to close combat if all else fails.

"The animated dead, skels and decaying bodies, can be destroyed with your regular steel weapons. Cleave through their center, and you will disrupt the force that holds them in sway.

"Ge-or?"

"Aye?"

"You have not fought such?"

"Nay, and the prospect is uncomfortable."

"Frightening?"

"In a way. I do not ken fighting something already dead. My father never spoke of it."

"It is wise to have a bit of fear, Ge-or. It helps us all keep our edge. However, unless there is more in this place than I think, we should not have too hard a time of it. Should we have to face the undead, keep this in mind – they have overstayed their time on this plane. Life is a process that we all pass through, and then move on. These souls chose not to embrace that cycle. We will simply be helping misguided spirits take the next step. They were afraid of what that might have been and have remained, by choice, locked into this realm of existence.

"The other thing, which I find a bit amusing, is that there are so many people who have the erroneous idea that they can take material things with them when they pass on. Fear not that we take from the dead. What they have coveted is no longer theirs to hold onto; and lest any of us forget, when we die, it will pass to others as well. Even these bodies we inhabit are only borrowed for a space. As all things, they will eventually be of the earth again." Sart smiled as he touched the ancient rood hanging from his neck. "It is the belief of my brethren."

"Still, it feels odd, disrespectful," Ge-or said hesitantly. "I have been taught to venerate the dead. It would be unthinkable to disturb the graves of our kin and friends."

"That is understandable, my friend, for we respect those we have known by honoring our memories of them. In many ways I, we," Sart gestured around the campfire, "share your feelings. We will despoil as little as possible. I do not disturb these places lightly, yet I also see little point in leaving that which is potentially useful and valuable in the 'hands' of those that have no need of it anymore. Worse yet, allowing it to be acquired by, and used to serve, the evil that threatens our world.

"You are an honorable man, Ge-or; and I see your wilderness upbringing in all that you are. Do not let me change that, for it is far better to question and ponder than to smash through one's life as if nothing matters. Everything matters – we have to put it into the context of what is most important for the moment in time in which we find ourselves. Live each as if it matters the most. Then you will have fully lived.

"My dear Ge-or, with your hesitation you have even given me pause to think more deeply on this quest. That is also a good thing. I thank you for it, because we all can get too wrapped up in our single-minded goals. You have helped me think about respect for all things, the living and the dead. Let us not forget to honor the fallen in the days ahead. Perhaps we can also help these lost souls find some peace. I will meditate on this tonight."

They entered the vale as the sun was rising above the hills to their right. The dell was an elongated oval with a single entrance to the south. Rocky walls surrounded the verdant center. Ge-or noted that if one did not already know where it was, it would have been almost impossible to find. It was an ideal site for something you wanted to keep from prying eyes. If Randaul hadn't written about it, it likely would have remained undisturbed for a long time. Already the earth, grasses, and shrubs had grown up, obscuring much of what had been built above ground.

With Sart in the lead, they moved single file down an animal trail toward the center of the vale. As they got closer, they could see a mausoleum set partially below the earth. Wide stone steps led down to two molded brass doors. They paused briefly at the top to readjust their weapons and to receive a final blessing from Sart.

Before descending, Stradryk took two torches from his backpack and held them while Ge-or plied flint to his knife. When lit, Sart gestured Ge-or to his right and Stradryk to his left. The two fighters drew their swords as they followed the cleric downward. Erno was to hang back at all times and only to come forward should Sart need his support.

Sart ran his hands over the door panels. Sensing no magic, he pushed the ornate handle down and put his shoulder to the right-hand door. It was unlocked and swung in easily. Stradryk only had to touch the other panel, and it swung in as well.

The crypt was rectangular in shape. It stretched ahead further than they could see in the mixed light. To their right and left were alcoves with marble busts on pedestals. Ge-or assumed these were of the family members who had been interred within the tomb. As far as they could see, the men all had a similar facial structure – thin, bony, with a prominent, almost hawk-like nose. Ge-or felt a shiver run up and down his spine. He was still uncomfortable with the whole idea of what they were doing, but he was willing to follow Sart's lead.

The cleric stepped forward slowly, looking to each side for any indication of trouble. After about ten paces, he gestured for Ge-or to hand him his torch. "Be ready," he whispered. The cleric brought the torch forward in his left hand; reaching under his robe, he drew out his heavy mace with his right. He took one more step forward when all hell broke loose, or so Ge-or felt.

The floor suddenly erupted in front of them. Three heavy marble panels flew straight at the adventurers. Though they were surprised, they were all easily able to duck out of the way. Erno, standing behind on the lowest step, had to dive sideways to miss the one that sailed over Sart's head. Following hard after the stone slabs, skeletal heads came up out of each of the openings.

Ge-or froze in place, convinced that death itself had come for him. Even in dreams as a child he had never imagined such a hell. It is one thing to think about a thing happening; actually seeing human bones moving as if alive WAS a living nightmare. He couldn't swallow; his mouth was as dry as the dust swirling in the air about them. Finally, the movement of his fellows into fighting postures awakened enough of his warrior mentality for him to follow suit.

The skeletons scrambled up out of the holes quickly. The first few were soon followed by others. They didn't have any weapons but reached out with their appendages as if they would claw their victims. Sart yelled, "Fight!" He stepped forward and swung at one that was bearing down on him. His mace smashed through the skull, and passed with relative ease through the rest of the brittle bones, snapping and breaking them apart as it plunged down. Stradryk also set about with his sword, hacking back and forth through the remains. With each swipe, the blade would crunch through another layer of bones.

Seeing his companions crushing the skels with ease, Ge-or shuddered violently once, throwing the skeleton aside that had clawed onto his shoulder. After that, Ge-or came to life. He entered the fray with his sword smashing down through the skull of the one closest to him.

The skeletons kept emerging from the floor almost as quickly as the adventurers turned them into piles of bones and dust. Still, the two fighters and Sart were able to fight their way forward toward the openings, eventually dispatching them as they emerged. Finally, the efflux slowed and then stopped. They each stood over a square hole in the floor of the tomb, looking down.

It was only a second later that Ge-or noticed the foul odor emanating from below his feet. He gagged, took a step back, and turned and ran toward the outer door. There he gagged again and lost his breakfast. Sensing that there would be no more attacks from below, and with their eyes streaming and noses running from the noxious fumes, Sart and Stradryk backed away from the open holes as well.

"Put the panels back," Sart gasped at Erno as they passed. The acolyte grimaced. Drawing a handkerchief from his robe he tied it tightly around his nose and mouth. "Up." Sart gestured for Ge-or and Stradryk to head out of the tomb. "I will help Erno."

"Demon holes," Sart said when they had all gathered at the top of the steps. "The less important members of a family do not merit a separate casket. With little ceremony, they are dumped into community tombs beneath the crypt. There they... Well, you get the picture. Now that the holes are capped, we will wait a couple of hours to let the fumes dissipate before venturing in again.

"There is magic in there," he said, gesturing at the tomb. "Skels are animated by a source of power. We may have more to deal with than I first thought. This uncle may have traded his life for unlife – becoming a minor lich, or at the least, a powerful crypt fiend. These are skeletal remains that have used magic to remain a part of this world after death. Our Recluse's uncle must have been at least a minor mage. We will need to be cautious as we proceed. I expect we will be assailed again, and by worse than animated dead.

"Are you all right, Ge-or?"

"Aye, that smell – the odor of death and rot is bad enough following a fight – that..."

"A century or more of rot and decay contained in a small space, and finally let out?" Sart said. "Aye, I reacted the same way the first time. It is not pleasant."

"You have encountered them before? By-the-gods!"

"I have even been down these kinds of holes before, my good half-elf. My quests take me to many unpleasant and dire places. It is often the price we must pay for knowledge. The past seems ever to impinge on our future. There are few enough of us that try to sway the tide now. Unfortunately, evil does not rest.

"Come, we should all relax while we wait. Here." Sart handed a bottle of dark brown liquid to Ge-or. "A little rum after a fracas is good for the soul."

Two hours later, as the sun was now climbing toward its zenith, they reentered the tomb. Sart instructed the three to roll heavy stones from above ground down the stairs and onto the three slabs of marble that marked the demon holes. He did not think anything else would come forth, but he did not want to take a chance at something coming up at them from behind.

In the same formation as before, they moved slowly further into the tomb until they saw large structures begin to emerge from the gloom. A few more steps ahead and they began to make out the formation of the stone caskets before them. As Randaul had described in his notes, limestone sepulchers were arranged around a much larger marble crypt in the center of the room.

From his position on the right, Ge-or had finished counting the twelve smaller caskets, when he heard a sharp grinding sound. Startled and still jumpy for being in a death chamber, he backed up two paces. He watched in horror as the lid of the tomb closest to him began to slide off. In quick order, the lids from the other caskets also began to move. Ge-or turned toward Sart for guidance as a richly clad skeletal figure began to rise from one of the now open tombs.

Sart shouted to them, "These are more powerful; stay back. Use your silver-tipped arrows, though they will have limited effect. Keep firing, I will engage them. Erno, back me up. Use your staff to keep any away that might get close." He moved ahead, meeting the first of the creatures as it stepped out of the stone sarcophagus. His mace rose and fell, crunching into the thing's boney shoulder. Sart brought it up again and smashed it into the skull.

Unlike the skels, this undead creature's bones were not brittle. Sart's heavy mace did do massive damage to the shoulder and to the cranium; but the skeleton still kept scrabbling ahead, trying to claw at the cleric.

Finally, the one to Sart's fore collapsed in a heap of bones and rags onto the floor. He grunted and turned to face another. "Keep those at bay that you can. These are nasty things and will take time to bring down."

Ge-or set his torch down on the floor, allowing both his hands free to bring his bow forward from off his back. He nocked a silver-tipped arrow. He had no idea what might be most effective; so he aimed at the biggest target he could, one of the skulls. The arrow struck home in the thing's forehead. It spun sideways at the force of the blow coming from such close quarters. Then it began flailing wildly about, as if it had lost some sense of orientation from the strike.

Encouraged, Ge-or fired arrow after arrow at more of the emerging ghouls. He was an excellent shot, and the targets were huge at less than ten paces distance. He only missed once, when an arrow from Stradryk's bow sent his target twisting in another direction.

Though the horrid creatures were far less deadly with arrows sticking out of their skulls, they were still dangerous. They appeared to have a sense, almost as if they were smelling the humanoids before them, of where to press their attacks. Sart was smashing away with his mace, but he was already tiring. Erno was also engaged, slamming his staff into one after another to send them backward. Unfortunately, they would recover quickly, reorient, and come back again and again.

Ge-or shot his last few arrows directly into the chest areas of a couple of the ghouls; unfortunately, this had little affect except to break his arrows and to briefly cause the deathly things to fall back. Stradryk, who had inched his way over so that all four of them were now in a semi-circle on the east side of the room, gasped out to Ge-or, "Use the stiletto. Stab into the chest area and quickly withdraw your blade. Try not to let the thing claw you; it will do more damage than you think. The magic of your blade may disrupt the force of the thing. I will join Sart." The half-gzk raised the hammer he had pulled off his weapon belt and grinned.

Slipping his sword from his back scabbard to use for blocking, Ge-or drew the silver blade from the sheath on his belt. He edged sideways and back, looking for a way to drive the magicked blade home through the chest of one of the two horrors facing him. He noted that they generally groped out in front, raking with their clawed hands as if they could not see, yet knew in which direction their foe stood. They were not agile, so Ge-or was able to time his jab. At the right moment, he lunged forward from the side, burying the blade in the closest one's left breast. There was a massive spark, and Ge-or almost had the blade fly from his hand at the shock of it. As he withdrew the dagger, the one he had stabbed sank to the floor.

Ge-or pressed ahead, stabbing the next closest to him. He kept an extra firm grip on the handle, and this time the shock of the released energy did not faze him. In quick order, he dispatched five more of the deadly ghouls, as he moved in and out of the sepulchers with the dagger flashing in the orange torchlight. Sliding sideways, toward the far side of the tombs, Ge-or saw that only a few of the ghouls were still moving. Sart was finishing off one that had been driven back to him by Erno's attacks, and Stradryk was polishing off another with hard hammer blows that were driving the thing down onto the stone floor.

Ge-or moved toward the west side to see if any others were still active. He stopped short when he heard a sharp grinding sound yet again. This time it was from the massive marble tomb in the center. He stepped toward it, hoping to stab the thing before it could leave its resting place. Sart's voice stopped him short. "Stand back, Ge-or. This thing is beyond your power, and mayhap that weapon you wield. I will have to wrest with it."

Sart sounded tired. He was breathing heavily as he came further around the near side of the large casket. "Erno," he said, "it is time."

The acolyte came to join Sart. Ge-or could see the young cleric was a bit the worse for wear, too. His brown robe was torn in several spots; and he looked to have been badly clawed on his right shoulder, for there was a good bit of blood soaking the heavy brown cloth. Yet, he moved up directly behind Sart, placing his hands on the cleric's broad shoulders.

"Ge-or?"

"Aye, Sart?"

"When it comes out, throw the stiletto at its chest. If nothing else, it will distract it; and it may do some damage. Hopefully, that will give us a bit of an advantage. Erno and I have to try to dispel the power that holds it here. Stradryk, stay back. If the battle sways in its favor, distract it with the vials of holy water... Now, Erno!"

Ge-or saw the acolyte's hands tighten on his mentor's shoulders. At the same time, Sart raised his rood, holding it in front of his chest with his arms outstretched.

The skeletal creature that emerged from the large tomb was not unlike the ghouls they had defeated, with one distinct difference – Ge-or could see an angry red gleam coming from its eye sockets. When he felt things could not get any more frightening or bizarre, the thing hissed out, "Who disturbs my rest?"

"Foul thing," Sart answered. "You do not ken what rest truly is. Go from this place and be at peace." Then he yelled, "Now, Ge-or!"

Shaking his head to clear the mental fog that had come on him as soon as the creature had spoken, Ge-or drew the stiletto back past his ear and in a quick motion threw it at the chest of the richly clad skeleton. The blade was not meant for throwing; but Manfred had taught his sons that in an exigency one had to know the heft and balance of any blade, because you might have to use it in a way that was different from the norm. Ge-or's training and skill proved: the blade buried deep, right in the center of the thing's breast.

At that instant, Sart pressed his attack. The horror fought back, hissing terribly. For fully five minutes, with what seemed to be unseen forces at play, the two vied for dominance. Later, Ge-or swore that he had seen a shimmering black wall of energy emanating from the undead fiend, which was met by a brownish-grey wall of force pushing out from in front of Sart's rood. For a long time, there was no gain on either side. Suddenly Sart gasped, his right foot slipped, and he almost fell. Shoving his left foot back to brace himself, Sart grunted, "Water, use your waters!"

Stradryk, seeing this happen from his position, reacted immediately. He shouted above Sart, "Ge-or, holy water. Now!"

Ge-or grabbed for the vials he had placed in his pouch. Pulling the stopper from one, he flung the contents in a swath up toward the figure now standing on the edge of the tomb. Stradryk did the same from the other side with the two he had left. The thing above them began to hiss even more loudly, brushing at its decrepit robes as if to put out a fire, though nothing was burning. The two fighters continued to strew the contents of their vials up at the skeletal figure, during which Sart recovered his composure and renewed his attack.

The hissing rose to a high pitch, followed by a loud explosion. The figure above collapsed inwardly, bones crunching into dust and fragments as its robes and the remains of a body too old to be whole fell and scattered about the tomb. Sart, releasing the energy he had used to send the undead soul beyond, fell to the cold marble in a swoon.

"Crypt fiend, as I feared," Sart said, shading his eyes from the late afternoon sun. Stradryk and Ge-or had carried him up into the bright daylight where he had recovered quickly. "Come, we had best go back in and have a look around before it gets dark. Let us explore the end, before we look for any treasure. I think we have had enough surprises for one day."

As it turned out, there only was one more tomb. It was set into the far wall with a molded façade of a woman plastering the vault shut. Sart translated the old language. Ge-or could read it well enough. "Here lies, Lizbeth, wife of Hugh of Randaully. A great beauty."

"I think we shall leave this unmolested," Sart added. "I believe she is at peace."

"Come, search amongst the remains and the caskets. No telling what you might find. I will climb up and see whether this device is still here; I will be surprised if it is not. Most grave-robbers would not have stayed to fight such horrors."

Ge-or and Stradryk looked into each of the tombs, leaving Erno, who did not have any qualms about dealing with the remains, to search the refuse of ragged cloths and splintered bones. There was little enough to find: a few trinkets of silver and bronze, several rings with stones of some merit that the acolyte uncovered, and a gold chain with a large emerald set in a florid pendant. They were bending over the small trove, when they heard Sart start to guffaw.

Looking up, they saw the cleric rise from his knees inside the coffin. "Hah! Surely some men are fools. Erno, catch." The cleric tossed an object down. The acolyte caught it in his left hand, while Sart continued to laugh.

"What is it?" Stradryk asked.

"A hairbrush, I think," Erno said, looking confused.

Sart above them laughed even louder. "Yes, a hairbrush. This fool, who obviously doted on his wife's hair, had a magical hairbrush. Heh, heh, heh! By-the-gods, a hairbrush! I'm not certain, but my guess, because it does emit a magical aura, is that it kept her hair from aging. Such are the whims of those blessed to be born noble. Well, my companions, this artifact should certainly prove of some worth in the kingdom's war against evil."

"Is there something else?" Erno queried.

"A moment… ahem." Sart bent over and searched the tomb further. "Yes, there is a small chest here. Ge-or, come up and let us remove it from this sad place. It is not magicked, so it should be safe to take it outside to open it."

The bound wooden chest that Ge-or carried up from the tomb was not large. It measured a foot or so wide, and perhaps ten inches deep. Sart directed Erno to gather a few smooth rocks from a nearby stream. When he returned, the cleric had them stand about ten paces back. "I used to be good at this. No sense springing a trap and spoiling our fun." He selected a medium-sized stone from Erno's out-stretched hand and took aim at the locking mechanism at the front. "Pow!" he said as the lock sprang open at impact. "There you see, opened with my first shot." Sart grinned. "At least, I still have a good eye."

The four of them moved forward to look into the case.

"Ah," Sart exclaimed. "Uncle Hugh does not disappoint. These must have been his wife's jewels – a pretty pile."

Indeed, the chest was filled with a wide variety of rings, necklaces, bracelets, and even solitary gemstones – a treasure that would have befitted the wife of a minor king. "Well, While I am disappointed in my own personal quest, we have done handsomely. These will fetch a fine price at market and auction. Come, let us be out of this vale. We will set out in the morn for Aelfric."

They kept to the edge of the mountains as before. Thankfully, except for waiting for several Qa-ryk patrols to move past their position below them on the mountain paths, their return to the border town was without incident. Once they were back and well rested, Sart drew them together to divide the spoils.

In spite of Ge-or's and Stradryk's objections, Sart and Erno would take no part of the treasure. "I am true to my word. Besides, this magical hairbrush, though bauble for the vain, will fetch a handsome price in the city, quite a handsome price I would hazard. We will be able to put the money to good use. The church will not go wanting."

Ge-or still felt uncomfortable for some reason that even he could not explain. He asked a question that surprised both Sart and Stradryk. "Does your church tithe?"

"Tithe? Nay, we are not like other religions in that sense. We ask for donations so we can help the less fortunate – each to what they will and to what they can afford. In most ways we are self-sufficient; many of our brethren farm, weave, make things, and so on. Why do you ask?"

"Do you have houses, places, where you care for the less fortunate of society?" Stradryk looked up at that, suddenly more interested in where Ge-or was going. "Good places?"

"Aye, we have several in each of the larger cities. Ge-or, what are you driving at?"

"I am uncomfortable with all that this quest has been. I don't know why, perhaps because we obtained this largess from graves. I do understand and appreciate that it was not needed by those in attendance there." He smiled wryly. "Also, because Stradryk told me of the needs of those… those who cannot take care of themselves. I come from a small village; and though my parents taught me much, there are things in this larger world that astound me. Nay, better said, they shock me. Not that our village was perfect, but all in all, we take… took care of our own. It is how we survived." He paused, looking up.

"This..." Ge-or waved his hands in the air as if to encompass the entire kingdom, "is almost overwhelming at times. I am ashamed that I have considered so little of anything else, anyone, except myself and my own desires since being thrust into this world."

"My good half-elf, we have talked at length, you and I; and what you say is not true. You have done many kindnesses and have been generous to others in a variety of circumstances, even if you do not see it. You are more selfless than most men I have met. You were brought up well. You were raised with honor in your blood, not a small thing."

"I would do more, Father. Will you not take ten percent of my share for your work?"

Sart looked in Ge-or's eyes, and saw that he was indeed earnest. "So be it. You..."

"And I as well, good Father," Stradryk jumped in. "I trust your judgment; and as you know, this is also important to me."

"I am moved by you both," Sart said. "This rarely happens anymore. One does become a bit jaded by the work one does. Ge-or, you often ask me for advice, yet I have learned much from you as well. I thank you. I thank you both.

"Come, let us say our goodbyes over a pint. I can bend Ge-or's ear a bit more about his future quest."

They were well into their cups, when Sart finally stood to say his goodbyes, which, as was his custom, came with some sage advice. "Ge-or, remember my counsel when we first met. You will have money for some fine armor and equipment now, but you must understand all that you can ferret of dragons before you go after so old a beast. Seek wisdom wherever you can find it." He clapped the two warriors on their backs, and motioned for Erno to follow. Duty called.

A Lesson in Humility

Ge-or pondered Sart's parting words for some time. With Stradryk's knowledge of the dealers and auctions in Aelfric, they did well selling the jewelry and gems from the treasure chest, though they each reserved a small handful of fine gems for exigencies. They amassed several thousand gold pieces over the course of the week's sales. Now, he was determined to find out all that he could about dragons and how to fight them, even if it meant buying beer or rum for half the old-timers in the city.

He quickly found out that there was little enough to glean from such sources. Two weeks later he still felt as if there were several insurmountable obstacles to his potential success: first, how to protect oneself from the beast's fearsome fire; second, how and where to best attack the monster; and finally, what to expect if the dragon actually could use magic. He had ideas, yet none of these translated into anything close to a chance at success. He needed to know more.

One evening, he and Stradryk were going through all they knew about the beast in question and dragons in general, when the half-gzk brought up an interesting idea. "What about Ordrake?"

"Ordrake? The seer, magician, the imbuer? He hardly…"

"He is much more than he seems, Ge-or. He was one of the great Wizards in the first Qa-ryk Wars. He is old and he plays the fool, but for a purpose. He is the wisest person I have ever met. And that includes many a mage on a great many quests."

"Do you think he would give us any help?"

"Give?" Stradryk answered. "Nay, he always wants something. The question is whether you can afford what he desires."

"He would want more than the money and gems I have?"

"It is not always wealth that he seeks. Just be warned, Ge-or. If we go there, he will likely have answers for you, the price will be high, and it mayhap be something you cannot or will not give willingly. Also, he can be cryptic in his advice."

Ge-or frowned, then grunted, "On the morrow I will see him; I would move ahead with my quest. Father's sword beckons."

Ge-or's second visit to Ordrake's hut started much the same as the first. When the magician finally appeared from behind the multicolored curtain, if anything, he looked even more oddly dressed – wearing a frumpy, squashed orange hat and a voluminous scarlet robe that almost overwhelmed his slight figure. As before, he waved off his and Stradryk's attempts at deference. "So, it's young Ge-or, son of Manfred, formerly of Thiele. Well, never mind that. Back again, so soon? Did the dagger work for you? A trifle – useful I hope?"

Ge-or stared at him. He could not remember having told the fellow his name on their first visit, and he certainly had not said anything about being the son of the famed fighter. Ordrake rattled on, so he dismissed the notion.

"You are here about that beast, Fis. Ran into him once – nasty creature. Old as the hills and mean, dangerous, bit of the old magic in him still. Best leave him alone, thank you. See you in a few years." Ordrake turned to go.

Ge-or stopped him by managing to clear his throat.

"Yes?" Ordrake turned back, raising his eyebrows.

"I… ah… mostly I desire information. He has my father's sword."

"Yes, yes, I know all that. Well, information I can give; the question is, 'Are you willing to pay the price?'"

"If I can afford the asking."

"Nay, my good half-elf, it is not the asking that costs so much; it is the giving. My price is simple, but difficult, as well. I would see the ring."

"Ring?"

"A gift so soon forgot! Tut, tut, my boy, the one your mother gave you."

"I… By-the-gods! My mother's ring!"

"Single-minded and simple-minded; can't trust fighters. Give them a quest, and they're gallivanting about the country with no thought to anything else."

"I…"

"… don't have it. Yes, I am quite aware of that. I would sense it. So, go get it. There are others after it, you know."

"My mother's ring?"

"Come, come, Ge-or. The task is simple enough in theory – go get your mother's ring. Bring it here so I can look at it. Hurry, will you; that idiot Aberon may actually think it through eventually."

"Aberon?"

"A nasty fellow, but don't fret about him; he's busy with other things. If you don't waste time, you will beat him to it. Go! Come back with it. I'll tell you more than you will ever want to know about dragons. Go!"

"That was the strangest conversation I've ever had in my life," Ge-or said, as the two walked back toward the Druid's Hut. "How does he know all this about me and my family. I truly believed the ring a secret, never shared by my brother, father, or me. And about my quest? Fis? My name and my heritage? Is he all-seeing?"

"Nay, Ge-or, not quite. He sees much, a great deal more than anyone who lives in this town might expect. The wise defer to him for many things; that is, if he is willing to give of his knowledge. What is this ring he speaks of?"

"I would think it would be a trifle to him. It is a small stone in a simple setting. My mother gifted it to me before she passed. My father was to keep it until I came of age. I would have gotten it last year or this. It must have been destroyed by the dragon's fire. He wore it on his little finger."

"I would warrant it was not destroyed by the fire. Ordrake seemed to believe you could, and should, find it. He is not often wrong about anything; and I'm guessing there is more to it than you think, else he would not be interested in it. Where might it be, if it survived?"

"I don't know. I... By-the-gods! It..." Ge-or stopped, glancing about. "Not here. Let us wait until we are in our rooms; then I will tell you a heavy tale."

Two days later, feeling about as low as he had ever felt, Ge-or set out for the north. To have forgotten his dying mother's gift, which was now likely lying at the bottom of the ocean out from their docks at Thiele – he felt he had shamed her memory. The truth was, since he had left Thiele, he had been rash, foolish, and single-minded.

Ge-or rode hard, due north, for many days. Though Stradryk had been willing to come with him, they had eventually decided that he would stay behind in Aelfric getting all that they would need for a winter trapping trek ready. Ge-or hoped to return by the early fall; if he was delayed, he planned to follow the half-gzk west as he had the previous winter. Whatever Ordrake might impart to him, he had decided he needed to scale that western peak when the beast was away feeding, so he could get a good look at the dragon's lair. He would need to know the ground he was to fight on.

Third Year

The Old Meets the New, Polyphony has its Place

It was the last evening before school. Jared, Karenna, and Simon-Nathan had decided to spend it at the Green Horse tavern. They had secured two rooms for the night and intended to have a grand party before diving into their studies the next day. Simon-Nathan, always on top of what was happening through all of his father's contacts, had found out that the upper-class students liked to grab rooms at the different pubs near the Hall and party until the gates opened the next morning.

Karenna had come back with Jared mid-summer. Since then she had been working with them at one of Simon-the-Elder's shops. After only a few days, her nose in books as always, she found all kinds of errors and discrepancies in the store's ledgers. Within a couple of weeks, she had been promoted to what Jared referred to as a "mobile accountant." She would spend one day at a store checking over its receipts and books, moving on when she was done. It kept the shopkeepers on their toes, and Simon-the-Elder was thrilled. He had agreed to pay for their entire night of revelry because of the fine work they had all done for him that summer.

By sunset, the tavern district was rollicking. They saw many of their friends and acquaintances from school as they hopped from one pub to another. The ultimate challenge was to drink at least one ale at each place and, hopefully, manage to find oneself back where one had started. Jared and Karenna convinced Simon-Nathan to return to the Green Horse after five moves, skipping the last two or three establishments. They were all sipping last ales before heading upstairs.

"Did I tell you my plans?" Simon-Nathan slurred.

"A least five times tonight," Jared said, bleary-eyed. Karenna was holding onto his arm with her head lying on his shoulder. He thought she was probably asleep.

"Well, don't forget. We could all go out on apprenticeship together if I stay the extra year to start my graduate work."

"I know, it's a good idea. It's just that…Well, never mind for now. C'mon, let's get you upstairs."

The next day they all discovered that perhaps the partying had its drawbacks. Their masters were none too sympathetic.

Jared was having the time of his life. He was actually enjoying all of his class work and lessons this year including theory, music composition, and history. They had moved on to studying the polyphonic masters of the past few centuries. It turned out that he had both a knack for playing the intricate pieces on the lute and lyre, as well as an innate understanding of the composition of these highly designed and controlled works. The interweaving melodic lines lacked the "harmony" or "verticalness" of the new music, instead they used strict compositional guidelines that created, in the best of hands, an incredible movement and flow and a wonderful ethereal sound. This was in large part due their linear nature and the emphasis on using the pure or "perfect" intervals of the fourth, fifth, and octave as a foundation for its "harmony". And much to Jared's preference, the intricate harmonic relationships of the "new music," that he had struggled with since first year, were not part of this "old" music.

Jared also found the period – sometimes referred to as the Modern Resurgence, though it was now considered "the old music" – to be fascinating historically, musically, socially, and politically. He read all the scrolls and texts Simon-Nathan passed on to him. The two became even closer friends through their work in the area of his friend's true passion – the study of what had been.

By mid-term, Jared was placed under the tutelage of Therin himself for lute and portative harp, albeit as one of his students who studied with both him and an assistant. With this arrangement, Jared actually saw the master for only one hour every two weeks. Because he loved the music so much, Jared had taken to practicing twice as much as in his first two years. He would sit for hours working out the interweaving contrapuntal lines. He even took it upon himself to find intricate accompaniments for the vocal compositions they studied in theory that combined both polyphony and the basics of the new harmony.

His new-found dedication to performance created some difficulties with his extra work in weaponry. He was able to keep the early morning workouts, as they had become somewhat of a ritual for his friends and a core of other students wanting to improve their fitness and fighting ability. Still, he had to give up the extra afternoon and weekend workouts. Elanar had progressed enough to draw inspiration and creativity through his own efforts, as well as from all those he sparred with. Occasionally, he and Jared would meet to challenge each other to a friendly spar to keep a fine edge. The elf was now sought after by some students as a long sword sparring mate, since he had won the Long Sword Cup two years running.

For those who really wanted to become Bards, one always had to consider the overall balance of their studies. So, Jared was working harder intellectually than he had ever done in his life. Unfortunately, that left little time alone with Karenna. They were both unhappy about it, too. Nevertheless, she was also incredibly busy trying to maintain her perfect academic record, while putting in what time she could, and was allowed, in weaponry.

True to his word, though the announcement had been delayed slightly due to more deliberations, Leonis did announce during the first convocation of the year that women would be allowed to participate in a one-year limited apprenticeship program. Limits were set based on the areas of the country where women were allowed to spend their time in residence. The reasoning – to keep the young women out of potential war zones – was actually fairly sound. They did not have the extensive weapons training that the young men had. Nonetheless, Karenna was a little put out that their choices were less free than the men.

All in all, the three best friends were having a great year. Simon-Nathan had actually grown over the summer, upward. And he appeared to still be growing. This had surprised all of them, Simon-Nathan the most. He stood a proud five feet nine and a half and was hoping he would make six feet, now that he was having a growth spurt. Jared still had him by four inches; he had topped out at just under six feet two.

The only thing missing for Jared was that he had not seen Thistle. She had sent him a note and requested his patience with her. She had said she would contact him when she felt she had better control of her emotions and the issues she was currently trying to work through.

He was surprised at how much he missed their once-a-month get-togethers. Though they had been innocuous enough, they had filled a void for him. He had to admit he missed seeing her, talking with her, being near to her. Karenna noticed.

Lying together on one of the rare weekday nights when they had been able to have an hour free with no one else about, she asked Jared, "You miss her?"

He touched her brow with his index finger, smoothing her hair back from her eyes. "I'm sorry, Karenna, I do. The odd thing is that it is not physical in any way. It's just seeing her, knowing she is well."

"You went through a good deal of trauma together; you are bound in ways that we aren't. I know that. I…" Karenna was trying to be her intellectual self, yet Jared could see it still affected her.

"Yes, perhaps. You and I have been through much more together in other ways. I love you, Karenna. You know I do."

"But…"

"Yes, I guess there is still a 'but'."

"You know, someday, you will have to choose. You will have to be with her as we are, if you are to know for sure."

"I don't know. I…"

"I do." Karenna pushed herself up and looked at him. "I know I may lose you, Jared. However, I may gain you completely as a result. It isn't easy for me to say this; I know that it is what must happen for us to have that chance."

"Shhh-h," he said, pulling her back close. "For now, you have me, totally."

She knew she didn't.

Defensive Magic

When Thistle and Alli disembarked at the dock, Sart was standing there waiting for them. Thistle threw her arms around his barrel chest and immersed herself in a huge bear hug. "Oh, Sart, I have so much to tell you. It was wonderful. It was just what I needed."

"I am glad, child. You look better, sun-burnt and happier. And your concerns?"

Thistle blushed. "Much better, much, much better. I still have some bad times, but I have enough control to get through them with less discomfort. I didn't even have to take any of your medicine."

"Praise the gods, child. You had me a bit worried." Sart took a deep breath. He would have sighed loudly, though he didn't want Thistle to see how worried he had actually been.

"I heard you had a bit of excitement out west," Sart said, releasing her.

"What? How? I expect the rangers must have sent a boat back to report. Well, it was nothing really. I did have to use a bit of magic to help out."

"Well, perhaps. Our dear Meligance thinks it is of some import. She wants to see you right away."

"And I thought you came down to see us back."

Sart reddened a bit. "Well, I did, or I meant to, until she summoned me and insisted. You know her; she wants to know what happened."

"Yes, I do, more and more."

At that, Thistle decided to change the subject. She was too happy to be weighed down when she was feeling so good. "You have gotten a bit of sun, as well, my good priest. What have you been up to?"

Sart laughed. "You are more like her every day, child. Come, we will talk as we go. I have been in the south and west…"

***

"Tell me," Meligance said, as soon as Thistle was fully in her study, having only nodded at Thistle when she had materialized in front of her.

"It was almost surreal," Thistle said. "What are the chances that I would pick the one day to visit Thiele that it would be re-attacked by Qa-ryks. The odd thing is, I did not feel afraid. When we first heard the attack against the stockade walls almost three years ago, I was petrified. This day, I reacted."

"Go on."

"Alli came riding back shouting that there was an attack. I took command and galloped ahead. Maybe I was angry; probably, now that I think on it. But I was also determined to do something. It was as if I wanted to have a say in this result. Somehow, I think I felt it would make up for being sent away during the first battle." She paused, thinking back to that day.

"And?"

"When I cleared the unfinished eastern stockade wall, I could see the fighting was centered to the south and west. There was a breach in the stockade, small, only five or six feet wide; and there was a knot of men and beasts struggling there. Other Qa-ryks were coming over the walls by scrabbling up the sides. I knew instinctively that whatever had made that small breech was not a red dragon. I also knew somehow that whoever it was, I could handle them.

"I remember riding up to the center of the compound and sliding off my horse. I immediately felt my own power well up. I took hold of it, reached out as I have done a hundred-hundred times, and drew power to me from the ether; this time it was easy to gather and focus it. I did it all in a gesture." Thistle demonstrated with her hand outstretched. As she had done that day two weeks before, she immediately felt and saw the power. She drew it into a tight ball. An intense orb of energy appeared in her hand. Then, with a snapping of her fingers, she dissipated the power.

Meligance blinked, nodding for Thistle to go on.

The girl blushed. "I'm afraid I was emotionally involved, and I drew a bit more power to me than I really meant to. I blew two sections of the stockade wall apart along with a number of the beasts climbing over it. That first time I did not think to use the energy in some form. I just hurled it at them. When I ran forward to get closer to the men engaged at the break, I said to myself, 'Control!' I got the young lieutenant there to pull his men back, and I quickly created another sphere of energy. I sent a more reasonable fire attack into the midst of the beasts who were massed coming through the breach. It was quite effective."

Thistle's eyes were gleaming. She appeared to be possessed again by the heat of the battle, as she relived her part in the fight. "After that, I kept drawing bits of energy to me, picking off the remaining Qa-ryks with bolts of lightning. At first, I wasn't positive whether they would kill the beasts, but they turned out to be quite deadly." Thistle stopped, dropping her arms to her side. "That was it. I don't think I was engaged more than a few minutes – four or five, maybe. If there were other beasts, or others outside the walls, they fled."

"You didn't see who or what created the breach in the wall?"

"No, ma'am. It was already there when I came around the stockade. There is one thing that puzzles me – why didn't they attack from the open side of the stockade?"

She mused out loud, "Perhaps it was the element of surprise and shock. The unfinished east wall faced the road. They would have been exposed for a much longer period approaching it, whereas they were able to sneak through the corn to the south to come up on the stockade quickly. I imagine the blast that opened the breach might have been a ploy to discourage resistance."

"Good, good. You are thinking things through." Meligance was smiling. "You did well, really well, Thistle. I am pleased by a number of things. First, you were able to focus and control, though it took you a little time to achieve complete control. More importantly, you used your emotions to strengthen the whole process – focus, control, power. That shows maturity. You have come a long way in a short period of time.

"Second, you did not panic and use your own power; you drew from a source without. Thus, you were able to strike again and again. Tell me, how did you feel afterward?"

Thistle thought for a minute, going back to the aftermath of the fight. "Powerful, initially. My personal energy was… Well, I guess best put, I felt alive. I was enlivened by it. The next day, as we were riding home, I was perhaps a little tired, yet still exhilarated. Nervous energy, I think. I was a bit afraid of what my father would think, and others at home when told the tale. I had kept my magic under wraps while at Permis. I didn't want to be seen as an entertainer."

"Good. Yes, well what you felt is fairly normal. Had the battle gone on, you would have tired more. You did well, amazingly well. You have moved to a point where I think we can begin the study of defensive magic in earnest. For had you been seriously attacked during such a battle, you would have been at the mercy of offensive spells, hurled or shot weapons, and even direct assault. Now, we will begin the long process of learning how to deflect all of these types of attacks, and eventually, to learn how to do so while you are yourself engaged in the offense. Once again, the heart of the matter is your control of the energy you draw to you, in other words, how you mold and use it."

"Yes, ma'am."

Thistle had thoroughly enjoyed her summer at home; nonetheless, it was good to be back. Having put up with several weeks of sore muscles, stiffness, and blisters during the first part of the summer, she resolved to not let herself get so soft ever again. She convinced Sart to find a place where she could stretch, run, throw her knives, and work with weights. The more she learned of magic, the more she realized how her good health and well-being were going to matter. Sart did her one better. He got her and Alli personal trainers.

While her woman problems were considerably better, there were still times when she suffered in silence. She discovered this often happened when she was working on magical incantations that were new, ones she did not control yet. It was as if she had to release a part of her self-control to focus more on what she was doing. She began to pay more attention to this. Over the first few months of the fall, she slowly got better; and the painful physical episodes became shorter and more bearable.

It was near the beginning of November when she felt well enough emotionally and physically to contact Jared. She sent him a brief note, asking him if he could meet her the next Solisday at the Green Horse.

Two days later, Thistle got a nice note back from Jared, warmly accepting.

Interference

Ge-or had chosen to ride light. He left his chain mail and many of his weapons behind, preferring to carry only his new sword, a couple of throwing knives, and the magicked stiletto. After his recent experience in the tombs, when he had to fight horrors from childhood imaginings and worse, he was taking no chances. He also left most of his cooking gear, preferring to stop at outposts and taverns.

It took him almost a week and a half of steady riding from dawn until well after dark to reach the north country. He rode along the west Borean highway, east of the King's Wall, looking forward to the relative comforts of the Wayfarers Inn on the outskirts of Cutter-by-the-Sea. It was the first of the wilderness coastal towns west of the King's Wall.

It was full dark and beginning to rain in earnest, when he rode up toward the flickering light of the single torch set by the door of the inn. He was weary and saddle-sore. He took his horse around to the stables, where he was met by the attendant. Slapping Sandy on the rump, he gathered his saddlebags and strode quickly along the dark path to the front door. The place was not busy; only a few horses and mules had been stabled, and there were no raucous sounds coming from the small open slit windows he passed. He was pushing in the heavy door when a slight shiver of energy along his spine and up his neck jolted him to full alertness.

Ge-or stopped, turning about. He stood there and scanned the shadows, waiting. Nothing moved; there appeared to be nothing out there. Yet he sensed something was not quite right. As a precaution, he took off the holding loop from the stiletto scabbard on his belt. Seeing nothing, he turned back and finished opening the door.

He paused again after taking one step into the large community room of the tavern. Scanning the place from left to right and back, he saw nothing out of the ordinary. There were two men sitting at the long bar chatting with the bartender, obviously locals, as they were dressed for farming. Another man, a traveler, sat at a table in the corner. Still in his riding clothes, he was sipping a tall mug of ale. Three others, perhaps fisherman, sat to Ge-or's left, playing cards.

Satisfied there was no immediate threat in the room, Ge-or approached the bar, laying his saddlebags on the surface. He waited until the barkeep raised his hand to silence the two conversing with him. "Well met, stranger. You seeking room and board?"

Ge-or nodded. "Private, with bath, and the lamb you're roasting smells good, with trimmings. I'll eat above." He nodded to the stairs to his left. As he spoke, he opened his purse and looked questioningly at the barman. "Stabling one horse, as well."

The barkeep stretched out his hand toward Ge-or. He was a big fellow, shorter than Ge-or, and several stone heavier. "Filled out," as they would say in these parts. He had a well-trimmed beard, and he was now smiling broadly at Ge-or. "Well met, I say again. I'm Brando. Frist born and raised. You must hail from the North Coast by your accent."

Ge-or took his hand. The big man pumped it enthusiastically. "Formerly of Thiele, I am traveling west to Permis."

The barkeep's expression changed to a grim visage. "Bad thing, that. Sorry for you. Were you away when it happened?"

"Nay, I got bashed in the head and left for dead. Luckily, I bled a lot. The beasts thought me gone. A cleric rescued me."

"Relatives?"

This time Ge-or shook his head. "Some friends made it out and east to Permis. I would see them before winter sets in. My brother is at Bard Hall."

"Aye, it is good to stay in touch with one's roots. No charge for the room, ye've been through enough. It's me pleasure to help a fellow northerner."

Ge-or took out a silver piece, easily twice what the charges would be. He placed it on the counter. "Buy the wife a present or help another. I have done well enough on my travels, and it looks like business is slow."

Brando placed his hand over the coin. He nodded his thanks to Ge-or. "Aye, it has been…" He looked up as the door opened. His voice trailed off and his eyes widened in alarm.

Ge-or spun around as two swarthy men wearing black robes and cowls pushed through the open doorway.

He could see no weapons, yet everything about these two screamed evil to him. Their whole demeanor spoke ill-will. He had sensed such before, in his youth; but never this close and personal. Not only did he feel their negative aura, they were weather-beaten – with mud-splattered robes and boots and several days' growth of beard. They looked not only weary, but annoyed, as if they had been put out by someone. Since they were scowling directly at him, Ge-or figured it must be him. He moved his right hand to the hilt of the stiletto.

Now that they were close enough to see in the torch light, they both looked almost emaciated. The bigger of the two, though he barely reached Ge-or's shoulder, growled. "A fine hunt you have led us, half-elf. Where is it?"

Ge-or looked at the man with no expression on his face; instead he did raise one eyebrow as if to say, "Huh?"

"The ring; our master wants the ring. And we're tired of chasing you all about the countryside."

Ge-or's mind kicked into gear. Aberon! What had Ordrake said about him? "A nasty fellow…"

Well, if this were that devil and a compatriot, they indeed looked nasty. Actually Ge-or felt no real threat from either of these two vagabonds. "You be Aberon?" he said, taking a slight step toward the two.

At that, the man who had spoken looked surprised. He raised his hand palm outward toward Ge-or's chest. A second later a bolt of energy exploded from the man's palm. It struck Ge-or full in the solar-plexus.

Ge-or was wearing his heavy leather armor above his tunic. The well-padded shell dissipated the energy bolt. It merely drove his body back about two inches. All he felt was a strong tingling rush through his chest and arms. Following the attack, the man took two steps closer to Ge-or, as if to follow up the energy bolt and finish his opponent off.

Ge-or reacted with elven quickness. He grabbed the still outstretched arm of the priest in his left hand, spun sideways, and thrust the man's hand down toward the top of the bar. With his right, he drew the stiletto. He drove it through the top of the fellow's hand pinning it to the hard wood. Before the other dark priest could move, he found Ge-or's sword resting against his throat.

"Down!" Ge-or commanded. The smaller of the two men went to his knees, thudding into the floor. "Watch him." Ge-or jerked his head toward the two farmers who were standing agape by his side, wondering at the speed in which the large fellow had reacted. The one closest to Ge-or took the proffered blade from his hand and held it, while the other drew a long knife and stepped behind the kneeling dark priest.

Ge-or turned to the man pinned to the bar. "Who are you, and what is it you want?"

The man scowled up at Ge-or. He tried to spit at him, but he missed as Ge-or stepped aside.

Holding the priest's pinned hand with his left, Ge-or reached out and calmly grasped the hilt of the knife. He pulled it slightly up and twisted it, driving it back into the wood. The priest screamed. "I'm waiting for an answer; as you may note, I am none too patient."

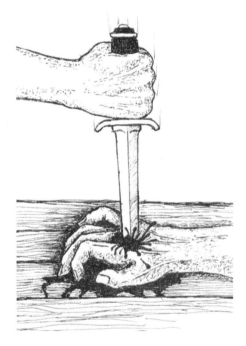

"A... an acolyte of Aberon. He wants the ring, that's all I know."

Ge-or reached for the knife. The man begged. "Please. It's the truth. We were told to follow you and... and to get it if we could."

"You decided to save yourself some trouble and take it for yourself?"

The man whimpered again.

Ge-or grabbed the man's cowl and hair, jerking his head back. At the same time, he yanked the stiletto out. With two quick slices of the blade, he carved a cross in the man's forehead. The priest screamed again and fainted. Ge-or let him slip to the floor.

He stepped toward the other. Grabbing his hair, Ge-or tilted his head back so he was forced to look into the eyes of an obviously extremely unhappy half-elven fighter. "Tell your master that I do not have it, and that I do not abide fools. If he persists in this folly, we will meet; and I will mark him like I have marked you both." With that, he cut this fellow's forehead as he had the other. "Leave, and take this other idiot with you. If I sense that you are on my trail again, your lives will be forfeit."

The man scrambled up, holding his forehead as blood trickled through his fingers. The two locals picked up the unconscious priest and dragged him to the door. They unceremoniously tossed him out into the now pouring rain.

Reunion

"It is so good to see you, Thistle. I was concerned. Last time you were so tired, distant – like you were fighting something inside yourself." Jared reached out with his hand toward her gloved one. She met him halfway and clasped his. Giving it a hard squeeze, she let her hand rest in his.

"You look beautiful."

"I am well, Jared. Much better. I was dealing with many things this past year, including, as I suggested before I left you last, women's concerns." She flushed slightly. "I have learned to control my, ah… concerns, and to control the magical issues that were exacerbating the problem.

"Meligance told me that the power within me, as well as my use of power, affects many things. I am different, Jared. There are things you should know."

She paused, looking into his eyes. Seeing only acceptance there, she continued. "Those with power find it affects the entire maturation process, from birth until death. This explains odd things that happened to me as I was growing – like my younger sister becoming a woman before me." This time Thistle did blush. "I was really late, and it has been very difficult for me. It was one of the reasons my marriage to Baldo was to be postponed for another year. The magic affects my emotions, physical tension, pain… many things. I am only now learning how to deal with that. It will never go away, but I can at least learn to cope with it.

"I will, also, according to Meligance, live longer because of the power within me. That, for us, if there is to be an us, is a good thing, since you are half-elven." Jared thought that he felt a slight squeeze from her hand again. "Unless of course, I do something stupid and get killed… That reminds me!" Thistle reached out with her other hand, and took Jared's. "I wanted to tell you. I went to Thiele."

She told him about her visit home, the joy of doing simple things again, the ride through the countryside to see the monument at Thiele, and the battle. She told him of her studies, her love of languages, and many other things.

He sat mesmerized, not by what she was saying – by the young girl who appeared to be changing into a woman before his eyes. The joy at seeing her at once as the same beautiful young maiden he had met and fallen for on their trek across the wilderness, and yet now, as a maturing woman whose words and energy reflected something far beyond her years, was almost overwhelming. In those few minutes, his love for her burst forth anew. He understood, perhaps for the first time, how different that was from what he felt for Karenna.

When it was his time, he spoke only about his studies. He told her of his love of the old music. He described in detail the intricacies of the interweaving melody lines, coupled with the strict adherence to the purest of sounds based on the nature of music itself. He told of his new-found love for the lute, his developing facility on all the string instruments, and his joy in singing.

Finally, he told her about his friends, because he sensed that she now understood he loved her with a depth of feeling that would never be dissolved by his relationships with others, only enhanced because he would learn to love her even more.

As the hour approached for them to part, they were both amazed that the time had sped by so quickly. Jared walked her out to her carriage, her arm resting in his. When they said goodbye, he wanted, felt, an overpowering need to kiss her, to touch her in some way, flesh to flesh. Even as the sense became a thought, she reached out with her palm to his chest. "Not yet, Jared," a tear and smile coming to her face at the same time. "Soon, I hope, my love. For now, let me touch you." She drew close to him and bussed his cheek, allowing their cheeks to brush ever so lightly as she drew away.

***

Karenna noticed there was a change in Jared after that. Not that their relationship changed, or that he was any less attentive or loving; it was almost as if his joy of life had risen a notch. She didn't tell him that she cried herself to sleep for many nights thereafter.

A Long Search

Aberon was furious. The fools had actually asked the half-elf about the ring, though he had expressly forbidden them even to be seen. Now they groveled before him, each marked, and... and useless. Well, maybe not entirely useless. There was always a use for carrion.

It was time to let Number Seven know what fear meant. The Qa-ryks could have the younger one. This one – Aberon kicked at the still only partially healed hand of the whimpering priest before him – he would slow roast on a spit for all to see.

Perhaps he should leave such a death for his next conquest. It was a foolish system they had anyway, a system based completely on power. Number Eight had been only a fly in his way. He was now fish food at the bottom of the southern marshes. That certainly had been a nasty trip. Aberon hated the heat. He far preferred the north country.

Hah! He would roast them both – Number Seven and this, this thing at his feet. That should put a scare into the rest above. When he was the One, there would be no balance of power, nor any rising in the ranks by deposing the next. He would rule with absolute power and inspire fear. Only then would they be able to destroy the kingdom. As their hierarchy now stood, the brethren were more concerned about consolidating their own power than they were about building the army they needed to annihilate the Boreans.

This fool had told him the half-elf denied having the ring. Whether he had it or not, he was now forewarned. "Idiocy!" For now, he had to play the power game. That treasure and his revenge would have to wait.

***

Ge-or had hoped to arrive at Thiele within a week and a half of having left the Wayfarer in Cutter. If he had ridden hard, he would have made it, but at each village along the coast he was asked to stay. They remembered him from his trek the fall before and wanted to know all about his adventures since. He found he thoroughly enjoyed the long evenings and early mornings, rising to help with the work of the village for a few hours before he broke his fast and moved on. It reminded him of his youth, of the kindness and resilience of these people he had long lived amongst.

It was on the thirteenth day out from Cutter-by-the-Sea that he left Permis at mid-morning and rode the trail toward Thiele. The villagers had told him of the new stockade being built there. He was encouraged that he might find some help in his search.

It was well after dusk when he rode up to the eastern wall of the stockade. Two soldiers met him with crossed pikes at the opening where the gate would eventually be set. "I am Ge-or, formerly of this village," he announced. "I would speak with your commander."

The men uncrossed their pikes, allowing him passage. One remained at his post, while the other gestured for Ge-or to follow.

The lieutenant in command stuck out his hand when the guard announced Ge-or. "Well met. What can we help you with?"

Ge-or explained his mission, seeing nothing wrong with letting the fellow know what it was he sought. "...and my best guess is that if it survived, it was in the barrels on the boat that I pushed into the harbor."

"The waters are already cold, and as you must know, fairly deep only a short way off the shore. It will be a monumental task to find so small a thing."

"Aye, but I have pledged to try. Can you offer any assistance?"

The lieutenant shook his head. "Unfortunately, we have too much to finish before the snows. We hope to have the first boat with winter provisions in before the sea ices up. We are pressed for time as it is."

Ge-or had an idea. "If you will give me two men to man ropes for me, after my search I will help in any way I can. I am strong and able, and used to hard work."

The lieutenant looked Ge-or over. "A couple of days. I cannot afford more, and we will take you up on your offer."

"I can pitch in whenever I am out of the water as well. I will not be able to stand the cold except for short dives."

"Good. Yes, that will help."

They shook on the bargain.

The next morning Ge-or set about his task to find the ring. As he had suspected, the water was bloody cold. It took him a day and a half to find the burnt husk of the ship's hull. He discovered that he could do several dives within a half hour span; after that he would have to take a long break. Though he was a strong swimmer, the cold and current took its toll.

On the second day, he was able to locate two intact barrels still in the hold. It wasn't until the third day that he found that the last barrel had fallen over when the sinking boat had rammed into the bottom. Most of its contents had spread over the deck of the ship and been dispersed by the tides.

The next day, with the help of the two men that Lieutenant Waltham had given him, Ge-or was able to enclose each of the two intact barrels in canvas to be hauled to the surface. It was a long, slow process. It took five or six dives each to complete the task. By the end of the two days in which he had the men's aid, the barrels were safely ashore.

Unfortunately, in spite of carefully sifting through the contents, he found nothing, just bits of melted metal and stones that had gotten in the mix when he had shoveled up the ash and remains.

He spent six more days diving whenever he felt strong enough. He was on the verge of admitting that the ring had either been incinerated by the dragon's breath or lost in the sea, when he saw a shadow of a different color in the murkiness down toward the stern of the boat. Needing air, Ge-or surfaced, immediately diving again, though this was one more dive than he had planned for the day.

What he discovered, as he made his way through a tangle of burnt beams and timbers, was that heavier objects from the overturned barrel had settled into the lowest section of the wreck. They were wedged into the point of the stern by the motion of the waves. As quickly as he could, he sifted through the odd assortment of metal objects. Finally, he found what he was seeking. Grasping out as another wave pushed him forward, Ge-or hoped he had retrieved it in the handful of metal, rock, and sand that he had when he surfaced.

Exhausted and freezing, he barely made it to the dock. He emptied his hand onto the wooden planks while he held on, gasping for breath and trying to gain back enough strength to haul himself up.

The ring was as he had last seen it. It was a perfectly formed stone in a plain gold setting. Whether it was his exhaustion, or simply emotions reflective of his family and all that had happened that suddenly overwhelmed him, Ge-or sat on the dock with his knees drawn up holding the ring in front of him. He wept.

True to his word, Ge-or spent the next three weeks helping the men finish the stockade. Unfortunately, his diving in the cold waters gave him a tremendous head and chest cold. An herbal tea Sart had given him helped him heal a bit faster as well as assuage the worst of the symptoms.

It was only when the boat came into the newly refurbished dock, that Ge-or said his goodbyes and nosed his horse back to the east. He was late; hopefully Stradryk had waited.

The half-gzk had indeed waited for him, and their next meeting with Ordrake proved an eye-opener. The Wizard merely acknowledged the ring when Ge-or showed it to him. He said that if Ge-or ever wanted to part with it, he was interested. He adjured him to keep it safe. Otherwise Ordrake would not answer any of Ge-or's questions about it.

After the short dialogue about Ge-or's ring, Ordrake waxed eloquent about dragons for well over an hour. The Wizard knew more than Ge-or would have ever imagined.

For the most part, Ordrake was straightforward about what he told them of dragons. Yet, he was a bit cryptic about other points. When Ge-or asked him whether the red dragon used magic, Ordrake hemmed and hawed a bit before answering. "They are magical," he said. "But not in any way like how we mages use magic. It is part of them, so to speak. It enhances what they are." He paused, thinking about how he might describe it. "It's like their ability to speak. Normally, a dragon could not form words as we do; they don't have the physical parts to do so properly. Their magic helped them learn the old language, and in some way helped them speak it. Such is the nature of the power they have. Do not fear that they will cast some dire spell. Their breath and claws are fearsome enough; that is what you must focus on, young man."

After they left the Wizard's establishment, Ge-or was curious why the mage hadn't demanded his ring in payment. Stradryk shrugged his shoulders.

Ge-or paid attention to everything Ordrake told him. He had many more questions to ask of the old mage, yet after one hour he waved them to be gone. Ge-or knew well enough that trying to get anything further from him would be fruitless. Afterward, considering all that the Wizard had told them, he realized that he was far from ready to go after the beast. He and Stradryk decided they would observe Fis again that winter. Ge-or would do what he could to find and explore its lair, which he did not expect to be an easy thing to accomplish.

Out of a need to stay busy during the long winter months more than any need for money, Ge-or and Stradryk trapped again. When Fis sallied forth for food, Ge-or tried gamely to scale the mountain to seek out its lair. Each time he made it further up and around toward the back, from where the dragon seemed to emerge and return, but the climb was too steep to get there in the time he had before the winged beast came back.

He was able to pinpoint more accurately where the red dragon disappeared. Over his three attempts, he also discovered better paths up and down.

On the third occasion, caught on the mountain when Fis returned, he hid under a rock outcropping for several hours while the dragon winged about the mountain, obviously enjoying its chance to stretch its wings in the bright winter sun. He got a good opportunity to see how it maneuvered; still, he did not reach its lair.

Stradryk convinced Ge-or that he would need aid in bringing the beast to bay. He offered to help him with his personal quest. Though he did not have the investment that Ge-or had in hunting the beast, he had become intrigued by the prospect of the challenge. When they returned to Aelfric that spring, Ge-or was more resolved to find a way to bring the dragon down. He was glad to have Stradryk's commitment to his purpose. After selling their furs, they bought what they needed for a long trek south.

On Stage

End of term for third years meant they were expected to perform in some way or another at one of the convocations dedicated to that purpose. They had each done their fair share of presenting or playing during bi-weekly performance or lecture classes; however, this was the first time Jared and Karenna would be featured at an all-school event in the main auditorium. Simon-Nathan was giving his senior thesis, which in history was considered the ultimate test for heading into master's work. The three of them were exceedingly nervous. They had sequestered themselves every free minute they had for the two weeks prior preparing.

Simon-Nathan was giving a lecture titled, "The Historical Significance of the Early Motet to the Religious Movements of the Eighth Century." Jared didn't understand half of it, but he dutifully listened as his friend went through the text for the twelfth time. As a fourth year, Simon-Nathan was in one of the earliest sessions. And though he had done a lecture the previous year, seniors got to invite their relatives and friends to the event.

"You'll be great, really. If I don't understand the half of it after twelve times through, believe me, your parents won't get any of it. What is important is that you sound convincing. Stand up straight, look like you know what you're doing, and speak loudly and clearly." Jared clapped him on the shoulder. "You'll be wonderful."

"You think it's too obtuse? Really?"

"Simon!" Jared used his friend's shortened first name when he was frustrated with him. "We've been through this. You know this is for the masters. They're the ones you need to impress. Anyone who doesn't understand what you are saying need only be impressed with your delivery, and you are the best presenter in your class. Why do you think Karenna keeps asking for pointers?"

"Yeah, well. It's good enough?"

Jared groaned.

Three days later, Simon-Nathan had received highest honors by the panel of judges, and now he sat anxiously in the audience waiting for Karenna to take the stage. She and Jared were on the same program. Since they typically did an hour or so of the ten-minute lectures before resetting for the musical portion, Jared was sitting with his roommate nervously twisting his hands. Simon-Nathan was almost as nervous.

Following her personal love of theory, Karenna had chosen "The New Music: Expanding Structural Modulations while Preserving the Integrity of Musical Flow," as the topic of her presentation. Simon-Nathan and Jared had both nodded as she tried to explain the intricacies of her thought and approach. Not even Simon-Nathan really knew what she was talking about.

She was noticeably nervous. When she started, it was difficult to hear her; however, as she continued, she gained in confidence. By the end, she appeared to have pleased the theory judges. They were all nodding and smiling as she left the stage. The rest of the audience applauded politely. Since Karenna was always on the cutting edge of what was new and developing in music, most of them had been lost after the first sentence.

Jared had chosen to improvise in the old style. It was a daring feat for a third year, but it was his true love. He had spent the latter part of the term playing with old melodies to see how he could twist and turn them about themselves. He had picked the lute for his performance. Though he was nervous, and did not know exactly what would come out once he sat down on stage and plucked the first strand of the melody, he settled into it.

Jared's true gift was the music that poured out whenever he sat down and began to play. He would never be an outstanding technical performer, having lost considerable advantage by not studying professionally when he was young; yet he could play beautifully. He lacked only the flare and dramatic fireworks of the truly skilled.

His performance quieted the auditorium. By the end of the first section, no one wanted to breathe, lest they disturb the effect. He came out of his trance-like state to thunderous acclaim.

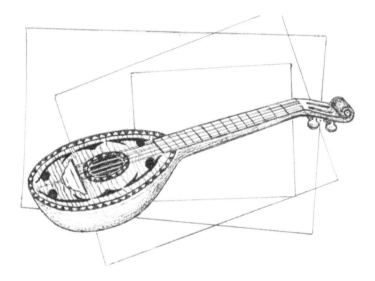

"Well, well, well. You know I enjoyed that quite thoroughly, young Jared. Quite thoroughly, indeed. It was enchanting and ethereal. You had the audience enthralled." Leonis smiled across his desk at Jared. He stood politely, having been corralled by the grandmaster at the end of the recital. "I see you have found your niche. Tell me, do you still wish to become a Bard now that you have seen what we do around here? You know you could make quite a comfortable living, and be acclaimed around the kingdom as a minstrel with your performance acumen. You know how to move people, my son."

"I do wish to be a Bard, Grandmaster. Learning is my life. This is my home. I want nothing else."

"Good, good. I was hoping you would feel that way. We will talk again next year. I want to be sure you head in the right direction. Think about what that might be, my boy. Enough! Off, go be with your friends. Very nice, very nice indeed."

A New Quest

One of a wide variety of things that Ge-or had learned from Ordrake was that he had no chance at all against a beast as old, wise, and dangerous as Fis, unless he possessed some really fine, fire-resistant leather armor or undergarments. The old fellow had told him, "You probably won't find any old dragon leather lying about, either. If there is any in the kingdom anymore, it is either in a museum where it has been left untended and unoiled for years and therefore is unusable, or perhaps the elves have some. You won't be getting in there any time soon either. So," Ordrake had caught Ge-or's eye, and winked at him, "that leaves fire lizards."

It turned out that the only place that fire lizards lived was deep in the marshes to the south. These unwinged, "miniature" dragons were, according to Ordrake, probably the ancestors of the true dragon. They did breathe fire but had to eat brimstone and coal to produce it. Of more importance, their skin was highly fire resistant, though not to such an extent as a red dragon's. "It will serve you," the old codger had said.

"Miniature" was of course in comparison to a true dragon. From what Ge-or was able to piece together from among many stories he had heard, they were almost as big as a small horse and quick afoot.

He and Stradryk discussed at some length the best time to head for the southern marshes. Ge-or was ready to charge out as soon as they had settled whatever affairs they needed to get done before they left. Stradryk urged him to reconsider. "That would mean crossing the desert during the worst of the heat. We wouldn't be able to join a caravan, and any other way south would be foolhardy. The chatts would attack all except a powerful party, and the heat would take you if they did not."

Finally, Ge-or acquiesced. They also discussed taking the long way around to the east of the great Bendir Plains, bordering the horse-people's domain. Stradryk, however, said that they would have to go far enough east to be free of their lands, as the Slivs did not abide strangers any more than the elves did. It would have taken them months to get south and back west to the marshes.

Finally, receiving word from Sart that he had a small adventure in the offing, they decided to wait for the late fall and the start of the merchant caravans before heading to the swamps.

Sart's business turned out to be another trek out west. This time it would be into the heart of Qa-ryk country to explore an old monastery that had lain empty since the first Qa-ryk expansion. The party included some of those from their expedition to the Recluse's citadel. Tyron was engaged as cook, and Ardan and Katelyn joined them from the north as they rode the western trail out of Aelfric.

Ge-or was more than pleased to see Katelyn. He had been complaining of late to Stradryk of missing having a regular relationship, though he had more than enough opportunities in the border town to bed women if he desired. There was something about the half-elf that drew them toward him. He learned quickly that a light touch on his arm, a flick of a woman's hips, or a blink of her eyes meant she was interested. If he wanted companionship for a night, all he had to do was walk into the merchant district and casually stride around. There were almost always young and beautiful, or older, handsome, experienced women, who were lonely because their husbands were "off on business here or there." Occasionally, Ge-or was obliged to help them out.

Still, Ge-or was more than happy that Katelyn wanted to renew their relationship as before. Ge-or found the young mage's fire was as intense as always, and the connection he felt with her was more satisfying than any momentary tryst.

They progressed slowly through the hills and rocky terrain westward. Sart wanted to avoid conflict if at all possible, so they circumvented known areas of Qa-ryk clan concentration, pushing southward until they were high in the foothills to avoid "The Valley of Death." Sart explained this was at one time a powerful cleric's domain. Unfortunately, something evil had taken over the citadel and valley after his demise.

Sart knew the route well enough. He told them that he had spent quite a few months in the general area chasing after an evil priest named Aberon. Ge-or perked up when he heard the name. He resolved to ask the cleric more about the fellow when they stopped for the evening.

"Aye, you are right, he is the one that was involved at Thiele and afterward. Your brother had the fortune, good or bad, to tangle with him several times. He is powerful, Ge-or. Do not take him lightly."

"What would he have with my mother's ring?" Ge-or asked, having told Sart of Ordrake's admonition and demand.

Sart fingered the ring. "I know not. This is magicked; I can sense it. Its import is buried deep within. I cannot divine what it is meant for. What was it your mother said when she willed it to you?"

"'Remember Ge-or, a life for a life. Use it only if you must. Use it for love.' That is all she said. I did not know what it meant. Nor do I now. She never explained before she died. My father wore the band until I was to come of age."

"I should take care of it and not let it out of your sight. Ordrake is an ornery old fool and a bit extravagant in his presentation, yet he is one of the wisest of the wise. He may know its purpose, and he is unlikely to tell you, not if he hasn't already. Often a magicked item will let on when it is to be used or what it is about. Keep it safe.

"As to Aberon, he seems to desire magical items. For what purpose, I cannot ken; it may simply be to get them out of circulation. He is wise enough to know that the old magic is the most powerful, and ancient magicked weapons could foil his brethren's plans. The man is ambitious and deadly. If you have a choice, stay away from him and his minions. He wields powerful magic and is quite dangerous. Someday, I am afraid, the wise will have to deal with him."

After three weeks of travelling through difficult terrain, Sart signaled a halt. They were approaching within a couple of days' ride of a wilderness fortress; he would ride ahead to signal the garrison before they were inclined to take matters into their own hands and bring their small group in forcefully. "They are really cautious, as I found out on another occasion I happened to be in these parts. They will likely send an escort, a troop of rangers, to bring us in to their fortress. Look for them in a couple of days. They may look a bit rough around the edges and worse for wear. It is an appearance they try to maintain. It is also possible they will insist you wear a hood or at the least a cloth over your eyes, though I will vouch for you to their leader.

"Stay alert, my friends. This is the heart of Qa-ryk country. If you have not seen or heard from the rangers or me in four days, head back at all pace. Something will have gone wrong, and it is best that you are safe."

Five days later, as the sun was reaching its apex, their small party, surrounded by twelve rangers, rode up to the gates of Xur. They were roundly welcomed by the populace of the outpost. Ge-or in particular, when they found out he was Jared of Thiele's brother, was approached by many. He was slapped on the back and had his hand and arm pumped enthusiastically, all to shouts like, "Jared, a good man," "A fine musician and a true hero," "You must be proud of him," and on and on.

Ge-or was dumbfounded. When he asked Sart what all the fuss was about, the cleric put him off with a cryptic, "You will find out tonight. From what Rux, the commander of this garrison, has said, I believe the new Journeyman Bard wrote a lay about that battle."

Xur was a fascinating fortress. After Ge-or had seemingly met almost everyone in the compound and had his back slapped so many times his shoulder was sore, Ge-or took the opportunity to explore the intricate fortifications and their defensive devices. His father had taught him and Jared all they knew about weaponry, but his knowledge of siege weapons had been limited. Ge-or was able to study at close hand a wide range of ingenious war machines, manufactured for specific purposes. It was dusk before Katelyn could draw him away, insisting that he come down and join the festivities in progress.

A lavish dinner, by wilderness standards, had been prepared for the visitors. And, as any variation in the rangers' hard existence was a cause for celebration, almost the entire garrison was present except for the evening's guards. Even these would be allowed to join in after their replacements had taken over.

There were copious amounts of food. Game of many types had been harvested and the mid-summer harvest was bountiful. Ge-or sat near the front of the hall, an honored guest. He ate stuffed quail and partridge, roast boar, stewed venison, rabbit and squirrel pot pie, and a plethora of freshly cooked, herbed vegetables. He was so full that when the music started, he was dozing in his seat.

He was poked awake by Katelyn when the resident Journeyman Bard began "The Lay of the Battle for Xur." He discovered that Jared had only a small part in the whole story. Yet his brother had played a crucial role at the end. He was proud that his brother was obviously considered not only a fine singer and performer, but also a stalwart and brave fighter.

They stayed in the fortified compound for two days while Sart held council with Rux and his lieutenants. Much had happened since the cleric had been there. The fortress had been rebuilt and refortified with double walls and supportive earth works. The intricate machinery had been revamped according to its effectiveness in the battle, and additional equipment had been brought in or built. Rux, who had returned from a short stint to report to the Commanding General in Borea, intended to remain a thorn in the side of the Black Druids and the Qa-ryk clans as long as was feasible.

Ge-or and the others enjoyed the comfort and safety of the complex. During the daylight hours they pitched in to help the inhabitants with daily chores. At night, they relished the luxury of hot baths and comfortable beds to sleep in.

On the evening of the second full day there, Sart gathered them together to announce a change in their plans. "We will still move west and north from here to the monastery, as I feel it is important to see if there is anything left in the place. On our return, I want to swing south to the ruins of Kan's citadel and palace. According to Rux, there is still evil lurking about the place. I would see for myself if perchance the altar we destroyed has been rebuilt or in some way continues to be used.

"It is an unholy place. If you do not wish to take part in this, Rux's men will escort you here until my task is complete. Else we will go directly there on our way back from the monastery, heading further south and east."

"I am game," Ge-or said. "I would see this place that my brother discovered."

"Aye," Stradryk said. The others all nodded, too.

"Good. Rux will send us on our way with a strong escort for the first two days as we ride west. Shortly after that, we will be past the heart of the Qa-ryk lands. On our way back, we will head south first, which will circumvent much of their western range, and then head east through the foothills. There we will have to be extra vigilant, though Rux will have men stationed at Kan's ruins in ten days' time. They will look for us.

"We leave at dawn, so rest easy and be ready to move out."

They reached the ruins of the monastery after six days of steady riding. Ge-or realized the place was only a few days ride from where he and Stradryk had spent the last two winters. It was a heavily forested region of evergreens – gzk country. The cloister had been built on the top of a large hill. The grounds, now overgrown by tangled masses of undergrowth and small trees, had once been cleared for over a thousand paces around it.

They spent three long days searching the old buildings, walls, and cellars to little avail. It had obviously been rummaged through any number of times by robbers, Qa-ryks, and gzks. Even the studies and library had been torn apart. There was little left except for scraps of an occasional scroll that were still legible. Sart had them carefully gather these. Unfortunately, he did not hope to glean much from them.

Elsewise, they found nothing of value. It was disappointing, as there is always the excitement on an adventure of the possibility of treasure. Sart had warned them that he had no knowledge of what shape the long-empty place would be in. The last of the monks had left almost seventy-five years before. They did not run into anything dangerous other than a plethora of large bats and rats in the cellars and the occasional large spider.

After a last search for any hidden passages or cavities, they left the next day at mid-morn, riding easily through the forest, heading due south. Stradryk took point as he knew how gzks operated and could give early warning should he sense their presence. Ge-or took the rear, making sure that nothing came upon them and caught them unaware.

Several times over the next few days, they drew into a defensive posture when either Stradryk or Ge-or saw the grey-green creatures flitting through the woods about them. Their party must have looked formidable enough that the creatures would eventually fade away.

They had been heading east for a couple of days when Ge-or's elven sense put him on alert. He signaled to those behind to stay alert. Drawing his bow forward, he set an arrow and watched. Nothing appeared to be moving to his fore, yet he continued to

255

scan the rocks ahead for several minutes until his eyes adjusted for the slight variations in color. He eventually noticed a subtle difference in the shading behind a large outcropping of brownish-red rocks. Ge-or could now distinguish the outline of its head against the similarly colored background.

Ge-or signaled the others to prepare for battle. He backed, nocking an arrow as he moved into a defensive position behind a large boulder. An instant later hoarse roars erupted from the rocks to their fore. The hidden beasts rose up and charged toward them. Ge-or and Stradryk were both able to loose several arrows into the chests of the three Qa-ryks leading the pack; and though they struck true, the hits only slowed the beasts.

Drawing their swords, the two fighters prepared to meet the charge. At that instant, two things happened in quick succession: a pack of timber wolves suddenly jumped from the rocks above and dove straight for the charging Qa-ryks, and a wall of energy about ten feet wide materialized along the pathway where Ge-or and Stradryk had been standing moments before.

The three leading Qa-ryks slammed into the wall of force, bounced off it, shook their heads in bewilderment, and ran into it again. Coupled with the arrows in their chests, the obstacle caused them considerable consternation for several seconds. Ardan yelled out from behind, "You can shoot through it." Ge-or and Stradryk quickly switched back to their bows, carefully picking out their shots. They aimed to disable at least these three while they had the opportunity.

Meanwhile, the wolves had disconcerted the remaining Qa-ryks enough that they paused in their rush forward. But as they were backing away, the illusion passed through them and dissolved.

Two Qa-ryks facing the wall of force were now thrashing on the ground with arrows in their throats and eyes, and the third's chest was sprouting arrows like a pincushion, yet the brute was still determined to get past the wall.

"I can't hold this much longer," Ardan gasped from behind.

Ge-or scrambled up a flat rock to get a better line of sight on the beasts now resuming their attack. He loosed another arrow as the shimmering energy dissipated. He saw that the beasts had fanned out and were moving to encircle their small group. There were at least twelve more, and the two mages and Tyron were not fighters. He knew they did not have much of a chance unless he and Stradryk could keep them at bay long enough for Sart to use his power offensively.

Ge-or switched back to his sword. Nodding to his partner, he leapt down and ahead to meet two of the creatures as they scrambled over the rocks in front. Stradryk dove into the fight next to him, his sword in hand.

Indomitable as ever, Sart swung his mace up, smashed one Qa-ryk in the side with a mighty swing and brought it up and back into another's head, as he tried to make room and time to bring his own energy to bear. Ardan and Tyron drew long knives and rushed to the cleric's side, knowing what he had in mind. Katelyn, her long brown hair blowing behind her, climbed to the top of a large boulder in the center of their small group. She began throwing knives at any beast she could get an angle on.

Ge-or, having grown in strength and fighting prowess over his time with Stradryk, met two of Qa-ryks with a crash, his small buckler slamming into the head of the one on his left and his blade stabbing into the chest of the other. He danced sideways blocking fierce swipes of their claws, while his blade flashed in and out and up and around. The two slow beasts did little damage to the half-elf. Ge-or's strokes quickly brought one down and had the other gushing blood from deep wounds. Still, by weight alone they forced him back. Two others were already scrabbling over their compatriots trying to get at the half-elven fighter.

Stradryk, a versatile, quick fighter, had also learned a great deal from his well-trained partner; but he lacked the half-elf's weight and power. He wove his blade in practiced arcs, keeping the beasts mostly at bay; unfortunately, two crunching blows from powerful arms caught on his shield had him buckling at the knees.

Despite Sart's efforts, he could not leave the fight long enough to focus his inner energy. Several claw swipes had already torn through his clothing, and he was as much trying to protect himself as the others.

Katelyn's expertise with her knives was impressive. She was able to send five blades into the torsos of three of the beasts coming up the sides. Unfortunately, the small throwing knives did little to deter the massive creatures as they came ahead. They brushed them aside as minor irritants and continued to push inward.

Ardan, too, was game with his knife. He kept weaving in and out with his blade until he was smashed aside by the swipe of a Qa-ryk's claw. He landed heavily against a sharp rock and sank to the dirt, unmoving. Tyron engaged the beast next, doing his best to duck, parry, and strike; but he was doing nothing to seriously hurt the heavy-legged creature he faced.

Exposed because the others had collapsed backward while fighting for their lives, Ge-or was facing three of the beasts all at once. He used his quickness and his father's admonition to always learn during a fight to dive, dance, and spin away. As a claw came sweeping toward his head, he found an opening. He managed to bring the hilt of his sword up to partially parry the blow; then he ducked under the attack, spinning and driving his blade into the beast's throat.

Stradryk, forced backward by the beasts he faced, was still fighting gamely. He had received several gashes to his arms.

As things began to look ever more disastrous, hoarse shouts came from the east, followed by a shower of arrows into the Qa-ryks' backs. A troop of rangers from Xur had come up behind, and they now charged into the beasts' ranks. When one of the Qa-ryks reared back with an arrow in its shoulder, Ge-or dispatched it with an upward stab to its gut. He continued to wade ahead, his bloody blade sweeping in practiced arcs.

The battle quickly wound down. Several of the wounded Qa-ryks managed to scramble up the high rock walls to the south. The rangers decided not to pursue them. They set up a defensive position, while Sart looked to everyone's wounds.

Ardan was in bad shape. He had been raked along his side and shoulder; and in the brief period between the ranger assault and the end of the battle, he had lost a lot of blood. Sart, focusing his healing powers, was able to bring him to a point where he was out of immediate danger; though Ardan would be quite sore and unable to help for many days.

Some of the others and a few of the rangers had wounds and serious gashes. Sart's heavy robes and chain mail had protected him from deeper cuts. Katelyn had to stitch one claw strike under his left armpit and several bad cuts Tyron had received across his left cheek. The gnome was more upset that the beast had ripped out a chunk of his long beard, than from the wound. Ge-or was unscathed; and Stradryk, thanks to his agility and his long hours sparring with Ge-or, had escaped with cuts to his arms

257

and a good many bruises.

It was late afternoon when they were finally able to move out. The ranger lieutenant in charge of the twenty men that had come to their rescue told them that they were only an hour or so from the ruins of Kan's fortress. They had been patrolling westward when they heard the roar of the Qa-ryks' attack and had immediately ridden toward the sound of the fighting.

When all had been done to help the wounded, the young commander and Sart decided to divide the force in two: one group to take Tyron and Ardan – the gnome would help care for the mage on their way back to Xur; the others would provide protection for Sart's remaining party as they explored the dungeons below Kan's ruined fortress. The two groups rode together for the rest of the day, and at dusk camped to the west of the ruined fortress in a small grove.

The next morning the group with the wounded headed for Xur, leaving the others to their explorations. Ardan, heavily drugged by herbs from Sart's pack, smiled feebly up at Katelyn from his horse-drawn sling as she held his hand. "I will see you anon, sweet Sister. Be safe."

She smiled, a tear coming to her eyes. She enjoyed Ge-or's company, but her twin was dearer to her than any other. She knew this had been too close a call.

Summertime

The summer was a busy one for Jared, Karenna, and Simon-Nathan. Karenna continued her duties as the book-minder of Simon-Nathan the Elder's stores. Jared worked doing manual labor and serving as a supervisor in the warehouses. This year Simon-Nathan the 10th pushed his son more into the offices and management of the company so he would finally be able, as Simon-Nathan complained constantly to the other two, "...to take over the family business once I have graduated." They were sipping some late evening ales at the Green Horse when he started in again bemoaning his predetermined fate.

"I don't want to be a businessman. I just don't."

"Then tell him, Simon. You're going to have to say something sooner or later." Jared had begun to get irritated with his friend. "We only have six weeks left before next term. If you're going to start graduate work in history, you'd better set this right. He thinks you're going to do your apprenticeship; and while you're wandering about the country, you'll be making contacts for him."

"How? He is so busy, and my sister is always in need of care. I..."

"Your sister is doing better, much better," Karenna said. "She has even shown an interest in doing more for your father. She's a whiz at the books, better than I am, and..."

"And my father won't hear of it."

"He might if you put it to him. Come on, Simon-Nathan, we're on your side in this; but we can't do it for you."

"I know. You're right. Maybe next week..."

Next week came the next day.

"You don't want the business, do you, son?"

Simon-Nathan looked up from the manual he was trying to fight his way through, startled at his father's words. "Ah... Father..."

"I hoped you would. I guess most fathers hope their sons will follow in their footsteps, yet you don't have the passion for it. I ken that." He spread his hands wide, gesturing at the large store below. They were sitting in the office loft of his largest mercantile outlet. "I have always had a zeal for buying and selling. At least, I'm not so blind that I can't see that it is simply an exercise, a burden for you. What is it you want to do, son? What is close to your heart?"

"Father?"

"Tut, tut, Simon-Nathan, your mother and I have seen how much you have been moping about the past few weeks. We both want you to be happy, nay, passionate, about what you do in this life. I can't buy that for you; perhaps I can smooth the way. You can always come back here and start afresh if you find that is what you want. What would you do now that you have graduated?"

"I... I want to be a master at Bard Hall. It is my dream, Father. Are you not disappointed in me?"

"Disappointed? By-the-gods, Son, you have excelled at everything. I couldn't be more proud.

"Of course, I am disappointed that you don't want to take the business over;

however, that is a minor thing, a vanity of a father, nothing more. I would keep the business in the family; well, that is vanity, too."

"What about Athena, Father?"

"Athena? She is frail, Son. She couldn't…"

"She could!" Simon-Nathan stood up. Closing the book firmly and placing it on the desk, he put his palms flat on the cluttered surface and leaned toward his father. Though his head was spinning at his father's words, and his heart had leapt into his throat, he was now brimming with enthusiasm. "She is brilliant, and she loves it, the business. She brightens up when she is here. Athena is as passionate about it as you are. And she has a knack of dealing with people – other merchants, the customers, bankers. Teach her, Father, and you will see her blossom."

"I fear for…"

"Give her a chance. Maybe she will have to do less than you, cut back in ways, or find those who can help her when you retire. I think you may be surprised at how strong and resilient she is."

"Your mother has tried to get me to give her more duties. Are you confident your sister would want to do this?"

"More than want, Father. Bring her here with you for the rest of the summer – every day, not just occasionally. Watch her; let her grow. I think you will be surprised and more."

"Well, well, well."

***

The entrance to the Altar of Kan was no longer shrouded by an illusionary wall. Still, it was impossible to see from below. One had to climb to within twenty paces of the entrance before the dark maw into the earth was visible. Sart took the three aside to explain their purpose. "This place is unwholesome. Though the altar itself was destroyed, evil permeates it. I want to descend into the depths again, where I hope in some small way to consecrate the altar room. Mayhap this will begin a process of tempering the evil that has long dwelt here.

"Also," Sart paused looking at each of them in turn, "be careful and touch nothing. The walls of this place are imbued with malevolence. When we first descended into these depths, we saw no doors or passages leading elsewhere. However, I believe there must be access points to other parts of Kan's dungeons. These may be shielded by illusions, as was this opening; or they may be safeguarded by other means or magic. As we ascend, I want to study the walls for hidden passageways. It will be tedious work in a hostile environment; but gaining access to whatever remains intact below may yield valuable information, perhaps even great treasure, that could be of value to the kingdom.

"Understand that I do not plan to undertake that mission now. If we do find access, at some time in the future I hope to bring a strong party here to explore the depths. If you wish, you may be part of that excursion."

"Soon?" Katelyn asked, concerned that her brother might be left out.

"I think not. There is much I have on my plate right now, and there are others who would prove valuable on such a mission that are not available for a quest of this nature. I will let you know. For now, should we find what I seek, I will place what wards I may to keep others out.

"Come, let us press ahead. I would do this as quickly as possible and be out again before dark," he said, looking at the sun, which was now rising above the tree-line to the east.

Sart led them downward. They each carried torches as the walls were pitch black; the eerie red luminescence Sart had encountered before was no longer present since the altar had been destroyed. As before, the priest could sense the evil exuding from the stone surfaces about them. None of them had to be told to stay in the middle of the stairwell. The evil feel drove them toward the safest place, the center of the route downward.

They went as quickly as they might while still being cautious. Since he had not encountered other creatures on his previous descent, Sart was not overly concerned they would be attacked. It took them almost an hour to make the descent to the cavern where the altar lay. Much to Sart's relief, the room looked as it had when he had been here last. The ebon slab lay split in two as he had left it.

At the time he had destroyed the Altar, Sart and the others with him had not explored the chamber. Wounded and weary beyond almost all endurance, they had left the dungeon as quickly as they could. Now, with no immediate threat, they had time to search the small cavern's recesses.

There was little to find or to see. What little was in the room had been focused on the altar. The chamber had been cut from the rock of the mountain. It was roughly rectangular, with the altar set in the center and aligned along its length. The only other structures in the room were long stone benches set facing the ebon slab.

Gesturing for the others to stand back and keep watch, Sart approached the broken altar. Taking vial after vial of holy water from his pockets, he strew the contents over the entire surface. Astonishingly to the others, the water bubbled and sizzled as it struck the stone, sending popping sounds echoing about the chamber. After emptying his eleventh bottle, Sart stepped back. Using his rood, he began a long prayer. For a half hour he stood with his arms raised above the stone slab, invoking the protection of Gaia, the Earth Mother, the Womb of the World.

Finally, obviously weary from his efforts, Sart stepped back. Withdrawing one last vial, he strew its contents along the altar's two halves. It still sputtered a bit, yet the surface remained wet this time. Sart sank to his knees and bowed his head.

An hour later, after having rested on the first platform above the altar chamber, Sart felt he was strong enough to continue his work. At each level upward they would pause, and they would all search the walls. Sart or Katelyn would pass their hands over the dark surfaces, searching for any hint of magic.

As Sart had suspected, on each platform there were well hidden, dwarven or gnome-crafted doorways cut into the stone. Upon careful examination, they would discover the fine lines where the sill and lintel met the surrounding structure. Upon each of these, Sart placed a rune ward – an explosive device that would warn by glowing red if touched. Hopefully, these would serve to keep all others at bay.

The atmosphere was oppressive. They hurried as they might -- the work, though, was agonizingly slow. The more time they spent below the depths of the evil fortress, the more the malevolence weighed on them.

It was getting on toward dusk when they finally emerged from the opening. The relief was instantaneous. They all felt like a heavy burden had been lifted from their shoulders. They wound their way down the hidden path to the bottom of the mount and took the road east almost a league before stopping for the night. There they were finally able to relax and recuperate, especially with some welcome libations Sart had kept for just such a purpose.

The rangers led them safely back to Xur where they spent a week recovering from their ordeals. By then, Ardan was well enough to ride. The small troop set off eastward on the long trail back to Aelfric. Rux allowed them an escort for five days, wanting to be positive they were safely out of the main Qa-ryk lands before his men turned back.

They arrived back in Aelfric as summer was beginning to wane and the first frost was imminent.

Fourth Year

Hard at Work

The entire fourth year was focused toward finishing successfully. For Jared, who wanted to be accepted into the Bard program, that meant excelling in at least three areas and making "Good-pluses" in most of the others. Karenna, who hoped to continue her studies toward a Professorship in music theory, needed "Excellents" in three academic subjects, and doing well enough in performance and weaponry, to pass to graduate level. Thankfully, they had Simon-Nathan's recent experience with the exams and performance trials to give them at least a perspective of what they had to accomplish.

Seniors were able to design much of their work around their aspirations; so Karenna was taking Advanced Modern Theory, Advanced Modern Composition, and Modern Orchestration, along with classes in History of the Modern Era, portative harp for her performance focus, and general weaponry. Jared had chosen Middle Resurgence History, Lore, Resurgence Contrapuntal Composition, Scoring for String Instruments – Ancient and Modern – and finally, after long personal debate, he decided to focus on lute as his performance major. He had been excused from weaponry finals as he had been promoted to instructor in archery and since he had won the Short Sword Cup two years running.

Simon-Nathan was happily immersed in his graduate work in history and lore. As a graduate student he was entitled to a place on campus to himself, or he could live in the city. He and Jared decided to continue to room together. Because Jared was already mentoring many students in archery and short sword, he was excused from typical senior duties associated with the newer students.

***

Thistle was working as hard as she ever had. Meligance was driving her pupil to concentrate ever harder on defensive magic. She would often stop Thistle in the midst of her work with the admonition: "Power is easy; control is not."

Though the magical aspects of defensive work were no harder than offensive, defensive magic appeared to take considerably more effort because one was rarely in a position to simply protect oneself. The old adage, "Offense is the best Defense," worked as well magically as it did with a sword in one's hand. Thistle had to learn to cast offensive spells while she was protecting herself, as well as be capable of defending others at the same time. It took tremendous concentration.

She made progress. And when Meligance was in a good mood, which was more rare these days, she would praise her student and give her time off for a day or two. Soon enough, they would be hard at it again.

Thus, she only got to see Jared twice before the Yuletide and had not been able to see him yet after. The last time they had met at the Green Horse Tavern near Bard Hall, they had both remarked to each other about how tired they looked.

It had been good to see Jared. Now that she had matured, and her womanly problems dissipated to the point that she could bear and control them, she once again felt a strong emotional and physical attraction to him. She kept these feelings to herself as best she might. She knew she wasn't ready. Her control of herself was still suspect; and though she and Meligance had not discussed it again, she knew she needed to gain command of defensive magic before she would be ready to be close to him again.

***

Jared and Karenna were working hard. The year flowed past. By February, they had reached a feverish pace, though their exams were still two months away. Occasionally, they did manage to find time together, as Simon-Nathan was often at home for entire weekends now. His sister had done remarkable things under their father's tutelage; but she tired easily, so he often stepped in to manage affairs while she rested.

The three of them were enjoying a brief respite one Solisday evening – Jared and Karenna snuggling together on Jared's bed, and Simon-Nathan perched opposite – talking about finding a day to spend out on the town, when a notion popped into Jared's head.

"Karenna, Simon-Nathan, this is somewhat difficult, yet I feel it is important. I was wondering if we could all meet with Thistle next weekend. It… it might be good for all of us," he kissed Karenna on the cheek, "if we all met and talked. I know it will be awkward at first. She is a good person and, well, I don't know…" His voice trailed off.

Karenna pushed herself up and slightly away from him; their legs remained entwined. "Oh, Jared, I…"

"Jared," Simon-Nathan jumped in, "don't you think that is really inconsidera…"

"No, No. NO!" Karenna slapped at Simon-Nathan's knee. "No! Jared is right. We should meet. Get to know each other. And it might make a difference in how you, we, feel. I see that, Jared. It's hard." Her voice hesitated, still she pressed ahead with what she wanted to say. "When you said that, I… so many emotions came up. I felt angry, sad, powerless, and ashamed of myself all at once. You have never hidden how you feel, Jared. Still, you know how I feel, too. It's hard."

"Karenna…"

"No. I mean, yes, let's do it. I would love to talk with Thistle, and I do think it is for the best. Please understand it will be hard for me, not just awkward, but hard."

"I know, Karenna. I know." He reached out and drew her close.

Simon-Nathan turned away, his face reddening brightly.

***

After parting company with Sart and Katelyn, Ge-or and Stradryk planned their venture south. Reluctant to do so, Ge-or gave his mare, Sandy, to a farmer he met at market who lived north and west of the border town. The old girl was now showing the wear of their recent adventures. The fellow had looked to be an honest man, who would use her in her waning years for light work on the farm. Ge-or sold his mule, and they both purchased horses and mules that were better suited for the dry hot climes of the desert.

They also purchased heavy, light-colored robes with wide-brimmed caps to ward off the worst of the sun, and a wide variety of other equipment, including extra water skins for their trek. Sart had given them, as a reward for their stalwart service, several rare herbal potions that he claimed would offer them some protection against

264

fire should they need it.

It was mid-autumn when they hooked up with a wine caravan headed south. Stradryk had explained to Ge-or that the chatts, dangerous at any time, were most active during the late fall, winter, and early spring. Thankfully, a heavily armed caravan typically dissuaded the aggressive creatures from attacking. They would be paid for providing protection for the month or so it took them to reach the far border of the desert. They would also benefit from the victuals and water that the large caravan wagons carried on the way south.

By Yuletide, they had reached Anada, the first large town bordering the southern mountains. From there they traded animals again and re-equipped for the journey further south through the wine country, and then up the passes to the marshes beyond. It was midwinter by the time they reached the edge of the Nolosh swamps.

Mettle

Jared, Karenna, and Simon-Nathan were in the Green Horse tavern enjoying a second round of beer waiting for Thistle to arrive. They were all nervous. Thistle had actually been enthusiastic about the meeting, though Jared perhaps was reading that into her note. Perhaps she had just been polite. "I would love to meet your friends, Jared. I know we will have a pleasant time together. I will see you soon. Regards, Thistle."

The "regards" had given him pause, yet after he had reflected on it, it was how she signed all her notes to him. He knew she would be gracious and kind. He hoped the meeting would not be altogether awkward and stilted.

Thistle entered the tavern on her own, having left Alli to take the carriage to go shopping with some extra coin she had gifted her. Sometimes her handmaiden was overprotective; and since they shared almost everything, Alli was concerned that her mistress would be upset by the "odd" meeting.

For whatever reason, Thistle did not actually feel that ill at ease about the whole affair. She understood Jared's unwritten, but suggested, reasoning – that it would help him, and her, gain a better understanding of how they actually felt.

The tavern was dark and smoky, so Thistle stood in the entryway for a brief period to let her eyes adjust. Unfortunately, three inebriated dandies at the bar caught sight of her. Dressed in the fashionable, overly ornate, current style-of-the-day with gilded rapiers at their sides, the young men were of a type that she often saw wandering jauntily about the castle, trying to impress one and all with their bravado. She had no use for courtiers who thought more of themselves than others, and she always ignored them. At the palace, they knew who she was and tended to give her a wide berth anyway.

These men, boys really at least in manner, saw her only as a prize beauty worthy of their immediate attention. When she began to walk up the passageway to the center of the large room to look about for Jared and the others, the three men decided that this young woman would be a perfect target for their attention. Nudging each other, they sauntered rakishly from their place at the main bar and quickly took positions, one in front and one on each side of her, effectively barring her progress further into the room.

The men's movement caught Jared's eye. As they left the bar and went up to Thistle, he slid from his seat and started toward her. His hand went to the knife at his belt.

At the same instant, Thistle saw Jared and the others. She gestured to him to stay where he was. The dandies saw her gesture, and they turned to see a tall young man dressed in common clothes start toward the beauty they had in mind of conquering. They noted he was only armed with what looked like an unremarkable utility knife. The one closest to Jared began to draw his rapier. Thistle's voice broke through the silence that had suddenly fallen. The few patrons in the bar were watching the now tense scene.

"Hold, gentleman; Jared, stand down." She looked at Jared and held her palm out toward him. "I am apprentice to Meligance, the Great White Wizardess of Borea. I suggest that you men return to your seats and drinks. I would not wish to harm you." She said it lightly, but firmly. The men, not too drunk to know that powerful name, stopped in their tracks. The one with the sword partially drawn let it slip back into his scabbard; though, as he turned back toward the bar, he gave Jared an angry look.

Thistle walked over to Jared. Taking his hand, she leaned in toward him and brushed his cheek with her lips. Next, she stepped to the table and offered her hand to Karenna, and then Simon-Nathan. Not waiting for Jared to seat himself, she sat down next to Karenna, which left the seat next to Simon-Nathan open.

As Jared sat down, he visibly relaxed. Not because of the resolution of the recent unpleasantness, but because he had not known what to do about where he or Thistle should sit. Wisely, she had taken the seat he would have preferred her to take, yet could not suggest, as it would have been a slight to Karenna if he had not sat next to her.

The first few minutes were a bit awkward. Nevertheless, as Jared had hoped, Thistle was both gracious and, ultimately, herself – a country girl at heart. Soon they were all enjoying an afternoon away from their work and were sharing stories of their experiences and endeavors.

The two hours they had scheduled went quickly, and Thistle was sad to go. She liked both Simon-Nathan and Karenna. She understood Jared's attraction to the girl. Karenna was smart, very good looking, and after the initial shyness, open and honest about who she was and what she wanted to accomplish in a male-dominated profession. Thistle liked her quite a bit.

After Thistle had gone, the conversation immediately turned to her. "Oh, Jared, I am so glad we did this," Karenna gushed. "She is wonderful. I do understand better now, how and why you feel the way you do. It… I guess I still feel a bit jealous, yet somehow this feels like it was the right thing to do. Thank you." She kissed Jared on the cheek; pulling his hand toward her, she kissed it as well.

"She is incredible," Simon-Nathan gushed. "There are few, I think, who could have pulled such a meeting off with aplomb and genuineness. I am glad we did this, too. I am glad to have had this chance to get to know her.

"Well, my friends, Father's books call to me; and I have a few hours left before sunset. Maybe we can do this again."

Karenna stared at Simon-Nathan; oddly, she felt something unexpected. She thought, Where did that come from? But they were all getting up, so she left it to think about later.

They paid for their drinks and headed, all three arm-in-arm, for the tavern door. As they exited, the bright sunshine made them blink and pause to allow their eyes to adjust.

"Ah, at long last it is the somewhat-elf that would rescue the distressed maiden," an unpleasant voice to their fore announced.

Jared blinked a couple more times before he could focus on the three men who had obviously been waiting for them to emerge from the tavern. The dandies had their rapiers and daggers drawn and were wagging the tips about in the air, looking like they wanted to have some fun with the country-bumpkin they had seen rise up to come to the witch's aid. Now that she had gone, he was not under her protection.

Jared pulled away from Karenna and Simon-Nathan, purposefully not letting his hand go to the hilt of his knife. "Come gentleman," he decided to take Thistle's approach and try to dissuade the intoxicated men from their fun, "you do not want to do this. I am studying at Bard Hall; this is unnecessary."

"A Bardling? Why even more fun." The one who had almost drawn his sword inside spoke, taking a step forward, his blade flashing in the sunlight.

"Please, this is not necessary," Simon-Nathan, shouted. "Stand down or you will get hurt."

"Stay out of this, merchant, or I will carve you up as well. Your father would not want his poor son spitted upon our swords today, I think."

Simon-Nathan blinked, surprised at having been recognized, though his hand did go to his knife.

During this exchange, Jared stepped further to his left away from Karenna as he drew his blade. Simon-Nathan was no knife fighter; and even if he had a sword in hand, he was no scrapper. He had learned a great deal about swordplay from his roommate, yet had never been in any kind of scuffle. These dandies might not be the best when it came to a real brawl; however, they did know how to use these lightweight blades. It was part of their upbringing to develop a "gentleman's prowess," with a "gentleman's weapon."

"Your knife, Simon." Jared's tone was commanding.

His friend was reluctant to relinquish it and leave the fight to his Jared, yet Simon-Nathan understood all too well how little he knew about real fighting. He tossed the knife hilt first to Jared, who deftly caught it in his right hand.

Circling ever more to his left, Jared tried, and succeeded, at drawing the three's attention away from where Karenna and his roommate stood. The foremost of the three struck first, launching a textbook attack with the rapier while the other two closed in from the side. Jared caught the fellow's blade with the knife in his right hand. Having the advantage of a shorter blade and the leverage it could afford up close, he stepped into the stroke, surprising his opponent. He let the knife slide down the edge of the rapier while blocking the fellow's dagger with the knife in his left. When he was close enough, he twisted his wrist violently in a quick circle. The rapier was wrenched from its owner's grasp. Jared caught the hilt as it was coming down. In the same extended motion, he tossed Simon-Nathan's knife back to him, hilt first.

Any who observed the scuffle, unless they were skilled at watching close-in fighting, saw only a blur of motion and a sword flying up into the air. A swords-master would have marveled at the skill of the maneuver and known immediately that the three men didn't stand a chance against this young half-elf.

Jared, ignoring the now disarmed dandy, leveled the rapier at the other two as they came toward him from the side. In a flash of lightening strokes, he disarmed both of them as well. He ended with the rapier blade resting against the throat of the last one to lose his sword. He said angrily, "Next time you pick a fight, know who you are fighting. It is the first law of staying alive." He sheathed his utility knife and then snapped the expensive blade across his knee and tossed the broken halves at the feet of the fellow who had attacked him first. "I don't want to see or hear of any of you again, and that goes for my friends, too." He turned his back on them and strode toward Karenna and Simon-Nathan, who were staring wide-eyed in disbelief at what they had just witnessed.

"Remind me never to get you angry," Simon-Nathan said as they turned to go.

Winter in the South

On the edge of the vast swamplands was a settlement of the oddest assortment of people Ge-or had ever seen. Stradryk, who had wandered this far south once before, was not surprised. "Aglimiville is the main trading post for anything coming from the swamp and for those who want or need the valuable plants, animals, and other things that are found there. Gnomes and dwarves from the mountains come for strong woven ropes from the fibers of various reeds, and baskets that hold liquid without leaking and withstand rough usage. Others are after the delicacies they make from the many plant species here, and so on. Clerics and priests come for the rare herbs and minerals only found in the swamps. The elves of the plains, and occasionally the Wapite of the steppes, find nutrients for their animals and colorful dyes for their weavings. Certain parts of the outlying forests produce, according to the wine merchants, the best cork available. It is a rich place in a strange sort of way. There is much here that one would not suppose.

"All of these peoples, and more, Ge-or, are serviced by the Aglimi, the swamp people. Come, we need to head to the main tavern-trading post to find one who is willing to take us on our quest for the fire lizards. We will need a scout if we are to head into the swamps."

Ge-or discovered that the Aglimi were a shy people. They were rarely seen in the open; and since they were semi-aquatic, they almost never stayed in a town unless their services were required. You were expected to meet them, by appointment only, in special rooms built in the rear of the tavern that opened at the back to the waters of the swamp. Here they would swim up and leave the water for brief periods to discuss your needs and to barter.

When it came time for their meeting, Stradryk and Ge-or entered the chamber and sat on the landside of a long table. On the other side of the table, the floor and part of the wall were missing; and the water lapped up onto the boards, pushed by the gentle winds sweeping in from the west. They sat for several minutes before they saw a ripple coming toward them from the murky waters outside the tavern proper.

A light green, yellowish-brown, mottled humanoid emerged from the water in front of them. Reaching out with its webbed hands, it pushed itself up onto the platform and onto a perch that had been formed to fit its unusual body shape. The creature was generally human-shaped, with two arms and two legs, the hands and feet of which were webbed and clawed. Its body was lean, yet with an extended belly and rump. Its skin appeared to be a cross between the flesh of a naked human and the broad scales of a large fish, though Ge-or could not see whether the scales were individual or simply an interconnected mass. Its face was slightly elongated, due to a protruding jaw, and it had bulbous lips.

The creature spoke to them formally, the words slurring slightly due to its physical anomalies. "Greetings, travelers. I am called Ooglu. I am a swamp guide of the Aglimi people. How may I be of service?"

Stradryk stood and bowed low, introducing himself. "I am Stradryk, half-gzk, and this is…" Ge-or stood and bowed as well, "Ge-or, half-elven. We wish to hunt the fire-lizard."

Ooglu frowned, then grunted. "Dra-ken-la, foul-breathed-one, we call it. They are dangerous. I do not recommend a hunt for them. Thank you. Good-day." The Aglimi began to slip from its perch. Ge-or raised his hand, palm outward.

"Hold! Please, Ooglu. We do not pursue such a creature for pleasure. I have need of the skin to… to fight a dragon that has dishonored me and killed my family."

Ooglu turned, staying where he was, still mostly on his perch. "An honor-quest?"

"Aye, the beast destroyed my village, killed my father, and took a family heirloom – a sword of great power."

"Honor I ken." Ooglu said, searching Ge-or's face. "However, you need to know this – the beast you seek is rare, extremely dangerous, and they are hard to find and incredibly hard to kill. The price is high for this type of venture. Have you coin or jewels?"

"Both."

"Let me see the jewels."

Ge-or and Stradryk opened their purses and withdrew the fine stones they had kept from the treasure found in the crypt. Ooglu stuck his hand forward and stirred at the contents in each man's hand, finally selecting two fine rubies and an emerald. "These for now and three others of my choice when we succeed in this quest. Be aware, this may take more than one season. The beasts you seek are deep in the swamp, and even for one as experienced as I, one of the best trackers in our tribe, they are elusive and hard to find."

"Season?" Ge-or asked.

"You are late. Humans cannot abide the deep swamp during the heat of the summer. Unlike my kind, you cannot hide yourself underwater for long periods to stay cool. We have two, maybe three months left to hunt before we will return here. It will take us a while to even reach the deep swamp where these creatures dwell. If we are

271

successful, well and good; if not, you will need to start next season, a month or more before your Yule-time. The cost will be the same, regardless of how many seasons it takes. We are an honorable people, and a bargain is a bargain. If you decide to call the quest off, you still have to pay the contracted amount. Agreed?"

Ge-or looked at Stradryk, wondering if his friend would commit to a possible long-term proposal. The half-gzk nodded. Ge-or turned back toward Ooglu and nodded as well. He stuck out his hand.

Ooglu shook his head. "Do not touch me. Our flesh-covering is caustic to humans, and it is dangerous for me to lose my protective coating. I will provide all your sustenance on the venture, though you will need to learn to eat many new things. Do you consume fish?"

Both Stradryk and Ge-or nodded.

"Good. That makes it somewhat easier. Bring your normal weapons, yet only as few as you feel comfortable with. Leave all except light leather armor. You will have no use for anything else, and it is dangerous to be weighed down. Buy some long, thigh-length boots of Igluani leather. They are waterproof. We walk, occasionally swim. There are no boats available for such treks. Travel light as you may; you will carry all. Meet outside this tavern on southwest side at dawn. Good day." He slid back into the water and vanished from sight.

Ge-or watched the ripples after he had disappeared, thinking how odd the whole encounter had been. Ooglu was obviously quite articulate and knowledgeable. Ge-or didn't know what he had expected, but he chastised himself for letting the alien-feel of the whole place influence what he thought. He had made judgments based on simply the fellow's appearance when he had come out of the water.

They were ready at dawn. Ge-or had lightened his load considerably, leaving only what he considered essential tools, equipment, and some minor pieces of cooking gear in his pack. Upon meeting up with their guide, Ooglu immediately began going through both their packs and tossing things aside. He threw out all the cook-wear, ropes, most of the spikes, all except a few of the tools, and other items, until what they had left probably weighed less than half of what they had started with. "Come," is all he said. They followed him into the swamp.

For three weeks they followed in Ooglu's footsteps. He obviously knew the swamps well, because they never had a misstep as long as they followed exactly where he led. They quickly learned that under the murky waters were long narrow passages of relatively solid ground that served as pathways through the muck. Sometimes these shifted; but Ooglu either could physically feel when they had changed their course, or he had a way of anticipating breaks in the normal paths that he had memorized over many years' time.

Though he did not talk much, he always explained what he could about things they encountered. When they ate, he talked of the fish, amphibians, mammals, roots, grasses, herbs, and vegetables that he harvested and what he was doing with them to prepare their meal. He also showed them how to purify water with a simple mesh sieve made from a particular plant species. Many things they ate raw. When he deemed something needed to be cooked for their palates, he took a certain kind of leaf and wove it into a pot that was able to withstand low heat; then they would have a stew or braised animal that he had taken. He cooked over a fire of dried leaves and branches he harvested from the almost perpetual canopy above. They became accustomed to many new practices under his tutelage; and they also realized how lost they would be without him, even after all they had learned. They would never survive out here on their own.

Ooglu had his own ways to protect against the many bugs, snakes, and other dangerous creatures they encountered. A certain plant, when rubbed on their skin, served as an insect repellant. Another, crushed and smeared on a bite or sting, eliminated the pain and itching. Snakes and poisonous lizards were avoided or killed if they came too close. Ooglu, however, did teach them what plants could serve as a tonic for this or that bite, or as an antitoxin for the more dangerous critters.

He also taught them a good bit of swamp lore so they could help along the way. A certain branch or cutting from a tall reed made an ideal spear for fishing when sharpened and hooked on one end. Another plant could be woven quickly into a long strong rope that was as sturdy and flexible wet as it was dry. There were uses for much of the vegetation they passed. Under Ooglu's tutelage they became more and more swamp-wise.

It was at the beginning of their fourth week in the swamp when Ooglu announced that they had arrived in fire lizard territory. The hunt was on.

Three weeks later, they had seen nothing of fire lizards. Plus, Ge-or and Stradryk had to admit that it was becoming increasingly more difficult to breathe in the humid, oppressive atmosphere of the swamp. It had been hot from day one, yet bearable. Now that spring was beginning up north, this quagmire that was currently their home was becoming almost unbearable. Finally, Ooglu stated firmly, "We must head back. It will take three weeks or more to return. By the time we get back the swamps will be too dangerous even for me to stay above water for long. Come, we must hurry."

It took them only two and a half weeks to return. By then Ge-or and Stradryk were almost delirious from the heat and humidity. Ge-or had lost almost two stone in weight, in spite of eating and drinking his fill; and he desired nothing more than to get on solid ground and feel a cool breeze in his face. Stradryk, though his wiry body had stood up a bit better, was also in bad shape. When they finally got back to Aglimiville, they were completely exhausted. Ooglu bade them goodbye and told them they could connect with him at the tavern in the mid-fall when they were ready to return.

Ge-or and Stradryk stayed in the swamp town for a week -- long enough to gain the strength to head into the hills and through the passes back to Anada where they decided to stay the summer. There they would be able to make short excursions with mining parties or provide protection for local dignitaries. They were too spent to think about making the trek across the desert with a late caravan in search of an adventure.

Exams, Tests, and Goodbyes

It was late spring, and Thistle had been put through a rigorous test of her skills by her mentor. The entire morning, she and Meligance stood in the courtyard below the White Wizardess' tower window. For a long time, the place reverberated with energy and power. Meligance had sent spell after spell careening toward her apprentice in what became effectively a controlled Wizards' battle. Thistle was required not only to block the spells aimed at disrupting her concentration, she was also to assail Meligance with energy of whatever form she chose.

Those few people who were brave enough to watch – Sart and Alli stood above looking from the ramparts that connected the wall and tower – saw bright flashes of energy snapping back and forth between the two figures, only to be either absorbed by a glowing globe, or bounced back as if they had struck a solid clear wall.

When Meligance was satisfied that she had tested her protégé enough, she held her hands up toward Thistle, palms outward. She had a grim smile on her face. "So, you are ready."

Thistle lowered her arms and stared, not knowing precisely what she was ready for.

Above them Sart clapped Alli heartily on the back. Realizing he had literally clouted the poor girl, he lifted her into his arms in a great bear hug. "Your mistress has done well. Come, let us prepare a lunch for when she returns. I have much to talk with her about."

A few minutes later, up in her tower room, Meligance addressed her student. "My child, you have made excellent progress this year on the use of defensive magic. I am pleased. It is time to move to your next phase of training – the use of energy that can produce both an attack and a defense at the same instant – to form energy in a way that it dissipates what is sent at you, and/or blocks as it forms into an attack. You can even learn to use energy that is cast at you. I…

"What is it child? You should be happy?" Meligance saw Thistle's facial features drop and her head dip at her words.

"I'm sorry, mum, I was hoping…," she said, blushing. "I was hoping you meant I was ready to see, ah… to be with Jared."

"Ah! Well, yes, I suppose you are, yet only to a point. You will need to learn control in this respect as well… Yes, I suppose you are ready. I am glad you brought this up, for it is time we spoke again on it. Let us talk on this more on the morrow. I imagine we are both tired. Go. Clean up and enjoy the rest of the day. I believe Sart wants to fill you in on all his recent travels. He has prepared a nice lunch and a surprise for you."

Thistle ran and skipped back to her rooms; and no one would have expected, unless they knew, that she was a new Wizardess of Borea.

"Rose. Oh, my little Rose!" Thistle scooped the girl into her arms. You've grown so big. It's been over a year. Thank you, Sart. Thank you." She burst into happy tears.

***

Exams, performances, and the Challenge Cup had been all they had thought about for the past four weeks. They had all done well. Karenna had excelled in all her academic subjects and done well-enough in performance – "Good-Plus", and weaponry – "Improved," that she had been accepted into the master's program in musicology. Simon-Nathan's first major master's paper in history had been lauded by his professors. And Jared had managed "Excellents" in all his classes for the first time. He had also taken his fourth Cup in archery, a new record. He had chosen not to challenge in the short sword, preferring to focus on his performance, which had been roundly acclaimed at this year's convocation.

With all of that behind them now, the three good friends sat together in their room looking decidedly downcast. Finally, Simon-Nathan stood up, and paced back and forth. He stopped suddenly in front of Jared. There was an angry tone to his voice. "You have to go back and ask him again, Jared. It was the plan."

Karenna, who was strangely sitting separated from both of them at one of the desks, flushed deeply red and looked down at her feet. She knew the truth and had badgered Jared for weeks to tell his roommate his decision. Jared *had* tried earlier, and Simon-Nathan had not wanted to listen. He decided to wait to see what the judgment would be. He had not tried to influence Leonis' decision one way or another.

"I can't do that, Simon. I never asked in the first place."

"Whaa-a? What do you mean, Jared?"

Jared stood up and faced his roommate. "Simon, this was always your plan. I never said I was for or against it. I tried to tell you several times that I didn't see myself fitting into it, but you wouldn't listen. Finally, I let it be what it would be. I was willing, always willing, to go where the committee sent me. Leonis made the decision, not me; and I think it is the right one. I need to see the world. I need to experience all I may if I am to be a full-fledged Bard one day. What you proposed for us," he glanced at Karenna whose head was still down, "is limiting."

His roommate stared at him, finally lowering his head in defeat. Karenna turned even further away, staring out the window. She was embarrassed, angry, and at a loss. She knew she was about to lose her lover and companion, and she didn't know what to do or say to be able to hold onto him for a bit longer. She wasn't positive she wanted to. Why had it come to this?

"Please understand, Simon-Nathan, your ideas are exemplary. What you have planned is ideal for you and Karenna. You will be brilliant and produce, I have no doubt, the most comprehensive and well-researched book on folk music ever written. It is a grand project for your apprenticeships; but it is work for historians, musicologists, and theorists, not for a performer. I will be happy to play the tunes I know for you; and I will be more than happy to go through and comment on whatever you pull together, as my travels and duties allow. Leonis, however, is right on many fronts. I am destined to be in the field. Not only now. It will be my life, even after I become a Bard.

"And not just in the field – far out in dangerous areas. I am an adventurer at heart, as Sart has told me my brother has become. I would be unhappy gathering folk music from village to village, writing things down day after day. I'm sorry Karenna, Simon-Nathan. We will be friends forever; elsewise our paths will diverge. I…"

"Friends!" Karenna finally gave in to her anger. She jumped up, her face redder than her hair. She ran up to Jared and began striking him on his chest with her small fists. He caught them and drew her toward him. She burst into tears. Simon-Nathan put his hand on her shoulders. Jared reached out and drew him into the embrace. They stood there for a long time, emotions swirling; yet all of them understanding, at the last, that this was as it should be.

***

Graduation day was a grand affair. Jared would be receiving his diploma, the cape of an Apprentice Bard, and a special award for weaponry. Karenna, besides her diploma, had taken academic honors and would receive a medal and the robe of a master trainee. Each of them was allowed to invite six people. Karenna had invited her family – father, mother, her two brothers and sister – and Simon-Nathan. Jared had sent invitations to Simon-Nathan's family and the only other three people he could think of to ask.

"You received one of these?" Meligance asked, fingering the ornate gold envelope with the fine elven script addressed to "Meligance, White Wizardess of Borea."

"I did, and I think I shall attend. I think you should, too. He is a grand lad; you should meet him. The way I see it, he will be part of your young lady's life for some time to come."

"Yes, I think you are right and wise as usual, my good cleric. It will create quite a furor at Bard Hall if I just show up." Her eyes twinkled.

"I should think it shall. Good for you, and I would warrant, good for them. Shall we go unannounced?"

"By all means." Meligance penned the acceptance as she spoke. "I should like to meet this young half-elf, after all. Do you think he kens what this means?"

"I should think he has an idea. Leonis says he has quite a sense of humor."

"Good. Then I shall like him."

There was a decided hush in the Grand Hall when Jared, leading a beautiful young lady dressed in a flowing green velvet robe, walked down the aisle followed by the stately Grand Wizardess of Borea herself, dressed in a long lavender gown that shimmered as she walked. She was in turn accompanied by a cleric, who, for once, was wearing the formal scarlet robes of his Office and Church. Even Leonis was surprised. He had to revise his introductory remarks on the spot so as to include the unexpected honored guests.

With all the pomp and ceremony over, most of the crowd had dissipated. Meligance was gracious to Jared afterward. She took him aside from the others for a brief time and whispered in his ear. After, when all were together again, she gave him, though he had expected nothing, a plain, well-tempered dagger "slightly magicked," as a graduation gift. Sart gave him at least three crushing bear hugs and presented him with "a minor ring of power" to help keep him safe on his travels. He also re-admonished Jared to keep the pendant and stone safe.

Before the party, courtesy of Simon-the Elder, the three friends went back upstairs to exchange gifts. Jared had made Karenna a fine bow with a dozen arrows, "to encourage you to continue your practice as a woman archer." He gave Simon-Nathan a magnificently bound scorebook to record the folk music during his apprenticeship with Karenna. Karenna received a beautiful lute from Simon-Nathan with a note attached that made her blush. She declined to show it to Jared. Simon-Nathan and his family

276

gave Jared a fine stallion for his travels. Jared gratefully accepted, though he knew his roommate had spent far too much. Karenna gave each of them a set of sturdy traveling clothes for their time away from the Hall.

A magnificent party was planned at one of Simon-the-Elder's buildings. The two families and all of their friends had been invited. Meligance had demurred, but Sart said he could not pass up such a sumptuous repast and planned to come.

At the last, Jared stood with Thistle outside Bard Hall. Most of the others had left. He wanted to walk over to the party with Thistle, allowing them some time alone to talk. He looked up at the magnificent building and smiled, a lump forming in his throat. He remembered when he had bidden her goodbye and entered Bard Hall for the first time. It seemed like a lifetime ago. Yet, he could remember every detail, including the cacophony of miraculous sounds he had heard flowing down from above.

Thistle took his hand and turned to face him, understanding intuitively what he was feeling and what this all meant to him. He looked down at her and another emotion took hold. She bent her face up to him and said, "Yes, you may kiss me."

So he did.

The End

Next, **Book III: The Making of a Bard -- Siciliana**

End Note

On Writing *The Chronicles of Borea*

In 1979-1980, I wrote the first book of *The Chronicles of Borea,* entitled *IXUS* (now the fifth book). At that time I sent this work out to a variety of publishers because it was still possible to do so. The book made it to several senior editors, from whom I received personal suggestions and comments re: revisions. Many of these were instrumental in the rewrites and the direction the series would go. Eventually, with my professional life taking up more and more of my time, I put this manuscript aside, and only sporadically returned to fiction over the next several decades.

The idea of a Prequel to *IXUS* crept into the picture fairly early. I finally wrote a short novel, entitled *The Making of a Bard*, for my young son.

Many years later, I envisioned expanding and finishing the *Chronicles*. From approximately 2007 to the present, I completely revised and expanded *IXUS* several times; and *The Making of a Bard* was extended into a series of four complete works: *Preludio; Gigue; Siciliana; and Ciaccona*. The initial drafts of the final two books of this series which follow *IXUS*: *Corrente; Civil War Threatens: Tempo di Borea; and The Great War: Grande Finale,* were completed in 2011. A short story, entitled, *The Hunter's Mark*, was completed in 2022 and serves as an introduction to the series.

As a musician and an avid Sword and Sorcery fan, this series was a natural for me. I think my love of this genre really solidified when I read T.H. White's *The Once and Future King*, Tolkien, Lloyd Alexander, and others, and also when I was introduced to *Dungeons and Dragons* ©. (I still have the original three book set from 1974 – Thank you, Gary Gygax and Dave Arneson, MYRIP). I owe a great deal to all of these "mentors" and many other figures in this arena.

Music, Magic, and the Warrior mentality play major roles in these works. Each is wrapped around the other, and they are threads that tie the entire series together. I have tried to detail the development and unfolding of the three primary characters, who forward these roles throughout.

Also, I have placed many references within for fun. I am not sure when all of this started, probably when I picked names for the first characters in *IXUS*; but it seems I like to play games with words, titles, names, sayings, and so forth, as well as, in an indirect way, give homage to authors and others that have influenced me through the years. Some of these are fairly obvious if your background includes the information to decipher them, e.g. Lassus is a Bard named in *The Making of the Bard, Book I* -- Orlando di Lasso, or di Lassus is a Renaissance musician (16th century). Others are much more subtle and personal, e.g. Aelfric (a town in my kingdom), was a dwarf character of a librarian (thanks Carol) in one of my early *Dungeons and Dragons* groups (as well as a real abbot and writer). I hope you will have some fun finding the hundreds of subtle underpinnings and references within these books. I write and insert them as I go.

As a musician, I also like the sound of words, so I tend to play around with that a good bit in my manuscripts.

I have been influenced by many writers and works. I hope I have offered a nod to all in my own way, for I cannot fathom the depths to which my imagination takes me. I write and it all comes out, typically flowing as fast as my two index fingers can fly over the keyboard.

A brief perspective: Tolkien's orcs have become a mainstay of gaming for a creature with certain characteristics. However, as it was pointed out to me by a senior editor of a famous publishing house, they are uniquely Tolkien. Therefore, as a way of offering homage to the Dean of this genre, I have twisted this type of creature to my own usage with "goblin" (used fairly synonymously with "orc" by Tolkien) as the beginning reference point. My goblins, gzks, and chatts are creatures who are from the same heritage, but were mutated due to their environs -- therefore, I have chatts of the desert, goblins of the caves, and gzks of the evergreen forests.

My sincerest wish is that my writing is first and foremost enjoyable to read. I love a good tale, and I hope these books satisfy that criterion.

Joe Koob

About the Author

Dr. Koob is a former college music educator, having taught: – Music Appreciation; Music History Course Sequence; Private and class Stringed Instruments –Violin, Viola, Cello, Bass; Music Education and Student Teacher Supervisor; Student Success classes; Interdisciplinary advanced seminars; and Music Theory. He also Conducted University-Civic Symphonies for many years and has performed in symphony orchestras in the United States and Europe.

Dr. Koob served in the United States Air Force during Vietnam as a C-141 Starlifter Navigator.

Education: Bachelor of Music – DePauw Univ; Masters Degree in Violin – Montclair State Univ; Masters in Counseling, Northern State Univ; and Doctorate in Education – Univ. of Illinois.

Writing Awards: *A Perfect Day – Guide for a Better Life*: **Winner – Best Book Non-fiction,** Oklahoma Writers Federation, and **Certificate of Merit**, *Writer's Digest* Self-Published Book Awards. Winner Various Local and Regional Writing Competitions

His background includes work as an Executive Coach and Motivational Speaker; Author of Music Educational Software, Music Texts, Manuals, and Adjudicated Articles; as well as many books and articles on "Understanding and Working with Difficult People." He has many additional interests, including bicycling, woodworking, painting, reading, archery hunting, fishing, and more. Joe is happily married and has two grown children. He divides his time between FL and MI.

Website: **chroniclesofborea.com**

Blog: chroniclesofboreabooks.wordpress.com

Made in the USA
Monee, IL
24 May 2023

33991981R00154